I0891487

TEDDY'S WORLD

GUERNICA WORLD EDITIONS 89

TEDDY'S WORLD

ANTHONY M. GRAZIANO

GUERNICA
World
EDITIONS
TORONTO—CHICAGO—BUFFALO—LANCASTER (U.K.)
2025

Guernica Editions Founder: Antonio D'Alfonso

Michael Mirolla, general editor
Scott Walker, editor
Cover design: Allen Jomoc, Jr.
Interior design: Jill Ronsley, suneditwrite.com

Guernica Editions Inc.
1241 Marble Rock Rd., Gananoque (ON), Canada K7G 2V4
2250 Military Road, Tonawanda, N.Y. 14150-6000 U.S.A.
www.guernicaeditions.com

Distributors:
Independent Publishers Group (IPG)
600 North Pulaski Road, Chicago IL 60624
University of Toronto Press Distribution (UTP)
5201 Dufferin Street, Toronto (ON), Canada M3H 5T8

First edition.
Printed in Canada.

Legal Deposit—Third Quarter
Library of Congress Catalog Card Number: 2025932052
Library and Archives Canada Cataloguing in Publication
Title: Teddy's world / Anthony M. Graziano.
Names: Graziano, Anthony M., 1932- author.
Series: Guernica world editions (Series) ; 89.
Description: Series statement: Guernica world editions ; 89
Identifiers: Canadiana (print) 20250145170 | Canadiana (ebook)
20250148307 | ISBN 9781771839426 (softcover) | ISBN 9781771839433 (EPUB)
Subjects: LCGFT: Historical fiction. | LCGFT: Novels.
Classification: LCC PS3607.R395 T43 2025 | DDC 813/.6—dc23

Dedication

Teddy's World is dedicated to all who have known the sting of intolerance for being deemed "different." But we know that in such difference there can reside a unique humanity, beauty, and potential.

And to Miss Helen Powell, Nyack Librarian from 1897 to 1957. In the 1930s and 1940s this genteel lady welcomed a scruffy little boy into her library and generously nourished my love of reading.

A Special Dedication
December 2023

To the memory of my lovely Sheila Grace
And our 66 glorious years together.

When I was born
They said I would be dull.
So they put me in a place that made me dull
And then they said
"See. He is dull."

(Unknown)

An early morning knock on the door
The police, a social worker, or a priest,
Sometimes, all three.
"It is time!" they say. "Come!"
And they take away your children.
There is nothing you can do about it.
It is the law!
The government bus drives off,
And takes away your children.

The vivid scene in red and black
The broken bird in Teddy's hand
The scarlet pearl oozing out
Teddy's tears that stain the ground.

Contents

Part One:

The Corner

Chapter One:

1953—A Hundred Clocks on the Wall

In the spring of 1953 Teddy was fifteen years old and already a target. He knew this, but not in words because thinking in words was not his strength. He knew it as rumbling feelings and dark images; but it was a certainty nevertheless, a never-distant dread.

On this Friday afternoon Teddy walked along Franklin Street to Mr. Spone's store, looking around for signs of danger, clutching the money Pa had given him to buy a pack of Lucky Strikes. "Here's a dollar," Pa had said, handing him the crumpled green bill. "An' don't lose the change!"

A big sponsabilty, Teddy reminded himself, like carrying a heavy rock that he must not set down, even for a moment, until he returned home safely with Pa's *sigrets* and change.

It was not a long walk, only a few blocks. Teddy liked going to Mr. Spone's store but, not so nice, was the *Bad Thing* waiting for him at the *Bad Corner*. Sometimes it grabbed him on his way to the store and, again, on his way home. Those were *speshul bad* days. But so far today nothing bad had happened, and Teddy felt relieved when he arrived safely at the store.

Now he faced *Ol' Green Door*, Mr. Spone's thick, heavy, wooden door that looked even older than Mr. Spone. *Ol' Green Door* stood there, solid and mute, blocking Teddy, challenging him to open it, to push down just right on that little thumb-thing on the handle and, at the same time, shove in with his shoulder and quickly hop over the door sill. It had taken him many tries to get those coordinated movements to work.

Determined to defeat *Ol' Green Door,* Teddy grabbed the handle, squeezed down on the latch with both hands, and pushed hard with his shoulder. He stumbled as the door flew open, banging against the wall, adding to the noise and clatter of Teddy's feet dancing on the old wooden floor to keep his balance. Once Teddy was inside, *Ol' Green Door* slammed itself shut with a window-rattling crash as if celebrating another victory over Teddy.

Teddy was not purposely making a racket, knowing that some people, like *Ol' Mr. D'veer,* the neighborhood grouch who lived around the corner on Maple Street, didn't like noisy kids, always chasing them away from his lawn. But Mr. Spone was nice, did not mind Teddy's clumsiness and clatter. In fact, Mr. Spone had a noise of his own, a bell, and when you went in or out of his store, the bell, on a spring above *Ol' Green Door,* jumped and jiggled like a puppy happy to see you. Teddy bobbed his head up and down, trying to catch the rhythm of the bell but never quite getting it right.

Maybe it's a cow bell, Teddy thought, *like that cow had around his neck.* (Teddy did not know that cows are girls.) He had met the cow when Ma had taken Teddy and his sister, Emily, to visit a farm. That had been a long time ago and he had no idea where that farm was, but he remembered a warm, sunny day and on their way home they had stopped for ice cream at a bright yellow place where people sat in the sunshine at little round tables on little round chairs made of wire, like the clothes hangers in Ma's closet, only thicker.

Going out for ice cream was a rare treat, and that was Teddy's first taste of an ice cream soda. Emily had strawberry but Teddy wanted one like that boy at the next table was happily scooping up, a *chawclit* ice cream soda, and Teddy was bowled over by that wonderful treat he had never imagined existed. His images of that day were golden-hued, and he remembered that despite the cool tang of the ice cream, a warm feeling had nestled inside him and embraced Teddy, Emily, and Ma as they sat close together at that little round table in the sunshine, Ma giggling at their conspiracy of stolen pleasure while poor Pa had to be at work.

That day Teddy had learned that cows are *real big,* not like those cute little black and white cows in his *picherbooks,* little cows small enough to pick up and put in your pocket. And when that big cow at the farm had ambled over to the fence right at him, head bobbing up and down the way cows do and making that deep "moo" sound, Teddy had yelped and run away but then was drawn back by the cow's tinkling bell and those big, soft, friendly, brown eyes. Later, he thought it was *real funny,* being afraid of that nice cow. Everybody had laughed, especially when the cow turned out to be so friendly after all.

Teddy liked remembering nice things in *pichers* inside his head, right *there,* right behind his eyes, bright *pichers* in bright colors, like the yellow and white ice cream place and the chairs made of wire hangers and the little white tables and the *chawclit* and the strawberry ice cream sodas and that friendly cow and the bell and all. He had lots of *pichers* in there and liked to look at them, like turning the pages of his own secret *picherbook* that nobody else could see.

"I got a picture book too," his sister Emily had told him. "Just like you. Right inside here," she pointed to her eyes. "And nobody else has one, just you and me, Teddy."

"Yeah," Teddy said, smiling. "Jus' you an' me."

"And," Emily added, "it's better than watching the new teevee Pa brought home because our pictures are all color and we can make them as big and bright as we want, not like those little gray teevee pictures that jump around and look like they're in a snowstorm so you can hardly even see them!"[1]

'Yeah," Teddy said. "Can't even see 'em."

Emily liked knowing that she and her little brother shared that. "Hey, maybe Pa has a picture book too, like us," she told Teddy. "Maybe we got it from Pa."

Teddy knew that Pa loved bright colors, liked to paint their bedroom walls in wild colors that Teddy and Emily loved but drove Ma crazy.

Real nice, Teddy thought, which brought up the image of that friendly cow. *Maybe there's a cow out back of Mr. Spone's store,* he wondered. *Maybe that's his cowbell over Ol' Green Door. Maybe the cow wants it back.* Teddy wanted to go and see Mr. Spone's cow but one day when he had shyly asked about the cow behind the store, Mr. Spone was puzzled, didn't know what Teddy was talking about. "Cow?" Mr. Spone had asked. "What cow?"

Now as Teddy stumbled into the store under the jangling cow bell Mr. Spone frowned, thinking, *Is no good, sendin' this boy all alone with money in his pocket. 'Specially here on-a Franklin Street. Got no sense, these parents today. But is nice to see Teddy. A nice kid. No like some o' them fresh kids aroun' here. Trouble-a makers. I worry about him. Eh, somebody gotta' worry about the poor kid.*

"Good-a' morn' young-a' man," he always greeted Teddy, even if it was really afternoon. That was a joke between them. Teddy was not sure what was funny about it, but he laughed and liked it anyway.

Mr. Spone was 66 years old and not very tall, a little pudgy with a bald head and a fringe of white hair around his ears. He frequently took off his wire-framed glasses to rub his eyes with the heel of his hand, making the glasses twirl around in little circles. "How you do today, Teddy?" he asked, carefully putting his glasses back on, squinting to get used to them again.

"Hi Mr. Spone," Teddy answered. "Thumbs up an' A-OK!" he said, completing their usual greeting and handing the dollar bill over the counter, his big smile lighting up his round face and almond-shaped eyes. Teddy did not know why thumbs had to be "up" and not down or just straight out, or exactly what "A-OK" was all about.[2] But no matter, he liked Mr. Spone, liked to visit him in the store and hear him talk. He was a nice man, friendly and funny, and no one else said things like *good-a'* and *how-a'* and *young-a'*. Sometimes at home Teddy talked like Mr. Spone. "Gooda' morn', 'allo, allo," he would greet Ma, Pa, and Emily. "An-a' how-a' you do today young-a' man? Eh?" he asked his Ma, but Pa always told him to "talk right!"

"Oh, don't be such a sourpuss," Ma would say, giving Teddy a hug. "Teddy's just having some fun. Right, sweetheart? Leave him be. Don't be such a grump."

So, at night in his room Teddy had quiet conversations in his Mr. Spone voice with Mr. Binky, his stuffed bear. *Allo, Mr. Binky. An-a how you do today, eh?* It was fun to talk like Mr. Spone, and Mr. Binky must have liked it, too, because he never got irritated about it.

When Teddy handed Pa's dollar over the counter, Mr. Spone put it in his big *cash rester* with the dinging bell and noisy sliding drawer. Then he'd smile and hand Teddy the pack of *sigrets, a* little book of red-tipped matches, *and shiny money!* More money than the *raggedy ol'* green dollar he had started with.

That was one of the nice things about going to the store, getting all that money to jiggle in his pocket. And Mr. Spone, with his nice smile and the funny way he talked, that was nice, too. But best of all was what gently greeted Teddy each time he entered the store, like walking into a cloud of sweet cherry breath mixed with honey and strawberries and vanilla, an invisibly inviting mist of joy. The old wooden floor squeaked as he walked on it, but sometimes it didn't want to, and Teddy had to back up and try again to find the right spot, pleased when the floor finally answered him.

"Ah, Teddy. You woke-a' him up," Mr. Spone would say, his part in their little game.

The small soda fountain was inviting, but Teddy knew he was there for another purpose and had never tried out one of the six stools on which, he suspected, you could twirl all the way around.

Each time he entered Mr. Spone's store Teddy sniffed the sweetness and smiled at Mr. Spone, who smiled back and tipped his head in greeting. They communicated in many ways, Mr. Spone and Teddy; words were not always necessary.

Teddy wondered how Mr. Spone knew what he wanted to buy, not knowing that his father telephoned Mr. Spone after Teddy left the house.

So, Mr. Spone knew which *sigrets* to pick out from all those colorful packs stacked in neat piles on the shelf behind the counter. One pack always caught Teddy's eye because it had a picture of a camel on it. Teddy had never seen a real camel but knew what it was from one of his books.

"See," Emily had told him, turning pages, pointing things out, and naming them for him. "That's a camel. He's kinda' like a horse and people ride on 'em and he has two big bumps on his back and inside them he carries water, like in big barrels, so he won't need to take a drink for a long time. And look, some camels only have one bump! Maybe they don't need so much water."

"Camel go drink water?" Teddy asked.

"No, he can't just go get a drink of water like we do because it's all dry there, like all sand. They don't have water, so he's gotta' carry his own."

Teddy imagined a place that was all sand. He knew he would not like it, especially if he had to have big bumps on his back to carry around his own water, and another image developed in his *picherbook.*

Be nice, he thought, *to take the camel sigrets to Pa instead of Luckies, like a surprise.* "That one," he told Mr. Spone one day, pointing to the package with the camel's picture.

"Ah, no, Teddy," Mr. Spone said. "You father, he no like tha' kind. Better you jus' take his Luckies, like alla time. OK?"

"A-OK!" Teddy agreed, smiling.

Pa's Luckies came in a shiny white package with a big red ball in the middle, a red stripe around the top and bottom and shiny black words on it. Teddy could not read the words but easily recognized the Lucky Strike package in magazines and signs. Someday he would have his own money and get one of those nice Luckies packs for himself.

Mr. Spone was an old man, and he grunted and rubbed his back when he reached to the shelf for the *sigrets.* Old people did things like that. It was funny when Mr. Spone said, "Ai!" in complaint and was so slow to straighten up, keeping his hand on his back and kind of scrunching up his face. But Teddy never laughed because Ma had taught him it was not right to laugh at people, although he wasn't sure why it was not right; people laughed at him plenty of times.

Teddy liked going to the store but worried that the *Bad Thing* might happen. He had never told Ma and Pa about the *Bad Thing,* but they must have known something because they argued, usually in fierce whispers, about sending him to the store by himself. Their arguments, always the same, made Teddy feel bad and he was starting to believe it was all his fault.

"Don't send him to the store alone like that, Frank. He's not ready to go by himself, crossing those busy streets with all those people he doesn't know!"

"Connie, he's almost sixteen for God's sake!"

"No, he's not, and you know it. He's a six-year-old in a fifteen-year-old body."

"I know that, but we can't keep him a six-year-old forever. We gotta' let him grow, spread his wings, learn, like walking to the store and meeting people. You need to loosen the apron strings, Connie, you're holding him back."

"Holding him back ...?"

"Yes, holding him back. You want to hold his hand forever? What's he gonna' do when we're not around? You gotta' let him man up, for God's sake."

"Man up? Oh, that's great. Frank, you don't understand your own son."

"I understand perfectly well ..."

"No, you don't! You're rushing him. Those are busy streets. He's going to get in trouble, get hurt or, or ... something. Don't send him off alone like that. Go with him, take a walk with your son, get off your rear-end and go buy your own damn cigarettes!"

She slammed her palm on the table. "What is it, Frank? You won't walk to the store with your son? Why? Maybe you're uncomfortable because he's not like other kids? Afraid of what other people will think? Afraid that somehow you failed?"

It was an unpleasant, repeated argument. Eventually to avoid it, Frank stopped sending Teddy to the store when Connie was home.

Teddy liked Mr. Spone's store and also enjoyed visiting the Rose Beauty Salon on Main Street where Ma worked three afternoons a week. "Miz Rosie's place," he called it. It was *real nice,* busy and bright with big mirrors, nice perfume smells, and slick black chairs with shiny chrome arms and footrests.

Miz Rosie's nice. I like Miz Rosie. Sometimes he'd go in to wait for Ma to finish with a customer. He liked to sit in one of Miz Rosie's chairs and look at the *pichers* in the magazines and listen to the ladies chatting as they sat under those shiny helmets like the high school football players wore, but bigger and shinier. He had asked Miz Rosie if he could wear one of the shiny football helmets, and she had laughed and said, "Oh, honey, those are only for ladies, to dry their wet hair, not for big boys like you!"

He liked to spin around in the chairs, but Miz Rosie made a rule, shaking her finger at him. "You get only two spins, young man, and slow ones at that. Then you gotta' stop. Don't wancha' bustin' my expensive chairs. Then you'd hafta' get your Pa's toolbox and fix 'em. You think you can do that? Fix my busted chairs?"

"Sure!" Teddy would answer, with his big smile and naive confidence. "Kin fix 'em real good!"

"I'm sure you can, Teddy," Miz Rosie said, smiling. "But, you know," she leaned down and whispered, like they had a secret, "maybe it'd be better if you don't break 'em in the first place. Dontcha' think?"

"Yeah," Teddy said, smiling at Miz Rosie. "Don't break 'em! A-OK!"

"Miz Rosie's Saloon," Teddy called her place.

"No, sweetie, it's not a sa*loon,*" Ma patiently corrected him, gently cradling his face in her hands. "It's a Beauty *Salon.* Don't go tellin' people your Ma works in a sa*loon!* What would our neighbors think if you told them that?"

But Pa thought it was funny and encouraged Teddy to call it Miss Rosie's saloon, just "to get Ma's goat."

Goat? Teddy thought. *What goat?* And that made him think of Mr. Spone's cow out behind the store. Teddy was not sure what a *saloon* was, anyway. Maybe that's where Ma kept her goat. Someday, he decided, he would ask her.

"Your Ma's gonna' be workin' at the saloon, today," Pa would say loudly, making sure Ma heard him. Then Pa and Teddy would cover their mouths and snicker like third graders.

Connie would glare at Pa, then smile at Teddy, give him a hug, ruffle his hair, and tell him quietly for the millionth time, "Sa-*lon*, honey, Sa-*lon*."

Ma worked three afternoons a week. Pa worked six nights at the power plant and was home all day until late afternoon. When he ran out of cigarettes and Ma was working in Miz Rosie's *Saloon*, that's when he sent Teddy to Mr. Spone's, like today.

Teddy imagined Pa being *The Boss* of the power plant, running those big machines that towered over Teddy when Pa had taken him one day to see the plant. He imagined Pa running everything from his big chair that could spin all the way around, even better than Miz Rosie's *saloon* chairs, watching a hundred clocks on the wall in front of him. Some of the clocks were running fast, their hands whirling around like Ma's *letrit fan* on a hot day; others had only one hand that moved slowly in little jumps, and some did not have any hands at all, just red and black lines. Having so many clocks was strange—you need only one clock to tell time, although Teddy couldn't tell time anyway no matter how many clocks he might have. But he was sure his Pa knew what time it was and what all those clocks meant.

The big wall of clocks was impressive, but it was the noise that overwhelmed Teddy, the thumping and whirring of the great machines that Pa tamed every night. It was loud, with booming echoes like those big drums the high school band pounded on when marching up Main Street on *forthajooleye.*

Pa was like the *train driver* who waved at Teddy from high in his giant black steam-hissing engine when he drove his train into Nyack's station. Pa had told Teddy that the engineer was Mr. Fiola and he lived on Brookside Avenue, just a few blocks away. Often, when he heard a train coming, Teddy ran down Cedar Hill to wave at Mr. Fiola but sometimes it was a different train driver. That was OK, and Teddy waved anyway.

To Teddy, Pa and Mr. Fiola were the men who ran the big machines, the *bosses* of everything. Pa, turning his chair, checking clocks, pushing switches, busy making *letrisity* for the whole town, keeping everything running and everybody's lights glowing all night. In his private *picherbook* behind his eyes Teddy watched Mr. Fiola driving his great black engine and Pa running his great machines, and Teddy was sure proud of his Pa.

Now with Pa's Lucky Strikes in his pocket, Teddy knew he had to leave the safety of Mr. Spone's store and start his journey home. He hesitated, frowned, and moved slowly toward the door.

Mr. Spone saw his hesitation. "You go straighta' home, Teddy," he said with a reassuring smile. "Straighta' home. OK? An' a' wah-chou' for da' cars!" He made sure Teddy put the change safely in his pocket, and gave him a penny candy from the big jar on the counter.

"Bye Mr. Spone. A-OK! Thumbs up!" Teddy smiled and opened the door, sending the cow bell jingling. He put the candy in his mouth, tasted its ginger bite and sugary sweetness. It was good. He looked back, waved at Mr. Spone. Teddy let *Ol' Green Door* slam behind him, jumping out of the way so the heavy door would not bump him, but it always did, making him hop and skip down the single step to the sidewalk. Teddy gave the door a stern look. Then, as Mr. Spone watched through the big window, Teddy headed home.

Chapter Two:

The Little Blue Bottle

In the 1950s there were still songbirds in the few remaining trees along Nyack's commercial streets and among the shiny green weeds and glorious goldenrod that grew tall in the empty lots that dotted the town. Teddy liked those lots—not knowing they had once harbored homes and stores, had been alive with vibrant families and exuberant children but had decayed in economic despair, their tumbled rubble sad witness to personal tragedies during the Great Depression. To Teddy the lots were islands to explore on his journey home.

One day a sparkle of sunshine had flashed and caught his eye. Using a stick, he dug out a small blue bottle. It was caked with mud, except for the spot that had sparkled at him, and had raised letters that he could feel with his fingers. *A treasure!* He ran home with it.

Washing the bottle made a mess that he did not notice until Ma came into the kitchen and said, in her patient way, like singing a song: "Oh Teddy, my Teddy, what have you done now?"

He looked up at Ma and down at the muddy water in the sink and on the floor, puzzled about how it got there. Ma smiled. "C'mon, Teddy, let's clean it up."

Teddy was eager to make up for the mess he had made, and they cleaned it in no time. Ma washed out the little bottle, dried and polished it with a towel. Then they sat at the table to examine his new blue treasure, turning it over and over so it sparkled in the sunshine streaming through the window over the sink.

"Real pretty!" Teddy said.

"It's an old perfume bottle," Ma explained. "Might be a hundred years old. I remember old bottles like this when I was little."

"Yeah," Teddy answered, seriously. "You're a hundred years old."

"No, sweetie," she laughed. "I am not a hundred years old. But I remember my Grammy had pretty bottles like this. You know, some of those bottles must have been very old because my Grammy was born before the Civil War."

"Yeah," Teddy said. "Silver War," his private *picherbook* already working on shiny images of whatever a *Silver War* might be. *Maybe like the shiny money Mr. Spone gives me.*

Connie laughed. "OK, sweetie. 'Silver War' it is."

"A-OK," Teddy agreed.

"And I remember," Connie continued, "Grammy had a little table in her room, with only three legs, one in the back and two in front; a table with only three legs, and I always thought it was going to fall down!"

"Table fall down?" Teddy asked, a new interest in his voice.

"No," Ma smiled. "It never did. Its three legs were perfectly good. And it was covered with a pretty blue cloth that my Grammy embroidered."

"Broyded?" Teddy asked, puzzled.

"Embroidered, sweetie. That means Grammy sewed it all up with a needle and thread, so it had lots of pretty colors in it."

Broyded, Teddy thought. A three-legged table sewn up with pretty colors began to form in Teddy's *picherbook.*

"And on the table," Connie added, "all lined up on that pretty blue cloth, Grammy had a dozen little bottles just like this one, only they were full of wonderful perfumes and powders and salts. And when no one was looking, I sneaked into Grammy's room to open them up and sniff how lovely they were."

Teddy picked up his bottle, sniffed it, and looked disappointed.

"Oh my, Teddy," Connie laughed. "Whatever nice perfume was in your little bottle a hundred years ago is all gone now."

"Yeah, all gone," Teddy said, looking sad.

Teddy kept his treasure in a wooden cigar box with a picture of a pretty lady on the cover. Mr. Spone had given the box to him after Teddy had said it was "real nice."

"See," he showed Ma when he had brought the box home. "Mr. Spone's lady smoked all the cigars. You smoke cigars, Ma?"

"No, young man," Connie answered, arching her eyes, "I do not smoke cigars."

"Huh" Teddy said.

"And I suppose you think I ought to be smoking cigars while I'm working in Rosie's *Saloon*?" Ma asked.

"Sure," Teddy said, a little uncertainly because of her tone, seeing in his *picherbook* the ladies in Miz Rosie's *Saloon* wearing their big shiny football helmets and smoking cigars. Maybe someday he'd get some cigars from Mr. Spone and take them to Miz Rosie's *Saloon* for the ladies to smoke.

Although he did not have a clear concept of "favorite," Teddy knew he liked blue the best. He liked bright colors wherever he saw them: flowers, birds, ladies' dresses. Teddy liked those brilliant blue birds with their black wings and those bright black and yellow birds and even the little brown sparrows who were not so colorful but chattered and hopped around in the back yard chasing after the breadcrumbs that he tossed out to them whenever he could. Little birds made a big racket chattering, hopping, and popping up and down like they were on springs and getting all mad whenever that big bully blue jay came after their breadcrumbs. *Bullies,* he thought. *Birds got bullies too.*

And birds made nice noises, not like the pounding in Pa's power plant. He liked their singing and chirping and even their squawking as he watched them from his bedroom window, keeping still so they would not get scared and fly away. *They peck all around,* he thought, like the little girl who went *peck, peck pecking down the street* in his favorite song that he heard on the radio, the one that lady sang, who was sad because she lost her little yellow basket.[1]

The bright red birds that sang from the highest treetops were around all year, even in the wintertime when you could see them best against the snow and the bright sky, and he knew their songs whenever he heard them. "All the other birds fly south in the winter," his sister had told him, and he imagined that south was a nice, warm place filled with all the colorful birds singing in the trees.

Teddy's favorite birds were the shy, quiet, ones, also in the tops of the trees. A long time ago, when he was little, he had seen a strange-looking car driving by. "It's a streamlined car," Emily had told him.[2] He wasn't sure what "streamlined" meant but he could see its shape and he decided that those shy birds were streamlined too. He had seen them only once because they liked to hide and were very quiet, so it was hard to find them. That one time he saw them he had stopped and held his breath, not daring to move even a finger for fear of scaring them away. He saw not just one bird, but a whole bunch lined up on two branches, one above the other. Some were turned his way and some away, some fluffing up their feathers or flapping their wings, or just sitting there. They were the most beautiful birds he had ever seen, perfectly combed and smooth, softly gray on top, gently fading into shades of pale-yellow underneath, with a splash of black and a bit of red and white here and there and a sweep of feathers on their heads as if they combed them straight back like the high school boys combed their hair, making them look like they were always running a race or facing a wind. Teddy stored the images in his *picherbook*. He did not know the birds were cedar waxwings, could not easily describe them in words, but he held them vividly in his *pitchbook*.

Emily, knowing how much he liked birds, had given him a bird book for his birthday and it had pictures of those beautiful quiet birds. Teddy could not read the words to name or describe them, but he knew they were *real speshul*, so much finer than all the others, never chattering and jiggling about like the silly little sparrows. But most interesting was what he discovered in his new bird book: "See!" he said to Emily, pointing to a picture of the bird. "He got a mask!" And, indeed, the bird was wearing a slim, glossy black mask that swept back right into the streamlined crest on his head.

Whenever Teddy came to his *speshul tree,* he stopped and walked quietly around it, looking up into the cool quiet green world of filtered shafts of sunlight, and the rustle of leaves as unseen birds moved through the branches. Teddy hoped to catch sight of those birds again, lined up in their world. Except for the blue jays and sparrows, he did not know birds' names or much about them. They were just there, in Teddy's world. "Birds are our special friends," Mrs. Kinsella, his next-door neighbor, had once told him. *Speshul,* Teddy thought. *Speshul friends.*

Now Teddy came to his *streamlined bird tree.* He carefully tip-toed around the thick trunk, stumbling on the big roots that he knew were there but tripped him every time anyway. Looking up into the leafy canopy Teddy held his breath, but the streamlined birds were not there. *Hidin'*, he decided. Disappointed, he patted the rough bark of his *speshul tree*, a big maple, although he did not know it was a maple. He did know, however, that his special tree, like so many others along Nyack's sidewalks, made its own *green snow.* Sometime during the year trees all over Nyack sent green whirly-things spiraling down, like a million butterflies covering the ground with a crunchy carpet of *green snow.*

"Seeds," Emily explained one day. "See, the tree makes seeds and puts wings on them and flies them down to the ground to make baby trees."

"Seeds got wings," Teddy said, "an' make baby trees." For Teddy, all trees were big trees. He had never wondered how they became so big—they just *were.* Now he pictured baby trees, and that made him smile. He could see them growing out of the ground, tiny trees not even as high as his ankle, just like the big trees but with tiny little leaves. He smiled at his picture of baby trees, storing it away in his *picherbook.* He tilted his head back to look up into the dark green jungle of the big maple expecting to see seeds with wings flying down but then felt dizzy as always happened when he looked up fast like that and he had to look down, so the dizzy feeling would go away.

What he expected to see did not go away, it had seeped into his *picherbook* to become a permanent image—a rich, mottled green, pleasantly warm snowstorm of seeds with wings silently drifting down all around him, covering the ground, bursting into tiny trees growing all over the sidewalk, causing him to be very careful where he stepped to avoid hurting the baby trees.

His *picherbook* image was vivid, but when he looked down at the ground, there were no baby trees! He had asked Emily, "Where the baby trees in the sidewalk?"

Emily had smiled. "That's concrete," she said. "Trees can't grow in concrete. They need soil to grow in. See, when the seeds fall on the sidewalk, they dry up and die. But, when they fall on soil, they grow into baby trees."

Teddy thought about that, feeling sad for the poor seeds that died. After that, when the green snow began to fall, Teddy tried to pick up every seed from the sidewalk and put them into the soil, usually into Pa's lawn, where he hoped they would grow. But there were too many seeds and after a while he stopped doing that, but occasionally he still rescued a few.

Teddy looked up into the big tree and circled it one more time, stumbling over the root as usual but saw no streamlined birds. Disappointed, he gave his tree another soft pat. "Bye, tree," he said, and walked on.

Chapter Three:

The Red Horse Bird

As Teddy neared the *Bad Corner,* walking home from Mr. Spone's store, that tight coil in his gut was starting up again. He squeezed the coins tightly in his hand to make sure they did not jingle, so they would be quiet and safe like the shy, streamlined birds hiding in the *speshul tree.* The coins reminded him of his *big sponsabilty,* adding to the unease that was growing inside him as he neared the corner of Franklin Street and Cedar Hill. Mr. Burt's gas station was just ahead, across the street, and he could see his favorite sign with its picture of the big red horse with wings.[1] Teddy's house and safety were near, just up the hill and around the corner. He was almost home.

Teddy wished he did not need to go to that dreaded corner. There were other ways home from Mr. Spone's store, longer, roundabout routes where he could not remember which way to turn at the unfamiliar corners. Maybe someday he would learn. Pa said he would. But for now, this was the way he was sure of—*stay on the horse-bird stre*et *to go home.*

He was pretty sure that horses don't have wings, don't really fly. Teddy remembered asking Emily as they leafed through the pictures in his bird book if she had ever seen a horse-bird.

"A what? A horse-bird? What's a horse-bird?"

"Red horse-bird. Mr. Burt's gas station. Red horse-birds got wings. Baby horse-birds in a tree. *That* horse-bird."

They both laughed at that, and Teddy looked inside himself to one of his *pichers* of a nest with the big red horse-bird and the little baby red horse-birds.

"Boy," Emily said. "A red horse-bird and baby horse-birds in a tree. What an imagination you have!"

"Yeah. Mashinashin." He wasn't sure what a *mashinashin* was, but suspected it was a good thing and was pleased that Emily said he had one. Teddy hugged his sister and leaned his head on her shoulder. Emily smiled and they sat there, quietly, for a nice, long moment.

Now, intent on getting safely home Teddy walked faster, reminding himself to *turn this way* when he reached the red horse-bird, pointing his left arm straight out, like a driver signaling a turn. He stopped, frowned. *No*, he corrected himself, dropping the arm and extending his right one. *This* way. If he did it right, his house, white with gray trim, would be there as usual, just up the hill and around the corner.

Twice while taking other routes from Mr. Spone's store, he had lost his way, and his distress had taught him to stay with this familiar, safe route along Franklin Street. The irony, that this way felt the safest but was really the most dangerous, was not understood by Teddy.

The *Bad Corner* was not always bad; sometimes he went through it quickly, with no problems. But he never knew when the safe times would be. Was it dangerous only some days, at certain times of the day? He could not untangle all that, think it through and plan to approach the corner at the safest times or console himself with thoughts like, *it doesn't happen all the time, I got a good chance of bein' safe*. What he *knew* for sure was, *that's the Bad Corner,* and Teddy felt the dread every time.

Now the *Bad Corner* was just ahead, only a few steps to go. Looking carefully around he saw no *Bad Thing* getting ready to leap out and grab him. Mr. Nichols' high hedge was there, making Teddy feel uneasy because he could not see behind it, see what might be hiding there. But everything seemed quiet, safe. He clutched the coins in his pocket and held his breath, not daring to make any sounds. Slowly, heart pounding, Teddy stepped carefully to the corner. He stopped at the curb. Nothing bad happened. Teddy looked, this way and that, straight ahead and up and down the hill; everything seemed *A-OK*. Safety was just across the street at Mr. Burt's gas station. He began to relax; his knotted stomach eased. Close to home, now, and no *Bad Thing*; another step, another. All was quiet; and then it was not.

The Bad Thing roared out from behind the hedge and leaped on him.

"Ha! Look! It's The Retard!" the *Bad Thing* screamed, its voice slicing through Teddy. Thoughts of birds and colors and nice days, and sweet, peppery candy and Mr. Spone's funny talk evaporated. Turmoil and fear boiled inside him. He ran blindly to get away from this tormentor who had been hiding behind Mr. Nichols' hedge, watching Teddy's approach.

Running away was new for Teddy. In the past when the *Bad Thing* had snatched him, he had turned rigid, his body stuck, frozen in place. Not knowing what to do, he had done nothing.

Not long ago, Roger had told him, "Run, Teddy. When they come after you, run as fast as you can and get home or to my house."

Roger was Teddy's best friend even though he was older and in college. Teddy had known him all his life. Roger had taken his young neighbor under his wing, played games with him, told funny stories, and protected Teddy from bullies and the everyday meanness of an ignorant world. Roger called Teddy "my little brother," and Teddy loved it.

Mr. Chisholm, Roger's father, had told the boys a story of a special day years ago. "You know, Teddy, you wouldn't think it now, but Roger was a little devil. Never listened to nobody about nothin', like being careful. Was always climbing trees and poles, swinging from branches, doing cartwheels on his roller skates, jumpin' offa' the garage roof, and just genr'lly getting hisself all banged up so's we hadda' run him up to the hospital just about every other week!"

Teddy was fascinated to hear all this about his friend Roger, his big brother. "One day," Mr. Chisholm continued, "when Roger was maybe six or seven, he went jumpin' offa' the garage roof like we tol' him a hun'red times not to, an' twisted his ankle bad and there we go again, up to the hospital to see Doc Wharton for the second time that summer."

Teddy beamed at this. "Dokker War'n. My fren!"

"Yep, that's him," Mr. Chisholm said. "And do you know, Teddy, while Roger was givin' Doc Wharton a hard time when the Doc was tryin' to bandage' up his ankle, do you know that a little boy was gettin' born right there in that hospital practically in the room next door? Well, maybe not right next door, but close by. An' you know who that little boy was?"

Roger knew, he had heard the story before. But this was new to Teddy.

"Well, that was you, m'boy. You, Teddy, gettin' born right there. An' when your folks brought you home to your house right next door to us, you and Roger, you got to be good friends right away and you been friends ever since."

"Yeah, frens. Roger got hurt an' I got borned an' Roger's my big brother." Teddy smiled. It all made sense to him.

One day Teddy learned that Roger and his father had the same last name.

"Your name," he told Roger, pleased with his new knowledge, "is Roger Chickins."

Roger laughed and, putting an arm around Teddy's shoulder, said, "Well, little brother, that's close, but not quite. Now, try it again. *Chisholm. Chis-holm.* See? Chis-holm. Try it."

Teddy worked on it. "Chick-ins" he said. Then, after a moment to collect his thoughts he added, "And your Pa is Mr. Chickins."

"No," Roger sighed. "Not *Chickens,* Teddy. *Chisholm.* Look, just call my Pa Mr. C. OK.?"

"A-OK," Teddy said, always happy to please Roger, although he did not understand why Roger's father was named *Mr. See* and not *Mr. Chickins,* like Roger.

That had been a long time ago. But right now, being threatened by *The Bad Thing,* Teddy remembered that Roger had told him "Run, Teddy. Run, when the bullies get after you."

Roger had tried to teach Teddy to defend himself, to throw a hard punch when the bullies started in on him. "See, like this. Make a fist. Real tight. Yeah, that's it. Then you gotta' throw your shoulder into it, twist your body, see? Not just with your arm. Your shoulder, your whole body. Watch me. Like this. See? Wham!"

"Wham!" Teddy shouted. "Wham!" showing Roger how hard he could punch. But his punches were weak, soft, and uncoordinated, and would never stop the bullies.

"Hmmm," Roger said. "Maybe you should just try to run away. Can you do that, Teddy? Run away? Run real fast?"

"Sure," Teddy said. "See?" Teddy ran as fast as he could around Roger's yard, certain that he was zooming along just like Roger.

"Real fast, huh?" he beamed, breathing hard from the exertion.

"That's good, Teddy," Roger told him, despite Teddy's slow and clumsy attempt to run.

Now remembering Roger's advice, Teddy ran, but in panic, heading blindly into the street. Here was Connie's private terror, her little boy running recklessly into traffic, his small body at the mercy of cars and trucks. Traffic was heavy at the Franklin Street corner, across the railroad tracks, past the Singer Sewing Machine factory and the Nyack Lumber Mill. But Teddy was lucky: just then no cars came around the corner or trucks from the mill, no train moved on the rails. Teddy made it across the street and began to run up Cedar Hill Avenue, close to home and safety.

But Teddy's tormentor was not yet finished. "Hah!" the bully laughed, rearing back on his heels, pointing both arms straight out at Teddy, aiming his fingers like a two-gun outlaw in the Saturday afternoon movies. "Lookit," he shouted to his friends, laughing, and pointing. "Lookit the Retard run! Looks like a chicken! Hah! Hey, Retard! You a chicken? Huh? A chicken?"

Gary—Teddy's *Bad Thing*—stood inches taller and pounds heavier than other boys his age. He was perfectly built for his favorite sport, menacing weaker kids. Teddy, with his peculiar appearance, short stature, clumsiness, and physical weakness was a tailor-made victim for Gary's enjoyment.

Gary mocked Teddy, wobbling side to side, flapping his arms and cackling like a chicken. "Where ya' runnin' Retard? Back to yor chicken coop? Huh, Retard? Yor chicken coop?"

Teddy ran as fast as he could just like Roger had told him, but his short legs and clumsy coordination made him no match for the bully who sprinted across the street, caught Teddy by the belt, hooked an arm around Teddy's neck, and pulled him off his feet, off the sidewalk, back across the street and behind Mr. Nichols' hedge. Teddy's legs pumped uselessly in the air like a wind-up toy. He was snared, netted, trapped, caught, held and going nowhere despite his pumping legs and flailing arms.

The bully laughed at Teddy's struggles. "Where ya' runnin', Retard? You inna hurry? Don'cha know you ain't movin', Retard? Ain't even goin' no place?"

Teddy tried to shout "lemme go!" but he could not escape the bully's grip and, feeling himself choking, could only make gagging sounds.

The bully enjoyed that and mocked him even more. "Guh! Guh! Guh!" he imitated Teddy's choking. Laughing, and squeezing harder, he leaned into Teddy's face, spraying him with spit.

"Cantcha' talk, Retard? Ya' scared, Retard? Huh? Why ya' scared o' me, Retard? I'm only bein' friendly! I'm yor friend, see?"

He squeezed his arm tighter around Teddy's neck, bringing on the panicked feeling of choking to death, like the bully did to him last time, making him go all loose inside and so scared that he had wet himself, right there in the street. The bully had laughed at that, and mocked Teddy even more, jumping away from the spreading wetness, pointing, and calling Teddy "Baby Retard."

"Oooh!" he had taunted. "Baby Retard needs a *dyyy-per*!"

"Ya' scairt, Baby Retard?" The bully breathed into Teddy's face. "Ya' gonna piss y'self again, like ya' done last time?"

But this time Teddy was determined to hold it in, controlling himself, he wasn't going to go through *that* again. His gut tightened and he struggled to escape but could not get out of the bully's tight grip. Teddy felt himself starting to cry, tried to stop but the sobs began to shake him.

"Hey," the bully shouted to his friends, Ricky and Tom. "Let's pull Retard's pants down." He laughed. "Make him piss right here inna' street, where everybody can see!"

"C'mon, Gary," Ricky said, feeling uneasy, looking around to see if anyone was watching.

Ricky was a slight, timid boy and no match for Gary, but he found some courage, stepped up to Gary and pulled hard on his arm.

"Leave the kid alone, Gary. He ain't done nothin' to you! You're hurtin' him."

Ricky pulled harder. "Let him go!"

"Shut up," Gary growled. Releasing Teddy, he savagely twisted Ricky's hand away and shoved his fist into the smaller boy's face.

"You want a knuckle san'wich pounded down your throat? Huh? Do ya? Huh?"

Ricky's bravery evaporated, and he backed off.

The interruption was enough for Teddy. He hitched up his pants and began running up the hill toward home. The nearer he came to his house the safer he would be, knowing that Gary—who wanted to be called "Gar" because that sounded like a tough guy in a comic book—was afraid to follow him to his house where Teddy's father might be home or, worse for Gary, where Roger might catch him.

Gary watched Teddy running up the hill, his awkward, slow, bowlegged gait making the bully laugh. He let Teddy escape, knowing that he could easily catch him again, like a cat torturing a mouse. Anyway, there would be other times to have fun with *The Retard.*

Chapter Four:

Fathers and Sons

Each day after school, Gary, Tom, and Ricky walked along Midland Avenue, down Cedar Hill and across the railroad tracks. They often detoured for some mischief at the Liberty Street Grammar School playground with its little-kids' swings, see-saws, and sand box. Mr. Walmsley, the custodian, would be working in the building after school hours. They taunted him by climbing the fence into the empty playground and pumping furiously on the swings, then twisting them up, knotting their chains together. They tried lifting a see saw from its supports to throw over the fence, but the thick wooden board was too heavy to lift that high.

Their commotion brought Mr. Walmsley running, shaking his fist at them. But the boys were fast and agile, easily hopped the fence and ran across the street, hooting and laughing at him. "Hey, Ol' Wormy Walmsley" Gary taunted, safely outside the fence. "Come and get me, old man!"

But on this day, as Teddy ran home, Gary found something even better.

"Hey, wait," he shouted to his friends, reaching down to the sidewalk, his eyes gleaming. "Wow! Hey! Lookit this!"

Gary held up his discovery. "Lookit! A whole new pack o' Luckies. Ain't even open. And matches. And money, too! Three quarters! Oh man! Retard musta' dropped 'em!"

Rickie's eyes widened. "What's he doin' with cigarettes, Gar? Ya think he smokes!"

"No, ya' dumbass! He musta' got 'em for his old man. Over at the Dago store, Ol' man Strepponey-Macaroni."

"C'mon!" Tom said, excited. "Let's go in my garage. My folks ain't home yet. We kin smoke 'em in there. Nobody's gonna' know."

Ricky was not sure about this. He knew kids should not smoke, had been warned that cigarettes could "stunt your growth" and "make you sick." But, at least for now, he was still in Gary's gang, and he reluctantly went along.

They ran across the tracks to Tom's house, excited by their new treasures. Cigarettes and money! "Who thought we'd be this lucky?" Tom said.

The boys huddled in Tom's garage, making sure the double doors were closed so Tom's nosey neighbor—*Ol' Biddy McQuiddy*, he called her—couldn't see them.

"She got a big ol' telescope in her bedroom,"Tom explained. "An' she's always spyin' on everybody in the neighborhood. 'Specially on kids, an' when she sees something she don't like, she goes and calls the cops on' us! She's really a ol' witch and lives all alone and nobody knows what really goes on inside her witch house!"

They fumbled open the pack, each taking a cigarette, Gary keeping the rest of the pack, the money, and matches. Gary and Tom had tried cigarettes before, but this was new for Ricky.

"I smoke all the time," Gary said, lighting his cigarette the way men do and puffing out a cloud of smoke but being careful not to inhale. Tom and Ricky knew he was just bragging, lying really, but dared not challenge him. The boys huddled around the burning match that Gary held out, fired up the Luckies, sucked in the hot smoke. But first Gary, always looking for a chance to torment someone, showed Ricky, the novice, how to do it.

"See, Rick," he instructed, putting an arm around Ricky's thin shoulders, and winking at Tom who knew what was coming. "You gotta' take a great big drag and you gotta' swallow the smoke real fast, all the way down. Go ahead. Try it."

Ricky, innocently following Gary's instructions, took a hefty drag on the cigarette, pulling the smoke deep into his lungs, and knew immediately he was going to die as the hot toxins seared his throat, and attacked his lungs and brain.[1] Gary roared with laughter, pounded Ricky's back, enjoying his friend's anguish.

Ricky slowly recovered, tears rolling, coughing, face red, certain he would not live another moment and resolved that if he did, he would never touch another cigarette the rest of his life.

Gary could not stop laughing, doubled over, holding his stomach, and pointing at Ricky. "Oh man, you shoulda' seen yor face. Man, oh man! An' smoke was comin' outa' yor ears too!"

Tom thought that bit of sadistic embroidery was hilarious. "Yeah," he said. "Right out of your ears, Rick. You shoulda' seen it!"

Ricky failed to see the humor. His image of Gary and Tom darkened. Shaky, he threw his still-burning cigarette on the floor.

Gary and Tom laughed at him, continued puffing, the smoke thickening around them, making them dizzy and a little sick which, of course, they would never admit. "Man, this is good, huh?" they told each other as they choked and coughed and turned red and green. In school they would brag how they had "smoked the whole pack" when, in fact, neither had been able to finish even one cigarette.

After several minutes Tom, feeling queasy, thought he had better stop before he got sicker, but could not admit that he was a weakling, a *pansy* like Ricky. "We better get goin', he choked out. My Pa's coming home and he drives the car in the garage an' we don't want to be here smokin' when he does."

"So what?" Gary asked. "You scairt o' yor ol' man?"

"Sure am," Tom said. "He catch us in here, he could get mad and make me stay in every day after school all week; probly make me spend all day Saturday cleaning out the cellar and cutting the grass or something."

None of that worried Gary. "You're a pansy. *I* ain't scaired o' *my* ol' man."

But they did leave the garage, careful to close the doors. Tom went into his house and to the refrigerator to see what he might find. After cleaning out a shelf of cold leftovers Tom went in his room and dropped onto the bed, dirty shoes, and all. His stomach, already riled up by the cigarette, was now in more turmoil from the bowl of congealed mac-and-cheese, a slice of cold pizza, and a big drink of cold milk from the bottle, all consumed in about four minutes.

While Tom's distress grew, his father pulled into the driveway. Relieved to be home after a tough day, he was looking forward to a relaxing evening. He turned off the engine, snuffed out his cigarette in the Plymouth's overflowing ash tray built into the dashboard, and set the emergency brake. Stepping out of the car he pulled open the garage doors.

Like all smokers he was not aware that fumes from his own heavy smoking permeated his hair and clothes, and filled his nostrils, leaving him barely able to detect the lingering smoke in the garage. But the boys had left ample evidence: a cloud of cigarette smoke hugging the ceiling, charred matches; three crushed cigarettes on the floor near a can of gasoline.

He stormed into the house looking for Tom, furious—not because of the smoking, after all "boys will be boys" and experimenting with cigarettes was a healthy, normal rite of passage, nothing to become alarmed about.[2]

Tom's father was furious over their carelessness around the gasoline, a disaster waiting to happen from a carelessly tossed match or cigarette. He had left the can there but could not accept his complicity in that potential tragedy. Turning his ire on Tom, he entered the house, slammed the door, and found Tom lying on his bed, pale and groaning in distress.

His anger evaporated. "What's the matter," he asked. "Are you sick?"

"Yeah,"Tom moaned. "Don't feel good. Stomach. Hurts. Head, too."

In a few moments Tom's father had the whole story of smoking and binge eating. *Well,* he thought. *Now's not the time to get after him for smoking around that gas can.* "I hope this teaches you a lesson," he told Tom. "I'll get you some of that pink stuff, it'll settle your stomach. And since when do you wear shoes in bed on your Ma's good quilt? Take them off before she gets home!"

An hour later Tom was feeling better because his stomach was settling, his father had not blown up and the feared punishment had not descended. In fact, his Pa had been really nice about it. Soon, Tom drifted off to sleep.

Chapter Five:

The Goldfinch

In the father we can see
What the son is soon to be

After leaving Tom's house, Gary and Ricky separated at Catherine Street. Ricky, like Tom, was not feeling too well. Gary, however, was in good spirits, although still a little queasy from the cigarettes. It was a beautiful day, but Gary seldom noticed such things. What he did see was a little yellow bird, a goldfinch, swaying gently on a goldenrod in an empty lot, pecking at seeds, an easy target. Gary picked up a sharp stone, reared back, and fired it—aiming to slice the little bird's head right off—but missed.

Stupid bird. Too dumb to fly away. I won't miss this time! He searched the ground and picked up a bigger stone, but the goldfinch had darted away.

Nuts! Gary blindly threw the stone across the street, not concerned that he might hit someone, like that kid on her tricycle. The stone zipped by the child, who looked up, knowing something had whipped by but not what or from where. Gary was alarmed by his near-miss, not for the little girl he almost hit but because he could have been in real trouble had he hit her with that stone. Gary looked around to make sure there were no witnesses and then ran to the safety of the next block.

He slowed to catch his breath and soon came to Gertie's house. At sixteen, Gertie had, seemingly overnight, developed an enchanting body and unguarded innocence that drove adolescent boys into breathless fantasies. Gary had heard what the older boys said about their imagined adventures with Gertie.

Gary had his own fantasies but no experience with girls. He wondered what it was like but wasn't sure what "it" was or how to get her to show him. He knew that Gertie, being stuck-up like all the older girls, was not interested in "kids" his age. *But who knows? Maybe ...*

So, he sucked in his belly, squared his shoulders, and swaggered past Gertie's house, hoping she might be sitting on her porch steps and would see him. He stuck a cigarette in a corner of his mouth, rolled up the left sleeve of his tee shirt and tucked in the pack, like the older boys did, leaving enough of the bright pack showing for Gertie to see. But Gertie was not sitting on the steps and missed Gary strutting by. *Nuts!*

Gary was thirteen, the biggest kid in the sixth grade and a full year older than his classmates. He did not think of himself as a bully. He knew he was mean, *wanted* to be mean, and wanted everyone to know he was mean because, he told himself, he was *tougher and stronger than anybody else.* It felt good making kids cry, like *The Retard*, to twist their arms and make them feel pain, just enough to make them beg and then be all thankful to him when he let them go. He was only having fun, *no big deal. Never hurt nobody.* The best part was the fear in the kids' faces. And they knew better than to go cryin' to their Pa or to the principal, *ol' Big-Beak Ascherton with his nose like a big-assed bird.* Gary warned his small victims—grabbing them painfully by their thin arms and digging his fingers into their elbow joints—that if they squealed on him, he'd really get them next time, and that kept them in line. But, anyway, when complaints had been made the principal brushed them off: "Boys will be boys," he said.

Gary made sure his victims were younger, smaller, and weaker than himself. *Older kids are no fun.* In truth, he feared kids his age and size; they fought back, so he left them alone.

Gary had his "gang" to back him up. When the three of them surrounded a victim, others knew trouble was ahead but could do nothing about it. Gary became so skilled at selecting easy victims that he won all those confrontations; his repeated successes made him bolder, meaner, and more pleased with his power. He swaggered along the street, as tough guys do.

Reaching home Gary looked up at the shaky wooden staircase tacked onto the old single-family house, long ago cut up into two small apartments. The old house sat uncertainly at a rutted dead-end street on a narrow lot squeezed between a depression-abandoned gas station and a junk-littered empty lot.

The stairs led to the second-floor apartment where he lived with his parents. Never eager to get home, Gary hesitated before reluctantly starting up, careful not to slide his hand on the rough wooden railing with its long, sharp splinters.

At the top he paused, looked down twelve feet to the ground where a bone-thin, dirty-yellow cat pawed at something in the weeds, probably a piece of garbage. *Wish I had a rock,* he thought. *I could really nail that scrawny thing.*

The cat ran away when two motorcycles roared into the empty lot, circled through it, and sped away down the street.

From his high platform, Gary saw the weeds struggling for life in the hard-packed dirt, the crumbling gas station, and the junk-littered lot. The street ended there, just gave out at his house, a dead end.

Gary pressed his ear to the door. All was quiet. He slowly opened the door, stepped inside, and found his father sitting at the kitchen table, his big hands wrapped around an empty beer bottle, its tip poking out between two fingers. A cigarette wrapper lay crumpled on the floor. Ashes and butts spilled from a cracked saucer on the table. Smoke drifted up slowly from a crushed, still-smoldering cigarette and hovered at the ceiling, like a drifting ghost haunting the dingy room.

Surprised, Gary stood rooted in the doorway. *What's he doin' here? This time of day he's usually over at Eddie Boot's Tavern gettin' drunk. Maybe they threw him out early today.*

Gary wanted to turn around, slam the door behind him, run down the stairs and escape, but it was too late to run; his father had seen him.

He stared at his father, a big man, thick, powerful, with heavy black stubble on his face. An acidly sour smell whirled around the room, the clinging odor left after each workday in the hot, toxic, glue room at the paper mill. *He smells even worse,* Gary thought, *after drinking beer at Eddy Boot's all night.*

As a youngster, Gary had admired his father's World War II[1] medals, a Purple Heart and a Silver Star, taking them out of their neat white boxes to look at. He knew the Purple Heart was because his father had been wounded in action but had kept on fighting, a real war hero. The Silver Star was even more special, for "gallantry in action against an enemy of the United States." That had made Gary proud of his father, and he dreamed of someday being tough and brave enough to win his own medals.

But his father was no longer that brave soldier. He had become this angry, abusive, alcoholic man who terrorized his family, and Gary had lost the admiration and respect he once had.

Now, in a voice like the slow growl of a menacing Doberman, his father demanded, "Where the Hella' ya' been, boy?"

Alarmed by his father's tone, sensing an attack about to be launched, Gary felt a blast of resentment. With unthinking recklessness, he snapped back, "In school. Where the Hell you think I been?"

The words had rushed out before he could stop them. Now Gary was afraid, realizing those disrespectful words would enrage his already-seething father, and that was never a good thing to do.

Uncoiling like an angry viper, his father shot from the chair, knocking it over, violently shoving the table against the wall. He pounded a big fist on the table and the house shuddered.

"Don't you sass me, you little shit, or I'll knock you on your ass!" he roared, shaking his fist, and belching a stream of alcoholic fumes in Gary's face.

Gary reeled from his father's outburst and beer-breath and felt his gut knotting up.

His father spied the pack of cigarettes tucked in Gary's sleeve. "Where'd you get them fags, boy? Give 'em here!" he demanded, reaching out his hand.

"They're mine ..." Gary started to say, backing toward the stairs.

With a speed that always caught Gary by surprise, his father lashed out, his big hand clamped on Gary's arm, twisting it, powerful fingers digging deeply into Gary's elbow where it always hurt the most: a grip of searing pain and control honed over the years on Gary and his mom.

Lightning streaked up Gary's arm, slashed into his neck and jaw. He yelped in pain, struggling to get away. With his other hand he pulled out the cigarette pack and threw it, skittering, across the table and onto the floor. His father lunged after it, releasing Gary's elbow.

Freed, Gary ran out, stumbled down the stairs, sucking in his breath when a long, thick, razor-sharp splinter from the rough railing slid deep into his palm. He heard his father shouting, cursing, staggering drunkenly across the kitchen, kicking the upturned chair out of his way, coming after him.

Gary pounded down the quivering stairs, ran past the crumbling garage and down the street, holding his pain-streaked arm against his side, his hand flaming from the deeply embedded splinter, his heart pounding in fear, tears of pain, anger, hate, and humiliation rolling down his face.

Chapter Six:

Frank's Epiphany

After escaping the bully, Teddy ran sobbing up Cedar Hill Avenue to Roger's house to tell him about Gar, *The Bad Thing*, but no one was home. Disappointed, Teddy ran through Roger's yard to his own door and quietly sneaked up the stairs to his room, out of breath, still sobbing but quietly so Pa would not hear. He hurt where Gary had held his neck and squeezed him so hard. *Why he do that? Why he don't leave me alone?*

Teddy dropped onto his bed and hugged Mr. Binky. Worn out in spots, missing an ear and the little brown stitch that once was his smile, Mr. Binky had always been in Teddy's world, a safe and familiar friend, still soft, still soothing. Teddy rolled over, covered his head with the pillow so no one could see him. Clutching Mr. Binky, he cried softly. His sobs slowed. Teddy wiped his eyes with his sleeve, reassured Mr. Binky that everything was "A-OK" and they were safe and feeling better. But that did not last long.

Teddy sat up, remembering; he reached into his pocket for the cigarettes and the change. They were not there!

Where Pa's sigrets?

He searched his pockets, the floor, under the bed. Teddy looked at Mr. Binky, but the little bear had no answers.

Oh no! Panic rising. Bringing home Pa's *sigrets* was his *Big 'Sponsability!* He knew he had put them in his pocket in Mr. Spone's store. *Where they go?*

His distress grew; he felt afraid, not like being afraid of the *Bad Corner,* but something else. It was all mixed up, feelings without understanding. Teddy's fear was not about Pa getting angry and punishing him; Pa was not an angry man and had never punished Teddy or his sister. Teddy's distress was about something else, but he did not know what, except that he knew he felt *real bad.*

"Bad!" he moaned. "Bad!" Teddy's body caved in; he slumped in guilt and failure, defeated, just as Pa walked into the room.

Waiting for his cigarettes, Frank had heard Teddy enter the house and climb the stairs to his bedroom. *He forgot to give them to me*, Frank thought, annoyed. He put down his newspaper and went upstairs to Teddy's room to get his cigarettes and to talk with his son, once again, about "responsibility." But when Frank saw Teddy's curled-up, defeated figure, and sensed Teddy's desolation—even Mr. Binky looked distressed—his annoyance evaporated along with thoughts of cigarettes and lectures about responsibility.

"Hey there, Teddy," he said softly, sitting on the bed and gently patting Teddy's shoulder. "What's all this about?"

Teddy looked up, surprised; he had not heard Pa come in. When Frank sat next to him Teddy felt another surge of emotion, this time of relief and love. Teddy collapsed against his father, hiding his face, his tears, burrowing into his father's strength and safety.

Frank was patient with his son, knowing that Teddy was easily alarmed, readily panicked into exaggerated distress over minor things, little problems that he could not handle. He put his arm around Teddy, held him quietly and gently sat him up.

"Now then," he said, his arm still circling Teddy. "Can't be all that bad, so let's get it all fixed up. Tell me, what's going on?"

The whole story came tumbling out: Mr. Spone's store, the *sigrets*, the change, the *Big Sponsability,* the *Bad Corner*, the *Bad Thing,* all of it.

Frank was furious, felt like he wanted to punch somebody for hurting his boy. But he hid his anger, did not want to add to Teddy's distress by showing his own.

Hearing what Teddy had just gone through and realizing this might have happened before, Frank began to face what he had long denied: his little boy, this sweet kid who has never hurt anyone, who simply could not comprehend the world's hard meanness, had been the victim of bullies so cowardly that they ganged up on easy targets, like Teddy.

Frank seethed. *Bullies! Cowards!*

But, *even worse,* he told himself, *Teddy is a* victim *of my stubborn ignorance.* Frank heard his own words: "Dammit, Connie," he had said many times, "when are you gonna' loosen the apron strings? You're babying him for God's sake. The boy's gotta' learn, gotta' man-up."

Man up, he thought. *That's smart. And at what cost? Alone, against a gang of bullies. How could I be so dumb?*

Connie was right; he had been pushing Teddy too fast to "be a man." He wanted to be a responsible father, usually was, but perhaps he was sometimes insensitive, challenging and overbearing. *I'm just like another* bully, he realized. And that jolted him.

I didn't understand. But now I do!

Frank's epiphany had burst upon him in that instant when he had entered Teddy's room and saw his son dejected and distressed. Now he fully accepted what Connie had understood and had been trying to tell him. *True,* Frank told himself, *Teddy is limited.* And *like all boys he has plenty to learn, lots of growing to do. Maybe he won't learn as much or as fast as other kids. He won't be President or run a power plant like I do. But he can learn. Lots of things. Like how to be a man, how to hold a job, whatever that job might be; how to be himself, do his best, run his life an' be happy with it. And I'm going to help him. Not by shoving him along too fast or ignoring the real Teddy, but by walking along with him, step by step, holding his hand when he needs it, letting go when he needs that. We'll get there, me and Teddy. We'll get there.*

And Frank did that for the rest of his life and the majority of Teddy's. Frank had not become a "new man." After all he had always been a good man, a decent person, a loving father and family provider. But he had also carried that unfortunate blind spot about

Teddy. He was not a *new* man, but a *better* man, a better father, a very good father to a special boy.

Teddy is what Teddy is, Frank told himself. *Teddy is Teddy. And, by God, I love him.*

After that Frank no longer sent Teddy alone to the store. Two or three times each week around three o'clock, in the hour before Frank left for his night shift at the power plant, he and Teddy walked to Mr. Spone's store or down to the park at the river.

The first time they had walked together down Cedar Hill Avenue to Franklin Street, heading for Mr. Spone's store, Teddy had been surprised. "C'mon, Teddy," Pa had said one afternoon. "Let's you and me go for a walk."

Me an' Pa walkin'! Teddy thought, excitedly.

When they reached the gas station at the corner of Franklin and Cedar Hill, Teddy ran to the big swinging sign. "See, Pa," he said, "red horse-bird!" He pointed at the gas station, "An' Mr. Burt. My fren'."

Teddy banged on the round metal sign, releasing the deep rumbling noise like thunder that made Mr. Burt look up. Teddy waved and Mr. Burt waved back, smiling. Frank did not know Mr. Burt, but he waved at him, too.

Huh, Frank thought. Seeing Teddy's horse-bird and his friend Mr. Burt, Frank had a glimpse of Teddy's world.

"Mr. Burt seems like a nice man."

"Yeah," Teddy said. "My fren'."

"Well, in that case maybe I should buy my gas from Mr. Burt, seeing as he's your friend and all. What do you think about that?"

Teddy was pleased about that idea. "Buy gas," he said. "Mr. Burt."

In his private *picherbook* Teddy saw Pa drive his car into the gas station and wave at Mr. Burt, who came out of his little house and stuck the black hose in the tank. He saw them standing there, his Pa and his *fren,* talking and smiling. *Real nice,* Teddy thought, as this new image settled in behind his eyes.

They crossed the street and came to Mr. Nichols' high hedge at the corner. "Bad Corner," Teddy mumbled, looking around.

Here was another part of Teddy's world that Frank had not known about, a distressing part, and now that he knew about it, he felt guilty for not having known it sooner.

"Don't worry, Teddy," Pa said. "It won't be a bad corner anymore. We'll fix that." He did not yet know how he would fix it, but he would fix it.

Teddy smiled. Now he felt no fear at the *Bad Corner*, no tightening coil in his stomach, no worries about the bully. As they walked toward Mr. Spone's store, Teddy took his father's hand. It was warm, strong, and felt *real nice.*

"See, Pa," he pointed. "Streamline bird tree. An' a blue bottle. An' a little yellow bird, he lives over there, an' . . ."

Mr. Spone was happily surprised to see them come in together, the first time that had happened. "Allo," he said. "Ana' what I can do for you today?"

Teddy and Pa sat at the tiny soda fountain with its six stools. Teddy, of course, had to spin around, nearly twirling himself off and, just in time, Pa reached over and steadied him.

"Miz Rosies' chairs," Teddy said. "Ladies' football hats."

"Ladies' footaballa' hats?" Mr. Spone asked, puzzled.

But by then, Teddy was absorbed with the magnificent chocolate ice cream soda—only the second one he had ever had—that Mr. Spone served up in one of his fancy glasses.

"I'll have a cuppa' coffee," Pa said. "An' a pack of Luckies."

He put a dollar on the counter for the ice cream soda, coffee, and cigarettes. Mr. Spone set down the cigarettes and matches, picked up the dollar and gave Frank 45 cents change.

Teddy and Pa sat quietly enjoying the moment. Mr. Spone, sensing something special, did not interfere. He thought, *So maybe he no so bad after all, this father.* Then he added extra chocolate to Teddy's wonderful soda.

Teddy's straw reached the bottom of the fancy glass and, like a little vacuum cleaner, searched for the elusive last drops, making loud noises that bounced around inside the fancy glass. Teddy glanced at Pa and Mr. Spone, then went back to his task.

Pa laughed, enjoying Teddy's pleasure. Mr. Spone smiled and leaned on the counter. "Alla' tha' noise you make, Teddy, tha' mean you really like-a tha' soda I make for you."

"A-OK! Thumbs up!" Teddy said through his chocolate-ringed smile, saluting Mr. Spone with the fancy long-handled spoon.

Frank was beginning to see Teddy's world through Teddy's eyes and, more importantly, saw Teddy. He watched his son, perched on the stool, happily vacuuming up stray drops. With a final loud slurp, Teddy finished the soda and smiled at Pa.

"Done!" he announced happily, and then his smile curved down as he realized his soda was, indeed, *all gone*.

"Don't worry," Pa said, reading Teddy's disappointment. "We'll have plenty more sodas. But not right now," he added, giving Teddy a gentle poke in his now slightly protruding belly, "or else you're gonna get a big, fat belly!"

Teddy laughed and grabbed Pa's hand and did not want to let go and felt *real nice* about everything.

Then, searching for another drop but not finding it, he reluctantly set aside his vacuum cleaner. For the next few moments all was quiet in the little shop. No one banged open *Ol' Green Door*, the bell did not jangle, no one intruded into their quiet moment.

Mr. Spone wiped the counter, washed the glass and spoon. *Eh,* he thought. *Maybe, jus' maybe, the world she no be so bad after all.*

On some days they walked down to Nyack's park at the river. Sitting on a bench, they watched big ships slowly going by. "See," Pa pointed upriver, "the big boats, they go north, up the Hudson all the way to Albany and," pointing the other way, "down river to New York City."

The big ships, stately and slow, went about their serious business. But Teddy liked the small boats best, zipping and bouncing all over the river, leaving foamy twin trails behind them.

"The big boats," Pa said, "they're workin' boats, takin' things up and down the river. But those little boats, they're not going anywhere special. What do you think, Teddy? Maybe they're runnin' around out there, just havin' fun?"

"Yeah," Teddy said, liking that idea. "Little boats havin' fun."

Real nice, he thought.

One day, before going to the park, Pa broke up some stale bread and put the crumbs in a paper bag.

"Here," Pa said, handing the bag to Teddy. "You carry 'em. They're too heavy for me."

"Yeah," Teddy said, taking the bag. "Heavy."

A few moments later Teddy smiled, getting the joke. He hefted the bag, held it up for Pa to see. "Not heavy, Pa."

"Well, I guess you're just a lot stronger than me."

"Yeah," Teddy laughed. "Strong," he added, and Frank chuckled.

As they started walking down Cedar Hill Avenue, Teddy opened the bag, looked at the unappetizing, stale bread. He frowned. "Gonna eat 'em?"

"You'll see," Pa said, mysteriously. "*We* won't eat 'em, but somebody will."

"Summbody," Teddy said, puzzled. "Summbody."

"Yep. Somebody. You'll see."

To Teddy's delight, when they reached the park Pa showed him how to toss the breadcrumbs high in the air to attract the seagulls that hung around the fishing boats. Once the breadcrumbs were airborne the gulls, nowhere in sight a moment before, appeared like magic, swooping, squawking and squabbling until a dozen or more were wheeling and diving overhead scrambling for the bread. Those aerial acrobats had Teddy and Pa cheering and laughing. Teddy's favorite was the smallest one, white with a black spot on his head, like he was wearing a little hat. Teddy named him "Little Blacky."

"But he's all white," Pa said. "Except for that little black cap on his head."

"Yeah," Teddy answered. "Little Blackie." He tried tossing the crumbs to Little Blackie, but the big gulls swooped in and snatched them away.

Aww. Big bullies, Teddy thought, not for the first time.

Teddy discovered that by tossing the crumbs away from them he could make the whole flock wheel around and change directions, going this way and that way, wherever he wanted.

"Look, Pa," he laughed. "Me an' the birds playin'!"

Frank taught him how to skip stones across the water and Teddy became pretty good at it. At one end of the park there was a long, narrow inlet where the river's constant motion was slowed. Standing on the shore Pa and Teddy skipped flat stones along that narrow stretch of water, like an oversized, wet bowling alley, counting how many skips each stone made, competing to see who could make the most skips. One day Teddy made the all-time high with an amazing seven skips—at least by Pa's generous counting—before the stone slid under water. Teddy exploded with excitement. Pa's best had been only three skips.

"Teddy!" Pa said. "I think you just set a world's record! Nobody's ever gonna' beat that!"

Teddy was not sure what a world's record was, thinking of his sister's music records that she played on her little suit-case wind-up Victrola. Maybe one of those was a world's record, too. That would be nice.

"Anyone who sets a world's record wins a prize," Pa said. "Let's see. Wonder what kind of prize you ought to get?

"Chawclit soda!" Teddy announced, holding his arms up in excitement. "Chawclit soda, Mr. Spone!"

"OK," Pa smiled. "That sounds about right to me. So, let's go up to Mr. Spone's and get your prize."

"A-OK!" Teddy shouted and started walking toward Mr. Spone's store.

"But" Pa paused, looking troubled. "I don't know if that's such a good idea."

Now Teddy looked worried.

"So," Pa said, putting his arm around Teddy's shoulder in a conspiratorial hug, "maybe we better not tell your Ma I been feedin' you chocolate sodas an hour before dinnertime. OK?"

"A-OK," Teddy agreed, much relieved. "Ma's workin' in Miz Rosie's saloon."

With that settled, they marched to Mr. Spone's store.

Everything went into Teddy's private *picherbook*—sounds, shapes, feelings, colors, the magical *chawclit* soda with the big cloud of whipped cream and bright red cherry, the boats on the river, the gulls, the skipping stones, Mr. Spone's funny talk, Pa's quiet little smile, and the warm feeling of just being with Pa. Teddy tried to share his *picherbook* with Pa, but words failed him and he never got it quite right. And Frank savored the gentle pleasure of being admitted into Teddy's world along with Ma, Emily, and, of course, Mr. Binky.

Part Two:

Decision

Chapter Seven:

1938—Fifteen Years Earlier on Midland Avenue

On an early summer's day in 1938, in Nyack's tree-shaded hospital on Midland Avenue, Teddy was born to Connie Gardner; and a protesting six-year-old named Roger was having his ankle bandaged.

"It's sprained, not broken," Dr. Wharton explained to Roger's worried father. Wharton finished wrapping Roger's ankle, looked sternly at the boy and said, "Now you listen here, Roger, don't go doin' all those fool things that get you all banged up, so your folks keep bringing you in here to get fixed up!"

He paused to see if his words had penetrated but, seeing Roger's steadfast focus on the floor and his fiercely stubborn expression, decided they had not.

"Ah, well, Roger," he sighed in resignation. "You're a good lad and we all like you."

Roger smiled, pleased at that.

"At least," Wharton added, with a raised eyebrow, "Most of the time."

Roger was not sure he liked that.

"And you listen to your mom and dad! OK?"

Roger maintained his silent defiance, his eyes aimed at the floor, his lips set, his scowl undiminished. He was not about to agree to anything, doctor or no doctor.

"You tell him, Doc.," Rogers' father said. "He don't lissen to nothin' we say. Maybe you can get some sense in his head."

He glowered at his son, but that did not conceal his pride: *Yessir,* his expression said, *I got a real boy here!*

"He is a handful, John," Wharton said, shaking his head as he stood up, grimacing at his creaking left knee. "Try to keep him quiet, keep his weight off the foot—and good luck with that. Bring him to the office next week. Should be fine by then."

He gave the unrepentant Roger another stern look and then, relenting, smiled, squeezed Roger's shoulder, and went to talk with Connie Gardner.

After Wharton left, Roger looked up at Laura, scowling. He was uncertain of her because she was a nurse—kind of like a doctor—but also a neighbor. Their back yards adjoined, and Roger often climbed over the rickety fence and dashed through her garden to get to his friend's house on Ross Avenue. Roger knew her well enough to stand his ground, nurse or no nurse.

"Where's my lollipop?" he demanded. "I always get a lollipop!"

"Lollipop!" she said. "What I oughtta' give you, young man, is a good spanking for jumping off your Pa's garage roof. And maybe a few extra swats for running through my garden. I'll bet your Pa wouldn't mind if I did! Right John?"

"Be my guest, Laura," he said, motioning toward Roger. "Maybe a good spankin' will teach him somethin'. You want me to wait outside while you do it?"

"Hey!" Roger yelped, alarmed. But he was pretty wise to adults' vacant threats, so he held his ground and stuck out his hand for the candy. Laura, trying to keep a stern expression, opened a drawer and pulled out a lollipop.

"Here," she said, "Be thankful I'm feeling generous today or you'd be getting nothing."

"Hey!" Roger complained. "This's green! I don't like green! I want a red one!"

"Well," Laura said, reaching for the green lollipop clutched in Roger's hand. "Do you think I have all day to go searching around for the one you want? Green is what I have, and green is what you get."

Roger did not like that. Green was not acceptable. He wanted a red one and he continued to glare at her.

"You don't like green?" she asked. "OK, then give it here and I'll save it for some other boy who'll appreciate it. Maybe I'll give him *two* lollipops, yours, and another for good measure. Maybe three!"

Roger felt that was completely unfair but, not willing to risk that she might mean it, quickly shoved the candy into his mouth, green paper wrapper and all, before she could snatch it away from him.

Roger's father rolled his eyes. "At least show some manners and say 'thank you' to Nurse Laura. And take that paper outta' your mouth!"

"Mmph gooroo," Roger mumbled around his lollipop, keeping it firmly trapped behind his clenched teeth, the little white handle poking out.

Roger's father hoisted him onto his shoulders, looking apologetically at the nurse.

"Thanks, Laura," he said, ducking under the doorway so Roger would clear it. "Hope we don't hafta' come back again this summer with somethin' else to fix."

Roger, sitting high on his father's shoulders, rode grandly out of the room, a king on his horse, happily sucking on his green lollipop and trying to push bits of sodden paper out of his mouth. As they disappeared around the doorway, Roger looked victoriously down at Laura and flashed his special smile.

"Did he just stick his tongue out at me?" she asked, aloud. "That little imp!"

As Roger and his father left the hospital, Wharton walked to Connie Gardner's room. It was a long corridor to the other section of the hospital, giving him time to think about Connie and her new little boy.

I hate this part of my work, Wharton thought, *giving patients bad news, trying to be helpful, supportive as they struggle to understand. Mongoloid, a mentally defective child. Nothing we could do about it. No one could have known. A lifetime of sorrow dumped on this poor child.*

Most of Wharton's understanding of Mongolism had been learned in medical school in 1923. He recalled a lecture in which the professor began:

"Mongolism is a degeneration, a throwback to an earlier, less developed stage. These unfortunates are sub-human creatures, idiots or imbeciles,[1] the lowest levels of human intelligence. The Mongoloid has no capacity for normal learning, cannot be fully civilized or taught useful skills, will never relate affectionately to anyone. Brief, degraded lives await those who survive birth. Few will reach their tenth year. If some do survive into childhood, they will likely become unstable and aggressive, will burden their unfortunate families and strain society. We can do nothing for them because Mongolism is an unalterable hereditary condition about which we understand little."

Then, quietly, in a subdued voice that seemed sadly resigned, he added, "A kind providence would gently reclaim that child's life at birth and the compassionate doctor will take no extraordinary measures to keep it alive. But if it survives, then, with compassion for the family and for that unfortunate little child, it must be placed in an institution for the best care available in its brief, illness-plagued, and unhappy existence."

That lecture had stimulated a late-night discussion among Wharton's roommates about eugenics, the cultural phenomenon that was sweeping through the country in the 1920s like a powerful new religion.

"Eugenics,"[2] Greg said. "It's Galton's greatest idea. It's brilliant! Revolutionary! Gives us the science to improve and even *perfect* humanity!"

"Perfecting humanity, huh?" Philip said.

"Yes!" Look at Davenport's eugenics lab at Cold Springs Harbor,[3] all the research they're doing, their latest studies…"

Philip interrupted, "I'll tell you what I think; in the name of 'scientific eugenics' some bad medicine is being practiced. We'd better take a long look at what your wonderful eugenics is doing to people."

Paul jumped in. "Phil, you are a left-over Romantic from a hundred years ago. This is 1922, modern America, modern science, modern medicine. We need to think of our responsibilities in a whole new context and you, Philip, you just don't understand."

"And you, Paul, you do understand?"

"But of course. Now listen," and Paul launched his lecture. "We know that health, intelligence, criminality, insanity, most of our traits, are genetically determined. Some people inherit the best of human genetics—the 'Well-Born' Galton calls them, the most-fit people. Some inherit the worst. Most get a mix of good and bad genetics. But for all of us, our genetic inheritance is what we are!"

"Oh, c'mon," Philip objected. "Genetics don't account for everything. What about experience and education ..." but Paul ignored him and droned on.

"Galton's genius was in recognizing that with selective breeding we can control human evolution! We can lift humanity to superior levels!"

"So now you want to create a master race?

"No. Not a master race—human improvement for *all*! Think of it, Phil. With eugenics we can eliminate epilepsy, blindness, insanity, feeble-mindedness, criminality, alcoholism, even poverty. We can elevate human intelligence, physical and mental health. We know who the well-born and the unfit are. Now we need to encourage the well-born to have more children and the unfit to have none. It's elegantly simple. It's pure genius! The key is to identify the unfit and keep them out of the gene pool."

"And" Philip asked, "how do we keep them out of the gene pool?"

"How? We euthanize the most severely defective newborns. For others, we put them in institutions where they will be well cared for; we surgically sterilize the females; we legally prohibit their marriage; we urge people who have defects in their family histories never to have children. And we need public education, involvement, enthusiasm for eugenics. That's how."

Philip was appalled. "Oh, wonderful. Make it a public spectacle. I can give you some good slogans for the next eugenics rally.

Imagine a brass band marching around and a dozen cute cheerleaders in short skirts bouncing along holding up a big sign:

Breeding Our Way to The Super Race!

Or, how about this one:

Breed the Best and Get the Most!

And here's my favorite:

If Farmers Can Breed Better Chickens,

We Can Breed Better Babies!"

"Hey," Greg said. "That's not bad! I like that one! And what's wrong with applying proven livestock breeding ideas to humans?"

"What's wrong? We're not chickens! That's what's wrong!"

Paul had to grin at that. "There you go, Phil, just like I said before, you're stuck in that old Romantic sentimentality!"

Greg added "C'mon, Phil, you know that biologically we're all animals, you, me, the chickens. And we're more alike than different. We obey the same natural laws. Look, you're willing to sacrifice all those little lab mice in research. Science learns a lot from them. We use animals all the time to get information about human health. So why not use what the animal breeders have been showing us for centuries? It's right under our noses."

"Here's what I think," Philip said. "I think your eugenics craze is getting out of hand! Did you see that eugenics film, five, six years ago, *The Black Stork*?[4] It's disgusting, inhuman. There's a scene of a newborn being set aside, *left to die*! Does a medical degree give you the right to end that baby's life, to decide it's a life not worth living?"

Greg broke in, "Phil, when a patient is essentially dead, when you've done all you can and nothing's left but pain or coma, then the humane act is to end his suffering! Keeping him alive while you try useless treatment is torture. We need to take compassionate, even *active* measures for the sake of our patients."

"You would take *active* measures? So, now Greg is God? You can decide to snuff out your patient's existence? What about the sanctity of life, don't you believe in that?[5] And the Hippocratic oath?[6] Aren't we committed to maintaining life rather than destroying it? The first principle, 'Do no harm!' Remember that? And let me point something out to you guys, euthanasia is illegal[7] in this country, and in most of the world."

"C'mon, Phil," Greg objected. "The 'sanctity of life' is a religious thing, for priests and rabbis. We're scientists, doctors—or will be, I hope. We're the best qualified to make those medical decisions. I know that when I see suffering, I need to do something about it. When my patient tells me he's had enough, I'll listen. And when he *wants* to tell me he's had enough but is in no condition to say it, then I'll listen to that, too."

Paul agreed. "Look, when you've exhausted everything you can do for that patient and all that's left are extraordinary measures to force him to live a little longer, that's the time to back off and let him go, let him find the end of his misery, find some peace or at least painless oblivion. Like someone once said, 'sometimes our best friend is death.' Think of the anencephalic newborn.[8] Is it ethical to prolong that poor baby's life? And even the great Clarence Darrow said we ought to chloroform unfit children, give them the same mercy we would show to a sick horse or cow."[9]

"Right," Greg added. "And how 'humane' is it to pressure parents into years of grief, trying to raise a disabled baby? An act of *benign neglect* is merciful and humane, it's what we must do for that poor child and the family. I don't like the idea, but it's our responsibility, our duty, to do it."

"No," Philip objected. "Maybe that makes some sense for an older patient with his lifetime behind him, who can have a say in that decision. But you're applying it to a baby who is just beginning life and has no voice to protect himself. You're robbing that child of his future! You call it 'benign neglect,' like it's a noble act, but it looks like murder to me! You'd just ignore that baby, set it aside, let it lie there slowly starving to death while you do nothing to help it? Not do what you'd normally do for any newborn?

"Oh, don't be so melodramatic, Phil," Greg answered. "It's not like we're injecting a lethal substance. It's not murder; it's letting nature take its course. Think of that poor newborn and its family, it's the kindest and most humane thing we can do for them."

"Humane? You can't hide the fact that you killed that child, and you can't wash away your guilt by saying it's *only* passive. Passive or active, it's the same thing. *You* are the one taking that life. We kill in wars, but I refuse to accept killing in my *healing* profession! Your eugenics campaign is a human disaster!"

It had been a heated discussion so many years ago, and now Wharton recalled another incident when, as a third-year student, he had been allowed to join a group of interns on hospital rounds led by Clinical Professor Hans Gelber. Proudly wearing a white hospital coat just like the interns, Philip was eager to learn from them. After stopping at several beds and discussing each patient, Dr. Gelber led them to a high-sided crib and asked Wharton to examine the small child curled up there.

Wharton felt anxious, being put on the spot by Dr. Gelber and watched by the interns who, until then, had ignored him. Carefully and gently, he examined the child, noting what he had learned from a textbook: the unusually rounded head and small nose, protruding tongue, poor muscle tone, slanted eyes, short, stubby fingers and hands, the "sandal gap" between the toes and the 'simian crease' straight across the palms.

"This is a Mongoloid child," Philip said, realizing how obvious his diagnosis was, knowing that he was not telling them anything they did not already know.

"Yes," Gelber said. "Quite right. And" he asked quietly, "had you been attending at the birth of this child, what would you have done?

I'm only a third-year student, Philip thought. *Who the heck am I to lecture a professor?* But, clamping down his anxiety he went ahead.

"I would," he answered Gelber's question, "apply all ordinary care for this child to the best of my ability just as I would for *any* newborn. But I would not subject him to extraordinary measures, like high-risk surgery, adding even more stress, in vain attempts to prolong his life."

Professor Gelber was silent, waiting for Philip to continue. The interns, annoyed because Gelber had chosen this student—who should not have been with them on rounds in the first place—enjoyed some satisfaction over Philip's unease. They looked at him and waited, and he felt even more pressured. But he was in it now and was not about to back off.

"After all," he continued, "this baby is a human being, no matter how damaged he may be!"

His voice trailed off, perhaps an admission of futility and, after another moment, Philip added, "I know that some doctors ..." Again, he hesitated, not looking at Gelber, fearing he might see criticism gathering in the Professor's eyes.

"Some doctors," Philip plowed on, "would deny this baby's humanity, deny his life, would say our efforts are wasted, that we can't make any difference, that *this* life is not worth living. But, to me, supporting the child's chance at life is the *only* thing to do."

Gelber looked at the interns, then at Philip. "Quite right," he said, nodding his approval. "Yes, that is exactly what you must do."

Then he added, with a smile, "Doctor."

Turning to the group, Gelber continued. "Our responsibilities as doctors often lead us into futile treatments which, nevertheless, we feel ethically and humanely bound to apply. But, how far? To what ends? This child's brief life will be pained by constant illness, possibly congenital heart defects, respiratory problems, intestinal disorders, auditory and visual problems, gum disease, hypothyroidism, epilepsy, repeated infections, muscular weakness, and of course feeble-mindedness. What are we to do, faced by that mountain of problems? Are we obliged to go beyond ordinary treatment and invoke extraordinary procedures? To what ends will you take your skills for this child? Each of us must answer that question. And each must know upon what philosophies we base our answers. Objective science tells us much, indeed more and more reliably than any other forms of knowledge. But science cannot tell us everything. You must, gentlemen, be not only scientific practitioners, but also philosophers and ethicists."

Now, more than a decade later, as he approached Connie's room, Wharton recalled those old lessons. Sadly, he recognized not only his profession's limited knowledge of mongolism but, also, of fate's final insult to this already wounded child—the irreparably deformed appearance of the Mongolian Idiot: the broad face, protruding tongue, slanted eyes, coarse skin, squat stature and clumsy movements, creating a presence that is more repellent than endearing, inviting a lifetime of rejection. *What,* he wondered, *can possibly justify so much disfigurement and grief heaped on one innocent little child?*

It angered him to know that the God people worship allowed—even *caused*—such misery to fall on children. Where is God's benevolence, God's special love for children that Father Murphy had told his young parishioners about in those catechism classes at St. Ann's school? He was stymied and frustrated because medical science was unable to understand, prevent or correct mongolism. *What is there,* he thought, *in religion or science to guide me in helping this family?* But he would try his best to console and advise them, to offer his medical skills for that baby, and be there for them so they would not be alone.

Philip Wharton prepared himself to give Connie the terrible news, suspecting that she had no idea of the nature of her baby. He must tell her and do so in a kindly, supportive way that left optimistic room for the family's acceptance and survival.

But Wharton asked himself as he reached Connie's room, *how in Hell do you give news like that in a 'kindly, supportive, optimistic' way?*

Chapter Eight:

1938—"I Know."

Still a little woozy from medication, Connie was happily overwhelmed. Gently loosening the soft blue blanket that Nurse Laura had put around her baby, she gazed at him, her perfect little boy, round, chubby face like all newborns. His big eyes were closed in sleep, but she knew they were beautiful. He had pudgy, cute little fingers and toes; she had counted them and all ten were there. There was just one thing to ask Dr. Wharton about, a gap between Teddy's big toe and the others. *Looks strange, but probably nothing to be concerned about.* She held him close, and he began to nurse.

Everything had gone well despite some comments that at nearly 40, perhaps she was "a little old" for new motherhood? Connie knew they were wrong. *Theodore,* she mused. *Gift of God, from Frank's Greek grandad, Theodoros, or maybe Teodoro. We'll call him Teddy. Our handsome Teddy.* She cuddled him and sang a sweet lullaby. Connie knew that Teddy was a perfect little boy.

Given Connie's uneventful pregnancy and easy labor, Wharton and Laura had been unprepared for this child. There had been no warnings. The baby was a Mongoloid and many of their colleagues would set the baby aside, focus on the needs of the mother and hope that a kind Providence would take care of things. But *benign neglect* was not an option for Wharton, and he and Laura tended to this newborn as diligently as they would any other. It was going to be a sad time, Wharton knew, when he explained to Connie the reality of her little boy.

Laura was an experienced professional and had assisted in many births but that morning when she saw Teddy she teared up. She had seen other Mongoloid babies and knew what was in store for that unfortunate family. Laura also had personal knowledge; years ago, her Aunt Jen had given birth to a Mongolian Idiot. That had been a trying time for the family, but they had listened to their doctor and to their priest and placed the baby in a state institution where it would be well-cared for.

Laura now realized that none of the family ever spoke of that little boy, a child seemingly forgotten. *My little cousin. I don't even know his name! Poor Aunt Jen, all these years living with that emptiness. And that poor little boy. I wonder where he is now, my little cousin, how he's doing? He must be 15 by now*. A dark thought reared up: *If he's even still alive.*

Laura sent up a prayer of thanks because her children were healthy. *There but for the grace of God go I.* [1]

She shook her head to cast out the troubling thoughts but, from then on no matter how much she busied herself, Laura would never forget her little cousin whom she had never known.

While Connie was in the delivery room, Frank had been anxiously pacing in the waiting room with Evan Longuil, a bewildered, first-time-father-to-be, walking in circles. The unshaven, chain-smoking young man was the mildly comical stereotype of worried and clueless expectant fathers whose proper role was to remain in frantic male ignorance of what goes on in those mysterious delivery rooms where only doctors and women are allowed. Frank had been through it with Emily's birth, and was now the experienced, older man, calming and reassuring his bewildered young companion.

But despite his experience Frank, too, was anxious and was alarmed when Dr. Wharton came out so quickly.

"Frank," Wharton said, pulling him into a room where they could talk in private. "Connie is fine, but ..." He sighed, shook his head. "I'm sorry, Frank, "the baby, a boy ..."

There was a long silence after Wharton's explanation. Frank collapsed into a chair, unbelieving, feeling like he'd been punched.

"But, but my little boy! And Connie. What will this do to Connie? What are we going to do? Oh, my God! My poor little boy. Does Connie know? Did you tell her? How can I tell Connie? This will break her heart. Are you sure? There was never a problem in the whole pregnancy! Not one! You know that Doc. Never a problem. What are we going to do?"

Wharton knew what answer he would offer, but it was a tough one: that no family could easily survive the unbearable demands, the repeated medical crises, the sadness over the child's brief life of deformity and illness. What must a family do when a Mongolian Idiot is thrust into their lives? In the best interest of the child in the family, let the state take over raising the child. That is what he advised Frank and that is what he must advise Connie.

Reaching Connie's room, Wharton knocked softly and entered.

"Hello," he smiled at Connie. "How are you feeling?"

"Fine," Connie answered. She looked it, good color, clear eyes, nice smile, rested and relaxed.

"He's so beautiful," she said. "Our little Teddy. We named him after his granddaddy. Theodore, it means 'love of God.' But we'll call him 'Teddy.' And he's so strong, our little Teddy."

Connie radiated love for her baby and pleasure at having given birth after all those months of waiting, wondering if a boy or girl would appear.

This poor mother, Wharton thought, *doesn't see the reality of her child. I need to tell her that her baby is a Mongoloid, not the 'perfect' baby she sees.*

"Mrs. Gardner," Wharton said.

Connie looked up at him, surprised at the unusual formality in his voice. This was not like Dr. Wharton. *So solemn,* she thought. Connie felt a buzz of alarm and her smile faded into creased lines of uncertainty.

"Yes?" she asked, hesitantly, waiting, searching his face. "Doctor?" she asked again. "What?"

At that point Frank entered, with a tight, anxious smile that flickered on and off, still feeling the punch of that awful news. How would Connie take this? What would it do to her? How could he protect her? Their future had been brutally compressed into this terrible and unpredicted moment of tragedy and confusion. He felt his weakness, not able to protect his family. *Is this my fault? A sickness in me that's come out and infected us? Is this my doing?*

Holding Connie's hand, he looked at her and their new baby through tears that he did not realize were his. Frank's face was gray, solemn, as if he, rather than Connie, needed to be consoled, to be put back together again.

"Connie," he began, choked up, stopped, began again but could not continue.

She looked up at Frank and Wharton, saw their struggle over how to tell her something dark that they knew she did not want to hear. But, by then, words were not needed. It was all clear to her. Connie *knew*.

She closed her eyes, pulled Teddy close and, finally giving in to the reality that she had been desperately denying, began to cry softly. In Connie's sobs Frank heard their world crumbling. His sorrow overwhelmed him; his guilt, his failure, his weakness was tearing him apart. Frank tried again to tell her but, again, faltered. "Don't," Connie whispered, reaching up, lightly touching his lips, her voice small, tangled up in her tears. "I know," she whispered. "I know."

Connie pulled her sleeping baby closer, tenderly protecting him from the awful truth that she had finally accepted.

Chapter Nine:

1938—Emily and The Strawrks

"I knew it right away, soon as I saw him, our poor little baby," Connie sobbed feeling small and vulnerable lying in the hospital bed. "But I couldn't believe it. God wouldn't do that to Teddy, to us. I tried to push it away, to convince myself it wasn't true, and I saw how hurt you were, and I knew you were trying so hard to tell me gently. Poor Frank. I love you so much. I feel so terrible for you, for Emily, for Teddy. I did something bad to all of you. I didn't mean to, Frank. I didn't mean to. It's my fault! Oh, Frank, what are we going to do? What are we going to do?"

An emotional volcano erupted inside her—compassion, love, remorse, guilt, fear, even anger; and from that boiling mix what finally distilled out and canceled everything else was an overwhelming love and compassion for this fragile and innocent little baby. Connie had created him and would be his protector and *damn anyone who tries to stand in my way!*

A Mongolian Idiot, they said. Feeble-minded. No chance of a normal life! No! Connie told herself. *No!*

"Frank, what an ugly way they see him! Whatever else they think he is, he's *our* Teddy!"

As small and vulnerable as she had been a few moments earlier, Connie felt a powerful maternal resolve to nurture and protect this little baby, to guarantee that no further insults would ever be hurled at her little Teddy. *I'll be strong. I'll fight the whole world if I need to!*

But over the next week, Connie's resolve would be tested, attacked, stretched, and broken by the incessant demands to give up her baby, to let the State of New York take over.

"Connie," people said, "you and Frank can't possibly shoulder the immense task of raising this Mongoloid child. The strain will tear your family apart. The state has greater resources than you. In the best interests of your family and this child, *you must give him up, immediately, before strong attachments develop.*"

Dr. Wharton offered his best advice in his quiet manner, always sensitive, never strident, and his message never varied: "Connie, it's best for the baby, best for you and best for your family. Give him up."[1]

From all sides Connie heard the relentless, heart-breaking message: *Go home. Leave Teddy. Rest your mind. They will know what to do.* It was tearing her apart.

The usual maternity stay in hospitals was up to two weeks; nine days had passed since Teddy's birth, and Connie had had enough. "I feel fine. I don't need to stay here. It's like I'm in prison! And Teddy wants to go home, too."

But her most pressing reason to leave was her growing horror over the message that she heard even in her sleep: *Give him up! Give him to the state! Abandon him!* Connie felt herself weakening and becoming terrified that if she stayed much longer, she would not be able to resist. By the tenth day, in growing panic to rescue Teddy, Connie climbed out of bed and, unsteady, nearly fell. Frank caught her, eased her back into bed and, with Nurse Laura's help, calmed her. Wharton ordered a sedative and Connie slept for hours as Frank anxiously watched over her. When she woke, Connie was dispirited, fatigued, and ready to give up.

Frank visited every day, depending on his schedule at the power plant. He knew her anguish and was distressed that she blamed herself for Teddy's condition. During most of Frank's visits, Connie slept while Frank sat quietly, holding her hand, letting her know he was there. Each time she awoke, Connie found her hand in Frank's, felt his strength and was grateful. They did not talk much, did not need to. Frank had some success reassuring her, trying to soften her feelings of guilt; but a reservoir of guilt remained for both of them.

Every day he spent what time he could with five-year old Emily who was staying with Grammy, Connie's mother. Each time he entered Grammy's house, Emily charged into him like a little cannonball, laughing, screeching happily, arms reaching up, demanding, "Daddy, pick me up!"

"Oof!" Frank said at Emily's impact, scooping her up, hugging and twirling her around to the music of his little girl's happy shrieks. "Look out," he said each time. "You're gonna' knock me down, right on Grammy's new rug!"

Catching her breath, Emily's first question was always, "Daddy, where's Teddy? Is Teddy in the car? Is Teddy coming in the house?"

Frank explained that her mom had gone to the hospital where Teddy would be delivered. But that had been ten days ago, a very long time for a five-year-old. Emily—always attentive, aware of whispered words, glances, and worried expressions—knew something was not right: something sad, even scary in the secret ways the grown-ups whispered, in the tense visits by her aunts and uncles, in the sad expression on the usually cheerful face of Mrs. Kinsella who lived next door, and in the solemn visits of Father Murphy who lived in the big church downtown. She did not like those dark whispers and currents like cold drafts coming under the door, blowing around her ankles.

But there was one thing Emily did know: her mom had been gone for a long, long time, and Emily was distressed.

Emily's life had tilted. What had started as a happy adventure—staying at Grammy's house, playing with Grammy's little dog Pudge, sleeping in Mommie's old bedroom, and getting ready for Teddy to come and play with her—was turning into a dark, puzzling, scary feeling.

During the first few days Emily's questions had been easily, if fancifully, answered.

"Grammy, where did Teddy come from?"

"From heaven, dear, where all babies come from."

"Did I come from heaven?"

"Of course, you did. You were our sweet little angel, right from heaven!"

"Is heaven far away?"

"Mmm. Well, I don't know. Depends on who you are, I guess."

Emily did not quite understand that but, for now, let it go.

"But, Grammy, how did Teddy get to the hospital from heaven?"

"The stork brought Teddy to your Mommy in the hospital. The stork brings all new babies, in pink blankets for girls and blue blankets for boys."

Emily pictured girl babies wrapped in soft pink and boy babies in blue, just like her collection of dolls. *Pink blankets and blue blankets, that's how you tell girl babies from boy babies.* That idea stopped her for a moment. *But,* she thought, *what, if somebody mixed up the blankets? How will they know that Teddy's a boy?* And there were other things to worry about, like the strawrk that Grammy had mentioned.

"But, what's a strawrk?"

"Stork, sweetie. Stork, not strawrk."

"Um. Then what's that?"

"Well, a stork is a big bird with long skinny legs and big strong wings, and he can fly all the way from heaven to the hospital, carrying little babies like Teddy."

"Did the strawrk bring me?"

"Of course, sweetheart, and in the prettiest little pink blanket."

"My friend Betty says her baby brother slided right out of her mommy's belly."

"Hmm. Well, I don't know much about what your little friends might say. But surely, you and Teddy were both brought to us by the stork, right from heaven."

That was reassuring for Emily; the idea of popping out of her Mommy's belly was a little alarming. Emily was satisfied with those answers, and she enjoyed her image of a big, funny-looking bird with long, skinny legs flying all the way from heaven, carrying Teddy in a blue blanket.

But there was something wrong with that image, more puzzling as she examined it, and she thought: *If the strawrk's wings are busy flying, then how's he carrying Teddy?* Emily inspected that image, turned it this way and that, poked and pulled here and there, erased this, added that, finally rearranging the picture and solving the puzzle of how the strawrks carry babies.

Educated by Grammy, five-year-old Emily came to understand what childbirth was all about: It was a big bird flying down to the hospital from heaven with his long, skinny legs dangling down and blue and pink-wrapped babies securely carried by his toes.

That image would stay with Emily her entire life. When a little older she would smile at that silly—but still lovely—idea, and she even painted some fanciful pictures of how those baby-bearing strawrks might look. But at the time Grammy had explained it to her, it was important information about the world and Emily was pleased with her new knowledge.

Emily waited for her new brother. As the days wore on with no sign of Teddy or Mommy, Emily's anxiety grew, her questions became more insistent and no longer so easily dismissed with nonsensical but entertaining tales.

"Why isn't Teddy coming home?" Emily demanded. "And where's Mommy? I want my Mommy!"

Frank and Grammy saw Emily's growing distress despite their efforts to shield her from the anxiety that was plaguing them, and they worried they may have handled it all wrong. But then, who knew what was "right"? How would it affect Emily, that her new baby brother whom she so eagerly had expected to come home and play with her would not be able to play at all, would be disabled, sickly, might never smile or talk, could be no companion to her? And what if he never came home! What would they tell Emily, how could they help this little girl understand and accept that? And, if he did come home, how would the strain of bringing a Mongoloid baby into the family affect Emily?

What were they to do? There was no help except the standard advice, "give him up!" Society did not want Mongolian Idiots. There were no handbooks—*"How to Raise a Mongoloid Idiot."* There was no encouragement and little support or sympathy for the family that decided to keep the child; there was only society's hard judgment that bringing him home would be an immense mistake.

Now Frank began to see the tip of the unpredictable complexities of this tragedy, the expanding circles of uncertainty and despair swirling around them like a violent whirlpool dragging down even their innocent little five-year-old.

Chapter Ten:

1938—Fatigue, Depression, and Surrender

It was on the tenth day that Connie had tried and failed to get out of bed, leave the hospital, and escape the pressures to abandon Teddy. She collapsed in resignation, dropped into her deepest gloom and lowest level of energy, no longer able to summon the will to fight. She was falling, blackness rushing up, wrapping around her. She watched herself fall, victim and witness, as in a bad dream, terrified of what was happening to her. But even as this dark world wrapped her in terror, it began to offer safety, silence, and a drifting softness like black cotton, gently blotting away the dreadful reality of her unbearable world. Connie found peace as she gave in to the soothing, soft, blackness.

Connie had been beaten down, had no strength left to feel horrified at the demands, was no longer energized by anger at those people, no longer resolved to "fight the whole world" for her child. *So tired. So tired.* She closed her eyes, burrowed into the soft blackness. *Let them do whatever they want. Let them do whatever they want. Whatever they wan…*

Frank was frightened at her descent into depression. Despite her small size—maybe because of it—Connie had always been strong, determined, never giving up on anything she valued. *She's a fighter, not a quitter,* one of the many things he loved about her. But Connie had given up, finally, and no longer cared about anything. Seeing her so withdrawn, so small and unmoving, curled up, hiding in that big hospital bed, was shocking and frightening. *Can a grown man cry? Yes,* Frank learned.

She's not fighting for Teddy anymore, not holding off the "whole world." This isn't my Connie!

"What's happening," he asked Wharton. "What's going on? What's wrong with Connie? Is this a mental breakdown, depression? Am I losing Connie to some kind of mental illness?"

"No, Frank," Wharton reassured him, although he was not feeling very assured himself. "Post-birth reactions like Connie's do occur, although Connie's reaction seems more severe than most. She's gone through pregnancy and childbirth and now her body is working to readjust, to get itself back to where it was before the pregnancy. It's a major physical and psychological readjustment, pushing her body and emotions to extreme highs and lows, even into depression. You and I, Frank, mere men that we are, don't have anything like it in our experience and when we see it in our wives after childbirth, we can't even begin to understand what they're going through."

"But nothing like this happened when Emily was born. Connie was fine. Nothing like this. Is it because he's, you know, a Mongoloid? Is that it?"

"That's part of it, yes. Not in a physical sense, but in how it makes Connie feel, the added burdens on her, on both of you. This baby is not like Emily, there are new issues here and it's been a heavy punch to Connie. You know how you feel; imagine what she feels."

"God. I can't imagine it. Poor Connie. She's not even talking to me anymore! Will she pull out of it, be OK after a while, or is this going to stay with her? With us?"

"What I can tell you, Frank, is that when this happens, and it happens even in some normal births, it's a temporary depression. I think she'll pull out of it quickly. We'll help her, mainly keep her calm, and rested. Wish we could do more.

"So, it's normal, not serious? I shouldn't worry about it?"

"I won't tell you not to worry, Frank. We need to take everything seriously, just in case. And worrying isn't all bad, anyway. You know, my dad told his patients that a little worrying is a good thing, helps keep us on our toes, so we're less likely to miss something important."

"Huh," Frank said. "I think your pa was right."

"I think he was. And I think Connie will be all right. But, Frank, there's still that big issue hanging over both of you, that you need to take care of."

"I know. It all comes down to Teddy. Our poor little boy. What to do about Teddy. God, I don't know, Doc. I don't know. We're damned if we do and damned if we don't. I can't bear to think of just leaving him here for some strangers to take him away, but I'm scared to death to take him home."

Frank was quiet again, struggling. Then, in a near whisper, almost pleading, he asked, "Do you still think it's best to give him over to the state?"

Wharton sighed. "I'm sorry, Frank, but yes, yes I do, for all the reasons we've talked about."

Frank nodded slowly, stared at the floor, not able to look at Wharton, whose dismal message never changed.

"I hear you," Frank said after a long silence. "And I hear everybody else who says the same thing, even Father Murphy who visits Connie. I know you're thinking of what's best for Teddy, but …" Frank nodded toward the nursery. "But you know, Doc, like Connie said, he's *our* Teddy in there. It's not his fault. He didn't bring this on himself, didn't make himself a Mongoloid. I don't know why this happened, what makes some babies Mongoloids. Maybe you can explain it?"

Wharton shook his head. "No, I don't know why this happens. We know it does happen, about two in every thousand births.[1] Someday science will tell us. But right now, we have only guesses and not even good ones. But what we do know is the dismal, short life for these babies. That, unfortunately, is their reality."

Frank felt helpless, defeated. "I'll never understand it." Then he was angry, he stiffened as if preparing to fight. "You know, Father Murphy says it's all part of 'God's plan,' and we don't always understand 'God's purpose,' and we need to 'have faith.' 'Faith,' he says.

Faith in God's plan. But you tell me, Doc, what the hell kind of lousy plan is that? To do that to a baby? That's not my God!" Frank covered his face and sagged against the wall, his eyes squeezed shut.

Wharton was surprised at Frank's outburst, the grief, helplessness, and anger exploding from this man who had always seemed steady, even stoic. But he understood emotional limits and saw that Frank had reached his. In Frank's outburst Wharton recognized his own anger about a God who would cast such misery on children. He wanted to say something helpful to Frank, console him, agree with him, support him, but could find no good words. He put his hand on Frank's shoulder, hoping that physical contact would help.

In a few moments Frank regained control, felt embarrassed by his outburst, and appreciated that Wharton had not tried to say something consoling; that would have been hard to take. Frank shook his head, wiped his eyes, tried to smile. He was still distressed, but his anger had stilled, for now. Frank's distress had been intense but, he knew, it was only a shadow of what Connie must have felt. And it had left him with a different outlook, as if his anger had pushed him beyond his confusion and doubts to a clarity about what he must do.

"What I know for sure," Frank said, now in a calm voice, "is that he's all alone in there. Teddy doesn't know what's happening to him, what people are planning, doesn't know the kind of life that's ahead of him and can't do anything about it. He's at the mercy of whatever we decide to do with his life, me and Connie an' you an' New York State and he's got nothing to say about any of it. About his own life. Nothing! So, we gotta' say it for him. What would Teddy say if he could? Where would he say he'd rather be, with us or with them?

"He's so small, innocent and he needs so much, so much of everything!

"And then, for us to pack up and go home and just leave him here? In the hospital? For the state to come and get him? Leave him with strangers to raise him but no family to love him? That's not right. Dammit all! We can't do that!"

Wharton saw that whatever decision Frank was reaching would take his family into a swamp of distress. He had thought Frank would be the rational one and would help to persuade Connie to do the right thing. But now he was hearing something else—emotion, love, resolve, and strength in Frank's struggles, reaching for what is "right," and a powerful note of empathy. Wharton had not considered what Teddy might want had he been able to voice it and, recognizing that omission, he felt deeply ashamed of his own position about turning this baby over to the state.

He saw a tormented father struggling under enormous pressure to make the right choice about the life of his child and the future of his family. The decision must be made and there would be no luxury of a second chance, no way to erase a wrong choice and pick a new one. Frank had to be right the first time.

"So," Frank said. "Here's what I want: we take him home with us, where he belongs, raise Teddy as best we can, help him to a good life for however long he lives. I don't know what to expect other than problems, big problems, plenty of them, for Teddy, for us. You made that clear, warned us. But it's Connie whose gotta' decide; she's the mother, and I'll give her all the support she needs, do everything I can, whatever she decides." He added after a beat, "That's what I think, bring Teddy home, do our best. And I know what Connie's gonna' decide, even if right now she's still confused and out of it."

Frank had faced that impossible choice. Damned either way, Frank had fought the demons and had made his decision. And Wharton knew this was not the time to challenge him.

Chapter Eleven:

1938—Eulalia Pritchett's "Little Trick"

It was Thursday morning, Connie's fourteenth day in the hospital. She had pulled out of her depression as Wharton predicted. Connie felt rested after a full day of healing sleep induced by Wharton's medications, but she was still troubled. Now she found herself in another distressing discussion about Teddy. Wharton was again gently advising her to let the state take over. Frank was opposed, and Connie still did not know what to do. "We're in this together," Frank had told her. "We're Teddy's family, you and me and Emily, and like you told me, we'll fight the whole world if we have to."

That had revived Connie and edged her back toward her original intent to take Teddy home. But, although bolstered by Frank's strength and no longer deeply depressed, she was still wrapped in sadness and indecision. Connie felt an immense love for Teddy, having bonded with him in the two weeks since his birth, and the thought of abandoning him was intolerable. She was grateful that Frank had reminded her of her earlier determination. But the persistent pressure by well-meaning people had left Connie bewildered and frantically wanting to *do what is best for Teddy*. She was not thinking primarily of herself or of Frank or, even, of Emily, which made her feel guilty about being away from her little girl for so long. Connie was thinking of Teddy's welfare. *Are they right? Can the State of New York give Teddy a healthier, happier, and longer life than we can at home? What's best for Teddy? What should we do?*

Here was the most heart-wrenching decision Connie had ever faced: *Out of our love for Teddy, must we abandon him?*

She agonized over it, had prayed for answers through long, solitary hospital nights while she ached for Frank to be there, next to her. She had talked with Frank, with the doctors, with her mother and, for a half hour one afternoon, with Nurse Laura, whose aunt had faced the same issue years ago and had been left with a bottomless melancholy. Connie had prayed with Father Murphy, but even God had no answers. *What should we do?* she asked, foundering in confusion, consumed by distress.

At that point, Miss Eulalia Pritchett walked in.

After a soft knock on the door Eulalia Pritchett pushed it open, crossed the room to Connie, politely nodding to Frank and Wharton. Following her was a pretty, teen-aged Candy Striper wearing a bright red and white striped uniform, like a peppermint stick in motion, carrying a large, sparkling glass vase with a huge spray of flowers so bright they lit up the room—orange, yellow, white, green, blue, and glossy blacks and browns. Frank's love of color instantly pushed his attention to the red and white swirl of stripes and the explosion of flowers that had marched in, like a Fourth of July parade, and he had the silly thought that the whole high school band was right behind them. He smiled at the sight of the flowers, their young bearer, and Miss Pritchett. He knew of Miss Pritchett, everyone did. But he had never met her and was surprised and intrigued at her unexpected appearance in Connie's hospital room.

"Thank you, my dear," Miss Pritchett said, smiling to the Candy Striper. "Please put the flowers on the nightstand where Mrs. Gardner can see them. You've been such a help, Joyce, dear, that vase is so dreadfully heavy, I could never have carried it."

Connie was staring at Miss Pritchett. Frank was entranced. Wharton had stopped talking and his eye-rolling glance at the ceiling suggested that, knowing Miss Pritchett as well as he did, he should have expected her to come barging in at some point, although "barging in" was an exaggeration, given Miss. Pritchett's softly respectful entrance.

Joyce set down the flower-filled vase, turning its most spectacular side toward Connie. "You're welcome, Miss Pritchett," she said. "Any time you need anything..." With a shy smile and a little wave at Connie, Joyce left the room, her striped skirt swirling around the doorway.

Eulalia Pritchett was a diminutive lady, like Connie but three decades older and a little plump in a pleasant grandmotherly way. Her silvery hair, short and beautifully styled, was the perfect accent for the cerulean blue of her elegantly tailored clothes. Miss Pritchett had a soft voice, a warm smile, and an easy, friendly concern for each patient she greeted during her volunteer hospital visits. The children's ward always had half a dozen young patients, most of them to have tonsils or an appendix removed—standard procedure in those days. The young patients were happy to see "Miss Ulie" enter the ward, bringing little presents for them.

Her manner was refined, even elegant, and if Nyack could have had a royal family, Miss Pritchett would surely have been its queen. The Whartons and the Pritchetts were old Rockland County families, wealthy through business dating from the Civil War. Eulalia Pritchett, now 70, was born soon after that war. Her father had survived wounding in the 1865 battle of Fort Myers and developed a prosperous business over the decades following the war, first brokering machinery and supplies to the expanding railroad industry then investing in the new phenomenon, aviation, after witnessing Orville Wright's 1909 demonstration of the *Wright Flyer III.*

Anticipating that a global economic depression would follow the First World War, Eulalia's father took steps to safeguard his company and wealth. He brought in Eulalia—47 years old and a recent widow—and her younger brother, Frederick, and taught them to run the business and protect their family wealth. When her father died in 1928, Eulalia became the senior partner and a business anomaly: a *woman* running a large, prosperous company for a quarter century. Having survived the 1929 market crash and the depths of the Great Depression, Eulalia, 68, and Frederick, 64, sold their company in 1936, equally sharing an immense profit. New York's business community was astounded—a major business coup by *a woman*!

Two years later, when Eulalia visited Connie on that Thursday morning, she was still an enigma and recognized by all as an unstoppable force. "Mrs. Gardner," she said in a pleasantly soft voice, "my name is Eulalia Pritchett. Perhaps you have noticed me wandering through the hospital. I like to visit with the patients, especially the children. I do hope you will forgive my intrusion, such poor manners, I know. But I wish so much to chat with you and perhaps brighten your spirits a bit with this little gift of flowers. I know flowers won't solve the concerns you are struggling with, my dear, but pretty flowers do brighten one's view. Don't you agree?"

Eulalia extended both hands to Connie. It was an invitation to reach up and grasp them, and Connie felt compelled to do so. Miss Pritchett had a beautiful, warm smile. Connie smiled back, drawn quite helplessly into her orbit of friendship. Captivated by Miss Pritchett, about whom she had heard much but had never met, Connie continued to stare. Finally, in some embarrassment, rousing herself, she stuttered, "Why, yes, of course, Miss Pritchett. Thank you for the flowers. They're so beautiful and they do make me feel much better."

"You are most welcome, my dear," she said, still holding Connie's hands. "May I sit down and share a few moments?"

Connie was surprised and pleased by Miss Pritchett's warm offer, and she certainly could use a new friend right now. Frank, equally captivated by their unexpected visitor and impelled by the good manners taught him by his parents, stopped staring and hurried from the room, returning with a chair for Miss Pritchett.

"Thank you, Mr. Gardner," she said, smiling at him. She sat down in front of Connie and released her hands. Turning a concerned look on Dr. Wharton, she shook her finger at him. "Philip, I was speaking with your lovely wife who told me you have been working too hard. You know, you do appear a bit pale. You must take better care of yourself; you will be of little help to Mr. and Mrs. Gardner and their new little boy if you allow yourself to become ill."

Wharton was embarrassed by Miss Pritchett's easy familiarity, especially in front of his patients; it made him feel like a little boy being corrected by his second-grade teacher. From anyone else it would have been patronizing but from Miss Pritchett it was genuine concern. He was not surprised by her manner and had expected that she would turn up in Connie's room at some point. It was her way, not of slighting or diminishing anyone, but of taking charge before others realized what was happening, defining their relationship: warm, friendly, familiar and at ease, with Miss Pritchett, of course, in control, the respected and capable grandmotherly figure. He knew she was good at that, having watched her many times, so skillfully creating whatever relationship she wished to construct.

At times Wharton had tried to head off her tactics by asserting his own importance as *The Doctor*. But Miss Pritchett could not be intimidated. "Good morning, Miss Pritchett," he said, with a little smile of surrender. "You have surprised us with your visit."

He had no chance to say more because Miss Pritchett, as was her way, continued her soft scolding. "You must heed Deborah, Philip. Wives know these things. Now, then," she continued, "if Mrs. Gardner agrees, I hope she and I might have a nice chat. If not, then I shall go on my way. In any event, my dear," she smiled at Connie, "I do hope you will accept these flowers and my best wishes."

The men heard the message, looked at each other, shrugged, and quietly left. Frank was puzzled but Wharton knew it was best to leave and not question whatever it was that Miss Pritchett intended. He would find out soon enough.

Connie and Eulalia sat facing each other, knees almost touching. Connie regarded Miss Pritchett who, in just a few moments, had moved her from a dark place of distress to a relaxed and gentle curiosity about her visitor, a much nicer place to be.

They sat quietly. The afternoon sun washed through the west window, changing pastel yellow walls to a softly tinted rose, bathing the room in a dreamy light. Connie smiled, thinking how Frank would correct her about the color: *No, the walls are more peach than rose,* he would probably say. *Can't you see that?*

"Yes," Miss Pritchett answered. "I do see it. Peach. A lovely soft peach. I see it, my dear, the warm sun on the walls. So relaxing, don't you think?"

"What?" Connie said, surprised. "Miss Pritchett, how did you know what I was thinking?"

Connie then realized she must have spoken her thoughts aloud. *How had that slipped out? Am I feeling so safe with Miss Pritchett that I don't need to hide what I'm thinking?* "Oh, my," she laughed, apologetically. "It's like I'm talking in my sleep!"

Connie marveled at how calm, how *smooth* she felt now in Miss Pritchett's company, sharing these moments of peace and trust with her new friend. *Friend? Trust? But we've just met! Where did that come from?* "I must be feeling safe with you, Miss Pritchett, like you're already a dear friend, to let things slip out like that."

"I'm flattered, my dear, and I, too, am feeling the friendship, here with you, Connie. May I call you Connie?"

"Why, of course, I'd like that, Miss Pritchett."

"Eulalia, please. If we are going to be friends, then we must use first names. That would be nice, don't you think?"

And with that Eulalia and Connie tacitly agreed that, from this point on, they would be friends. Having arrived there they began, as good friends will, to share, to seek and to give support, advice, affection, soon finding so much in common.

At one point Miss Pritchett spoke sadly of loss and a lifetime of never-fading sorrow. She seemed to be looking far away at some other time and place. "You know, my dear, after that dark day, every new day opens with a shock of misery, of rehearsing one's self-accusing regret, overpowering no matter how many years have gone by. Sometimes it is a faint tremor, an eddy of sadness. But every day one confronts the never-fading question; and every day it goes unanswered, left unresolved in permanent tension, a pool of misery."

She stopped for a moment. Then, still looking somewhere beyond the room, Eulalia said, "Over and over one asks oneself, could I have prevented it? Was there anything I could have done to make it never happen? It stays with you, my dear. The grief, the guilt. It never leaves. My dear Connie, *loss is forever*."

Connie felt a deep foreboding of what personal misery Miss Pritchett was about to reveal, not at all sure she wanted to hear it.

"My husband," Eulalia continued slowly, haltingly, "and our young son, Emmett, only five years old. Named after his granddaddy. 'Little Em,' his sisters called him. It was a train derailment. To this day the only one, ever, on that line. They had left the house early that morning in 1901. It was a Saturday. That was 37 years ago, on a happy father and son excursion. They never returned."

"How awful!" Connie said, tears welling, bringing her hands to her face, and then reaching out, gently touching Miss Pritchett. "I'm so sorry; but surely, you can't blame yourself?"

"No," Eulalia answered, with a sad smile. Then she seemed to shift, and was back in the room with Connie, looking at her again. "I ought not blame myself, not in any reasonable way. But you know my dear, one's memory of such awful reality is not controlled by reason and, thus, one does blame oneself."

They were quiet for a long time until Eulalia added, gently clasping Connie's hands, "you know, my dear, loss is forever. But sometimes, if we are strong, if our minds are clear, we can make it not happen. *We can make it not happen*."

Connie was so saddened, so overcome that she did not know what to say to her new friend. *Losing a child*, she thought. *Dear Lord, that's the most terrible thing imaginable. Thank God I have never* … "and then Connie thought of Teddy, *Teddy, given to the state*. She heard Miss Pritchett's words: *Loss is forever. But sometimes, if we are strong, if our minds are clear, we can make it not happen*. And now Connie knew what she must do. *But can I do it?*

Miss Pritchett's words hung between them, like a slowly fading after-image at a fireworks display.

"But let us speak of happier things," Eulalia said, smiling. "Oh, I have some wonderful memories like marching with my sister suffragettes, demanding our right to vote. My first march was in 1888, I was just twenty. So young. So long ago." She laughed, remembering.

"We just took over the streets! We dodged horses and policemen and push carts. Annoyed men and little boys made fun of us, and little dogs ran alongside, happily yapping at our heels as we went marching along. You know, my dear, I do believe those little boys and yapping dogs quite enjoyed us, like discovering an unexpected holiday entertainment."

Connie laughed with her.

"We wore long billowy white dresses, quite dreadful and silly, elaborate hats that were all the fashion but were only in our way. We sang and marched and waved our signs and, in 1920, my dear, we prevailed! We won, as we knew we would, despite all the smirking men and shouting boys and little barking dogs!"

Eulalia smiled at her memories and Connie enjoyed the images that formed in her mind. "Oh," she said, leaning forward and clasping Eulalia's hand. "How I wish I could have been there with you, in those early days. Such glorious memories and what satisfaction for you and how much you did for all of us, for all our sisters!"

"Do you know, Connie, the marches had started long before my time. My mother, as a teenager, had marched for the vote in 1850, before the Civil War, and she became friends with Susan B. Anthony and Elizabeth Stanton!"

"I didn't know the marches started that long ago! In a way, then, you and your mother were sisters, marching for the vote!"

Eulalia laughed at that. "Yes, mother and daughter but sisters in spirit, and a generation apart. But it seems only yesterday. And our work is still not finished. Do you know the name, Alice Paul? She and Elizabeth Stanton are major figures in the women's suffrage movement."

"Oh yes. I've heard of her."

"Well, Alice is quite a bit younger than I. And a human whirlwind! In 1923 after the women's vote was affirmed, Alice Paul and Crystal Eastman drafted and proposed another constitutional amendment, prohibiting discrimination based on sex. And do you know that their proposal has been introduced in every session of Congress since then![1] But it always fails, blocked mostly by Republicans and a lot of Democrats, too, old men sitting on their backsides, looking fearfully over their shoulders as they hear us catching up to them!"

They laughed, enjoying that image.

"Now, fifteen years later, it has still not been approved by Congress![1]

"Oh, my," Connie giggled. "Old men sittin' on their backsides, I guess," and they enjoyed another laugh at that image. "But, Eulalia, you said 'we', are you working with them?"

"Oh, yes, I'm but a minor part. I no longer have quite the energy I once had. We meet several times each year to see where we are. But none of us can keep up with Alice. She's all over the country and off to England and Europe, even Australia, working for all sorts of women's causes. With people like Alice, it will surely become law someday."

Now Connie smiled, a bit shyly and with a hint of mystery.

Eulalia looked inquiringly at Connie whose pleased little smile made Eulalia suspect that Connie was about to reveal a treasured secret.

"We are linked," Connie said in a wondering voice as she realized something quite marvelous. "Your mother, you, me, Susan B. Anthony, Alice Paul, Elizabeth Stanton and all the others, we have a history together!"

"Linked?" Eulalia looked at her.

"Yes. There were still women's suffrage demonstrations in 1915 while states were voting on the amendment, right up to 1920. I was fifteen and I marched too! Just like you! We had only one small parade in Nyack, not like the big marches you had in Washington and New York. But it was so thrilling! I sneaked out of the house so my father wouldn't know. I was afraid he'd get mad. Then, as we marched, I saw him standing on the sidewalk, watching me with a big smile on his face, and he gave me a thumbs up! I guess he was a man before his time only I didn't know it.

"And I remember my little brother, Andy. Andy the Pest. He thought I was losing my mind, and he was so embarrassed he didn't even want to be seen with me. Andy and his fresh little friends and, you know, you're right about little yapping dogs, too. They chased our parade up Main Street, from Broadway to Highland Avenue, and all the way Andy pretended he didn't know me!"

"Oh, my, Connie, does your brother still remember that?"

"Oh yes, and we still laugh about it, although at the time I was so mad at him. My little brother, Andy the Pest."

"You and I share such rich memories, my dear and if not in the same parades or the same decade, we truly marched together in spirit!!"

"We are sisters," Connie said, smiling for the first time in days, since before her slide into depression. "I knew we had a connection, sisters for 20 years, but we never knew it!"

Eulalia nodded. "Yes, indeed. And today is rather like a reunion, don't you think? My dear mother would have loved this. And Connie, do you remember how we sang, how we shouted our marching songs? We felt so strong, so inspired, we were changing the world, and nothing was going to stop us!"

"Oh, I do! We were ready to fight the whole world! And I remember some of the songs, our version of the *Battle Hymn of the Republic*." That memory of youthful determination twenty years earlier was a message about herself, about Teddy. But, caught up in their exciting recall of the suffragettes' marches, she veered away from it, at least for the moment.

Connie began to sing, recalling the words bit by it, then with growing vibrancy. Eulalia joined in.

Rise up women for the fight is hard and long
Rise up in thousands, singing loud our battle song
Glory, glory, hallelujah, glory, glory hallelujah
Glory, glory, hallelujah! Our cause goes marching on!

Their voices rose, they pumped their fists, feeling again their proud defiance and ultimate victory. After several loud verses they realized what a ruckus they were making and, gasping with laughter, they quieted down, telling each other this was "no way for respectable ladies to behave in a hospital."

"Oh my!" Eulalia said, happily, breathlessly. "I haven't thought of those songs in years!" She leaned close and whispered to her co-conspirator, "I wonder what the nurses think is going on in here?"

"I don't know," Connie said. "But I bet they'll be poking their heads in here any minute to find out."

And, sure enough, Nurse Laura walked in, carrying Teddy. "It's nursing time, Connie," she announced, handing the baby to Connie and looking suspiciously at the two of them. "My goodness, Miss Pritchett, you have certainly cheered up our patient. Sounds like you two were having a party in here. Should I be looking under the bed for empty gin bottles?"

Eulalia laughed. "Oh no Laura. No gin bottles. At least not that we will admit. But I suppose in a way it is a party. You see, Connie and I have good reason to celebrate what we achieved years ago."

"You and Connie, years ago?" Laura asked, puzzled.

"Yes, both of us. Years apart, and we did it together. But there is so much more to do. Do you realize, my dear Laura, that here, today, in this modern world of 1938 we still have no equal rights amendment? And, *we still have not elected a woman president!*"[2]

"But we will!" Connie added, raising a fist. "We will!"

Laura arched an eye at Connie: *What's gotten into the two of them?*

Connie and Eulalia knew there would be no woman candidate in the 1940 presidential election. FDR would certainly win that.

"Maybe in 10 or 20 years, Connie said, "we'll have a woman president."

"Definitely within thirty years," Eulalia added. "By 1970! That's a whole generation from now! Absolutely! It will happen, we will have a woman President of the United States by 1970!"

A woman president? Laura wondered, shaking her head as she left the room. *How had those two come up with that crazy idea? But then,* Laura thought, stopping in mid-stride, *why is that so crazy?*

Why not a woman president? Look at Eleanor Roosevelt. I'll bet she'd be a great president if she ever had the chance.

Connie and Eulalia now were quiet, focusing on Teddy, who was hungrily nursing. He had some difficulty, the problems with his tongue and mouth making it a slow process. Wharton had anticipated problems, but Connie saw little of that. Indeed, she had told Wharton after Teddy's first nursing, "He's so strong."

The sun had dropped lower in the sky, no longer streaming through the west window. The room's soft peach atmosphere had faded to the walls' original pastel yellow. As if the shift in the light signaled a change in Connie's mood, she realized that they had arrived at what had been Miss Pritchett's goal all along—Teddy, and the decision still to be made.

Just an hour ago Connie had floundered in irresolution. Now, after Eulalia's magic, she was energized, eager to confront and, finally, to settle it. *Like marching with our sisters,* she thought. *We were determined. We knew we could do it. We were ready to fight the whole world!*

Miss Pritchett's words of warning and encouragement came back to Connie, like echoes that had circled the globe and returned: *Loss is forever, my dear... but if we are strong, if our minds are clear, we can make it not happen!*

So, what of Teddy? They talked for another twenty minutes about everything needing to be discussed, clarified, and settled, examining the implications of the question that Connie must now answer: Who can best raise Teddy: Frank and Connie or the State of New York?

"The state offers so much," she told Miss Pritchett, sadly. "They have the best resources, everything good for Teddy. They have doctors, nurses, around-the-clock caretakers who will take care of him when he's ill. They'll know what to do in emergencies. And we know he will be sick much of the time, will need special care and expensive treatment, as Doctor Wharton explained. What can I offer at home compared with all that?"

"You know, my dear," Eulalia answered quietly. "It seems to me that you've been thinking about this so much, for so long, so many words, over and over, getting all tangled up in them." She paused a heartbeat. "May I offer a bit of advice from one who has lived many years?"

"Why, of course," Connie agreed, and Eulalia answered, "Connie, do not let all that thinking get in the way of your feelings."

Connie was puzzled. Eulalia seemed to be telling her to stop trying to think it through, to make that important decision without more thinking. *How can that be? How can I decide if I don't think about it?"*

"Now," Eulalia continued, "here's a little trick I have found useful whenever I'm muddled about something. Instead of thinking in words, use pictures. Given what you are trying to decide, use pictures of your family. Close your eyes, Connie. Picture Frank. Picture Emily. *See* your house, in your mind go inside and *see* the rooms. See your Frank's atrocious painted walls you told me about. Build up those pictures in your mind. Put yourself and your family right in there and *see who you are,* see those pictures. And when they are sharp and clear, take a breath, relax, and let your *feelings* about Teddy, your family, your home, just float up, right into those pictures."

Connie was puzzled but intrigued. "I'll try," she said. "But what will that do?"

Eulalia smiled. "My dear, when you have done that, you will know what you have to offer Teddy, what the state can never give him."

Connie closed her eyes and did as Eulalia had suggested. She had always had a good imagination and skill at creating mental pictures. Connie worked at it, a pleasant exercise in imagination and not difficult to do, forming images of her home and family. She saw her kitchen and for a moment even caught the aroma of a bubbling beef stew on the stove. Mentally roaming through the house, she smiled and shook her head at the wild colors Frank was painting on the walls of Emily's room, and she had to laugh at their enthusiastic five-year-old who was gleefully jumping around and cheering him on.

Bright, sweet pictures were taking shape. She brought them into focus, like adjusting a telescope. Then, still prompted by Eulalia, Connie took a deep breath, relaxed, and let her feelings about Teddy, Emily, and Frank rise into that image, like warming sunshine rising at dawn. "Yes," Connie whispered, eyes closed, smiling at the surprising result. "Yes. I see. I see what's there, what's been there all the time, but I didn't see it before because of all the *noise*!"

Eulalia's "little trick" proved to be a potent exercise bringing Connie to a new level of clarity. She enjoyed the images, lingered over them, then slowly opened her eyes, and looked at her new friend with gratitude and affection and with a great respect for Eulalia's wisdom.

They talked quietly a bit longer, and after a while Eulalia left, promising to visit in the morning. Laura came to take Teddy to the nursery. Connie, now alone, warmly uplifted by "Eulalia's little trick," continued the mental exercise, creating images so inviting that she ached to return home to Emily and Frank, to their sweet home, to their world. *Home,* Connie thought. *In the morning, in just a few hours Frank will come and get me. We'll leave the hospital. We'll go home!*

It was nice thinking about going home, but sadness again dropped over her. *Frank and I will go home,* Connie corrected herself, tears filling her eyes. *But will Teddy come home with us?* There it was, the unanswered question, the decision to be made: *Will Teddy come home with us?*

Alice Girard, the hospital's social worker, would arrive in the morning, bringing papers to sign to give Teddy to the State of New York.

Time was up. Connie must decide.

The next morning Connie was dressed and ready to leave. Alice Girard had come and gone, the papers packed into her briefcase. Frank arrived, parked his old Dodge at the patients' entrance, and went in to get Connie. They thanked the staff, and Frank gave them a big box of chocolates. He picked up Connie's suitcase and paused, looking around at the pale-yellow walls of Connie's brief home. Miss Pritchett was there, too, to see them off and walked with them as Nurse Laura pushed Connie in the wheelchair to the lobby.

Then they went home: Frank, Connie, and Teddy.

Part Three:

The Legacy

Chapter Twelve:

1938—The Better Babies Tent

They drove home from the hospital on that warm summer morning in 1938, a ten-minute ride along Nyack's quiet, tree-shaded streets, neat lawns, and tidy houses. Connie smiled, gazing at the passing canopy of dappled greenery. *What a lovely world,* she thought, hugging Teddy, a warm little bundle in a soft blue blanket.

But the world was not so lovely. The road from the first World War to the next had been building for twenty years while Germany nursed its humiliating defeat.[1] By Teddy's birth in 1938, the German people, enthusiastically supporting Hitler in their frenzy for revenge and honor, were ready to destroy Europe. Hideki Tojo was disemboweling Asia. Mussolini, Hitler's fascist mentor, had invaded Greece, Egypt, Albania, Yugoslavia, and Ethiopia. Franco and Salazar were strangling young democracy in Spain and Portugal. Stalin was killing two million of his fellow Russians—shooting, starving, hanging, torturing, and suffocating them in mobile gas chambers.[2] Fascism and communism, authoritarian brethren, stalked the globe, determined to kill democracy. Such was the world in the 1930s.

As the world slid into fascism and the next global war, another war was in progress: eugenics. A powerful pseudoscientific movement of the early 20th century, eugenics was a war against "the unfit." The military war and eugenics also were brethren, a fact little appreciated at that time.[3]

For Connie and Frank, fascism and the world's savagery were remote rumblings, and Japan's sneak attack on Pearl Harbor [4] was nearly four years in the future. Eugenics, however, fifty years in development, had already invaded their lives, but they did not know it. Eugenics was a popular cause in the United Staes, but Connie and Frank knew little about it and had no idea that their country and Germany were well into eugenics campaigns to exterminate people like Teddy, with Germany well ahead of the U.S. Neither had they any idea that, were Teddy born in Germany, he would soon be euthanized.

As they drove home, Frank and Connie were not ready to talk about what they knew they must talk about: Teddy, who was sleeping securely in Connie's lap. Connie glanced at Frank. He was busy driving, intent on the road; she knew his mind was whirling, like hers.

Are you scared too, Frank? she wondered. *Like me?*

"*Mongoloid*," popped into her mind and Connie batted it down. *I don't care!* she thought, angry for allowing that terrible word to arise. *I don't care!*

No. She corrected herself. *I do care. But it doesn't make any difference.*

No. That's not right. It does make a difference in how Teddy will grow, what kind of life he'll have, what sort of parents we'll be. It does make a difference. But then, it really doesn't. Oh! I don't know! I don't know!

But I do know! It makes a difference for Teddy, but no difference in how much we love him, how we'll take care of him.

There. That's it. That's what I mean.

Teddy whimpered softly. *You must be hungry, Sweetie,* Connie thought. *OK, we're almost home.*

Connie gazed at their special little boy. *You're so small,* she thought. *So helpless. So much in need of your Ma and Pa. I know we'll have lots to learn; wish things were better. Better,* she repeated, which reminded Connie of her family's visit to *The Better Babies Tent,* many years ago. She had been fascinated.

As the eugenics campaign was growing early in the twentieth century, another campaign began, the *Better Babies Contests. Making Better Babies!* "What a wonderful idea that was," Connie said.

"What?" Frank asked. "Sorry. I wasn't paying attention. What wonderful idea?"

"Oh, nothing," Connie said, shaking her head, surprised that she had spoken aloud. "I was just thinking of a county fair we went to a long time ago when I was a kid. Nothing important."

"Um," Frank said and continued driving, wrapped in his own thoughts about Teddy and their future.

Connie's trip to the fair had been in August 1912. *Oh my,* Connie thought. *Was it really 26 years ago? Was I really twelve years old, so young? There we were, my folks, my little brother, Andy the Pest, and me, enjoying a Sunday afternoon at the county fair, our annual outing.* Connie remembered her excitement over the crowds, the exhibits, the enthusiastic country bands, and their once-a-year fancy meal in a fancy restaurant with fancy waiters and all.

The scene came back in lively detail; Connie could still hear her Ma announce, "There's a new exhibit I want to see. The Better Babies Tent. It's over there," she pointed, "where all those people are going."

"Oh, a babies' tent! Yes, let's go," Connie said, not knowing what to expect but eager to see the babies.

"A babies' tent!" Andy the Pest protested, rolling his eyes, and sticking out his tongue. "Yewww! Yukk! Gaah'! Who wants to go see a bunch o' ol' babies inna' tent! I wanna' go to the shootin' gallery over there an' win a prize!"

"Babies aren't old, dopey," Connie corrected him. "And I want to go see them."

Pa agreed with Andy, and started walking to the shooting gallery, but Ma grabbed his arm. "Come along," she said, and marched her family to join the crowd at the *Better Babies* tent.

As they approached the tent, they saw signs announcing the nearby Champion Hogs exhibit.

Better Breeding Through Modern Animal Husbandry!

Scientific Breeding Gets Results!
See What Better Breeding Can Do!
Better Bacon through Better Breeding!

Approaching the *Better Babies* entrance, Connie could see two long lines of tables inside the big tent. Babies aged 4 to 48 months were arranged in two rows along the tabletops, like an assembly line, younger babies in one row, older babies in the other. Stripped to diapers or undergarments, the children sat, stood, or lay on the tables, those at the head of each line being examined by teams of doctors and nurses. Their parents stood by proudly but anxiously, eager to learn how their washed, combed, and prettied-up babies compared with the others. Most of the babies tolerated the examiners' probing but a few objected loudly to such intimate contact with strangers.

Connie was intrigued watching the doctors and nurses examine each child, measuring and recording height, weight, chest and cranial circumference, skin tone, blemishes, physical deformities, and general appearance, evaluating each child's physical and mental health, and even judging their moral development. The examiners engaged the children in activities to judge their responsiveness, alertness, personality, and intelligence. They awarded points to each child: up to 700 points for physical condition and appearance, 200 points for mental and psychological fitness, and a hundred points for a variety of other characteristics.

Children who scored 1,000 points were declared "Perfect Babies," and were awarded *Perfect Baby Certificates* and shiny little trophy cups while their parents beamed proudly.

Everyone came away with something; all received a score card showing how their child fared on each measured characteristic, much like a report card in school. Even the lower scoring families were "winners," learning their children's strengths and weaknesses, which attributes needed to be improved and how to do so. They received information about nutrition, hygiene, safety, sleep, good health practices, common childhood illness. They were urged to get regular medical examinations and to understand the value of education.

"Everybody seems so happy in there," Ma said, smiling. "Even the babies are enjoying themselves."

"Well, there's one that's not," Andy said, pointing to a loudly protesting two-year-old. But Ma's observation was generally accurate, and the atmosphere inside the tent was one of enjoyment in sharing this activity with like-minded good people.

As they entered the *Better Babies* tent, a tall lady with a stack of brochures peered down at Andy, smiled at him and asked Ma, "Are you going to enter this young man in the contest?"

It was a joke, a simple pleasantry. But Andy did not think it was funny, picturing the indignities of being stripped to his underwear and set on a table with all those babies to be examined by strangers right there in front of everybody! He slid behind Pa for protection, watching the lady for any move she might make toward him.

"Oh no," Ma laughed. "Andrew is six years old, much too old for that, don't you think?"

"Hmm," the lady said, still appraising Andy. "Yes, I suppose he is."

Handing Ma copies of the brochure, she pointed to the far end of the tent. "See where those people are seated? The lecture will start there in about fifteen minutes. While you wait, please look at this brochure. I think you'll find it interesting."

As they filed into the tent, Andy edged as far away as possible from the lady.

Waiting for the lecture to begin, Connie and Ma read the brochure: *Mary de Garmo: Education is The Key to Making Better Babies!*

Connie was fascinated. *Making better babies? What's that all about?* At twelve, Connie had reached marriageable age.[5] She had not thought much about her future as wife and mother but knew they were natural roles, *nothing you need to go to school for; nothing you need to study. Everyone just did it!*

Connie had recently learned about suffragists, powerful women demanding the right to vote and social justice, women determined to change the world! And described in this brochure was another woman crusader, Mary de Garmo, unknown to Connie until that moment. A flash of pride brightened Connie: *What we women can do,* she thought, proudly.

The speaker was Mrs. Georgeanna Gwynne, chairlady of the local *Better Babies* program. With silvery hair and the pleasantly rounded look of everybody's grandma, Mrs. Gwynne smiled at the audience.

"Welcome," she said, in a warm voice as if inviting the audience into her parlor for afternoon tea. "We are so pleased to meet you, so many fine parents, so many beautiful children on this lovely Sunday afternoon. Welcome, everyone. Welcome."

Holding up a brochure she said, "Here is a picture of educator and crusader, Mary de Garmo. Just four years ago, in 1908, Doctor de Garmo created our Better Babies Contests at the Louisiana State Fair. It was an enormous task, creating something so completely new and complex, bringing together doctors, nurses, educators, parents, and children, spreading her exciting ideas, training the examiners, filling them with enthusiasm, creating the settings, inventing new examination procedures, and much more.

"Using the State Fair was another stroke of genius because America's fairs are our most popular and well-attended annual events. The Better Babies Contests at all these fairs, are Mary de Garmo's portals to America's families.

"Parenting is surely our most important responsibility but is not very high in our nation's priorities. We do not pay it the respect it deserves, we provide mothers with little guidance or family support. Parenting is a demanding, task. We mothers do our best, but many strive under difficult conditions, with meager knowledge about good parenting. And our elected officials? They are all men, caught up in politics and business, at times even playing at war, and they have little interest in parents' struggles or childhood issues.

"As a result, tens of thousands of America's children are undernourished, under-protected, and undereducated. Too many are forced into dangerous child labor in factories, farms, mines, and even on treacherous city streets. Children need to be in school![6] And too many children suffer the stings of our most common methods of raising children—the woodshed, the birch rod, the Cat-O'-Nine-Tails.[7]

"Malnutrition, disease, physical punishment, injury, forced labor, inadequate schooling, little medical care and a lack of concern by officials degrade our children's lives and many innocent youngsters do not survive their few years of childhood."

Mrs. Gwynne paused, letting that sad note sink in. No longer the soft grandmother, she was a woman saddened by the hard realities of American childhood, angered at those who allow it, determined to change it all.

Can that be true? Connie wondered. *Is childhood in America really like that?* What the speaker described was nothing like Connie's experience. For Connie and Andy life was smooth, healthy, and rather fun, despite Andy being a pest. *A lot of kids in school talk about getting whipped pretty good by their folks, but that never happened in my family!* She shuddered, just thinking about it. And Connie had never heard of a *Cat-O'-Nine-Tails,* but the image it created in her active mind was frightening.

Children forced to work in factories, in the streets? Maybe out there alone, at night? Even with the total mess in Andy's room, Ma and Pa never make us to do much work, just a few chores around the house. And kids being undernourished? If anything, I'm too fat! My family's not like that. But are other families like that? Connie's creative imagination drew dark images of other children's lives.

Connie looked at her parents. *Ma and Pa knew all along about better parenting, long before Better Babies Contests!* Connie would never forget that Sunday afternoon and that insightful moment of magnified respect for her parents.

Mrs. Gwynne ended: "The Better Babies program is sometimes seen as part of the eugenics movement. I believe Mary de Garmo sees it that way. There are similarities, of course, but they are two trains on different tracks, starting in different stations but moving toward a shared destination: improving the well-being of future generations, helping our children become stronger, healthier, happier, making our nation stronger. The key in eugenics is *biology*; but the key in Better Babies is *education*. Doctor de Garmo's vision rests on education, educating the parents."[8]

Connie and her parents had been impressed. Only Andy had not been. As they filed out Andy warily edged away from the tall lady at the door and, when safely past, demanded, "Now can I go an' shoot the guns?"

It had not occurred to Connie that no dusky or dark-skinned, foreign-looking or poorly clad parents and babies were in that tent. And babies with physical, intellectual, or mental disabilities were, by definition, not welcome to compete as Better Babies and would never sit in the winner's circle.

They ended the day pleasantly weary, strolling in the waning sunshine, enjoying cool scoops of ice cream in crisp cones called "cornucopias" by the older folk, rescuing the sweet, melting drips before they could get away.

"*A perfect end to a perfect day*," Connie thought, recalling a favorite poem.

Chapter Thirteen:

1920s—The Better People's War

In 1919, Philip Wharton and Frank Gardner were among the four million U.S. veterans who returned from the war anticipating a peaceful and prosperous future. They found, however, that President Wilson, eager to return to a peacetime economy, abruptly canceled wartime government contracts, leaving farms, factories, and warehouses with unsold stockpiles and no buyers. Plant closings and unemployment surged in a world already in deep recession.

By 1926, Wharton completed medical school, earning a comfortable future in his father's practice. But Frank struggled in the worsening economy that was crushing millions of working families, farmers, and small businesses.

It had begun—the 1920's descent to the Great Depression.

"What the devil's going on?" Frank asked, as did everyone he knew. The common answer was all around them, carried on the winds of long-held prejudice, new fears, and economic disappointment. He heard it from his friends, relatives, politicians, radios, and newspapers: *Look around, Frank, see who's taking our jobs, turning our cities into slums, stealing our money, corrupting our children; the Coloreds pouring up from the South,*[1] *the immigrants breeding like rabbits, the Jews stealing our money, the lazy freeloaders, the crippled and feeble-minded, all worthless mouths to feed. They're dragging us down, Frank.* They *are why you don't have a job;* they *are why our country is bleeding into the gutter.*

Millions of Americans shared that message, and the 1920s became a war against the weak, the poor, the foreign, the disabled, the *different*. Frightened and angered by their economic decay, Americans blamed *Them* for their miseries.

African Americans were the most visible, immigrants the most feared, the feebleminded and disabled the most disdained, and Native Americans the most hidden—all were targets and easy victims, persons to be controlled, deported, incarcerated or, in other ways, eliminated.[2]

Frank was certain that he was not prejudiced but, immersed in the 1920's xenophobic culture, he absorbed much of that world view. Without much thought, Frank accepted what he was hearing.

There was one exception in Frank's thinking: Jewish people. In the war Frank had served with Jewish soldiers; he now had Jewish acquaintances and had grown up in a two-apartment house sharing it with a Jewish family who became good friends with his family. They were all very much like him, like his family, and Frank knew that the negative things said about Jews were wrong.

But Frank had no Black friends, had never shared a house with a Black family, had never served with Black soldiers. He knew there had been some Black soldiers in the war,[3] but had never seen one. With little contact with Black people, Frank had nothing to counter what others believed.

The Black people Frank saw in Nyack were poor, the men working low-level jobs or not working at all, wearing shoddy clothes, and blaming their problems on the lasting effects of slavery. *They're wrong,* Frank believed. *That's just an excuse. Slavery ended 60 years ago, can't possibly still affect them!* He accepted what everyone believed: *The problems of the Colored are due to their own limitations, like their low intelligence and laziness.*

Nyack's Black residents lived crowded in unpainted wooden tenements on Franklin Street—dilapidated, dreary, two-storied, ancient wooden buildings that looked like props from an old western movie. Their apartments sat above sad-looking, dark, one-room stores for "the Colored." On the east side of Franklin Street, some Black families lived above a live-chicken market that you could smell a block away and hear the squawks of chickens hanging upside-down, their feet tied together, beating their wings against the wall. One could not miss their strangled cries as they were slaughtered, although people walking by tried not to notice. One night the market burned down and the smell of burned feathers and flesh hung over Franklin Street for weeks.

As a youngster, Frank had wondered how the Colored could live there, *with all that noise and stink. Why don't they move to a nicer place?* He had walked along Franklin Street to and from the Liberty Street grammar school, seeing Colored people, old and young. But few of them walked on Nyack's quiet streets like his, of neat houses and green lawns. Frank accepted that. *That's just the way it is,* he thought. *Their problems aren't my problems. After all, I'm free, white, and 21.*[4]

Frank, like millions of Americans in the 1920s, carried the unexamined beliefs that such people threaten the country, and something should be done about them. But Frank did not think he was prejudiced.

Late in the spring of 1921, Frank and two friends worked several days picking green peas on a West Nyack farm. Their earnings were meager but better than nothing at all.

"When I got out of the army," Al said, "I didn't figure I'd be picking no peas!"

"Me neither," Charlie added. "But maybe we're not so bad off. You guys hear about that big Colored riot out there in Oklahoma? Coloreds went crazy, tore up their own neighborhoods. Burned the whole place down, even their own houses! Bunch of people killed. Don't make no sense, wrecking your own neighborhood. What kinda' people burn down their own houses? What the Devil's wrong with them Coloreds?"

"I don't know," Al said. "They're rioting all over the country. At least here in Nyack they seem quiet. But I don't know if they'll stay quiet."

"Maybe not," Charlie said. But I'll tell you what I think, it's all those Colored guys comin' back from the war, thinkin' they're as good as us and we owe 'em somethin'."

"Hmm" Frank said, "maybe we do," surprising himself and his friends.

They looked at him, puzzled. Al started to argue, but decided to let it go, asking instead, "So, what do they want, the Coloreds? They stir things up an' then they go rioting. Why they always rioting?"[5]

None of them could answer the question. But the descriptions of what had happened in Tulsa's Greenwood brought Frank back to scenes he had stepped into during the war: blasted cities; shattered farms; forlorn, homeless, wandering people, all victims of events too powerful for them to handle. He came away thinking of them not as enemies, but as victims. And now he thought about those people in Tulsa.

"You know," Frank said slowly, as if trying out a newly-discovered idea, "I can't believe they did it to themselves. It makes no sense destroying your own world, tearing up everything you own and even getting yourself killed."

"Well, that's what they did," Charlie said.

"I can't believe that Charlie. Look, there were White gangs in there, and they went in shooting."

"They were there to keep order, to control the rioters, to defend the place."

"You think so? Why would White gangs defend Black neighborhoods? No, something else is going on there. I wonder if we'll ever know the real story."[6]

But there was a bright spot for Frank: In the summer of 1921 he met Connie, lively, lovely and a joy to be with. Frank had seen her years earlier in high school but, being a senior and she only a freshman, had paid little attention. But now she was *different*, grown up and beautifully so, and Frank was falling in love. He wasn't sure if Connie felt the same about him, but she was willing to have a soda at the drug store and take a Sunday walk around Riverside Park. *Not very exciting,* Frank thought. *But I had enough excitement over there in the war. And all of a sudden I'm 25. How the heck did that happen? Time to settle down. But now's not the best time to get married, not with this recession and me with no job. Everything was supposed to be great after the war. What the devil's going on?*

Chapter Fourteen:

1926—The Wedding and the Great Depression

By the end of 1922, Connie had decided that Frank was, indeed, *The One* for her, but she had not yet told Frank or anyone else. Connie's Mom, however, knew it even before Connie.

"You know, Dear," she said. "We rather like that young man, Frank, you've been seeing. I think you should invite him over for Sunday supper."

"Oh, Ma. I don't know..."

"Well," Ma said. "If you don't, I will."

"Ma! Don't you dare," Connie said, her face turning red.

It is not clear who invited him but, no matter, Frank happily accepted, and frequently joined the family for Sunday supper. They were quiet, pleasant, simple meals and gentle conversation. After supper Frank helped Connie with the dishes while her parents and Andy discreetly withdrew to the parlor where Pa wrestled with his Atwater-Kent radio receiver to pick up news broadcasts from New York City. Things were happening in Europe and Pa wanted to know "what the devil's going on over there."

Pa liked Frank well enough but wasn't sure that a young man ought to be washing dishes. But who knew about this younger generation? Ma, however, was pleased at how nicely Frank treated Connie. Andy was 19 by then, no longer *Andy the Pest,* and was happy to have another young man in the house, even if only for these few Sunday hours.

With the dishes finished, Frank joined Pa and Andy for a spirited round of cutthroat checkers. Frank was good at the game and always won, even when playing against two opponents simultaneously. "The army taught me three things," Frank said, "how to shoot a gun, peel potatoes, and play checkers."

One Sunday when they were alone in the kitchen finishing the dishes, Frank finally said what he had tried for weeks to find the courage to say. It is not as if he had planned it for this moment, had worked out what to say, how to say it smoothly. The words had just suddenly jumped from his mouth, taking him by surprise and leaving him bewildered and worried about what might come next.

Perhaps it was the sweet domesticity of it all, standing so close to the prettiest girl in the world, sharing this most ordinary of all activities, *washing dishes*. Frank had never imagined he would look forward to washing dishes on Sunday evenings. It had become a deliciously intimate interlude, a few moments' relief from the tough world to a sweet place where only Frank and Connie existed, their hands in a dishpan of warm soapy water, their arms lightly touching as they quietly worked. And when Connie wiggled her nose to dislodge a soap bubble that had floated up and settled there, she looked so endearing that Frank melted completely, lost all reason, and blurted out in a rush of words, "Conniewillyoumarryme?"

Connie looked up, losing her concentration on the soap bubble, and said nothing for the longest moment of Frank's life. He kicked himself mentally: *What did I do? Did I just propose marriage? What a stupid way to propose marriage. Washing dishes! I should have had an elegant speech, something romantic. I should have had flowers or music or candlelight or something! Anything! Anything but washing dishes! Anything but blurting out a dumb question out of nowhere! What'll she think of me? She'll send me away for being a stupid, dumb clod. Oh man, I really blew it. I'm done here! I'm finished!*

Connie dropped the dish she had been scrubbing. It fell into the water, floated for a moment, rocking like a small boat on a stormy sea before it took on enough water to dip an edge and sink to the bottom, disappearing into the depths of the dishpan.

Frank watched it go. *Sunk!* He thought, miserably. *Sunk. Just like me.*

Connie turned, looked at Frank for another long, silent moment, then grabbed him, hugged him tightly, ignoring her soap-and-water-covered hands, and said, "I thought you'd never ask."

Frank was bewildered, surprised. He had expected she would need to think about it for a while, that she would say something reasonable like, "I'll get back to you on that." He had asked the question but now was not sure what to do with the answer. "Is that a, a, 'yes'?"

"Of course, it's a 'yes,' dopey!" Connie laughed and Frank whooped and hugged her, and they stood there for a long, delicious moment in that happy—if soapy—embrace, standing at a kitchen sink full of dirty dishes.

At that moment Connie's mom walked into the kitchen, looked at them, turned around, and walked out. As she reentered the parlor, she raised her arms in victory and, with a huge smile on her face, bent down and kissed Pa on the top of his bald head, interrupting his struggle with the Atwater-Kent radio receiver. Pa looked up, rubbed his head, and asked, "What the heck's *that* all about?" having no clue as to the major event that had just occurred in the kitchen.

The Twenties, that wild and disastrous decade, was not the best time to marry, so they delayed it. But in 1926 they refused to wait any longer for the Republicans' promised prosperity to "trickle down" to the common people. "We'll take the risk," they said, "and make the best of bad times."

Following an afternoon ceremony in St. Ann's Church officiated by Father Reilley, they celebrated at the fire hall. Platters of home-made sandwiches, cookies, and a beautiful home-baked wedding cake were brought into the big meeting room above the highly polished red fire trucks. Connie's mom set out a fruit punch; hard liquor was not allowed in the fire station, and it was still prohibition. But Frank and Connie's uncles Joe, Johnny, and Bill sneaked in a dozen bottles of *Ol' Alky* they had lovingly created in a tub in

Uncle Joe's cellar. They spiked the punch and passed the remaining bottles around.

The band consisted of the fire hall's battered old upright piano, two ukuleles, one banjo, a saxophone, and a snare drum. Frank's friends and Connie's brother Andy played them, an unlikely combo. Cousin Lou, a professional jazz pianist, carried along his enthusiastic amateur musicians, but *The Bumblin' Banjos,* as they called themselves for the evening, would not win many competitions. However, after several rounds of *Ol' Alky, everyone* agreed they were a fine band. Father Reilley was heard several times telling Uncle Joe, "Why, yes, thank you, Joseph. Indeed, yes, I'll have just another wee drop."

Bride and groom sneaked out early, leaving everyone to party into the early hours until only the three uncles, the five would-be musicians, and Andy remained. They were finally ushered out by Henry Willis, the fire hall janitor who, invited by Uncle Johnny, had set aside his broom, joined the party, and happily sampled the three uncles' creation.

Finding themselves out in the street at 3:00 AM and having nothing better to do, they formed a ten-piece marching band minus the piano and proceeded down Main Street, banging out a good deal of noise, Henry Willis leading, waving his broom like a drum major's baton, until an angry Mrs. Santoloro who lived above the Woolworth's 5 and 10 shouted out the window, "I'm calling the cops, you bums!" That sent them quietly home.

The young couple's honeymoon was a blissful but incessantly raining four days of camping in a New York state park in a little tent borrowed from Uncle Bill. "It was all rain and bugs and wet and cold!" Connie later complained to Uncle Bill. "All we could do for four days was huddle in your little tent!" But, for obvious reasons, she had loved it, and Uncle Bill wisely made no comment.

"Our honeymoon," Frank smiled years later, "cost us all the cash we had between us, two dollars and forty-seven cents for food, the park fee, and the four gallons of gasoline to get there and back. But the two bottles of Uncle Joes' bubbly didn't cost us anything!"

They returned to Nyack, penniless, happy, and a little afraid of the future. Frank searched for work, found only low-paying, temporary, part-time jobs, and they lived for six months crowded in the small house owned by Connie's folks.

Frank was discouraged with each day's unsuccessful search for work but, one day, he came home and jubilantly announced, "Guess what? I got a job at the paper mill!"

"Whooie!" Connie shouted, jumping up, knocking over a bowl of apples she had peeled and sliced, destined for a pie.

"Easy come, easy go," Frank observed bending down to clean up the apple, sugar, butter and cinnamon mess. But Connie hardly noticed the spill or Frank's precarious position, wrapping her arms around him, nearly knocking him over.

"I start tomorrow morning at six. Pay is low but we'll have a steady pay envelope every two weeks. Things are looking up!"

Six months later they rented a small three-room apartment across the street from the railroad tracks at the foot of Clinton Avenue in South Nyack. The sound of trains going in and out of the Nyack station became their normal background.

"It's nice to have our own place," Connie said, looking around the three empty rooms and picturing them filled with furniture. A train rumbled by, shaking the windowpanes.

It sure is nice," Frank agreed, pretending to stumble from the train's vibrations. "Especially with these earthquakes every half hour."

"Oh, don't be silly, Frank," Connie said. "It adds color to the place, atmosphere. How many people have trains going right by their door?"

"Going through their kitchens, you mean," Frank said. "But, yes, color! That's what this place needs, color!"

It was expensive, but Frank bought three gallons of paint—white for the ceilings, a nice yellow for the walls, a soft crème for the woodwork—and turned their little apartment into a cheery three-toned home.

"Is a nice job you do here, Frank," said their pleased landlord, Domenico Carbone, who credited the $6.50 for the paint, turpentine, plaster, scraper, sandpaper, putty, and brushes toward the $12.00 monthly rent.

They spent another nine dollars at the Salvation Army store for a small kitchen table and two wooden chairs, a used oak icebox, and an old three-drawer dresser with a cloudy mirror. Connie explored her folks' attic and basement, discovering a box of curtains, old dishes, pots, pans, forks and spoons, a worn but still colorful oval rug, and a lumpy couch. Frank brought in his old, dilapidated bed. "Not the finest," he said, then leered at Connie and added, "but it will keep us off the floor."

"Hmm," Connie smiled. "Why don't we see how it works?"

Later Connie said, "Now what we need is a pretty little cat all curled up in the middle of the old oval rug in the parlor. Wouldn't that be a nice picture?"

"Oh, great." Frank grumbled. "Another mouth to feed!"

"Frank, how much can a little cat eat?"

"Too much on my wages. But, on the other hand, maybe the cat could just eat the mice, so it wouldn't cost us anything to feed him."

"Frank, that's disgusting. The poor little cat!"

"And, what about the poor little mice?"

"Them, too."

"But then," Frank said, "the mice will be scared away by the trains running through the kitchen all day, so we won't need a cat after all."

"You're impossible," Connie sighed, raising her eyes to Frank's newly painted white ceiling.

Frank liked the idea of a cat. *A nice calico would add just the right touch of color to that old rug,* he thought. But they never did get a cat.

One day on their return from shopping at Mr. Raso's grocery on Franklin Street, Frank shouted from the bedroom, "Hey, somebody stole our bed!" Connie rushed in. Frank's sagging old bed was gone, replaced by a new, big double bed and matching night tables they had admired in Brown's furniture store on Main Street but could not afford to buy immediately. They had put five dollars down on a "lay-away" plan, with the understanding that Mr. Brown would deliver the set when the total ($93.99) was paid. It had a maple headboard and footboard, a mattress, spring, four soft pillows, was flanked by two matching night tables, each with a new reading lamp. A small maple rocking chair completed the set. A handwritten note placed neatly in the middle of the bed explained:

To Connie and Frankie,

Remember what we told you Frankie.

But you got to get your own sheets and blankets.

With All Our love,

Your One and Only Three Uncles

Frank smiled, feeling the love from those sweet old men. He recalled their advice, cornering him alone just before he and Connie had sneaked out of their wedding reception. By that hour the three uncles had been warmed and mellowed by *Ol' Alky*.

"Frankie," Uncle Bill had said, stumbling over his words and poking Frank in the chest. "Lissen here, Frankie. We gonna' give you the best advice for a good marriage you ever gonna' get."

"Yeh," Uncle Johnny added. "Listen to us, Frankie. We gonna' tell you the faks o' life." He put his arm around Frank's shoulder, leaned in and stage-whispered through fumes of *Ol' Alky*. "Frankie, now you lissen good. Ya hear?" Then he paused, flustered, forgetting what he was going to say.

Uncle Joe came to his rescue. "What that befuddled ol' man means," he said, pointing his thumb vaguely at Uncle Johnny, "if he could remember what he wanted to say, is this advice we gonna' give you from us ol' guys 'cause we know what's what, you know? We been aroun', you know? Been through it all. So, lissen good, Frankie. You lissen." He paused another moment, straightened his shoulders, poked a finger at Frank and said, solemnly, "The secret of a good marriage, Frankie, is a good mattress!"

"You bet, Frankie," Uncle Bill chimed in. "An' you better b'lieve that's the best advice you ever gonna get."

"An' don' tell nobody else," Uncle Johnnie added, putting a finger to his lips, and looking around. "That's jus' for you an' Connie."

The three uncles nodded sagely to each other, clapped him on the back, hugged him and, with tears of happiness and *Ol' Alky*, said, "On your way, Frankie Boy. On your way."

"What was that about?" Connie asked later. She had seen them huddling outside, whispering secrets. Frank explained the uncles' advice about mattresses.

"Oh, fine!" Connie said. "And what other intimate things about us have the four of you been giggling over?"

Chapter Fifteen:

1928—Poverty Will Be Banished From This Nation.

From 1926 through 1928, the economy boomed along for many Americans. "Prosperity for everyone," they said. But Connie, Frank, and tens of millions of other Americans continued to have a different experience.[1] In August 1928, Frank and two friends were discussing the coming presidential election—Republican Herbert Hoover and New York State's Democratic Governor, Al Smith.

"Did you guys hear Hoover?" an infuriated Charley Claussen asked. "Damn Republicans picked him to run for president, and you know what he said in his acceptance speech?"

"I'm sure you gonna' tell us," Al answered.

"Yeah, well, it's here in the paper, see? What Hoover said? I can't believe it. He said the Republicans are wiping out poverty! He said there's almost no more unemployment! He said everything's going great! What the devil's the matter with the man! Don't he know what's going on in his own country?"

"He said that?" Bob Greggs asked. "He actually said everything's goin' great?"

"Yeah, he sure did. Here, read it for yourself."

Charlie folded the paper to the article and Bob read aloud those soon-to-be-infamous lines. "Unemployment is widely disappearing... We in America today are nearer to the final triumph over poverty than ever before in the history of any land. The poorhouse is vanishing from among us...with the (Republican) policies of the last eight years, we shall soon, with help of God be in sight of the day when poverty will be banished from this nation.'"[2]

"Well," Frank said, shaking his head, "Hoover's not living in my world. What I know is that the mill's cutting hours again, our pay envelopes are getting thinner. And I know guys even worse off; laid off completely and can't find jobs. Nobody's hiring anymore. Henry Korell, I went to school with him, the bank went an' took his house. They have two kids. Eight years paying their mortgage every month without fail, always on time, an' then they couldn't keep up, lost everything. What are they gonna' do now, no job, no income, no place to live?"

"Yeah," Charlie added. "People all over the country been losing their homes. My cousin, he got a farm over in West Nyack. Been in the family over a hundred years. Says they're gonna' lose it. Bank's gonna' foreclose 'cause farmers, they can't make no money no more. Says in the last five, six years, been hundreds o' thousands o' farm foreclosures and farmers, they been struggling since the end of the war.[3] The politicians, they don't say nothin' about the farmers, an' they don't know nothin' about us, they just go on an' on about how great the economy is and how everybody's making money. An' it ain't true!"

"Well," Frank said. "I guess it's true for some people, those already rich, playin' the stock market and livin' good. And they have no idea what the rest of us been goin' through."

Connie and Frank, like so many others, fell behind on their rent and feared they would be evicted. But Mr. Carbone was patient.

"You know," he told them. "Carbone, it means coal. So, I'm suppose' to be hard, like a lump o' coal. But I'm jus', how you say? A' ol' softie. You been good tenants, *so* you pay me what you can, maybe half, an' when this crazy business she be over, you pay the rest."

As the country prepared for the 1928 presidential election, investors continued riding high, prosperity seemed to have no end—for some—it was one wonderful, booming, party! But below them, among the working families, unemployment, home, farm, and small business foreclosures grew, and more families, stripped of everything, fell invisibly and silently into poverty.

The Republicans won the 1928 election, their third consecutive hefty victory, and Herbert Hoover became president. Then, a year later, on October 25, 1929, finally hearing some rumblings at the upper economic level, President Hoover assured the country that all was well, the Republicans had everything under control. He said: "… the fundamental business of the country … the production and distribution of commodities, is on a sound and prosperous basis."[4]

Four days later, the stock market collapsed and $32 billion of the country's wealth disappeared. The Great Depression had started, and the insulated rich, comfortable and untroubled for so long, began to taste some of the bitterness that working families had known for years.

The 1920s had been tough for working families but the 1930s would be worse. Desperate parents, hungry children, abandoned pets, long breadlines, silent factories, empty stores, and the wandering jobless formed the picture of the Great Depression; and a quarter million homeless children wandered the streets. President Hoover, only a year in office when the market collapsed in November 1929, would serve three more years while the country fell apart. "Hoover" came to mean poverty, hard times, starving children, while the politicians—well-off themselves—remained blind and deaf to everyone else's suffering.

One morning Frank met his school friend, Henry Korell, who had lost his job and home. Henry said he was living with his wife and kids in one of the hundreds of tar paper "Hoovervilles" that had sprouted across the country, filled with distressed, hungry, hopeless families. *Henry doesn't look too good, unhealthy, and, like, depressed,* Frank thought, aching to help his friend, but what could he do?

It was a world-wide economic depression, not any one person's doing, but in the United States, Hoover, our most unfairly maligned president, was blamed for it all.[5] He tried various measures, but had no solutions for the country's miseries.[6]

"Damn Hoover," Henry said, and Frank agreed.

In November 1932, Frank, Connie, their families, and all their friends voted for Franklin Roosevelt and the Democrats, having had enough of Hoover and his Republicans. The next day a happy Charlie Clausen waved the *Journal News*:

FDR WINS! DEMS TAKE ALL! CONGRESS, GOVERNOR, STATEHOUSE.

"Hoover an' his Damn Republicans," Charley crowed, "got themselves plowed under by FDR!"

"Now," Frank said, elated at the Democrats' victory. "Roosevelt will get things done and end this Depression, get us working again."

But the Depression continued. Early in 1933, as Roosevelt's administration was getting organized, work at the mill was cut to less than three days a week. "I don't know what we're gonna do," Frank said. "We don't even have enough to pay half the rent this month. There's talk the mill might shut down. What'll happen to us?"

But even their dismal world of economic decay held a bright spot: In September 1933, Emily was born, bringing them a little oasis of happiness. Frank walked around their tiny apartment, gently cradling his little girl. "It's a good thing, my beautiful Emily, that you didn't come out looking like me," he said to the sleeping infant.

"How true," Connie said.

"Hey!" Frank said, insulted. "You didn't have to agree with me, you know. And anyway, I was talking to Emily, a private conversation over here, if you don't mind."

Connie's pregnancy and Emily's birth, with the help of Dr. Wharton and Nurse Laura, had gone perfectly. The new parents brought Emily home, a beautiful child with a sunny disposition right from the beginning of life. She was a contented baby, seldom fussed, was never cranky, and didn't keep them up at night. Of course, she cried when hungry and complained when she needed changing and wailed over a distressing gas bubble. But, otherwise, Emily was a happy child. And Frank was completely enchanted by his little daughter.

"Frank," Connie told him. "You're going to spoil Emily, picking her up and carrying her around like that all the time.

"Yep," Frank smiled. "I sure am."

They knew that Emily was a bright little girl, but they were surprised one evening when her high voice came floating from her crib carrying her first clear word, "Binky," a combination of vowel and consonants advanced for her seven months. This was no random babble; she was using the word with purpose. Binky was Emily's stuffed bear who was at that moment lying on the floor. Emily was peering down at him from her crib, saying, "Binky, Binky."

"Frank," Connie said later, "it was like Emily was calling him to get back in the crib. I couldn't believe it. How in the world does she even know his name, let alone call him to get up?"

As surprised and pleased as she was at Emily's precociousness, Connie felt a little aggrieved that Emily's first word had been "Binky," and not "mama." But she never admitted that to Frank.

Binky had joined the family in 1931, two years before Emily's birth, on a hot August Sunday at the Rockland County Fair. "Come on," Frank had said, "let's forget this damned Depression for a few hours and go see the county fair."

"But Frank, we need money to get in. How much does it cost?

"Twenty-five cents each," Frank said, digging in his pocket and finding a quarter. "Hey, look at this! I've got just enough for me. See you later Connie."

"Oh, ha, ha, my funny, funny, Frankie."

"OK, OK, so maybe we should dig around and see if we can find another twenty-five cents. I think there's some change in my work pants."

Soon, they had a little pile of change on the table. "One dollar, sixty-nine cents," Connie counted.

"And a paper clip," Frank added, tossing the clip on the table. "That's less than the $2.47 we scraped up for our honeymoon seven years ago."

"We're going backwards!" Connie said. "We have less now than we had then!"

"Never fear, Connie dear," Frank sang, wrapping her in a big hug and dancing her around the kitchen. "We will live on love!"

"Sure, Frank. You go live on love. I need money to run the family."

Laughing, they linked arms and went off to the fair.

As they walked along the midway Connie stopped, delighted. She grabbed Frank's arm and pointed. "Frank, look! It's Mr. Binky!"

"Who?" Frank asked, puzzled, peering at the crowd. "Who the heck is Mr. Binky?"

"There," she said. On the top shelf of that booth! See? It's Mr. Binky! He's sitting there all alone, and with the same goofy expression he had when I was little. I had a stuffed bear just like him. 'Mr. Binky' I named him because I just *knew* that was his name. Oh, Frank you have to rescue him, to get him for me! You *must*!" In growing excitement, she dragged Frank to the booth.

Two spring-loading pellet guns were on the counter, challenging young men to step up, take aim, and impress their young ladies. Twenty feet away at the rear of the booth, a paper target waited.

"Atta' girl!" the Carny said, seeing Emily's interest. "Bring him on over here Missy. What's your big fella's name?"

"Frank," Connie said.

"Here ya' go Frank," the Carny coaxed, holding out a rifle. "Only a dime, one thin dime gets ya' three shots and ya' look like yor just the man what can do it! C'mon, step on up Frank, an' take yer shots. Ten cents. Make the pretty lady happy!"

Smiling at Connie, Frank put a dime on the counter and picked up the rifle. "Let's see if I learned anything from all those hours on Uncle Sam's firing range. What about those prizes on the top shelf? Like that goofy-looking stuffed bear?"

"Frank," the Carny said. "I knew right away you wuz a better man than most. Them is the Special Prizes, Frank, a bigger challenge, tougher to get. Twenny-five cents for three shots and a smaller target. Tougher all around, but worth it if you win!" He pulled up a target half the size of the original.

Frank added fifteen cents. Raising the rifle, he squinted along the sights, aimed at the center of the target, and smoothly squeezed off three shots, watching to see where the lead pellets hit the backboard.

Huh. He thought. *Damn gun pulls high and right. I wasn't even close.*

But the Carny beamed. "That wuz real close, Frank! Only missed by a hair! Don't give up now. Try again. I bet you get it this time. Here, try a different gun."

"No thanks," Frank said. "I'll stay with this one." *Now that I know which way it's rigged.*

Frank dug in his pocket and put down another twenty-five cents. *Huh,* he thought, *already cost me half a buck tryin' to win a little stuffed bear I could buy in the store for less. But Connie really wants this one, so...*

Frank aimed just at the left edge of the target and a little lower, to compensate for the gun's high-right bias. His shot missed. *A little more left,* he thought, fired, and again missed.

Oh no. Connie tensed, pressing her fists against her chin. *C'mon, Frank. C'mon.*

Only one more shot. Damned if I'm gonna' spend another twenty-five cents trying to hit a target with a rigged gun! Gotta' get it this time.

He steadied, relaxed, aimed, squeezed the trigger as he had been taught in the army, and his final shot punched dead center through the paper target.

Connie laughed and clapped her hands like a happy child. A small crowd had gathered and cheered Frank's success.

The Carny beamed and congratulated Frank. Lifting the goofy-looking bear from the top shelf, he handed it to Frank, calling to the young men in the crowd, "See that you fellas? See how easy it is? C'mon and give it a try. Jus' twenny-fi' cents fer three shots."

Frank swept off his hat, bowed to Connie, and presented the little bear to her. She gave him an enthusiastic hug and a kiss with the poor bear squeezed between them while the little crowd cheered.

"Now that's what I call a bear hug!" the Carny said, making everyone laugh.

Impressed by Frank's success and energized by the good feelings, a dozen young men eagerly crowded around the booth, each offering a quarter to the very happy Carny.

Connie loved that little bear, her new Mr. Binky, a soft, cuddly bear who brought back wonderful childhood memories. And every now and then Connie would happily remind Frank how he had rescued Mr. Binky from his lonely perch on the Carny's top shelf and brought him home, "just for me. My Hero!" She sighed each time, giving Frank an appreciative hug and kiss.

Two years later Emily was born, came home from the hospital, and Mr. Binky was there, waiting for her. Soon Connie's Mr. Binky was Emily's Mr. Binky and, from then on, wherever Emily went, whatever Emily did, so, too, did Mr. Binky.

"Sweetheart," Connie explained one day to her adamant two-year-old. "I don't think you should take Mr. Binky in the tub, with you. Bears don't like soapy water."

"Mr. Binky need a baff!" a determined Emily said, and in he went.

After the bath, a sad Emily tried to soothe the poor, sodden bear and she remained contrite for a week until Mr. Binky, on the clothesline in the back yard, had dried out enough for Emily to hug and carry around again.

Chapter Sixteen:

1935—Thursdays with Sophie

It was 1935, deep in the Depression. With work at the mill reduced to three days a week and Emily to raise, Frank searched for extra work around town: clearing snow, mowing lawns, washing windows, doing handyman jobs. He was good at it, worked hard for people not much better off than he. Depending on the nature of each job and who was paying him, Frank earned about 15 cents an hour, when he could find work; not much, but it helped.[1]

Connie wanted to work too, but how could she, with Emily to care for?

"Margie Sutton works at home," Connie told Frank. "She gave me a name, Ben Krivitz. He hires people, puts a sewing machine in your house, and every week brings material to sew, like handbag linings, coat collars, gloves, things like that. The more pieces you finish, the more you earn."

"Piecework," Frank said.

"Yes, and I can work here while Emily's taking a nap and at night when she's sleeping."

"I don't know," Frank said. "I don't like turning our home into a factory."

"Oh, don't be silly Frank, it wouldn't be that at all. The machine's quiet, doesn't even have a motor. Has a foot pedal. No noise, no smoke, no dust. I don't know how much I'll earn but, whatever, it will help."

"Well, OK," Frank reluctantly agreed.

Connie began working at home, and Emily was lulled to sleep each afternoon and evening by the smooth whirring of the machine and the steady clanking of the pedal as Connie pumped it up and down. The kitchen floor sprouted piles of fabric, scraps, and neatly finished pieces.

Ben Krivitz, a small, energetic man, 60 years old and always in motion even when sitting down, became a weekly visitor. He held an unlit cigar between the second and third fingers of his left hand. When he talked, he waved his hand. The cigar circling around his head drew attention, and everyone wondered if he ever lit it up and smoked it. He never did.

At 2:00 each Thursday Ben Krivitz knocked on the door, bringing boxes of material to sew, instructions for the following week, and payment for the week's work. His greeting was a cheerful, "Hallo Missus. How are you and your family this week? And how is your little girl? Everything is good, yes?"

If Connie said Emily had a sniffle or other minor ailment, he was concerned and the next week would bring a gift—a toy, a trinket, nothing expensive, but always something a little girl would like.

"So, Missus," he would say, waving the cigar stub and offering his gift. "Little Emily, she will like this? Yes?"

He wore a black yarmulka and an aging, neatly brushed gray suit that he had once filled out more fully. Krivitz complimented Connie on her work, counted out the money she had earned, gathered the finished items, and left with a wave of his cigar, saying, "Until next Thursday, Missus. Yes?"

"He's a nice man," she told Frank. "I like him. But you know there's something about him, he's always rushing, like he's afraid to stop, like something's after him and he needs to keep moving. But he never says anything about it. He's always pleasant, asks about Emily, checks over the work, pays me, and then he's gone, maybe fifteen, twenty minutes. No time to waste. I wonder what he thinks is after him?"

Krivitz never met Emily because that was her nap time. But Emily knew about *Mr. Kivvies,* was curious about the never-seen man who sometimes left little presents for her. Creating a bright mental picture, she knew *zackly* what *Mr. Kivvies* looked like. Determined to meet him, Emily insisted, "Me an' Mr. Binky no take nap!" But, to her disappointment, she always fell asleep at nap time, as did Mr. Binky.

Connie had been working at home for ten months when, one Thursday, Ben Krivitz failed to appear. Sophie Krivitz, Ben's wife, introduced herself. "Ben is very ill. We will keep bringing work, but who knows for how long? Today I came to tell you. But starting next week, Leon Geyle, one of the men in the shop, will come. He's a nice young man."

Sophie was in her early 50s, well-spoken, with a German accent and a manner suggesting an educated European woman. Connie wondered about that. *She carts around cardboard boxes of gloves and pocketbooks. Just another worker, Like me. But she talks so nice! Like a teacher.*

Connie was concerned about Mr. Krivitz. "We like Mr. Krivitz very much," she said, "and enjoy his visits. And Emily wants to meet him. Please tell him we hope he gets better soon and comes to see us again."

Sophie smiled sadly. "Thank you, Mrs. Gardner. That was very nice of you to say that."

"Please," Connie said, "sit for a minute."

Unlike her husband, Sophie was happy to linger and talk, and the two women discovered a warm connection. The next week, instead of sending Leon Geyle, Sophie returned, and *Thursdays with Sophie* became a weekly tradition.

They enjoyed Connie's coffee and the wonderful slices of Sophie's home-baked *Streuselkuchen*. "Sophie," Connie said. "This cake is wonderful! I've never had anything like it."

Sophie was pleased. "Good. *Kaffee und Kuchen,* it is my country's traditional little ritual among friends. Enjoy."

"Oh, I do, but Sophie, I'm afraid it'll make me fat. Then what?"

"Then you'll be a little bit more woman, no? And I think your Frank would not object."

For half an hour they shared *Kaffee und Kuchen,* talked about children, families and the price of groceries, religion, history, world events, and even the future of humanity. Connie loved their discussions. She learned a great deal and marveled at how much Sophie knew and how well she spoke. Connie was not accustomed to handling weighty, abstract ideas. It was heady, challenging, but she rose to it. *Thursdays with Sophie,* she thought, *it's like being back in school with a good teacher.* She was impressed by her new friend.

"I don't think Sophie is just another worker," she told Frank.

"Sophie," she asked one day. "How do you know all this?"

"Ah," Sophie explained. "For a time before and after the war, Germany allowed some women into a few universities. There were so many bright young women, eager to learn, to explore, to join Germany's wonderful intellectual life. Many were Jewish. I was fortunate to share in that for a time. Oh, how exciting it was."

As their friendship grew, Sophie talked more of Germany, revealing a world Connie had never imagined.

"How can I begin to explain?" Sophie said. "How we loved the country that hated us? How can others understand? It is too much, too much. In 1918, almost seventeen years ago, I was 35, about your age, Connie. The world celebrated the end of the war. But not Germany. What had we to celebrate? A lost war? A country destroyed? Two million dead soldiers? A struggling democracy? [2]

"We were a grieving, humiliated, defeated people choked by inflation. Paper money was only good to light the stove in the morning. In 1923 I carried a laundry basket filled with *Reichsmarks* to buy a loaf of bread! And even as we waited in line, the prices doubled right before our eyes! It was *ein Wahnsinnsland,* a crazy land, a frightening, distorted world where each moment brought new distress."

Poor Sophie, Connie thought. *Those poor people. And we think we have it rough? What must they have gone through?*

Then an angry thought blazed up: *But why should I feel sorry for Germany? They brought it on themselves! They started the war!* [3] *Caused so much misery. They have no right to complain!*

Connie immediately felt contrite for such uncharitable thoughts. *No! That's not fair! Sophie didn't start the war! She was a victim. She suffered too! Oh, poor Sophie!*

She reached out and gently held Sophie's hand.

"I will tell you," Sophie said. "It is a sad story. After the war, in 1920, there was chaos! Atrocities! Terror! Street gangs; Nazis and communists fighting each other. Innocent people beaten, left for dead or dragged away, never again seen. Jewish shops firebombed. Viciousness without limits, and the police, blind and deaf. We cowered behind locked doors and shuttered windows, fearing their fragility, afraid to venture out."

"How awful!" Connie said, shocked at Sophie's tale.

"Yes, but Connie, worse was to come. In 1923 an armed insurrection to overthrow the Weimar Republic failed, its leaders convicted of treason. But the old-line conservative judges, believing the insurrectionists were 'concerned patriots,' gave lenient sentences for treason. Among the traitors was 35-year-old Adolph Hitler, a war veteran and Nazi party leader. He was sentenced to prison for treason and, we could not believe it, was released just nine months later! While in prison he held court with his supporters and together they wrote that terrible book, *Mein Kampf.*

"Back on the streets, in 1924 Hitler and his Nazi thugs resumed their campaign of lies and hate over the next nine years. They became 'legitimate,' winning elections, gaining power. Hitler is no philosopher, no intellectual, no great thinker, but he is a powerful speaker. Good people we had known for years, our neighbors, our employees, our customers, all ordinary Germans, lost their senses and cheered a monster.

"But Hitler is no ordinary street thug, Connie. He brings emotions to a boil, feeds the fear, resentment, and anger that *already exists* in the people. He shouts that Germany is in ruins and blames the feebleminded, insane, diseased, but mostly he blames the Jews. His lies became the truth. Not everyone believed the lies, but how many believers do you need to create havoc in the country?

"Hitler did not create the deep hatred of Jews and Roma and

other *inferiors.* Hitler was not the one who originated the programs to round up and lock away *inferior* people, like the feeble-minded, epileptic, insane, blind, and deaf. And Hitler did not originate the mass sterilization of *inferiors* to cleanse Germany of the Jews and other people they declared to be diseased organisms.

"It was all there before Hitler. His terrible genius is not in creating the *Big Lie,* the hatred, but in recognizing and using the power of hate, sharpening it and offering it to the country. He embraced, magnified, incessantly and loudly repeated the *Big Lie* that the Weimar Republic was an illegitimate government created by rigged elections, by fraud, deceit, treachery, and treason committed by the racially inferior Jews and other traitors who had weakened Germany from within, like a spreading cancer, causing Germany's defeat. The election was stolen from him, Hitler screamed; the Weimar government is not legitimate!

"Hitler and the Nazis embraced and magnified the hate that was already in our culture and made it their party platform, telling us what they would do when they gained power.[4] Hitler used what was there, the *Big Lie*, nourished it into a colossal monster and unleashed it, like a great, hungry beast.

"He is an evil man, Connie, he threatens the world. And in defiance of the Versailles Treaty, he is now rebuilding the German military. What do you think he is going to do, driven by his delusion of Aryan supremacy and Jewish deceit, once he has a powerful military under his control? I know what he will do to us, Connie. To the world. But the world is blind; the world must wake up!"

Connie shuddered. "Sophie, you make it sound so frightening. Are we all in danger? Can Hitler really be that bad? I've read about Hitler in the newspapers. Frank hates him; says he's like the Germans who ran the war. I never knew all that about Hitler, that he was imprisoned for treason. But the people elected him president, right?

"Ah, no, Connie. Not elected, appointed. Just over two years ago, 1933. A terrible mistake. By then Hitler's Nazis were the strongest political party. President Hindenburg was 85, old and tired and he despised Hitler. But, pressured by Germany's old-guard conservatives who favored Hitler's violent nationalism, he appointed Hitler as Chancellor. Then Hitler declared himself not just Chancellor, but Germany's *Führer,* the absolute ruler, banned all political parties but the Nazis, took over the courts and the media, ordered the military to swear allegiance to *him*, rather than to the country or to the constitution. And Germany's democracy was dead. But Hitler's Nazi Germany will fail. Dear God, *must* fail! For the sake of the world, *Hitler must fail!*"[5]

Connie was moved by Sophie's intensity, by the tears in her eyes and the waves of sadness, fear, and anger flowing across her face. Still, she said, "But Sophie. What I hear people saying is that Hitler is doing a lot of good for Germany. Like Mussolini did for Italy. Healing the country, uniting it. And thousands of people in the United States admire and support him and even send him money.[6] They say he's solving Germany's problems, rebuilding, going to 'make Germany great again!'[7] So, why do you call him a monster and want Germany to fail?"

Sophie was quiet for a long time, thinking of how to answer. She knew there were tens of thousands of Nazi supporters and Hitler admirers in the United States, hoped Connie was not one of them, and was reassured to learn what Frank thought of Hitler. "Connie," she said. "Hitler has only one idea and everything he says and does flows from that. It is not rational, has no factual support. It is very much a national delusion in Germany, but it is a powerful idea that drives the Nazis and is becoming the central drive of Germany. That idea is this: *The Aryan race is superior to all others; it is threatened by inferior races, primarily the Jews, and it is the duty of the Aryan race to eliminate Jews and other inferiors.*

"That's a terrible idea!" Connie had heard superiority ideas but never stated so boldly.

"And" Sophie added, "for Hitler, it justifies everything and anything. Eliminating inferiors, he says, is necessary for Germany to survive and to gain our rightful place of superiority over the world. There is no limit to what Hitler will do, all stemming from that delusion."

"And Hitler started all that?" Connie asked. "Just one man did all that, took over a whole country and led the people to such terrible beliefs?"

"Oh, no, Connie. As I said, Hitler did not create those ideas. They have long been in German culture: racial superiority, Aryan heritage, humanity threatened by racial inferiors, primarily by Jews. Even before Hitler came to power our Weimar government was rounding up and locking away inferior people. They came for the children first, those who were feeble-minded, insane, epileptic, blind, deaf. They took them away, Connie, the children. Then they came for the adults, with marriage restriction laws and legal sterilization of feeble-minded women and other defective people; to prevent racial mixing, to stop the 'poisoning' of Aryan bloodlines by 'the unfit,' to cleanse the nation! They restricted the rights and freedoms of Jews and Roma, and did it legally, with new laws that we copied from the United States! Laws the United States had developed for 200 years to restrict your Negro people, your feeble-minded, Jews, and immigrants. Our leaders even before Hitler liked what they saw you were doing in the United States."

"We gave Germany those ideas?"

"No, Connie. What you gave us, and gave to the world, is how to enshrine the hatred into laws, to make hatred legal, to turn the *idea* of restricting certain people into the *reality* of oppression. The hate culture in Germany and your legal guidance was well under way long before Hitler."

Shocked by Sophie's story, Connie did not know what to say. *Sterilizing women to 'cleanse the nation'? First, they came for the children? Took them away? How can such things happen? I'll never again complain about my little problems,* she thought, now that she had a new, unsettling glimpse of the world. *But the idea that we showed Germany how to do it? No! That can't be!*

"But, Sophie, we don't have laws like that in my country! We don't do that here. We don't treat people like that!"

Is Connie so naive? Sophie wondered. *Can my friend not see what is all around her?*

"Connie," she gently answered, "when it became clear in the 1920s what our government was doing to people, your country criticized Germany. They were right to criticize, but their own hands were not clean. The German leaders answered, quite correctly: 'How can you criticize us? You have been doing the same things to your Negro people and to your Indians for 200 years, and to your Jews and your disabled, and now to your immigrants.[8]

"Our German leaders admired your racial laws, your marriage restriction laws, your forced sterilizations, your drive to euthanize defective children,[9] your terrible repression of Native Americans,[10] your barriers against Jews, your Jim Crow laws. You showed us how to write laws to repress people, diminish them. Our leaders liked how you carried out your repressions especially in your southern states. We copied your laws. You were our guide, our model."

Connie was shocked but now realized those terrible things were real in her own country; and the truth flooded over her.

"Ben got caught up in it. They hated his success, his factory, our beautiful home. Ben was outspoken, a mistake. 'Why should I be afraid?' he said. 'Our family's been here five generations! I'm as good a German as anyone.'

"They hated everything about us. *Juden!* they screamed. One day in 1928, thugs dragged Ben from his car, beat him terribly. Set fire to the car, the poor driver, Erik, barely escaped. Ben was never the same after that, injured, terrorized, always looking over his shoulder, afraid of being beaten again. And they wouldn't leave him alone, kept tormenting him, threatening our family.

"But we were fortunate. Ben managed to get our children out, to Canada. They are married, now, with their own children. Then Ben arranged our escape to England, then here. That was 1930, you could still buy your way out if you were wealthy. It cost us everything we had. *Everything,* Connie. They said we did not belong in the new Germany. Five generations and we did not belong!"

And Connie began to understand what Ben Krivitz was running from.

Chapter Seventeen:

1936—Uncle Joe's Bubbly Under the Sink

In September 1936, they celebrated Emily's third birthday. Connie's parents, Andy, and Sophie Krivitz were there, and Mr. Carbone, their landlord. A widower, his children grown, he had become a lonely old man—until these young tenants moved in and he had become a family friend and regular visitor. He was captivated by little Emily, who reminded him of his own daughter. "Gampa Bone!" Emily greeted him, with a gleeful hug each time he visited. *Ahh, what joy a child brings*, he thought, feeling thankful to be allowed part of it.

Frank moved the two kitchen chairs and table into the small living room. Connie, Grammy and Sophie sat on the couch, Mr. Carbone and Grandpa on the kitchen chairs. Andy and Frank sat cross-legged on the floor. Emily, happy in Frank's lap, held Mr. Binky up so he could see what was going on. Emily was delighted when Sophie put her beautiful cake on the table, admired by everyone. It was an unusual cake, being oval rather than round.

"Hmph. Looks like *ein Straußenei,*" Sophie said, critically eyeing her creation. "Not what I planned, but it will taste just as good."

"A *straw* what?" Andy asked.

Sophie laughed. "*Ein Straußenei.* An ostrich egg!" That made everyone laugh and eager to find out what Sophie's ostrich egg might taste like.

The plump cake was covered with pink sugar flowers and was layered in white frosting so thick and curly that Emily saw a white fluffy bunny with many pink eyes and several noses, an impression so vivid that Emily gasped and reached protectively when Connie cut the first slice. Emily knew it wasn't really a bunny but still felt sorry for the pretty cake. But that didn't stop her from enjoying it, liberally smearing her face and hands. Frank was not spared a sticky coating of icing nor was Mr. Binky who, Emily insisted, must be fed his own little piece of cake on his own little plate. For two happy hours the raging Depression was kept out and Sophie's past was curtained off.

But reality soon returned. Ben Krivitz' condition grew worse, and Sophie struggled to keep the business going. Work at the paper mill was cut again. Frank and Connie dropped closer to the economic bottom. And Europe continued marching toward the next war.

Then, Frank caught a break.

Harmon Garrison, manager of the electric power plant, was one of Frank's gardening customers. When Garrison returned from work one day, Frank was cutting the lawn. They talked for a while, and Garrison noticed a strange-looking scoop attached to the oak handle of Frank's lawnmower.

"What's that?" Garrison asked, pointing.

"Oh, just something I rigged up. It catches the grass clippings kicked back by the reel. Saves me a lot of raking. I empty it over there behind your garage, making a compost pile for Mrs. Garrison. I know how she likes to garden, growing flowers. The compost will make rich soil for her flower beds."

Garrison was impressed, had never seen anything like it. "You know," he suggested, "you ought to try for a patent. Might be a good thing for you. I'll be happy to help you with that."

Frank was pleased but did not take the suggestion seriously. Garrison did, however. He made phone calls and checked the Nyack library for references to patents, only to learn that grass catchers had been patented in the 19th century and Frank's device was neither an original idea nor a significant improvement. Garrison gave up on the patent idea but continued to be impressed by Frank. *A hard-working young man,* he thought. *Responsible, reliable. Takes good care of his family. Bright, too. But held back by this Depression. Should be doing better than cutting lawns.*

They had other conversations through that summer, and Garrison's good assessment of Frank increased.

On a Friday afternoon in October 1936, Frank bounced into the house, high stepping through the kitchen, waving an imaginary baton as if leading the high school marching band. He plopped his big gardening hat on his delighted three-year-old Emily, scooped her up and twirled her around singing, "Happy days are here again!"[1]

Connie, laughing at his antics and Emily's happy shrieks, asked, "Frank, what's going on? What's gotten into you?"

"I quit the mill! I quit the mill, ta da! That's what's gotten into me! I-quit-my-job at-the-pay-per-mill! I-quit-my-job-at-the-pay-per-mill!"

Emily sang too, "Pay-per-mill! Pay-per-mill!" having no idea what it was all about but having great fun joining in.

"You quit your job? Frank, what do you mean you quit your job? Why? What are we going to do without your job? Frank, stop jumping around! Tell me what's going on!"

"Mr. Garrison's gotta' get somebody else to cut his lawn! That's what's going on! No more lawn-cutting for me, that's what's goin' on! Ta Da!"

"Mr. Garrison? What's Mr. Garrison got to do with it? Frank, if you don't start making some sense, I'll, I'll, throw this towel at you. I will!"

"Oh no! Not the towel!" Frank quavered. Then, setting Emily down he squared his shoulders, puffed out his chest and said, dramatically, "My dear Mrs. Gardner and," bowing to Emily, who giggled appreciatively at his silliness, "to the lovely Miss Emily, Mr. Garrison has offered me a job at the power plant: the first opening they've had in three years. Two openings, in fact. I start Monday. He says I can apprentice as a lineman, or I can start inside the plant assisting the Assistant to the Engineer. The lineman's job pays more right off, but the other job is inside and less dangerous and has good advancement possibilities. There's a lot of training involved because it's a complicated job, and Mr. Garrison says he knows I can do it. Why, just picture this, Mrs. Gardner, your one-and-only husband will have a big desk with a long sign, *Mr. Frank M. Gardner, Assistant to the Assistant to the Chief Engineer!* Think of that! Why, that's gonna' be a mighty big desk to hold that mighty long sign!

"And maybe not much to start, but could lead up to Shift Supervisor, monitoring all the equipment, and the starting pay is more than I make at the mill! And the power plant's essential, no more worry about lay-offs. Connie, now we can start looking for our own house!"

"Our own house! Oh, Frank, let's start looking right away!"

"Whoa, hold your horses. I haven't even started the job yet. First, we gotta' save some money and then we can start looking. But right now, we need a toast, a celebration. Where's that bottle of Uncle Joe's bubbly we saved from our wedding?"

"There," Connie pointed. "Under the sink, gathering dust for ten years."

"Well, it's time to open it," Frank said, retrieving and wiping down the dusty bottle, being careful not to shake it.

"Well aged," Frank said, in his *wine connoisseur* voice, holding the bottle up to the light and peering at it. "Vintage 1926. Ah yes, a fine year for Uncle Joe's bubbly."

"And for our wedding," Connie added, smiling.

"That, too."

While Connie set out two glasses, Frank struggled with the resistant cork, finally pulling it out with great difficulty but in several dried-out pieces.

"Uh oh," he said, disappointed. "No 'pop!' Not a good sign."

He sniffed at the open bottle. "Phew!" Our wedding wine went sour! Rancid, not even good for vinegar! I guess under the sink's not the best place to keep Uncle Joe's premium vintage 1926 bubbly. Oh well, so be it. We don't need a drink anyway!"

Smiling, he turned back to Connie and his smile disappeared. She was standing, stiffly, a stricken look on her face.

"Connie, what's wrong, why are you looking like that?"

She was slow to answer. Frank asked again. "Connie, come on now. What's the matter?" He put his arms around her.

"I don't know," she finally whispered, leaning into his shoulder. "It was so sudden, Frank, this feeling, so awful. Came over me, like a horrible black shadow, when you said our wedding wine went sour. Like a premonition, a sign, or something, like something bad is going to happen to us, to our family. Frank, it's so frightening."

Frank was deeply bothered by that idea, but mostly he wanted to calm her. "Connie," he said. "That's just superstition. C'mon, Hon, you don't believe that stuff. You never have. Look at you, you're shaking for God's sake!" Frank held her tightly, reassuring, calming.

"Me too! Me too!" Emily demanded, pushing her way into the embrace. She had brightened at her Pa's obvious happiness and silly antics but now was distressed at her Ma's turn to something dark and frightening. Emily did not understand what was going on, but knew she had to be in there, close, with her Ma and Pa, whatever was going on.

Frank swooped her up again, hugging and kissing his two girls, and Emily felt reassured. "Who needs a dusty ol' bubbly from under the sink?" Frank said. "I got all the sweetness I can handle right here!"

Emily giggled and Connie finally relaxed and smiled. But she never forgot that moment.

A year later, in 1937, with Frank securely employed and some generous help from their three uncles, they bought their house. Frank, overwhelmed by the uncle's generosity, protested. They waved away his protests.

"Frankie," Uncle Johnnie said. "So, maybe together we got a little money saved up, you know? Like three old misers. So, what's three old misers gonna' do with money? Hide it down the cellar in the coal bin? What do we need it for? It's yours, Frankie. You and Connie and Emily. For the down payment. An' maybe a little extra for good measure. The rest, you gotta' pay by yourself."

"A loan," Frank said. "A loan. I'll pay you back and I'll pay you interest."

"Sure, sure," Uncle Joe said. "You pay us interest."

"Yeah," Uncle Bill added. "Maybe 100 points a week, you know like the mafia. Then we gonna' get rich on your money! That would be something!"

"It's a deal." Frank said. "At 100% interest a week you'll be rich in no time."

"Sure," Uncle Johnnie said. "Coupla' months. Then, with all that interest you pay us, we take you onna' world cruise, an' everybody gonna' be happy."

"See," Uncle Bill summed up, "everything works out good."

They laughed at their silliness. Connie, overwhelmed, grabbed the three old men and hugged them, repeating through her tears, "Thank you, thank you."

"Hey, hey, Connie, watch out," Uncle Johnnie complained. "Look, you got my collar all wet over here!"

Later, Frank asked Connie, "What did we ever do to deserve those three wonderful uncles?"

"I don't know," she said. "I love them so much."

"Yeah, Frank said, "me, too. And don't forget, two of them are on *my* side of the family."

"I'll buy that," Connie smiled and gave Frank a hug.

They paid Mr. Carbone the back rent. He was happy for them and brought a bottle of his best home-vintage red wine and half a dozen ripe figs from his pampered fig tree that he had smuggled into the country many years ago as a tiny twig. Frank and Mr. Carbone drank the wine until both wore silly grins. Connie and Emily ate the figs. Emily was entranced by the juicy, sweet, pink fruit that was new to her. "Figgies," she called them, insisted on hand feeding one to Gampa Bone to the old man's delight, and decided figgies were much nicer than her old favorites, strawberries.

Their new home was a small, two-story, wood-frame colonial on Cedar Hill Avenue built before 1900. It had a slate roof, three small bedrooms, a large kitchen, a water closet,[2] entry hall, and a small parlor with a fireplace. Connie liked the wide, roofed porch stretching across the front, a family place for lemonade and rocking chairs on warm summer nights when neighbors strolling by would stop to chat for a few moments. *Just like when my Grammy was with us,* she thought, enjoying that image of long ago and the opportunity now of recreating some of it.

A garage—actually, a converted horse barn that still had two big barn doors—framed one side of a large back yard that was perfect for Emily's play area. Repossessed by the bank four years earlier, the previous family's misfortune, the house needed a good deal of work. Frank and the uncles would do that. Connie loved the house, picturing it after the renovation. The bank, with no other buyers, had been paying its taxes for years and welcomed Frank's ridiculously low offer.

For Connie and Frank life had brightened, but the Great Depression continued to overwhelm their world. It rolled along every street, into every home, grinding a million families into uncertainty, making people suspicious and hateful, all of which was turned against the usual easy targets.

Chapter Eighteen:

1942—Emily's Woolly Cloud

Teddy, born in 1938, was weak and sickly, had feeding problems, fussed, and cried constantly with painful ear infections, abdominal and respiratory ailments. It was distressing for Teddy and his parents who, trying their best, had little success soothing his pain. Wretched helplessness became their companion.

He slept only brief periods. Toilet training was a disaster, and at age seven he was still wetting and soiling himself. Teddy was a fountain of mucous and saliva, ignored it or smeared it on sleeves, blankets, and furniture. Developmental milestones were delayed: eye contact, smiling, rolling over, crawling, standing, walking, weaning, talking—all were late for Teddy, prolonging his infancy, keeping Connie and Frank diapering, feeding, and pacing through sleepless nights.

Teddy was easily upset, impossible to console, and had such limited understanding of language that words could not calm him. When Teddy began to speak, his tongue refused to cooperate, making his speech indistinct and difficult to understand, causing Teddy to break down in wailing frustration. In time they adapted to his speech, and Teddy's frustration over language decreased but never disappeared.

It was during one of those long screaming episodes when Teddy was three years old that Mr. Binky transferred his allegiance from Emily to Teddy, or rather, when Emily gave up Mr. Binky and assigned the little bear to become Teddys soothing companion.

Teddy was screaming, stiffening, twisting, flailing his arms and legs, arching his back, pulling away from Connie, resisting her attempts to calm him. Emily was distressed, and, after several minutes, came to a decision. Speaking quietly, Emily, gave instructions to the little bear, then gently placed him against Teddy's chest. "Don't cry, Teddy," she said, "Mr. Binky's gonna' make you all better."

The little bear made no immediate impression on Teddy, who continued crying for a while and then fell asleep. An hour later he woke up, found Mr. Binky in the crib with him and apparently contented, wrapped his arms around the bear and went quietly back to sleep. After that, Emily's Mr. Binky was Teddy's Mr. Binky, and wherever Teddy went, as Frank said, "Mr. Binky is sure to go."

Now it was Teddy and not Emily who carried Mr. Binky all over the house. And whenever Emily and Teddy sat quietly together, Mr. Binky was snuggled warmly between them, his arms out, as if trying to hug them both at once.

"What a sweet, generous thing to do, Emily!" Connie praised her. "We know how much you love Mr. Binky but you gave him up for Teddy, to make Teddy happy."

"Yeah," Emily said.

"Do you miss Mr. Binky?"

"No! Um, Maybe. Well, I guess. Yeah, I do miss him, Mommy."

"Well, I'll tell you what. Why don't we get another Mr. Binky just for you?"

Emily was jolted by that, could not grasp the idea of another Mr. Binky.

"Oh no," she said. "There's only *one* Mr. Binky! An' anyway, he's still in the house and I can see him anytime I want. An' anyway I can talk to him when he's not busy with Teddy. An' anyway..." she paused a long moment and added, wistfully, quietly, "an' anyway, I'm gettin' too old for stuffed bears..."

"Oh no, Sweetie. People never get too old for stuffed bears!"

"Yeah? I can still play with Mr. Binky?"

"Of course, you can. Even if you are practically eight years old."

"Prakitly?"

"That means *almost*," Ma explained.

"Yeah," Emily said. "Prakitly."

Then, another thought occurred to Emily: "Mommy, are you too old to play with stuffed bears?"

"I am absolutely not too old to play with stuffed bears. In fact, before you were born, Mr. Binky was my sweet little bear, and I played with him all the time!"

"Yeah?" Emily said, intrigued.

Then Connie told her the story of how Frank had rescued a lonely Mr. Binky from the top shelf of the Carny's booth and Mr. Binky became the family's favorite bear. Emily was enchanted by the story, and when Frank came home from work she ran to him, hugged him with more force than usual, and gave him an extra-big kiss. "My Daddy," she said, and hugged him some more.

"Wow!" Frank said, filled with pleasure, as Emily ran off to play. "What was that all about?"

"My Hero!" Connie said, hugging Frank like Emily had. "Remember? Mr. Binky and the Carny? Now you're Emily's hero, too."

At birth Teddy's length and weight were normal but the short, squat, underweight, and weak body typical of Mongolism soon prevailed. When Teddy began walking, he was clumsy, knocking things over, dropping and breaking them, tripping, falling, running into door frames and furniture, creating pain and bruises. Ordinary childhood achievements like playing catch or riding a bicycle were beyond him. Teddy was nearsighted, and that contributed to his clumsiness. Eyeglasses became an expensive problem as he lost several, forgetting where he had left them.

Teddy accumulated scrapes and bruises, like a wind-up toy unable to change direction once in motion. His persistence was not from determination to gain mastery, but from an inability to learn from experience. Teddy never learned that he could not run under the dining room table without banging his head. Twice, fearing concussions, they had rushed Teddy to Dr. Wharton. No concussions, but Teddy suffered bruises, swelling, and throbbing headaches that drove him to inconsolable distress. But he continued to run headlong under the table.

Learning was delayed. Eating, for example, remained infantile for years. Mastering a spoon was difficult: Teddy dragged his fingers through his food and thrust them into his mouth. Family meals were sloppy, patience-taxing times.

Teddy did not understand common dangers, like running into busy streets or hugging stray dogs—many such unfortunate animals roamed Nyack's neighborhoods in the post-depression 1940s. He was bitten once, needed stitches in his right arm, and was left with a scar and fear of dogs. That was one time Teddy did learn from experience.

When Teddy was eight, thirteen-year-old Emily's quick rescue, putting her life in jeopardy, saved him from injury. For Connie, the chilling sounds of screeching brakes, squealing tires, Emily's screams as she ran into the street after Teddy, and the loud *whump* of a car ramming into another were etched into her mind and remained her private terror.

Underlying everything about Teddy was his *feeble-mindedness.* His thinking was slow, his understanding, muddied, and infantile. Had Teddy been examined by a psychologist in the early 1940s, the report summary might have read:

> DIAGNOSIS: "Mongoloid Mental Retardation; Imbecile, Estimated IQ 35-40, Maxium Mental Age 3—5 years (lowest 2 % of the intelligence distribution).
> PROGNOSIS: This Mongoloid boy has a life expectancy of about 9 to 11 years with severely limited physical, intellectual, emotional, and social development. Normal physical growth, emotional relationships, academic achievement, employment, or independent living are not possible. Life-threatening illness and hospitalizations associated with Mongolism (e.g., heart defects, hyperthyroidism,

> metabolic disorders) are highly likely.
> RECOMMENDATION: Permanent placement in a residential institution for the feeble-minded.

Raising Teddy involved an unrelenting barrage of demands, fatigue, frustration, and sadness. Connie and Frank knew that Teddy was as the professionals had warned, but professionals did not know everything. Doctors and social workers had the outlines right but failed to see the truth about Teddy and other Mongoloid children. That truth would emerge as Teddy grew and as Connie and Frank struggled to do their best for him.

Everything about Teddy was slow. He took forever to learn the simplest things, and never did master many of them. It was heartbreaking for Connie and Frank to see the incomprehension in his eyes when they tried to explain something to him. At times they knew he wanted to understand, strained to do so, but could not. It saddened them, but they accepted his limitations, and maintained a patient, gentle, and sensitive persistence with him.

Teddy's slow thinking was no surprise to them, but they puzzled over it and wondered how to help him. It was Emily, with her skill for creating mental images, who explained it to her parents, giving them a useful, if fanciful, way to think about it and to guide them with Teddy.

In 1943, they celebrated Teddy's fifth birthday, the year most children begin school. There were no schools for Teddy. He was not "educable." He would stay home. While they enjoyed a rich chocolate birthday cake with five candles, plus one for "good luck," ten-year-old Emily announced, "I'm gonna teach Teddy how to read! I'll be his teacher, like Miss Jeffries teached me when I was little."

Thus began a wonderful interlude. Each evening after helping Connie clear the dinner dishes, while Frank was working the night shift at the power plant, Emily sat with Teddy on the living room rug. Connie turned on the big Philco radio for them and music played softly from WQXR, a classical music station across the Hudson River. Emily's picture books were scattered all around them.

At first Emily's sessions lasted only a few moments before Teddy, impelled by his short attention span, ran off. But then, something changed: Teddy began to enjoy being with his sister, listening to her stories and looking at the pictures as she turned the pages. And the music, too, was nice. He snuggled against Emily, holding Mr. Binky, captivated by Emily, their physical closeness, her voice, the stories, and the pictures, particularly the colorful birds and flowers. Gradually Teddy grew more attentive, stayed longer; within a few weeks they were enjoying a daily half-hour evening tradition of sharing words, ideas, images, music, and love.

Connie enjoyed watching them, a sweet picture of her children and Mr. Binky. But the scene also exposed a terrible falsehood believed even by the doctors: that Teddy, a Mongoloid, would never develop affection for his family. But here he was, each evening snuggled against his sister, attentive much of the time, loving it all of the time.

Where had the idea of that other Teddy, the one destined for an institution, come from? It made Connie angry to think of that destructive picture of "Mongoloids." *How could they be so wrong? So cruel? How many unfortunate mothers had they convinced?*

Emily, always patient, read to her little brother, made up funny stories, and explained the pictures. They turned pages to reveal beautiful flowers and strange animals—and some scary ones, too. They saw people in brightly-colored clothing; giant trees and mountains and tiny white cows and goats and blue oceans and whales and fish that looked like flowers and just about everything that could be pictured in bright colors; and they giggled together, enjoying whatever silliness they came across.

One evening Emily pointed to two words and asked, "Teddy, what does this say?"

"Blue bird!" he answered immediately.

Emily was ecstatic. Teddy was reading! Over the next several days he read more words: "freight train," "cow," "zebra," "red rose," "camel," "tree," "bear," "mouse," "funny man." But Emily's excitement soon faded as she began to suspect that he was not reading the words but responding to the pictures. At Pa's suggestion she showed Teddy the words without the pictures, and he did not know them.

Teddy never learned to read. An experienced teacher might have taught him, but in the 1940s such teachers were not readily available to children like Teddy.

Emily was disappointed but not discouraged. *So he can't read. But he remembers names of things in the pictures, so he's really learning stuff!* She continued their daily lessons knowing that although Teddy was not reading, he was learning about animals and flowers and people and the big world out there. Each day, guided by Emily, Teddy's world grew a little richer, fuller, more colorful; and each day, Emily and Teddy grew closer.

Connie and Frank were enormously pleased, and they praised Emily for being so good with her little brother. "Teddy's getting so much out of it," they told her. "And we know it's hard to be patient with him, he can be so slow."

"That's no problem," Emily said. "I just have to wait for everything to get through the woolly cloud."

"Woolly cloud?" they asked.

"Yeah, a woolly cloud. It's thick an' it's got all shadows and stuff, like a cloud an' it's so thick sometimes you can't even see through it."

Connie was intrigued. "So, where is this thick woolly cloud? I've never seen it."

Emily rolled her eyes. "Mommm," she said, dragging out the word. "You can't see it. It's not really there. It's just the way I think about it, how I picture it. I see it like a cloud that's all wrapped around Teddy's mind, and that's what slows him down. Most kids don't have a woolly cloud but kids like Teddy do. They're just born with it, it's part of their, you know …" Like Connie, Emily hated the words "Mongolism," and "feeble-minded," so she just slid past them.

"It's just part of him. Of Teddy. See? Teddy really wants to understand the stories and the pictures and stuff. His eyes and ears, they're taking everything in alright, but then it's all gotta' get through the woolly cloud. And it's hard for stuff to get through it. Like walkin' in deep snow. The words and stuff get all slowed down and sometimes get lost or mixed up and some never do get through. But lots do, and then Teddy understands and when he does, he feels good that he did. See? I just wait, see how much gets through the woolly cloud. And stuff that doesn't, I just hafta' send it through again. Gotta' be patient, that's all. An' keep on trying."

They were impressed by Emily's creative image of what made Teddy's thinking so slow. But they were no longer surprised by their bright little girl who was always at the top of her class in school.

The more they thought about Emily's woolly cloud, the more helpful it was in understanding not only Teddy's slow thinking, but his entire mental difference from other kids. His store of knowledge, general understanding, reasoning processes and judgment were limited, incomplete, and immature for his age, less developed, always trailing his age-mates. Why was this? Emily's analogy gave Connie and Frank a way to think about it, to understand how Teddy processed information; in short, how he thought.

"Emily's woolly cloud really helps," Connie said. I've been thinking about it."

Frank smiled. "You keep doing that and you'll get as smart as Emily."

"I doubt it," Connie laughed. "But it helps me understand Teddy and gives me some direction for helping him."

"How?" Frank asked. "What kind of direction?"

"See, Emily says that everything Teddy sees, hears, feels and thinks, gets filtered through the cloud; everything slows down, and some things get lost or mixed up and what finally gets through is often not quite right, a little off or incomplete, not what everybody else sees and hears. Everything Teddy learns gets filtered through that cloud and that slows everything down and bends some of it—but not all of it—out of shape. So, what's left in Teddy's mind, his memories, his thinking, his understanding, isn't just slower than other kids, it's also *different* from other kids. That's how Emily explains it."

"So," Frank said. "Even if we tell him something straightforward and clear to us, and he says "A-OK," we don't know what kind of twist or filtering might happen to it in his mind? What he ends up with isn't necessarily what we thought we were telling him?"

"Yes, that's what I'm saying. Teddy hears us OK, but the message travels slow and some of it might get lost in there. And even the part that gets through might be twisted up a little. And we need to remember that. If we rush him he'll get things wrong, mixed up, all confusing and upsetting for him. But if we're patient, give him time, then Teddy can think it through and understand just about everything that's important."

Helped by that understanding, they became better parents for Teddy, more patient and tolerant, holding to their basic rule—*slow down, be patient, give him time.* They never formalized an educational plan as a teacher would. They were just good, loving parents who exercised mature judgement, made plenty of mistakes and then corrected them. Add a tolerance for trial and error, and a good sense of humor, and they went ahead and did what was needed.

While Connie and Frank knew Teddy could learn, develop, and enjoy life at home, many professionals believed such children could not be trained, taught or "humanized," and their best advice for parents was to accept the futility of trying. Connie and Frank had no illusions about "curing" Mongolism, but they were determined to do their best to help Teddy have as satisfying a life as possible, given his biological limitations.[1]

But even as Teddy was showing some unexpected positive development, he still had serious health problems requiring frequent medical treatment. Each illness reminded them of Teddy's short life expectancy. Teddy was turning six, already closing in on those limits.

On Teddy's sixth birthday Connie made his favorite cake. She smiled at how Teddy would react on seeing his cake: both arms raised high, his huge smile, and loud, gleeful shout, "All chawclit all over!" She pictured, too, how pleased Teddy would be with their little party. Ma, Pa, Emily, Grammy and Grampa, Miss Pritchett,

Miss Sophie, and Mr. Carbone, all of Teddy's favorite people, would be there, and Mr. Binky, sitting happily in his little chair.

Connie spread the rich chocolate on the cake, but her hands began to shake. *My God! Six! How quick his years go by! How many are left to my little boy? Four? Five? And I can't do anything to slow them down!*

Teddy had already endured three hospitalizations. His parents were thankful each time he returned home. They paid the bills but with increasing difficulty. Finally, they were driven beyond their financial limits.

It was April 1944, soon after Teddy's third hospitalization. The Second World War was burning to its finish, still a year away. Frank, nearly 50, was Nighttime Supervisor at the power plant, 4:00 PM to 2:00 AM, a long ten-hour shift, six nights a week.[2] He was home by 2:30, tried to unwind and tune in war news on the radio but found mostly static. He looked in on Teddy and Emily. *No sweeter sight than a sleeping child,* he thought, smiling, but feeling regret that his schedule allowed time with Emily only on weekends, when she was not in school. *Maybe when this war is over, I'll have a daytime shift an' see my kids more.* Frank went to bed about 3:00, was up by 9:00, leaving 6 hours for his family and household chores before going to work at 3:30 in the afternoon.

Walking downstairs that morning, Frank knew that Teddy waited for him to "rustle up" something good to share, even though Teddy had already eaten breakfast and would soon be sitting down to lunch. He smiled, thinking how Teddy was getting a little chubby, enjoyed eating, always with a messy enthusiasm. Frank loved his daily breakfast with Teddy. Connie, seeing how much they enjoyed it, quietly tolerated the mess her "boys" made each morning.

To Teddy, his Pa was the best cook in the world. In truth, Frank knew how to make only scrambled eggs, cold cereal, apple pancakes with maple syrup (his specialty), and—if Ma was not there to see what they were up to—some of that left-over chocolate cake from the other night.

Each day started with a game; Frank offered Teddy "a bowl o' beetles n' bugs," "a plate o' peas n' porcupines," "a sip o' snail soup," or Teddy's favorite, "spaghetti n' spiders," making Teddy laugh and Connie roll her eyes. But whatever outlandish meal they decided to make, it always looked and tasted like scrambled eggs, pancakes, or cereal and milk. That was fine with Teddy, it all tasted good and breakfast with Pa was fun.

Frank entered the kitchen on that day in April, saying, "A-OK, Teddy, my boy, what'll it be today? A nice bowl of spiders an' ...?" but he stopped at the sight of Connie sitting stiffly at the table, looking defeated. She held a crumpled letter; Teddy was glued to her, his face buried in her shoulder, his arms wrapped tightly around her neck. Frank could not see Teddy's expression, but the scene radiated distress. Teddy was still not talking well but they had noticed his growing sensitivity to their emotions, and the beginnings of some appropriate feelings in response, like his enjoyment of Emily's "teaching" sessions. It was another happy surprise, like his emerging sense of humor, unexpected and wonderful.

Frank saw it all: Connie was distressed by that letter; Teddy, sensing her distress, had wrapped himself around her, seeking safety and comfort. It would be a stretch to think that Teddy was trying to comfort his mom—that degree of empathy was probably still beyond him. But, still, it belied the professionals' prediction that Teddy would never feel or share normal emotions with his family.

Frank did not know what the letter said but, seeing the hospital letterhead, had an idea what it was about. The floor crumbled under him, he dropped into a chair, no longer thinking whimsically about spaghetti and spiders.

"It came today," Connie said, pushing the letter across the table, her voice flat. "Three thousand, two hundred dollars. How in the world can we pay that?"[3]

Frank stared at the letter, not wanting to touch it, feeling like he was sinking in quicksand. "My God, that's more than I earn in a year!"

They were silent for long minutes, thinking the same thing, afraid to say it. Finally, Frank surrendered to the hard reality: "We'll have to mortgage the house. It's worth five thousand in a normal market. But now, who knows? We might get 70 per cent, about enough to pay the bill. Maybe need to scrape up a little more somehow."

"Oh, Frank," was all Connie could say, her eyes tearing up.

"It'll take twenty years to pay off the mortgage. I'll be seventy by then, if I'm even still alive. And, Connie, you'll be what, 65? And if there's another emergency, another expensive hospital treatment that Teddy needs? Or maybe Emily, or one of us? What then? We won't have a house to mortgage, won't be able to pay hospital bills or even get medical treatment."

Millions of people had lost their homes to the banks in the Depression. A dozen years ago their friends Len and Sarah Miller had seen their West Nyack farm taken by the bank, their equipment and livestock, their livelihood, their home of three generations back to the Civil War. Everything.[4]

With hard work, generous uncles, and some unexpected good luck Connie and Frank had survived the ravages of the Depression, and by 1940 were debt-free homeowners. But what they had avoided was now about to devour them.

Chapter Nineteen:

1944—The Space Between[1]

Several days after receiving the hospital bill, Frank told Edwin Speer in the hospital's billing office that he would pay the bill after completing the bank's paperwork. Leaving Speer's office, he met Dr. Wharton in the lobby, and they talked for a few moments. Wharton saw Frank's distress, did not ask about it but seeing where Frank had been, had a good idea of what it was about.

Wharton had no business in Frank's finances; he was their family doctor, not their financial advisor. But Nyack was a small town, the hospital community smaller still. People talked and it took only a few moments chatting with Ed Speer to learn that Frank and Connie were going to mortgage their home to pay the hospital bill. *That's terrible,* Wharton thought. *After all they've been through! It's not right. But I warned them, advised them to give custody to the state.*

That evening after office hours Wharton thought about the Gardners. He knew he should keep his nose out of their finances, but he could not. They were his patients; he had ushered Emily and Teddy into the world and that made him feel some responsibility for them.

But there was more: The Gardners were the first family in his practice with a Mongoloid child. They had defied conventional wisdom, chosen their foolishly heroic path, and that made them noteworthy, a most interesting family. Wharton wanted them to succeed, and despite his training in objectivity, he had become emotionally invested in their success.

"I warned them you know," he told Deborah. "I told them what would happen. They didn't take my advice."

Deborah, patient enough to listen, wise enough to understand, had helped him through knotty issues over the years. Philip was grateful for her patience and good sense and often said, "we're a winning team, Deb." He had no problem discussing his patients with her, undoubtedly a breach of confidentiality, but that's how it worked in real life.

The Gardners, he told Deborah, had been foolish. "They should have given custody to the state. It's not possible to travel the path they chose; tilting at windmills, doomed to failure. I didn't do enough to convince them to let the state take over."

"You did all you could, Phil. They made the decision they thought was best. Anyway, do you really think it's so impossible? Keeping their child out of an institution and raising him at home?"

"Yes," Wharton said. "I do. Or at least, I did."

Wharton had been taught that Mongoloid traits were biologically caused, and no medicine, training, or a family's good intentions could change it. "They thought they could do it and look what it brought them, losing their home!"

"They're mortgaging their home," Deborah said, "not necessarily losing it."

"Well, maybe not. But it's a risky thing to do."

"And yet, Phil, you told me their little boy seems healthy now, or at least healthier than you expected. Is that right?"

"Yes, Teddy's six now and doing better than I ever imagined. I had doubts he'd even survive this long."

"Sounds like they take good care of him,"

"They do. They keep him healthy, active, and even happy in his own way, raising him as much as possible like a normal child. They even have him doing chores! Connie says they need to remind him all the time, but he likes doing them, makes him feel proud, grown-up. Whoever thought a Mongoloid can feel pride, can have any idea of what 'grown up' means? And they take him places, for fun, like a normal child, with his sister Emily. She's a sweet little girl and as bright as can be, and she's decided she's going to teach her brother how to read! Imagine that! Of course, he'll never learn."

"I'll bet he loves the attention," Deborah said. "Sounds like they're enriching his life."

"They are. And with good success so far. How the devil did they know how to do that?"

"I don't think it's much of a secret, Phil, I think they're just *doin' what comes naturally,* you know, like the song says?[2] If you start out with love, the rest follows."

Wharton thought about that. "Maybe," he said. "I don't know. But if it's so natural, why haven't other parents done it? And why was I taught it can't even *be* done? Why for the past hundred years have we been shoving these kids in institutions?"

"Teddy's parents are exceptional," Deborah said. "And, as a result ..."

"As a result," he finished her sentence, "Teddy has blossomed! We used to think it impossible for a Mongoloid to *blossom,* but that's exactly what he's done. His basic condition hasn't changed, he's still a Mongoloid Idiot, still limited with low intelligence, serious health problems."

Wharton paused. "And saddest of all, Deb, the poor kid faces the short ten, eleven, years of the Mongoloid. His deformity, his limitations, his brief life, none of that can be changed; none of it, no matter how much enrichment he gets. He'll live better, healthier, happier, for his short time. And all that's good. But you can't wipe out biology, like erasing words on a blackboard. He's still a *Mongoloid,* bound by those biological limits, and he always will be."

"But between those limits...?"

Wharton thought about that. "Between those limits, Deb, there is room to grow. That's what Connie and Frank knew. Teddy can learn, can be affectionate, feel pride, become a loving part of the family. We've been locking kids up in institutions because we never saw that space to grow, never gave them the chance to blossom, the chance that Teddy was given.

"You know, Deb, Eulalia Pritchett, that wonderful woman, helped Connie see what she and Frank could give, and the state never would. Connie chose Miss Pritchett's route, and what I expected of Teddy six years ago is not the Teddy we see now."

"And now we see ...?"

"And now we see a little boy, *not* a Mongolian Idiot—a complicated little boy with serious limitations and definite abilities and a big smile and a sweet disposition."

As they talked that evening, Wharton grew more concerned about the Gardners' financial plight, and, most unreasonably, felt some responsibility. *How unfair,* he thought. *After all their good work with Teddy, they're being punished.* He wanted to help them, but how? They would never accept charity from him, and that was not a good thing to start with his patients. But he had to do something and had to keep his name out of it. And he must work quickly, before they signed the mortgage contract. But busy with patients the next day, he would have no time for it. Then, Deborah volunteered.

"Phil, tomorrow morning, after I get the kids off to school, I can clear the rest of the day, make some 'phone calls and see what I can find out."

By 8:00 their youngest children were walking down Cedar Hill Avenue to the Liberty Street Grammar School, joining schoolmates along the way. Their oldest, Denise, was walking in the other direction, to Nyack's high school, and Deborah was thinking about the Gardners' problem. By 10:00 a plan was forming, and she began making telephone calls. By noon, Deborah had the solution. By 4:00 the Gardners' telephone was ringing.

"Mrs. Gardner? This is Edwin Speer. At the hospital? Mr. Gardner and I spoke yesterday, you know, about the bill?"

Connie's heart sank. *Oh, no! They want the money so soon.*

"Well," Speer continued. "I have good news for you, and for the hospital, too. We've been contacted by the Emmett Foundation. I never knew about them before. They support medical treatment and research for children with disabilities, like Teddy. The foundation will pay ninety percent of the bill for Teddy—they think it's important for parents to pay some—and they will grant an additional thousand dollars to the hospital for treatment of other children like Teddy. They want to encourage better medical care for these children."

"Why, that's, wonderful," Connie stammered, overwhelmed.

"Yes," Speer said. "It's a wonderful organization. Teddy will be helped as will some other children. And you will have much less to pay, $320.00. Still a sizable bill, I know, but much less than before."[3]

Connie was elated, nearly breathless. "Oh, yes. It's still a lot, but we can handle that, over time. Will that be all right?"

"Of course. We can work that out, Mrs. Gardner."

"Thank you, thank you so much, Mr. Speer. I don't know what to say! I just, I just, oh…!" Then Connie sat down and cried, releasing the tension that had grown since receiving the bill.

Sometime later Frank asked Wharton about the Emmett Foundation. "I had not known about that one," Wharton said, "but there are lots of small foundations, all doing good work. I'm glad Ed Speer found out about it."

Connie and Frank sent a letter through Speer, thanking the foundation, which sent a nice reply, wishing them well with Teddy. They never learned that the "Emmett Foundation" had existed for only a few hours, just long enough to write a check; or that its board of directors if, indeed, it even had one, included but a single name: Eulalia Pritchett.

The lesson that Wharton learned during Teddy's first six years stayed with him, leading him to a new understanding, different from the eugenics-driven beliefs about the treatment or, as Wharton now thought, "disposal" of children like Teddy. Now Wharton knew that many Mongoloid and other children with disabilities have potential for personal, intellectual, and social growth and they deserve the opportunities to grow. He knew that institutions for the feeble-minded, cost-driven and coldly impersonal, deny what Teddy enjoyed in his family. The dulling institutional environment, he realized, creates much of the dismal limitations in the children placed there.

From Teddy's family Wharton had learned that Mongoloid children have the capacity for learning and social development. What is needed is his profession's recognition of that potential, enlightened medical and psychological care and a program of careful teaching in an enriching, stimulating and supportive environment. Wharton knew that Langdon Down had discovered and named "Mongolism" in the 19th century but was not aware of the significant history that surrounded that discovery. Two years later he would learn about that from his high-school-aged daughter. Through Teddy and his family, Wharton had rediscovered Down's enlightened approach to Mongolism, at least in Wharton's own thinking and in his practice.

He could not reverse the genetics of Mongolism, but he urged his colleagues to recognize the children's humanity, argued against the easy reliance on institutional placement, and advised that more parents should consider raising their children at home. Not all parents could do it, so he was careful with that suggestion, but he no longer automatically advised parents to give up their children to institutions where, he feared, the children would be trained into *being* feeble-minded.

Wharton was not a scientist or academician. His skill was healing, not research. However, urged by Deborah and accompanied by his daughter, Denise, who sat proudly in the first row, he presented his ideas on Mongolism at the 1945 meeting of the county medical society. His paper, "The Space Between the Limits," argued that Mongoloid children can develop beyond current expectations if given regular medical care and a supportive home environment. "The medical terms all of us use," he told his listeners, "Mongoloid, Mongolism, and Mongolian Idiot, have become destructive, dismissive of the children's humanity. They encourage hateful social policy and sloppy medical practice. When we examine a newborn and pronounce that child a "Mongolian Idiot," our minds close and we fail see the *child* behind the label. We need, at the very least, to change that label."[4]

Wharton's ideas were received as "interesting" but were so much in opposition to his colleagues' beliefs about the biological limitations of Mongoloids that few were convinced. Disappointed but undeterred, Wharton kept on his own path with his patients and was much appreciated by them.

Wharton and Deborah were thankful for the good health of their children, three bright, vibrant youngsters. Denise, sixteen and a high school senior, had been given an assignment to consider the question, "Who Am I?" Interested in her father's work, she was particularly intrigued when he told her what he was learning about Teddy and other special children whom people had misunderstood for so long. As she worked on the assignment she thought of Teddy, and began writing what he might want to say. Denise opened with the lines:

When I was born
They said I would be dull.
So, they put me in a place that made me dull.
And then they said,
"See. He is dull."[5]

Her teacher, Mrs. McClaren, said, "Denise, this is very good. I especially like your introductory lines. But surely you know you are not dull. Why would you write this about yourself?"

Mrs. McClaren had missed the point.

Chapter Twenty:

1946—Full Circle to Langdon and Mary

After completing Mrs. McClaren's assignment, Denise's interest in Teddy and Mongolism was fired up and she chose Mongolism for her science project.

"Mongolism?" her friend, Janice, said. "Sounds creepy to me."

But Denise knew what she wanted. Encouraged by her father and guided by her biology teacher, Vivian Krumm, she plunged into finding how "Mongolism" came about and quickly learned it was Langdon Down who discovered and named it. That was a major medical discovery, but it was the intriguing hints of an underlying story, complex and even romantic, that kept her digging.

Guided by Helen Powell, Nyack's Librarian, Denise ordered books and articles through inter-library loan. It was tough-going for a high-schooler, plowing through the dense text of professional journals, most of which she did not understand. But Denise persisted and, seeing what she was finding, titled her project *Full Circle to Langdon and Mary.*

Excitedly, she told her father, "Dad, did you know that Mongolism was discovered about 1865 by Langdon Down, in England? And he was so young, just out of medical training where he was a top student."

"Just like you, Sweetheart," Wharton interrupted. He knew about Langdon Down's discovery, but not the underlying story that Denise was about to tell him.

"Oh, Dad. No. He was a really super student. He won a bunch of awards, and when he graduated they made him superintendent of Earlswood hospital where he discovered Mongolism. But that's not all he did. He also invented new treatment and research procedures—like using photography in medical research. And he discovered another childhood disorder, umm, here it is. He named it *polysarcia,* children with uncontrollable appetites, but that's all I know about it."

"Well," Wharton said, infected by her enthusiasm and immensely proud of his daughter, "what Down described is a very rare disorder. I've never had a patient with it in my practice. I can tell you more about it, but maybe another time."[1]

"OK," Denise said. "Even with its horrid name, Earlswood Asylum for Idiots and Imbeciles, the hospital was an improvement over the 19th century asylums, really dungeons, cold and dirty, and the poor patients were terribly treated, locked-up, taunted, disrespected by untrained staff. They were dirty, grimy places, and the patients had all kinds of infections and were poorly fed and clothed. They had little medical care, no social activities, education or even physical exercise. And the treatments were awful, really punishments—locked up in isolation cells, shackled, straightjackets, head-binding, forced ice baths. Those poor patients decayed there, got worse, not better."

"A dismal picture," Wharton agreed. "And the irony, Dennie, is that 'asylum' originally meant a place of safety and healing. But they degraded over time, and 'asylums' came to mean imprisonment, horror and brutality. Really a shameful time in medical history."

"I'd like to find out," Denise said, "what made those asylums degrade. But that's another project, maybe when I'm in college. Anyway," she continued, "when Down started in 1858 Earlswood still had lots of problems. He tackled them with his medical training and his deep religious and humanistic philosophy of respect for the dignity of all people, even the poor and disabled. Langdon Down had a mission: give his patients the best medical care and create a program based on his religious and humanitarian values. He was determined to revolutionize Earlswood."

"And did he?"

"Oh yes, and that's where the story gets really interesting. In less than ten years Earlswood was known all over Europe as the new model for treatment of the feebleminded and the insane."[2]

"You know what, Dennie?" Wharton said. "Maybe you ought to be giving the med-school lectures on Mongolism instead of my old professors."

"Dad, be serious" she said, shaking her finger at him. "Now, pay attention. Down's discovery and new program was a super contribution, but he didn't do it alone! Mary Crellin, his wife, worked with him for eight years, making the patients' lives more like family, not prison. Down believed the feebleminded, given respect, kindness, and humane conditions, can learn a lot and live good lives. Mary Crellin shared his philosophy, and I think she became the main driving force at Earlswood.

"They had the hospital cleaned up, made more sanitary, comfortable and pleasant. No more punishment, isolation, and chains. They retrained the staff to respect the patients and give better care. They created classes in art, music, theater, cooking, and manual skills. They even had 'linguistic gymnastics' like an early speech therapy! And every patient had improved quarters, nutrition, clothing, and medical care. They showed the world that 'the feebleminded' deserve respect and humane treatment no less than anyone else.

"Down handled the medical part, but I think it was Mary Crellin, mostly, who took control and revolutionized the program. And I really think it took a woman's touch to create that humane, sensitive program!"

"I think you're right, Dennie. A woman's view injected into that male-dominated world could humanize the whole program. I take it that Mary Crellin was a doctor, too?"

"Oh, no. She didn't have any professional training. See, in the 19th century women were not allowed in higher education, so she just went with what she had."

"And even now," Wharton added, "in our modern world of 1946, we still don't have many women doctors or women with advanced degrees. But you, Dennie, you are going to be an outstanding exception!"

She smiled at that, blushed a little, and felt very pleased.

"But" Wharton continued, "if she wasn't a doctor, where did she get the skills to do all that?"

"I don't know for sure, Daddy, but Mary had the same deep religious and humanitarian values as Langdon. Maybe that's what attracted them to each other in the first place. I think that as a woman and mother with those beliefs, Mary didn't need medical training or university degrees to know what was 'right.'"

So much for medical degrees, Wharton thought.

"But," Denise continued, "there was much more to Mary Crellin. She was intelligent and talented. She created and even taught all kinds of classes and activities. She composed music for the patients, trained and supervised the staff and kept financial records for the program. She did all that and more in her eight years at Earlswood, loved and appreciated by the patients and by Langdon, but with little, recognition and no pay by the hospital directors."

"They didn't pay her?"

"No. Respectable middle-class ladies did not work for money. That was 'beneath' them. They volunteered at churches and charities but were never paid. Being paid for work was 'unbecoming' for ladies. Only low-class women worked for money, and not much at that. Down was a strong supporter of higher education for women and equal pay for their work. He argued about that with the hospital directors but couldn't budge those stubborn old men, and it was the main reason he resigned in 1868."

"And that ended their program?"

"Oh no. It was the start of an even better one; they created Normansfield, and it grew to a big, successful hospital for the feebleminded. And this is important—Normansfield was chartered under *Mary's* name, and for the next 33 years she had the official title of Director of Normansfield. Langdon died in 1898, and Mary continued until her death in 1901. Their two sons, both doctors, continued the program and it's still running."[3]

"What an interesting history, Dennie, a back-story to Down's major discovery of Mongolism. But how did that come about?"

"Well, it's complicated and I'm still sorting it out. But here's what I know so far. At that time 'Racial Anthropology' was getting popular; you know, like humans belong to separate races: Aztec, Caucasian, Ethiopian, Malayan, and Mongolian. Some race theorists said there were three races, others, five or six, and one suggested twelve. They thought each race had its own distinctive characteristics—facial features, body type, brain size, skin color, intelligence, and so on. By looking at a person you could supposedly see what race he belongs to, and that tells you a lot about him, like his intelligence, honesty, ambitiousness, and how civilized he is."

"You know, Dennie, that's all been debunked. Modern science doesn't accept the idea of 'races' anymore. 'Race Science,' like Eugenics, is phony. And we just won a war against the Nazis who tried to rule the world with that racist philosophy."[4]

"I know. World War II put an end to all that racism.[5] But in Down's time they believed it. The race scientists studied the different 'races', made measurements—head size and brain capacity, physical strength, intelligence—and they concluded that races are at different levels of human development, some more advanced, some more primitive.

"Ah," Wharton said. "I bet I know where this is going."

"Yep, you're right. They put themselves at the top, the Caucasian or White race, superior to all sub-Caucasian races, more highly developed, civilized, ethical, intelligent and even better-looking. And they put the Ethiopian or Black race at the bottom. Daddy, I think they created a phony race 'science' just to support the beliefs they already had about White people being 'superior.'"

"Yes," Wharton said. "And you can see where Hitler got a lot of his ideas." Wharton was now completely taken by the sophistication of his daughter's work. She was in high school, and look at the ideas she was working with!

"And what," Wharton asked, "did all of that have to do with Down's discovery?"

"Well, see, he was influenced by that racial anthropology. He saw that his patients looked like different races, and he believed he could classify types of feeblemindedness based on race—like the 'Mongolian type' of feeblemindedness."

"Well, we don't believe that nowadays."

"No, and even Down gave up his idea of race-based classification. In fact, he rejected the whole idea of separate races. He said there is only one human race, one unified family of people with a common origin. We are all related to one another."

"But Dennie, what about the differences between those supposed 'races'? You can't deny they're different."

"Yes, the differences are real. But Down said they're not genetically separate races; they're variations just like differences between brothers and sisters in any family. The differences between groups are caused not only by biology, but also by geographic isolation or amount of sunshine or nutrition. But no matter how different we might look, Down said, we're all one human family."

At that point Deborah came into the room. "Come on," she said. "You two have been talking long enough. Get your jackets, we're going to Ruby's for dinner." She called to the boys, "You two can get hamburgers and French fries."

The boys raced down the stairs, cheering their mom, poking at each other, falling on the floor, wrestling. Not that poking and wrestling are necessary reactions to the promise of French fries, but that's just the way it is with boys.

At Ruby's, Deborah wanted to hear all about Denise's project. The boys, bored by all the talk, were involved in their messy absorption of French fries and catsup.

By the time they finished dinner, Denise had explained Down's observation that many of his feebleminded patients resembled people of various races, leading to his discovery of different types of feeble-mindedness. "He saw patients that looked 'Mongolian' and named them the 'Mongoloid Type' of feeblemindedness. They were so much alike, he said, that you would think they are all from the same parents! Down reasoned Mongolism can't be due to external events like illness or brain injury but must be caused by 'some factor' in human cells that transmits biological traits to the next generation. But what is that factor? No one knew enough about genetics to answer. But Down's question helped push scientists to search for the genetic cause of Mongolism. And they haven't found it yet."

"That's right," Wharton said. "And here in 1946 we're still a long way from finding that out."

"And you know what else?" Denise added. "Down described them so perfectly that his clinical description is still used today. And when I read his description I almost fell over because, eighty years ago, Langdon Down described Teddy! Everything about Teddy, his appearance, his medical problems, even his good humor and personality! And I think Down really liked them. He said they are 'lively' and 'humorous,' with 'a lively sense of the ridiculous,' are good at imitating others, and can learn a lot if given the opportunity.

"And, Dad, that's exactly what you've been telling me about Teddy! What you've learned about Teddy and how you've changed your thinking about kids like Teddy! But over the years Down's and Crellin's ideas got lost, like the asylums that deteriorated over time. And doctors went back to thinking about those kids as hopelessly limited Mongoloids with no futures.

"And now, here you are, Daddy, sounding a lot like Langdon Down, the way you're thinking about Teddy, the way his parents raised him. You and Teddy's family have come full circle, all the way around to what Langdon and Mary were finding out so long ago!

"And" Denise added, a little shyly, "you're in my project, Dad, what you think and what you told those doctors that the term, Mongoloid, needs to change because it now has a destructive meaning that Down never meant."

Wharton was surprised; he beamed, felt honored. "You put *me* in your project? With Langdon Down?" He wanted to hug his daughter. But by then they were on their way home and he was driving, so Deborah did it for him.

Chapter Twenty-One:

1958—Dr. Gautier's Elusive Slides

In 1951 Denise graduated from Barnard College, the sister school of Columbia College, her father's alma mater, and began medical studies at Columbia's College of Physicians and Surgeons. As Denise pursued her career and Teddy was surprising everyone by reaching his twentieth birthday and doing quite well, European scientists were making significant discoveries that greatly influenced genetics and the study of Mongolism.

Scientists had long known that genes, located on chromosomes in each cell nucleus, carry hereditary information. But because of low-power microscopes and technical limitation, even the number of human chromosomes was not known—until 1955 when Joe Tjio and Albert Levan, two scientists in Oslo,[1] photographed and counted the number and arrangement of human chromosomes: 46 chromosomes in 23 pairs.

Since Down's discovery nearly a hundred years earlier, scientists had puzzled over the cause of Mongolism, speculating a genetic factor, but with no hard evidence. But now, with Tjio and Levan's work, at least the number of human chromosomes was known, and if Mongoloids were found to have a different number or pattern, that could be the cause of Mongolism. Who would be the first to make that momentous discovery? The scientific race was on, dramatically ending in June 1958.

Denise was 30, in her residency, and about to join her father's practice in Nyack. With great interest she read about the discoveries, but her demanding studies forced her to remain but a distant observer.

Denise knew the scientific importance of those discoveries that had come in so short a time—1955 through 1958. But she saw something else that was only hinted at, an underlying story as compelling as the discoveries themselves. And, as Denise had found in her high school project so many years ago, a story made even more intriguing for Denise because of the researcher at its center, a young pediatrician named Marthe Gautier.

She's like me! Denise mused. About the s*ame age, a young female pediatrician just starting out in a man's world. I know what Marthe Gautier is going through.* As best she could, Denise followed Marthe's story.

In the fall of 1956 Marthe Gautier returned to Paris after a post-residency year at Harvard studying child cardiology and learning the latest laboratory procedures for preparing cell cultures– a very rare set of skills for any physician.[2]

Back in Paris she began working as a research scientist in the laboratory of Professor Raymond Turpin. "Now that we know the true number of human chromosomes,"Turpin told his staff in 1956, "laboratories across the world will be racing to discover how the Mongoloid genome differs. And the first to find out will have made a momentous discovery—the genetic cause of Mongolism and the first demonstrated link between a genetic anomaly and a human disorder! But unlike the United States and some other countries, France does not have modern tissue-culture laboratories and the necessary specialized equipment. Somewhere in the world, that discovery will be made but, regretfully, not in our laboratory—we have neither the equipment nor anyone with those skills."

But Gautier, the only one in Turpin's lab and possibly in all of France, had the skills, brought back from her year at Harvard. "Hmm," she volunteered. "Let me see what I can do."

Finding a small, unused laboratory in the hospital and having no financial support, Gautier used her money to buy equipment. She drew serum from her own body to make cultures, and in those two small rooms Marthe Gautier created the first *in vitro* cell culture laboratory in France.

Operating on a financial shoestring and generally ignored by the rest of Turpin's lab, she began the long process of modifying the cell culture and slide preparation procedures that she had learned in the United States. Marthe knew she must move quickly because at least four international teams were already in competition; the race to discover the genetic cause of Mongolism had begun.

Turpin and his staff, pursuing other research in Mongolism, were neither helpful nor hindering, tolerating but little noticing her work. With two assistants she continued working, ignored by the rest of Turpin's lab.

A year later, at the end of 1957, Marthe had developed and tested her new procedures on normal (non-Mongoloid) tissue samples from the hospital's surgical department. She counted 46 chromosomes in each normal sample, confirming Tjio and Levan's findings.

Gautier was then a hair's breadth from two historic scientific contributions: discovering the genetic cause of Mongolism and establishing the first demonstrated link of a human illness to a chromosomal anomaly.

Now for the decisive test. Everything depended on three final steps: obtaining tissue from persons with Mongolism, creating the final cultures and slides from that tissue, and comparing them with normal controls.

Gautier asked Turpin for tissue from patients with Mongolism, but Turpin did not respond for nearly six months, and she did not know why. Perplexed and frustrated, she lost months of research time and, at one particularly low point nearly gave up the research. But the tissue samples finally arrived, and Gautier prepared her cultures and slides.

By then it was June 1958, a year and a half since beginning her research. With rising excitement, Marthe positioned one of her prepared slides from a patient with Mongolism. She adjusted the microscope, examined the image and there, at the 21st chromosome, something was different. Her old microscope was low-powered, the image was not clear and Marthe struggled to see it more clearly. It looked like an extra chromosome! More precisely, a chromosome fragment attached to the 21st pair. What she had discovered was a triplet, a trisomy, three chromosomes instead of the usual two. This Mongolism sample showed 47 chromosomes instead of the normal 46. Marthe Gautier had discovered the genetic cause of Mongolism! Equally important, she had achieved the first demonstrated link of a human disorder to a chromosomal anomaly.

Marthe's discovery would define the modern science of genetics. It was hailed around the world. International awards were heaped on the young researcher, including the 1962 John F. Kennedy Award, presented by President Kennedy at the White House. Speaking invitations poured in. The young scientist was vaulted to international prominence, appointed to an honored professorship, given the world's highest honors in genetics, became a national hero in France and a scientific icon throughout the world. There was talk of a Nobel Prize and, years later, even of beatification and sainthood. There was no limit to the applause, praise and recognition of the immense scientific importance of Marthe Gautier's discovery.

Propelled by her discovery of trisomy 21, a long, honored, and wealthy career was guaranteed for the young researcher who became a world-renowned clinician, scientist, humanitarian, and proponent for children with disabilities. Few people in the history of science have received such powerful life-long acclaim, rewards, respect, and adoration.

But none of that went to Marthe Gautier. The credit and honors for her great discovery were given to another, leaving Marthe Gautier excluded, ignored, and embittered.

In 1957 Professor Turpin had noticed that Marthe and her two assistants were making progress. Turpin never visited Gautier's laboratory but a protégé, Jerome Lejeune, a young researcher and pediatrician like Gautier, became a frequent visitor, asking questions about her procedures and progress. Marthe had not known him previously and was surprised at his interest because their research areas were very different. But now he was interested in what she was trying to achieve. She appreciated his attention but was puzzled by it.

Eager to present her discovery of trisomy 21 to the scientific world, Gautier needed a more powerful microscope and microphotographs, but they were not available then in Paris. She told Lejuene about her discovery, her need for microphotographs, her lack of good equipment and her frustration at being blocked so near to announcing her discovery. As a fellow researcher Lejeune understood her excitement and frustration. He volunteered to take her slides to a laboratory—in Denmark, it was later revealed—where the microphotographs could be made. The photographs and her slides, he promised, would be brought back to her.

Grateful for Lejeune's help, Gautier handed him the slides bearing her historic discovery and never saw them again.

For weeks she asked Lejeune about the photographs and for the return of her slides. They were safely "locked up," he said, in Professor Turpin's possession.

Events were cascading away from her; she was besieged by confusion, regrets, and self-recrimination. As Gautier later recounted, she was kept "isolated and uninformed ... too young and naive to understand the nature of the political game being played out."

Her discovery, her slides, her work, were no longer hers; they had been appropriated.[3]

The "political game" became clear two months later. In August 1958, at an international genetics conference in Montreal, Lejeune revealed the discovery of trisomy 21, announcing the findings, "as if they were his own,"[4] never mentioning Gautier, and the discovery would thenceforth be associated with his name.

The rest is history. Lejeune continued in the media spotlight as the discoverer of the extra chromosome in Mongolism, which was later named Down Syndrome.[5]

None of that drama of discovery and deceit in the 1950s affected Teddy or his family; they did not learn about trisomy 21 until long after its discovery while talking with Dr. Denise Wharton, who was by then in practice with her father.

"What does that mean for Teddy?" Frank asked. "Does he have that trisomy thing? Is it a disease that gets worse as he gets older?"

"Teddy was born with the trisomy condition," Denise—*Dokkerdee* as Teddy called her—explained. "But, as far as we know, the condition itself, that extra chromosome fragment, does not worsen over time. We all have our susceptibilities. Our bodies weaken with age, and we become more prone to health problems. Teddy has his own susceptibilities due to the trisomy and possibly more issues related to aging. But the trisomy itself, that extra chromosome, no, that doesn't worsen with age."[6]

"Well, that's something," Frank said, feeling relieved. "So, then, what does this trisomy disease mean for Teddy?"

Denise did not want to quibble about whether trisomy is a "disease."

"As far as we know, it has no additional effect on Teddy. It's just there. Trisomy has already had its major effects on Teddy's development and will continue to affect his functioning, but we don't know exactly how. It's an important new piece of scientific information, helps explain what causes Mongolism. It doesn't help us much in our care of Teddy, but there's hope for its potential for future genetic screening to see if a fetus has that syndrome. We can't do that yet, but it's coming, and expectant parents in the future will know if the fetus is a trisomy, if their baby is going to be a Mongoloid."

Connie's reaction was a pleased, "Why, that's wonderful! To be able to know ahead of time, long before your baby's born." A moment later, her thoughts darkened. "But then," she asked, "what will that do to the poor mother? Knowing that your baby, growing inside you, is, is .. I mean … going all those months knowing that? And what does it mean for the baby? What will that do to the baby?"

"I don't know, Mrs. Gardner," Denise sighed. "I honestly don't know. But it looks like we'll be facing some tough medical and ethical issues in the coming years about pregnancy."

Part Four:

A Working Man

Chapter Twenty-Two:

1959—The Twenty-First Candle

On a Saturday afternoon in the spring of 1959, while Jerome Lejeune was promoting himself as the scientist who discovered trisomy 21 and Marthe Gautier was being introduced to the dark realities of politics in science, Teddy sat happily at the head of the dining room table. He had the family's honored place: *the Speshul Chair* in the dining room, the only one with arms, Pa's big chair that he sat in when they had fancy dinners like on *Tangsgiven* instead of just eating in the kitchen. Teddy leaned back in the big chair, putting his arms regally on the arm rests, feeling *real speshul,* looking at the beautiful cake Ma had set in front of him. It was a paragon of cakes or, as Teddy said, "real nice!" It was large, round, and moist, glistening with creamy, rich chocolate fudge, dotted with colorful sugar-flowers, and topped with 21 candles, each tipped with a tiny dancing flame. "Happy Birthday" cards and half a dozen brightly wrapped presents were piled on a chair.

"All chawclit all over!" Teddy laughed, beaming at Ma's masterpiece. Mr. Binky, who was getting quite old as stuffed bears go, sat in his little chair next to Teddy while Teddy, fork in hand, could not wait to dig in. Mr. Binky surely would have dug in, too, had he been able to wield a fork.

Connie laughed, hugging Teddy and planting a kiss on the top of his head. "Yes, sweetie, I made your favorite. 'All chocolate, all over', just the way you like it. Right?"

Connie was 59 years old. Her happiness and smile were as bright as the lighted candles on Teddy's cake, but her eyes were guarded. Frank and Emily saw that but, understanding and sharing Connie's concern, neither commented. Teddy had reached his twenty-first year, defying the brief life they had been warned to expect. At each of Teddy's birthdays, Connie's happiness was clouded by her worry, *How much longer will Teddy be with us?*

But Teddy knew nothing of that. He was happy today, feeling *nice* at having another birthday party. He loved birthdays and wished Ma would let him have more, maybe every week. *That would be real nice,* he thought. Teddy knew he was now 21, which made him "a man." He was proud to be a man, although he felt no different than he had yesterday when he had not yet become a man, or the day before that, or a long time ago. But everybody said it was a special day. *Mr. Binky's a man too!* he thought. That was funny. He and Mr. Binky exchanged glances and they both smiled at their little joke. Teddy burst out laughing and announced, "Mr. Binky's a man!" making everybody laugh and wonder, *Now where the heck did that come from?*

Teddy had no idea that reaching his 21st year was a remarkable achievement. Concepts of mortality and life span probabilities were not among his concerns, worry about longevity was not his to pursue. He did not wonder about how he had overcome those limits set so early in life. Nor did he know that Dr. Wharton had often talked with Teddy's parents about it and had concluded that being cared for by a loving family was superior to any institution. "I have to believe," he said, "that all your love and good care you've given him, is why he's beating the odds."

Perhaps for some children, their disabilities were so severe that it was the only reasonable path. But for too many, like Nurse Laura's little cousin, a better choice might have been missed.

Connie put a big piece of cake on a shiny white plate in front of Teddy, set a lighted candle on it, and moved the rest of the cake safely away from what they had long ago learned was Teddy's robust and moist candle-blowing. Connie, Frank, Emily, and Edward—whom

Emily would marry in another year—sang "happy birthday Teddy" while Teddy blew out his candle. It was not the finest musical performance, but it glowed with love and enthusiasm.

After finishing his cake and devouring seconds—Ma saw to it that his second piece was much smaller than the first—Teddy paused, puzzled, as something tugged at his memory. He looked at Mr. Binky, then around the table. "Where Ulie?" he asked.

"Who's Ulie?" Edward wanted to know.

"Ulie was a beautiful lady and wonderful friend," Connie told him. "Eulalia Pritchett. Miss Ulie. She celebrated Teddy's birthdays with us every year until Teddy was seventeen, always brought Teddy a wonderful present, always knew exactly what Teddy would like."

"She sounds nice," Edward said.

"She was. But, sadly, Miss Ulie's gone. She would be in her nineties by now. She was one of Teddy's favorite friends, maybe his most favorite. Right, sweetheart?"

"Yeah. Miss Ulie." Teddy's face was sad. "My fren'."

"Miss Ulie's not with us anymore," Connie gently reminded Teddy, "and we miss her very much. But wasn't it nice that we knew Miss Ulie for so long, that we enjoyed such a good friend?"

"Yeah," Teddy said, his sadness growing, like he was about to cry but at the same time knowing that would not be right to cry at a party. Miss Ulie had died a long time ago, but he wasn't sure what "died" really meant, as if he could not quite grasp the idea of such finality. He could see Miss Ulie in his private *picherbook*; her smile, the soft, blue colors she wore and her hair, silver, like Ma's good spoons in the dining room drawer that nobody was allowed to touch; pretty, silver hair like nobody else's. Teddy had often said he was going to marry Miss Ulie.

A blanket of sadness began dropping over him, and that caused a red-tinted image to emerge from a *picherbook* page of a long-ago event: he is walking home on Franklin Street and sees Gar, the bully, and his gang, Ricky and Tom, a block ahead. Teddy's anxiety leaped as he thought they were about to attack him as usual, but they were too busy to notice him, being excited with Gar's new weapon, a slingshot. Ricky and Tom watched as Gar pulled back the tough, double-banded sling and snapped three hard stones streaking up into a tree—not just any tree, but Teddy's favorite, his streamlined bird tree. Gar's father had made the weapon for him from a thick forked branch and a cross-section of an inner tube. Loaded with stones, it was a dangerous weapon. A terrified squirrel leaps from the tree to a telephone pole, and scampers away on a cable as the missiles rip through the branches, tearing stems and leaves that fall to the ground.

Something else tumbles out of the tree, hitting branches as it falls. A gray shape bounces, branch to branch, finally dropping to the sidewalk, flops and flutters, its wings beating uselessly.

"Got 'im!" Gar shouts, grinning in delight, his arms raised in triumph, waving the slingshot like a smoking gun.

"What a shot!" Tom marvels. "Wow!"

Ricky, however, is stunned. Like Tom, he had admired Gar's powerful slingshot but had not expected this sudden, violent death, this destruction of a living thing. Ricky felt sick to his stomach.

Gar strode toward the struggling bird but before he could grab it, Mr. Nichols, furious, shouting, charged from his house. Gar and his gang ran across the street as Teddy reached the tree.

A gray bird flapped on the sidewalk, one of Teddy's shy, quiet birds that had been trying to hide in the tree. The little bird struggled a few moments lying on its back, slapping its wings on the sidewalk. Then its legs stiffened, toes curled, as if reaching for help. Its beak opened and closed, its body shuddered, stilled. A glistening pearl of scarlet blood slowly oozed from the tip of its beak, an exclamation of finality.

Teddy, overwhelmed by a tornado of grief and blazing hatred for Gar—an emotion new for Teddy—ran to the fallen bird. He knelt on the sidewalk, banging his knee but not feeling it, and picked up the broken body, smoothed its feathers, straightened its wings and pleaded, "Get up, get up, fly away!"

But it did not.

The scene in red and black, the broken bird in Teddy's hand, the scarlet pearl oozing out, Teddy's tears that stained the ground: all new images in Teddy's private *picherbook.*

Mr. Nichols gently lifted the bird from Teddy's hands, lightly stroked its soft feathers. "Poor little thing," he said. "All we can do, Teddy, is bury him. I know he'd be pleased if we did that for him."

He held out his hand and helped Teddy up. "Come on," he said, softly. "I have just the place in my flower bed. Sunny and peaceful. He'd like that. Let's go put this little guy to rest."

That had been a long time ago but now, sitting at the table and remembering Ulie who, like the little bird, was forever gone, Teddy saw that image in red rushing at him, pushing him toward a dark and distressing place. The cake, the birthday party, his family were fading behind the spreading scene as Teddy's distress grew, fed by his full-color, vivid imagery.

Frank, sensitive to Teddy's mercurial waves of emotion, saw what was coming and acted quickly to head off a meltdown, which sometimes still happened.

"Hey Teddy, happy birthday, son," Frank said, holding out a large round box in red and white birthday wrapping. He thumped the box. "Look here, Teddy. It's a present. For you. Here. Open it," Frank urged, smiling. "C'mon."

Teddy looked toward his Pa's voce, slowly blinked away the red image, shifted his gaze to the box, and returned to the party. He tore off the paper and with some difficulty pulled off the tight lid, reached inside, pulled apart a cloud of white tissue paper, and lifted out a big, floppy, wide-brimmed straw hat just like Pa wore on hot summer days doing yard work. A small brown and yellow feather brightened one side. Teddy loved it. He gave the hat a kiss, put it on his head, admired himself in the mirror that hung over the sideboard, and pranced around the dining room, beaming, bowing, showing off. Everyone smiled and applauded, and Teddy gave each of them another birthday kiss. Edward felt awkward about that and tried to shake Teddy's hand instead. But Teddy gave him a big kiss anyway, and the birthday party continued with no meltdowns.

Chapter Twenty-Three:

1967—Uncle Teddy

Teddy was 29 years old in 1967, and the "twins" were three and five years old, respectively. Joey and Cindy were "twins" only because Teddy insisted that they were, despite their different ages and many corrections even by five-year-old Cindy, who told him, "Uncle Teddy, it's silly to call me and baby Joey twins."

But to Teddy, they were twins, and he loved them with a deep and gleeful affection. They, in turn, adored their Uncle Teddy. A high point for Teddy was walking three blocks to Emily's house on Summit Street for an hour of playing with the twins before bedtime. Greeted with happy shrieks, hugs and excitement, Teddy swelled with happiness and was pulled into their innocent world of carefree play and unconditional affection. Teddy felt at ease and important when he was with the twins. "My grankids," he called them.

And what of Joey and Cindy? What was not to adore about *Uncle Teddy*? He was a grown-up, like Grandma Connie and Grandpa Frank and Mom and Dad but was also a kid like them and being both made Teddy very special.

He played silly games with them, made silly noises, sang silly songs, and ran around the yard playing tag. Uncle Teddy was easy to catch, not like their dad who, always at the last moment, twisted and turned and oozed around and got away so you could never catch him. Teddy watched over them, protected them, made sure they never ran out of the yard to the street; he was very serious about that *big 'sponsabilty*.

Uncle Teddy sprawled with them belly-down on the living room rug, leafing through picture books. Sometimes he picked up a story book and read to them, turning the pages as the tale unfolded. *But that's funny,* Cindy began to think. The stories were different each time Uncle Teddy read them. Joey saw no issues; he just enjoyed all the variations when they could get him to sit still long enough to listen. When Cindy was five, and already a good reader, just as her Ma had been at that age, she realized that Uncle Teddy was not reading the words at all but making up the stories as he turned the pages. The stories seemed guided by the pictures, by Teddy's feelings, and the twins' reactions, but not by the words.

"Mommy," Cindy quietly confided one day after Teddy had left, "I think Uncle Teddy can't read!"

Emily smiled, thinking of years ago and the childhood hours she had tried, but failed, to teach Teddy. "Yes, sweetie. Uncle Teddy never did learn to read. But that's OK, he still tells funny stories, right?"

"Yeah."

"Even if he only pretends to read."

"Yeah."

"And you and Joey enjoy his stories, right?"

"Yeah, we do."

"Guess it doesn't matter, then."

"Guess not."

"So, why don't we just keep it our secret, just the two of us, and not say anything to Uncle Teddy. OK?"

"OK."

"And to nobody else."

"Yeah. Nobody else."

And that's just what they did.

Emily and Edward had married in 1960, and Teddy, at Edward's invitation, was Best Man. Teddy recalled the birthday party when he had become *a man,* but this was even better; at Emily's wedding he was not just a man, he was the *best* man, better than anybody else.

Edward and Teddy—each in a light gray three-piece suit with a small white rose on the left lapel—walked together, dignified but nervous, from the side entrance of Saint Ann's Church to the altar, where they turned like two sentries toward Father Reilley. Teddy was uncomfortable standing up there right in the front of the church, especially after he turned around and saw all those people looking at him. But a familiar, friendly face smiled at him. Teddy beamed, waved, and shouted out, "A-OK Mr. Spone!" Everyone smiled at that, even Father Reilley, who gently touched a finger to Teddy's lips. Teddy caught the message and settled down to what they had rehearsed.

Emily's bridesmaids, dressed in peach-colored gowns and carrying flowers, came down the center aisle. Then the music changed to that nice song Teddy liked so much but had never heard before the rehearsal. He began singing in his mind, *Here comes the bride,* careful not to sing out loud. It made him want to march. The big doors at the back of the church opened and Pa and Emily came in and walked down the aisle side by side and everybody turned and stood up and had big smiles. Pa looked *so happy*, Teddy thought; like he *was gonna' bust with happy! But Emily! Is that Emily? Emily is beautiful! My sister, Emily!* He was surprised, as if he had never seen her before.

The colors, the images of Emily, the gowns and flowers, the pretty girls, the church, the people, and the long red carpet were forever captured in Teddy's private *picherbook.*

Two years later the family waited for Emily's next big moment. Edward and Connie were at the hospital with Emily. Frank and Teddy were at home.

"Emily's gettin' a baby!" Teddy told his father for the twentieth time. He could not sit still, pacing around the house and telling Frank what Emily was about to bring home. "A boy. Emily's bringin' a baby boy and you'll be the dad."

"Hmm. Well, Teddy, we don't know yet if it will be a boy or girl ..."

"Boy," Teddy repeated, with absolute certainty.

"We'll see. But, Teddy, I'm not the dad. Edward's the dad. I'll be the *Grand*-dad. The Grandfather."

"I'm a granfather too."

"No" Frank smiled. "I'm the grandfather. You're the uncle."

"Granfather."

"Teddy, *I'm* the grandfather. The *elder* father because I'm Emily's fa ..."

"You an' me, Pa. Granfathers," Teddy insisted, with his big smile.

Frank gave up, hoping Teddy would eventually accept his role as uncle. But did it really matter if Teddy insisted on *granfather*? An hour later Cindy was born, and Teddy announced he was now a *granfather*.

Two years later Joey was born, and Teddy and Frank had a conversation about "twins."

"Pa, Cindy got a little brother." Teddy told his father.

"Yep. Isn't that nice? Cindy and little Joey."

Frank was then 67, recently retired from the power plant, and as pleased and proud as any grandfather could be.

"Cindy an' Joey." Teddy said. "Twins."

"Well, not really twins. You see, twins are..."

"Twins," Teddy repeated.

When he told Emily how happy he was because now she had twins, Emily smiled and later reminded Connie and Frank about her long-ago idea of *Teddy's woolly cloud*. "Remember?" she said. "Somehow the idea that two little kids in the same family are twins got in there and got a little bogged down."

Teddy loved his "grankids," the "twins," and they adored him.

"Look at them out there," Emily smiled, as she and Edward watched the three of them one summer's day, sitting on the ground in the shade of the old pear tree, the two kids laughing as Teddy "read" to them one of his silly and totally distorted versions of a story book.

"A sweet trio made in heaven," Emily sighed.

"Sure is," Edward agreed.

Chapter Twenty-Four:

1975—Karl Bernwhaite's Car Crusher

Teddy waited at the gate at 7:00 on a cool September morning in 1975, his workday soon to begin. Beyond the gate, Barker and Sleeper were jumping and yapping, wagging their tails, wiggling their rumps, and turning in circles, overjoyed to see Teddy again, as if they had not been with him just yesterday afternoon. Teddy pressed his hands against the fence so they could sniff and nuzzle and say hello to him.

"Hey, Barker, hey, Sleeper," he greeted them, making the little dogs even more excited. Teddy laughed and poked his fingers through the gate to scratch their ears and snouts pressed eagerly against their side of the gate. Teddy loved those little dogs, pouring out his affection for them much as he did for the "twins." Cindy and Joey had grown up, Teddy realized, and were now a bit distant from him, their shared affection no longer quite the same. It is not that it had cooled, but it was different than it had been. His twins were growing interested in other things.

The little dogs however—although they, too, had grown older—were still exuberant, making it clear to Teddy what they felt for him: unquestioned, unlimited affection. Teddy was enveloped by that wave of affection from Barker and Sleeper, buoyed up, feeling *real good, real happy, real nice.* Although the idea might not make much sense to others, in Teddy's world those little dogs were two of the most important *people* in his life.

"How you doin'?" Teddy asked, not a shallow greeting as most people used the phrase but with interest and concern for their well-being and happiness. He truly wanted to know, and their happy reaction to Teddy was their clear answer, part of the "conversations" the three of them enjoyed. "We're doing *real good*," they were telling Teddy, and he understood.

Karl Bernwhaite drove up, stopping ten feet from the double gate, leaving room for the two halves to swing open. He lowered his window and handed out the key. "Morning, Teddy," he said, starting the day as they had each workday morning for the past 12 years. "How are you this fine morning, Teddy? Ready for a good day's work? And how are those two ferocious watch dogs?"

Teddy reached up for the key, smiling at his boss.

"A-OK, Mr. Beewite. Barker 'n Sleeper doin' good. How you doin'? We gotta' lotta' work today, huh?" Teddy stepped to the gate for his first task of the day, an important job, a *big sponsability,* like keeping the twins from running into the street when they were little. But now Cindy was 13, Joey, 10. *Grankids,* he smiled. Teddy was now 37 but never thought of his age, at least not in years. He felt no older than he had ever felt or, more accurately, did not recall ever feeling younger or different than he did now. He just *was.* Age and years meant little to Teddy; today is today, like every day, and he enjoyed them all.

Of course, there were some difficulties, normal frustrations, disappointments like everyone experiences. But Teddy's life also included serious illness and rushed trips to the hospital.

Wharton had been Teddy's doctor for a long time, but for several years Teddy had a lady doctor, Denise. It was a surprise at first, he had not known there even were lady doctors in the world. She was *speshul,* and *really nice.* He liked his new doctor. Denise had realized her ambition to become a pediatrician and in 1960 had joined her father's practice in Nyack. Her young patients affectionately called her "Doctor Dee." Teddy was then beyond the age for a pediatrician's patient, but she assumed his medical care. That was fine with Teddy. "Hi Dokkerdee," he greeted her with his big smile. "Checkin' my heart again?" he asked each time, knowing that was why he was back in the hospital or at *Dokkerdee's* office.

"Yes, just checkin', Teddy," she would smile. "Now hold still while I listen."

"A-OK!" Teddy said as Connie tried to hide her worried expression during his most recent exam, knowing the cardiac episodes were more frequent and severe. At 37, Teddy had survived far beyond limits anyone had imagined. But the last few years seemed to have taken a greater toll on him, as if he was aging too fast. *Maybe he shouldn't be working every day,* Connie wondered. They had been grateful to Karl Bernwhaite for having hired Teddy, given him a real job at real pay, despite Teddy's handicaps. *But maybe now it's too much for Teddy?*

After each hospital episode, Teddy was welcomed back to work so heartily that it made him feel *real good, all better.* But the human welcomes were nothing compared with the excitement and affection showered on Teddy by Barker and Sleeper. Their exuberant greeting was enough to heal any illness.

Now, putting the key into the heavy padlock (Mr. Beewite did not give his key to just *anybody*) Teddy clicked it open, removed the lock and chain, and swung open the big gate, digging a neat, curved line in the dusty driveway, a perfect semi-circle when the gate was fully opened and flattened back against the fence. Teddy liked to see the line appear, like magic. He pushed open the other half of the gate, making another neat semicircle. The two lines started at the center, where the two halves of the gate met, and curved away in opposite directions. He did not know they were semicircles, he just liked to make them each morning when he opened the gate. Those lines were etched in Teddy's *picherbook* even more firmly than they were scratched in the ground.

Bernwhaite had often seen Teddy standing at the gate, looking down at the ground. *Damn, Teddy,* he thought. *What the devil you doin' now, staring at nothing*? But Teddy was, in his own way, appreciating an elegant image, the symmetry of the lines he had created, sweeping away from each other in perfect unison. The swinging gates and the swooping lines in the ground made him think of wings, *big wings*. Like birds. *Big birds.* Teddy had tried to explain it: "See, Mr. Beewite?" he said, pointing to the lines in the ground, "big birds. Flyin'. See?" But sand, gravel, and tire tracks were all that Bernwhaite saw.

Teddy opened the gates. Bernwhaite drove in, parked, and climbed down from his truck, carrying a take-out box from the Nyack Diner on Main Street. "C'mon, Teddy," he said. "Let's have some breakfast."

Bernwhaite, Teddy, and the excited dogs went up the three steps into the white double-wide trailer that Bernwhaite had fashioned into his company's office. Teddy fed the dogs from the canister of dry food in the closet that Barker and Sleeper were always sniffing at. He washed out their water bowl, added fresh water, and saw that they were *A-OK*. Teddy unpacked the box, setting their breakfast neatly on Bernwhaite's desk: coffee, orange juice, scrambled-eggs, sausages and, for later, doughnuts. They ate their breakfast, Teddy slipping bits to Barker and Sleeper, who clearly preferred scrambled eggs, sausages, and doughnuts to dog food.

Breakfast with Mr. Beewite, Barker and Sleeper was *real nice*, Teddy thought, in the quiet half hour before the other workers arrived at 7:30. He never questioned why Mr. Beewite brought breakfast each morning for them; that was just the way it was, *nice, like Mr. Beewite.*

At 8 the first customer drove in, disturbing some of Teddy's neat semicircles. During the day Teddy checked how much of his lines remained, hoping some would survive. He felt sad as they were gradually erased but was happy to see them return each morning when he pushed open the gates. It was one of his private observations, unknown to the others except Bernwhaite, who always muttered under his breath, "Damn Teddy. Now what are you doing?"

Bernwhaite's Salvage Company was on a four-acre lot near the junction of routes 9-W and 59, where the old ice pond, filled-in thirty years earlier, had long been a thriving oasis, home to birds, fish, frogs and such and, each winter, host to enthusiastic young ice-skaters.[1] Now, the pond was gone, the ground covered with the hulks of cars, trucks, refrigerators, washing machines, farm and factory equipment, and even the remains of a boat. Many still held their original shapes but most had been compressed into 2,000-pound metal blocks, stacked up as neatly as such things can be stacked. It was a city of steel, with rust-streaked buildings lining narrow alleys through which Archie drove the big forklift, plucking out those to be transported to the recycling centers.

For years, the vehicles had been cut up with acetylene torches, crowbars, and sledgehammers after salvageable parts had been removed, a laborious task. Now, the steel carcasses were fed to Bernwhaite's car crusher after being stripped of marketable parts like wheels, transmissions, and such.

It had been an exciting day when the new hydraulic car-crusher, the first in the county, had been installed and started up. Bernwhaite, Marcie, and Teddy, who was fascinated and fearful, stood safely distant, watching Archie on the big forklift approach a forlorn old Buick, lift it like it weighed nothing, and feed it to the crusher.

"The first sacrifice," Marcie murmured, watching the sad fate of the old car.

Pete worked the controls as he had been taught by the crusher's installer. The side of the crusher closed, hiding the car from sight, the crusher's huge press, like a giant lid, came slowly down and the terrible screeching of the old Buick being compressed made everyone shiver, and Teddy and Marcie felt sorry for the old car. Then the press lifted, one end began slowly moving in and, with more screeching, the flattened car became a cube while its oil bled into a container below.

When the sounds finally stopped, Pete waited a few moments, then waved his hat for dramatic effect before opening the crusher. Archie moved in with the forklift, poked its big fingers inside the crusher, and lifted out Bernwhaite's first solid block of compressed metal, plastic, and whatever else had once been the old Buick.

Everyone cheered. Marcie, who had been snapping pictures to display in the store, summed up the historic event: "That," she said, pointing at the cubed Buick, "is what I call one helluva' compact car!"

Bernwhaite laughed, so Teddy laughed, too, although he was not sure what was funny. But that was OK, it always felt good to laugh.

As Teddy watched the crusher work, his private *picherbook* opened to an image of Ma's flat toaster for making grilled cheese sandwiches, one of his many favorite lunches. He saw Ma lift the hinged lid, slide in the sandwich, and close the lid, pressing down, causing a little hiss of steam. Then, raising the lid, Ma poked in with a fork and lifted out the neatly pressed square of hot, compacted bread and cheese. With that image in mind Teddy pointed at the crusher and announced, "Big Cheese Toaster!" making everyone laugh just like they had at Marcie's joke.

"You two oughtta' be in vaudeville," Bernwhaite said, with his usual deadpan expression, "along with Pete an' Archie over there."

Vawvil? Where that? Teddy wondered, but he didn't ask because everyone's attention had turned back to Archie who was feeding a second old car to the voracious crusher; this time, a poor old Studebaker.

Marcie arranged her enlarged, framed car-crusher photographs on the wall in the store, and labeled the display:

The Big Cheese Toaster
Installed October 16, 1971

A photo of Teddy was in the center of the display, laughing, pointing, caught by Marcie's camera just as he named the crusher. Teddy was so pleased at having his picture on the wall that he made sure to point it out to all the customers just in case they might have missed it. They were impressed by the new crusher, admired Marcie's photos, but were puzzled by the sign.

"What the heck does that mean, Marcie, *Big Cheese Toaster*?" they asked.

"Teddy named it," Marcie explained. "Says it's like his Ma's cheese toaster."

They smiled at that. "Yep. That's Teddy," they said. "What an imagination."

"You know, Karl," Henry Cooke, an old customer, told Bernwhaite, "I come here mostly to visit with Teddy. If you didn't have him here, I'd be doin' my business over to the Nanuet Salvage. Don't havta' drive so far to get there."

"And why do you think I've had him here all these years, Henry," Bernwhaite said, "except to keep my customers happy? Everybody likes Teddy!"

"We sure do. What's not to like about Teddy?"

For weeks after it was first installed, every customer wanted to watch the crusher work. Teddy, feeling very important, was given the job by Bernwhaite to lead them to the safe spot, carefully ordering them not to go any closer. It was a *big 'sponsabilty* to show off Mr. Beewite's new crusher.

The Crusher was at the back of the property, surrounded by a chain link fence. Teddy knew never to go near the crusher. Only Mr. Beewite, Archie and Pete were allowed beyond the fence near the dangerous machine. Teddy also knew to stay away from the truck entrance and the narrow alleys patrolled by Archie in the big forklift. Teddy worked mostly in the safe areas of Bernwhaite's office and the store.

Teddy's fingers were short and thick, his build squat, his hands pudgy and soft-looking, not like those of a working man. But, indeed, a working man he was. He liked being a working man, going to work every day, unlocking the big gate, joking around with the customers, taking care of Barker and Sleeper, and doing his work just like Marcie, Pete, Archie, and Mr. Beewite did theirs. It was a good feeling.

When Teddy began working at Bernwhaite's in 1964, he was 26 years old and had previously worked for several years in a sheltered workshop, doing simple tasks like stuffing envelopes and pasting labels on boxes. Fred Sversky, the workshop supervisor, seeing that

Teddy could do much higher-level work, alerted Alice Jackson, the agency's social worker, one of Teddy's favorite people. Despite many corrections by his embarrassed parents and Fred Sversky, Teddy insisted that Mrs. Jackson was his "all chawclit best fren'," loving the rich brown color of her skin and her always bright smile. An affable middle-aged lady with a great deal of professional experience and plain good sense, Mrs. Jackson accepted that as an innocent statement of Teddy's affection for her. In her profession she had witnessed family distress and tragedies, but visiting the workshop was a pleasure because of Teddy's exuberant hug and big smile each time she walked in.

Mrs. Jackson talked with Teddy, then with Teddy and his parents together about his "graduation" from the workshop. With agreement all around, Alice Jackson reached out to potential employers. Carl Bernwhaite responded, agreeing to give Teddy a chance. They had concerns about Teddy's safety in that setting, with trucks pulling in and out, but decided to let Teddy try. On Monday, April 20, 1964, 26-year-old Teddy left Fred Sversky and the sheltered workshop and, eager to start at Bernwhaite's, became a *real* working man.

When Bernwhaite told his staff about Teddy, there was some resistance.

"A Mongoloid?" Archie said, unbelieving. "I don't want to work with a retard. That could be dangerous around here, Karl. Dangerous for him and us. And what could a kid like that do here anyway? He ain't gonna' handle a cutting torch or drive a forklift or write up orders. Poor kid would just be in the way."

Marcie liked the idea of hiring Teddy and was annoyed at Archie, but knew he had a valid point. "You might be right. But you'll see," she told them. "He'll be just fine if we help him out, watch out for his safety, teach him. There's plenty of work he can do in the store while you two are out there playing with your machines. Let's give the kid a chance."

"Yeah, there's gonna' be some getting' used to having him around," Bernwhaite said. "And Archie, you're right about his safety.

And I also know you too many years to believe you're really like you sound, calling him that name."

Archie looked sheepish, although he thought "retard" was a perfectly good word. *Everyone uses it and not in a bad way. It was just telling it like it is.* But now Archie was getting a different message.

Bernwhaite spoke quietly, seriously, lightly tapping his desk for emphasis, and leaving no room for argument.

"So, let's understand that we will never again hear that word around here. We won't say it; we won't *think* it. An' we won't let anyone else say it either, customer or no customer. Take it as a new rule of the Bernwhaite Salvage Company. In fact, take it as the number one rule around here from now on."

Marcie, Pete, and Archie were curious about Bernwhaite's defense of this new kid who was about to join them. They all had the same thoughts: *What's got into Karl? What's he got at stake with this kid? What's going on?*

Bernwhaite eased up, seeing he had made his point. Knowing that his employees were good people, he asked for their cooperation and suggestions. "His name's Teddy. Seems a nice young fellow. I'll tell you a few days before he starts so we can be ready for him. Marcie you and me, we're going to figure out what he can do in the store. I have some ideas, an' I know you do, too. We'll all work with him, treat him right, help him out. He wants to work. Like Marcie says, there's lots of things he can do around here. If you have suggestions or concerns, you tell me, and we'll work 'em out. You're all too decent not to help him out, so let's just treat him right. He's gonna' be your fellow employee. Marcie, you're right about givin' him a chance. But he's not a kid, like you said. He's 25, 26, so we won't treat him like a kid. He's a young man, wants to work. Eager to work. OK?"

At first, Teddy was pretty much a *go-fer,* doing what everyone told him to do, running errands and fetching things. Within a few months he had learned a set of duties set out by Bernwhaite and Marcie that defined his job, and he did them well because, he knew, they were now his *big 'sponsabilty.* It was his job to open the gate in the morning, take care of the dogs, straighten up and sweep the office and empty the wastebaskets into the big dumpster. Then he raked the driveway, removing the tire-threatening bits of metal that fell from shipments of scrap, being especially careful in the driveway entrance and the parking area in front of the store. Teddy did his work carefully, knowing he had an *imporant job.*

Each day after raking the driveway, Teddy inspected the fence around the four acres, looking for damage. By then it was lunchtime. Like breakfast with Mr. Beewite, Friday's lunch was Teddy's favorite time. On the final Friday of each month, Teddy and Mr. Beewite drove down to *Bob's Chicken Nuggets* on Franklin Street to buy takeout for everyone, including Barker and Sleeper. They relaxed for an hour in the office or at the picnic table on the small patch of grass that was tended by Teddy behind the store and had their lunch. One person had to stay in the store, and they took turns.

Teddy worked the rest of the day in the store, helping Marcie, getting things from shelves, running purchase orders back into the warehouse, keeping the floor swept, the windows clean, and helping customers carry or wheel things to or from their trucks.

One of his important mid-afternoon tasks was to walk down to the post office on Broadway with the key to Mr. Beewite's post office box in his pocket and retrieve the business mail. On cold, wet, or snowy days Bernwhaite drove him, but Teddy carried the key, unlocked the box, and brought back the mail in the important-looking briefcase that had Mr. Beewite's name stamped on it.

Teddy also accompanied Bernwhaite to pick up and deliver things, helping to load and unload the pickup truck. Sometimes they drove all the way into New York City, an extravagant place of giant buildings that seemed to lean right over Teddy, ready to fall on his head. The streets between the buildings were packed with traffic, a million cars snorting and honking and a million people darting all over the place. Teddy loved those trips, although they were a little scary. He sat up, alert, looking around, not wanting to miss anything as Bernwhaite, cursing the traffic, muttered, "Damn, Teddy! You see that? Damn taxi damn near ran into us!"

One morning on his inspection walk around the property—this was before Barker and Sleeper had joined Bernwhaite's crew—Teddy discovered that the fence had been cut. Thieves had entered during the night, had tried but failed to break into the warehouse, and had left empty handed, but not before ransacking Bernwhaite's office. The police came and Teddy, feeling very important, led them to the damaged section he had discovered. The culprits were never caught; Pete repaired the fence, and Bernwhaite praised Teddy for having spotted the damage.

Bernwhaite installed motion-detection security sensors and video cameras along the fence and, after training Teddy, gave him the job of checking the video tapes each morning as part of his fence inspection. Teddy liked that job, discovering that all sorts of little creatures were busy around the fence at night, like mice and rabbits, a cat who showed up nearly every night, and even a family of foxes. An unsuspected nighttime world was out there, in shadowy gray tones. The animals moved as if no one was watching them, their luminous eyes bright as headlights whenever they triggered the lights and cameras. *Spooky,* he thought, but he liked watching them.[2]

Checking the fence was one of his favorite tasks, especially with his two canine companions. It was a daily adventure, the three of them setting out each noontime—Teddy with his favorite walking stick, a heavy knobbed one he had found inside an old car on the lot—and marching outside the fence along the sides of the four-acre property. The dogs enjoyed it, too, like a country hike. They sniffed and dug and barked at things, chased birds and mice. One day even a raccoon who ran up a tree and reproachfully looked down at them, waiting for them to leave. It took Teddy 20 minutes to get the dogs away from there. "Damn, Teddy," Bernwhaite said, when They returned to the office. "What took you so long? Damn near sent out a search party for you."

While inspecting the fence on a cold December day in his fourth year at Bernwhaite's, Teddy heard noises, animals in distress. With growing concern, he searched through the underbrush and found a cardboard box stuffed in a tangle of bushes, flaps closed and taped shut. He picked it up, listened, and heard scratching and whimpering sounds. Anxiously, and without proper caution, Teddy pulled off the tape, opened the box and found two puppies. They were cold, distressed, thin, dirty, and hungry. Teddy picked up the little dogs, petted them, crooned soothingly, and put them inside his jacket to keep them warm. Forgetting about inspecting the fence, he hurried back to the office to show Bernwhaite what he had found.

Plenty of things annoyed Bernwhaite to the point of unleashing a few curses during a business day: a delayed order, a wrong shipment, some knucklehead at the railroad getting a boxcar number wrong thus delaying its loading or unloading. But Teddy had never seen him this angry when he showed him the puppies and described the box. "Damn, it to Hell," Bernwhaite exploded. "Some rotten, good-for-nothing sonofabitch left those poor little dogs to die. I'd strangle him if I got my hands around his rotten, no-good, damned neck! Good thing you found them, Teddy. Good thing."

After Bernwhaite settled down they agreed that the dogs would be Teddy's responsibility. Teddy knew all about '*sponsabilty* and accepted it. He named them Barker and Sleeper. When Bernwhaite asked him why he called them Barker and Sleeper, Teddy said, "'Cause, that's their name."

For several months the little dogs lived in the office where they were safe, romping all over and entertaining Bernwhaite. Marcie told him he had become a much nicer boss since the pups had joined them.

"Hmph," Bernwhaite grunted. But he liked having them there and was pleased that Teddy was taking good care of them and keeping the place clean. When the pups had grown, Teddy dragged a big wooden packing crate from somewhere on the property and placed it next to Bernwhaite's office. He made a bed for the dogs using a seat pulled from the back of an old DeSoto,[3] placing it inside the box, against the rear wall, leaving plenty of room for the dogs to stretch and for their bowls and toys. Archie and Pete closed gaps in the sides and bottom and sealed the top against rain, using a salvaged piece of corrugated roofing. They set the big box on bricks to keep it off the ground so the wood would not rot.

Teddy liked the new doghouse, walked around admiring it, the excited dogs following him. Kneeling, he looked through the small, low doorway that Pete had cut into the front. It had an arched top and looked pretty fancy. "Real nice in there," Teddy said to Barker and Sleeper. "Go in," he motioned to them. But they held back, fearful of entering the box.

"Betcha' they'll go in if you go in first," Archie said.

Puzzled, Teddy looked at Archie, then at the little doorway that was far too small for him. He could not get his head through there, let alone his whole body. He looked back at Archie. "Can't," Teddy said.

"Sure, you can," Archie said. "That's a surprise, see?" Reaching, he pulled open the entire front, swinging it out on two hinges.

"When you gotta' get in to clean or something," Archie explained, "just open the front, like a door, see? And go on in."

Teddy was delighted and, bending down, crawled inside. It was not high enough to stand up, but he could sit comfortably on the old DeSoto's seat. The dogs, reassured by Teddy's presence, scampered in after him, jumped on the seat, one dog on each side of him. They nuzzled Teddy, wagged their tails, circled twice, and curled up to sleep. Teddy, equally happy, put an arm around each dog, closed his eyes, and leaned into the cushioned back of the seat. "Nice couch you got here," he told the dogs.

Everyone at Bernwhaite's liked the dogs, but it was clear to all including Barker and Sleeper that they belonged to Teddy or, perhaps, that Teddy belonged to them.

Despite its refinements the new doghouse was still a drab-looking packing crate. Teddy decided it needed something more, color, maybe. In his mind he saw his Pa, many years ago, happy among his paint cans, mixing, stirring, and creating wild colors to try out in the house until Ma started hollering. Now, Teddy rummaged through the opened paint cans in Bernwhaite's warehouse, selected several, hauled them out, and painted the doghouse with neat, wavy stripes of orange, yellow, brown, and white, making it look like a bright awning waving in the breeze.

"Damn, Teddy," Bernwhaite said. "Looks like a circus tent! What are people gonna' think when they see that thing sitting next to my office?"

"Yeah, Circus!" Teddy said, smiling, pleased because it did look like a circus. "For Barker and Sleeper. A-OK Mr. Beewite. Circus tent!"

Bernwhaite went into his office, hiding his smile. *Damn Teddy,* he thought. *Did a nice job, painting that doghouse. Never knew he could do that. Maybe I'll have him paint the office. Needs it. But I better' pick the colors or it'll end up looking like another damn circus tent.*

Barker and Sleeper lived comfortably in Teddy's circus-tent doghouse. In the winter and stormy weather, they spent nights snugly in a similarly decorated but much smaller box in the office. Most days they followed Teddy around because, as pups being rescued from that cardboard box, they had quickly bonded with him. Teddy soon lost his old fear of dogs from many years ago when he had been bitten by a frightened, lost dog that he had rushed at and hugged.

Bernwhaite's was closed on Sunday, and each Saturday afternoon Teddy took the dogs with him to the group home where he was by then living. Miss Jane, the House Parent, explained it was "against the rules, no animals allowed." But she was a lady of good sense, liked the little dogs and recognized the pleasure they brought to the other residents. Thus, each weekend, Miss Jane "never noticed" Teddy's rule-breaking, and the tail-wagging dogs enjoyed their weekends of attention and pampering by their group-home friends. That pleased Teddy, like a proud parent showing off his children.

Teddy looked forward to every second Friday, when Bernwhaite gave Teddy his pay envelope. It was half of his two-week's wages. The remainder, as arranged by Teddy, his folks, and Bernwhaite, was deposited into a savings account at the Nyack Bank and Trust to earn interest. Teddy, not sure what that meant, asked Bernwhaite if his *intres* was *A-OK.*

"Yep," Bernwhaite told him. "Won't make you rich, Teddy, but it grows a little bigger every day."

Real nice, Teddy thought, imagining green ivy climbing up a white wall, sprouting new leaves, growing bigger every day—another image for his *picherbook.*

Having money in his pocket and lots of time to spend it was nice. He bought little gifts for the twins who were by then too grown up for the childish trinkets he selected, but they smiled and thanked him so as not to offend their Uncle Teddy. He also bought toys and chewy treats for Barker and Sleeper who enthusiastically accepted them and carefully stowed away the plush toys in a growing pile inside their circus-tent doghouse. And he sometimes splurged on his all-time favorite meal, a take-out box from *Bob's Chicken Nuggets* on Franklin Street. But what he liked best were the chocolate ice cream sodas at Mr. Spone's. Sometimes he took his *speshul fren'*, Debbie, and bought a soda for her, too—although she always ordered strawberry—showing her first how to open *Ol' Green Door.*

They sat on the stools at Mr. Spone's small counter, enjoying their sodas. "Me an' Pa," Teddy told her, smiling as an image emerged from his *picherbook.* "We always got chawclit ice cream sodas from Mr. Spone." Then he paused and added, softly, "Pa, he's not here anymore."

Mr. Spone said, in his gentle voice, "You father, Teddy, he was a nice-a' man," and that helped to lift the touch of sadness that had dropped in.

Teddy often thought about Pa, saw him in soft images. There was Pa, cooking his spaghetti 'n spiders for their breakfast, and there they were, walking down Cedar Hill Avenue, waving at Mr. Burt, and at the park, watching boats go by, and skipping stones over the water, and cheering for Little Blackie and the other seagulls that whirled in the air chasing breadcrumbs.

He saw himself and Pa sitting on the edge of Teddy's bed, Pa softly talking, making a hurt go away. Pa always was good at that.

He saw Pa at Mr. Spone's counter, quietly smoking a cigarette, smiling, enjoying a cup of coffee while Teddy vacuumed-up his chocolate soda.

He saw Pa painting beautiful colors on the walls of Teddy's room and Ma, shaking her head, looking not too happy.

And there was Pa, beaming with pleasure at the head of the dining room table in his big chair, the one with arms. Ma, Pa, Emily, Edward, the twins, Mr. Binky, and Teddy were all there, happy, celebrating Pa's retirement from the power plant. "Yeah," Teddy had explained about retirement to everyone that day. "Pa, he got tired from workin'." And that made everybody laugh.

Then, one day, Pa wasn't there anymore; just like that; just like Miss Ulie.

Gray images: a big, fancy, black car, a stranger driving; other cars following, small flags flapping on little flag poles stuck to their fenders. Ma dressed in black, a soggy white handkerchief all squeezed up in her hand. Emily crying and Teddy, at first in confusion and then, with growing understanding, a deep grief.

For a long time, Teddy felt empty. His *picherbook* stayed closed and the only world was the one outside of him. But, slowly, over many months, a page at a time, it opened again, and his emptiness began filling with *pichers* of Pa and Ulie and everyone and everything else, all still there for Teddy, in his *picherbook*.

The last time he and Debbie had walked to Mr. Spone's store, *Ol' Green Door* was closed and locked. A new sign hung in the window, but neither Teddy nor Debbie could read it. He asked Ma why Green Door was closed.

Ma explained, "Mr. Streppone retired and closed the store."

Teddy thought about that. *Mr. Spone got tired. Like Pa.* Now he missed Pa even more, and Mr. Spone, and chocolate ice-cream sodas with Debbie.

They had met at the group home where they lived with five other young adults and the two house-parents. Teddy had been there for three years, Debbie for two, and she had become *speshul* for Teddy. They enjoyed being together and eventually decided to get married but were not sure how to go about it. Teddy told her about Emily's wedding, how beautiful she had looked walking with Pa down the aisle. He had a colorfully vivid *picherbook* image of Emily and now he created a new image: the same setting and colors, but it was Debbie walking down the aisle.

"You're beautiful, too," he told Debbie, holding her hand early one spring evening. "Real nice, beautiful dresses an' flowers an' the pretty girls all dressed up an' the nice song an' everybody all happy in the church." It may have been Teddy's longest sentence, and he had a warm feeling, almost like the times he and Debbie were alone and could touch each other all over without anybody interrupting them. That was *real nice.*

Debbie was excited about getting married but, like Teddy, did not know how. "Gonna' ask Ma," she said. "Ma knows how."

Debbie never did get around to asking her mom, and time wore on. They continued talking about getting married, were certain they would, someday, but never did. It was nice, though, to talk and think about it, and feel *real good.*

Chapter Twenty- Five:

1976—Teddy's Truck

Teddy finished his morning work around 10:30, and by about 4:00 completed his day in the store helping Bernwhaite and Marcie. The store was a long, narrow space across the front of the warehouse, a no-nonsense, plain, gray space with a concrete floor, unpainted cinder block walls, and two plate-glass windows flanking the wide front door facing the dusty parking area. A high counter ran along the length of the big room, its front panel scuffed by years of customers' steel-toed work boots, its top discolored, scarred, cracked, and cratered by metal parts being pushed across it. Cigarette burns in the countertop added to the well-worn feel of the place. The only decorations were Marcie's "Big Cheese Toaster" photographs and a fading, five-year-old calendar showing a pretty girl leaning against a shiny red Dodge pick-up truck.

Except for Marcie's presence, it was a thoroughly masculine, angular, functional place. Marcie threatened to hang lace curtains in the windows. "Big pink ones," she said, "to soften up this place."

Teddy thought that would be *real nice.* "A-OK, Marcie," he encouraged her, smiling at his image of that splash of bright pink curtains across the big windows. But nobody else, including the customers, thought much of that idea.

"Pink lace!" said a horrified Sammy Parkhurst, one of Bernwhaite's best customers. "Marcie, you want I should walk inna' place what's got lace curtains? *Pink* ones? No way!"

Nevertheless, every now and then Marcie threatened to do it, supported by Teddy's enthusiasm, but she never did get around to it.

The customers, all men, were comfortable in the unpretentious setting, greeted each other by name, and shared friendly insults just as men do in their neighborhood bars. In fact, the long counter suggested a working-man's bar, often prompting some joker to shout out, "Hey Marcie, a couple a' cold ones over here!"

Teddy, like Marcie, Pete, Archie, Barker, and Sleeper, was part of the Bernwhaite setting. The customers liked Teddy for his cheery eagerness to help, and Teddy, in his own way, joined in the good-natured joshing. He did not understand much of it or get many of the jokes but that was OK. It was during those hours working in the store that Teddy felt grown-up and accepted. It was a good feeling, being a working man just like everyone else.

One would think that a place of such masculine disregard for decorative niceties or anything non-functional—a place dealing in salvaged parts of cars, trucks, machines, and such, where the customers, mechanics of one kind or another, had grease-rimmed fingernails and hard calloused hands, and wore oil-stained coveralls—would be a dusty and messy place, downright dirty, with grimy, opaque windows. But that was not the case. It was Teddy's job, supervised by Marcie, to keep the store reasonably clean, wiping up grease and oil, brushing dirt and debris from the counter, cleaning the cobwebs from the walls and corners, sweeping and mopping the concrete floor and keeping the windows clean. Teddy did his job well and the customers, ordinarily not concerned about such unnecessary tidiness, were impressed by Teddy's industriousness, and appreciated that Bernwhaite's, compared with other salvage stores, was remarkably clean.

Teddy had his private place in Bernwhaite's four acres, his "office" he called it, "just like Mr. Beewite's." It was a large wooden packing crate, like the doghouse but much bigger. Teddy did not know what had once been packed in it but whatever it was, it must have been *really big,* like a *really giant frige rater* or something.

Having decided it would be his "office," he painted it white, *jus' like Mr. Beewite's.*

His workday ended about 3:30, and Teddy, trailed by Barker and Sleeper, disappeared into his office until 5:30, when Marcie closed the store and Bernwhaite gave Teddy a ride home. The dogs, tails and ears drooping, watched from behind the fence as Bernwhaite's truck drove off, taking Teddy away. They were much happier on Saturday afternoon when Teddy took the dogs home with him so they would not be alone through the weekend.

Teddy's office and what he did there for so many hours each week was a mystery that intrigued Archie and Pete. Bernwhaite had to stop them when, driven by curiosity, they planned to sneak up on Teddy and find out. "No, you're not gonna' do that," Bernwhaite said. "That's his private place and none of us is gonna' go snooping around. OK? So, stay away."

Marcie agreed, shaking an accusing finger at Pete and Archie. "You're like two little boys, sneaking around, looking for mischief! Leave Teddy alone. He's not bothering anybody in his 'office,' and it's none of your business!"

"Oh, come on, Marcie," Archie wheedled. "It's all in good fun. We like Teddy, you know that. We're just curious."

"Marcie," Pete asked, "ain't you even a little curious? You don't wanna' know what's he doin' there every afternoon? And, anyway, how come we don't all get our own private office, why just Teddy? How come he rates?"

"Because" she answered, "Teddy needs his space. You two lunk-heads don't. You wouldn't know what to do with two free hours if you couldn't hot-rod around on that forklift or squash some poor old car! And, anyway, Teddy gets his 'office' because Karl says so."

"You know," Bernwhaite added, amused at Pete and Archie, "if you two feel like you need to go out there and sit in a packing crate for two hours every afternoon, that's OK by me. Just make sure it's on your time, not mine."

Marcie smiled at that, picturing the two of them, each sitting in a packing crate among the junked cars, just because Teddy did.

They were all protective of Teddy. Recognizing his limitations, they helped him when he faltered, which was less often as he grew into his job. But Bernwhaite had gone much further: he had created a job for Teddy, paid Teddy for work that was helpful but not crucial to the business, shared breakfast every morning with him and bristled at even the slightest criticism of Teddy.

"Man," Archie remarked one day, "you'd think Karl's got Teddy for his prodigy or somethin'!"

"And if he did," Marcie answered, "that's his business. And, anyway, Archie, the word is protege, not prodigy!"

"What's the difference?" Archie asked, confused.

Pete laughed at Archie's ignorance, but he did not know, either.

Pete and Archie were hesitant to ask their boss about his protectiveness of Teddy, but they did ask Marcie if she knew what was going on.

"Whatever it is," she said, in a typical Marcie answer, "if it's anything more than Karl's good nature and concern for Teddy, it's none of your business, or mine, either. So, let's just leave it alone."

"Thus spake Marcie-thusela!" Archie said, rolling his eyes to the ceiling and slapping out a drum-roll on the counter.

"Spake?" Marcie asked. "Thusela? Since when you been talking like that?"

"Just something I heard in a movie. What it means is, *Marcie, she thinks she knows everything.*"

"And," Marcie said, arching her eyebrows, "has it ever occurred to you that maybe I do?"

"Ah, wee, wee, Mar-cie," Pete said, trying to imitate a French accent, doffing his cap and bowing toward Marcie, who couldn't help laughing.

But Bernwhaite's protectiveness of Teddy remained a mystery.

Soon after Teddy had started at Bernwhaite's, his mom had asked him, "Sweetie, you seem to like your job. How are you doin' there? Is Mr. Bernwhaite nice to work for? How about the others? You like them?" She still called him *sweetie* although he was then in his mid-twenties.

Teddy's enthusiastic response made it clear that he was happy with his job and the people there. "Yeah, Ma," he said with his big smile. "Like it. Real nice. Real, *real* nice." A double "real," for Teddy, was a superlative.

Teddy's world was expanding through his work and his relationships with his boss and co-workers. Teddy knew, in feelings if not words, that he now played a bigger, more important role in his world than ever before. Teddy's greatest pleasure was being accepted into that little group of workers at Bernwhaite's. He had become *one of us.*

Teddy recalled a birthday when Pa had told him, "Now, you are a *man*," and he remembered feeling no different on that day than he had before becoming "a man." Then at Emily's wedding he had been the *Best* Man. That had really been something! But none of that compared with his new status—*Working Man*—just like Pete and Archie and, most importantly, just like Pa had been. Teddy did not understand it in any intellectual sense, but his new status made him feel different, better, even bigger, and more important than ever before.

Teddy felt a powerful ownership of his job. If, for example, Archie or Pete suggested they instead of Teddy would walk the fence inspection one morning, or Marcie emptied a wastebasket into the dumpster, Teddy quickly reclaimed control of those tasks which were his *'sponsability,* his job. Teddy's message, although not in words, was clear: *I don't do your job; you don't do mine!*

Teddy's job did not require the highest levels of skill nor was it the most important, but it was a useful job, needing his consistent, responsible performance. It was real work, a real job, and as Teddy grew into his enhanced identity, he felt increasingly pleased with life.

At birth Teddy had been destined to a single, all-encompassing identity—*Mongolian Idiot.* He would never, people said, develop and enjoy the complex give-and-take of normal human roles like *son, student, friend, working man.* They said he was, and would remain throughout his short life, a *Mongolian Idiot* and nothing more.

That label said it all, what more did one need to know about Teddy? About Mongolian Idiots?

But destiny played out differently, and by 1976 Teddy had grown into a 38-year-old man who had mastered several complex roles; he was a good son, brother, uncle or, as he preferred, *granfather* to the *twins.* He was friend to many and, especially, *boy fren* to Debbie. And now he was a working man and wage-earner, a complex, multi-role human being like everyone else. Teddy could no longer be seen as a one-dimensional *Mongoloid.*

But now in his twelfth year at Bernwhaite's, Teddy was slowing down. He did his work, but more slowly, and found it more difficult to carry out some of the heavier tasks. He felt out of breath more than he used to, was more tired, a little slower. His heart sometimes pounded too fast, and he felt occasional pangs of tightness in his chest, sometimes downright painful, and he was having more moments of mild confusion and forgetfulness. Teddy noticed these changes, particularly being so `tired and wanting to lie down and sleep. But he was not alarmed because he quickly recovered each time, and he saw each incident as a brief, separate event-of-the-moment. Teddy did not see the trend that was gathering—his advancing weakness, exhaustion, and cognitive softening.

Teddy did not know what was happening to him. Both Doctors Wharton did: an age-related acceleration of physical and cognitive problems linked with his trisomy condition, congenital heart defects being the most life-threatening, cognitive weakening being the most distressing. Teddy had surprised everyone by surviving 38 years, extraordinary for his 1938 cohort of infants with trisomy 21. But now it was catching up with him.

Marcie was the first to notice. "Karl, I think Teddy's having problems, slowing down. I don't mean neglecting his work, nothing like that, but I think he's not feeling so good. And sometimes he gets confused about things that he's done a hundred times with no trouble. You noticed any of that?"

Bernwhaite was alarmed. "Hmm. Now that you mention it, yes. I been wondering about that but didn't think it was so bad. We all forget stuff, confuse things now and then. But you think it's different with Teddy? What do you think we should do?"

"Maybe I should ask him. He doesn't mind when I ask him how he's doing. Or maybe we ought to talk to his mom. Or his sister, Emily. I know they're close. He ought to go get a check-up."

"I don't know. That would be goin' over his head, don't you think? We should talk to Teddy first, ask him if everything's all right, ask him to let his mom and sister know, and suggest maybe he should get a check-up."

While their concerns grew, Teddy was well into what had become his major project—his "love affair," Marcie called it, with an old Ford F-100 pick-up truck that he had been working on for three years. It had started late one afternoon when Harry Haight drove his flatbed car-carrier into the lot just before closing time, delivering the vehicle.

Harry turned off the engine, gathered his folder with the title documents, and swung down from his truck. He stopped to pet Barker and Sleeper who had come running to greet their friend. "Hey, how you guys doin?" he laughed, bending down, petting the little dogs as they happily wriggled around his legs. "Hey there, Teddy," he called out, as Teddy came out of his "office" to see what the dogs' yapping was all about.

"Hey, Harry. A-OK!" Teddy waved and smiled. "Got more cars?"

Harry's flatbed, a familiar sight at the lot, bore an old pick-up truck. It grabbed Teddy's attention. He did not know why; it just did.

Harry went up the steps into Bernwhaite's office. "Sorry to be so late, Karl, catching you at closing time. Slow traffic on 9-W, accident or something."

"No sweat, Harry. What you got there on the truck?"

"An old Ford F-100 from the Munsey Depot. Shoulda' been here couple days ago, but there was some delay, some ownership hassle to get cleared up."

While Harry and Bernwhaite were finishing the paperwork, Teddy walked around Harry's flatbed. The old truck sat high on the flatbed like it was King O'The Mountain, pulling at Teddy, and he could not stop looking at it.

Harry came out of the office, climbed into his truck, and drove around to the drop-off area just outside the fence around the car crusher. He tilted the flatbed, winched the vehicle to the ground, and unhooked the final chains that had secured it. Then he leveled the flatbed back to transport position, climbed behind the wheel and, waving to Teddy, drove away, leaving the old Ford to wait for its appointment with the crusher.

Intrigued by the old truck, Teddy ignored Harry's exit, did not shout out his usual, "A-OK, Harry. See ya' later."

Twenty years earlier, in 1956, a Ford F-100 pick-up in gleaming *Raven-Black* finish rolled off the line at the Chester, Pennsylvania assembly plant.[1] It weighed 3,250 pounds on a 110-inch wheel-base with a 6.5-foot cargo box. It had a standard 3-speed manual transmission, and its V-6 engine delivered 133 horsepower. The truck began its 20-year working career for three different owners, accumulating dents, scratches, rust, worn-out and broken parts, and over 150,000 miles before becoming a faded and forgotten old work-horse on its final journey to Bernwhaite's crusher.

Teddy continued circling the truck, touching it, running his hand along its side, discovering a remarkably smooth, still-glossy spot on the left-rear fender, a little reminder of what the truck had once been. Teddy polished the spot with his sleeve, admired how it shined and polished it again. Then, continuing his examination, he was surprised when his finger poked through the heavily rusted bottom edge of the passenger-side door.

After several circuits around the truck, he opened the driver's door and climbed in. He turned the steering wheel, grunting with the unexpected heavy effort needed, making the soft, nearly flat tires crunch on the gravel. He stepped on the brake pedal which slid all the way down to the floor with no resistance at all. He pressed the clutch, or tried to, it was solidly stuck. Then Teddy pulled down the sun visor, tried to lower the window, flash the lights, and sound the horn; but none of that worked. As he poked around the dashboard, the glove-box door popped open, seemingly on its own, making Teddy laugh.

Teddy sat in that old truck, looking through the windshield, his hands on the wheel, pretending to turn it back and forth as if he were driving down the road. In his private *picherbook* an image formed: Teddy, driving the truck, but it was gleaming-new, just as it had been off the assembly line. From then on what Teddy saw when he looked at the old truck or even thought about it was not its flat tires, dulled, rusted, dented, and aged reality, but his *picherbook* image of the shiny new truck of twenty years ago. At that moment, without forming any words, Teddy knew that this beautiful vehicle was *Teddy's Truck.*

From his office window Bernwhaite had watched Teddy circle the truck, inspecting, seemingly *caressing* it, finally climbing into the driver's seat.

Damn, Teddy, Bernwhaite wondered. *Why are you so interested? It's just another old truck. What the devil you doin' now, sittin' in there? What's goin through your head? What are you imagining, Teddy? What?*

Bernwhaite had no way of knowing that in those moments Teddy had wrapped his life around that old truck. There is no explaining how or why it happened, and so quickly. Teddy, never having developed much capacity for self-reflection, did not question it. It was love at first sight.

Teddy welcomed that old truck into the small circle of treasures that made up his world: Ma and Emily, and his best friends—Mr. Binky, Roger, Debbie, Barker and Sleeper. There were other important people there, too: Mr. Spone, Doc Warn, Dokkerdee, Mr. Beewite, Marcie, Archie, and Pete; and, of course, Miss Ulie, Miss Sophie, and Pa, all three of whom now lived forever in Teddy's *picherbook.* Teddy developed a new afternoon routine: finishing his work, he spent the next two hours either in his office or *fixin' up Teddy's Truck.*

"What," Archie asked Bernwhaite, "are we gonna' do with Teddy's truck? It's in the way, taking up space by the crusher. He'd be unhappy if we compacted it and shipped it out like the other old wrecks. Why don't we move it someplace where he can get to it but won't be in our way?"

"Yeah, Archie, you're right," Bernwhaite said. "Teddy decided that old Ford is his truck. He doesn't bother anybody when he's fooling around with it, and he does that on his own time, not during work hours. So, we let him do whatever it is that he thinks he's doing."

"What he thinks he's doin'," Archie said, "is fixing it up, getting it running again, an' you and me, an' everybody else around here, we know that ain't never gonna' happen."

"Who knows, Archie, who knows?" Bernwhaite said. "Stranger things have happened. But you're right, it'll never run again and it's in the way. And he'd be sad to lose it if we shipped it out. So why don't you get up on the forklift,' take the truck over there by Teddy's office, set it down for him, out of our way, and forget about it."

Archie did that. Teddy was pleased and showed Archie where to place the truck so he would have no trouble someday driving it out of the lot.

"Sure thing, Teddy," Archie said. "I'll put it down just right so's you can drive it out o' here soon as you get her all fixed up."

"A-OK Archie," Teddy said, sincerely thanking Archie for his help but completely missing his sarcasm.

Teddy's determination to repair the old truck and drive it out of Bernwhaite's lot developed gradually as he worked on it many afternoons over the next three years. Teddy poked here and there, checked the oil just like Pete and Archie did with their cars. He tugged at drive belts, peered into the radiator, and added water. His clanging and banging could be heard as he worked under the raised hood, but no one knew exactly what he was doing under there. He swept out the cab, cleaned the windows, hosed down the truck, washed and polished it until it gleamed like new, at least in Teddy's imagination if not in realty.

It was never a systematically developed, rational plan, but a flow of gradually emerging images in his private *picherbook,* like a video with a soundtrack of emotions that solidified his absolute certainty that he would fix up the truck. At some point in those afternoon hours *fixin' the truck* became Teddy's most important focus, and his favorite image was driving his beautiful new truck with his *best frens* Debbie, Barker, and Sleeper all enjoying the ride.

Occasionally Pete and Archie, feeling sad at Teddy's innocent belief in his lost cause, helped him to fix some small thing and even showed him how to drive the old Ford if ever he got it going. They never criticized him or belittled his labors, and Teddy continued working on his truck.

Chapter Twenty-Six:

1976—A Cold Day with Snow in the Forecast

It was late Thursday afternoon, November 11, 1976, a cold day with snow in the forecast, when Teddy finished his work on the truck. Satisfied, he closed the hood with a rumbling bang and wiped his hands on the oily rag carried in his back pocket, just like Archie and Pete did. He walked slowly around the truck, inspecting it as he had three years ago when Harry had brought it in. He ignored that rusted, brittle place along the bottom of the door where his finger would go all the way through, but did stop to polish that still-shiny spot on the left-rear fender. Teddy smiled, satisfied, opened the driver's door, and climbed in behind the wheel.

Marcie was in the store, finishing up. It was closing time. The final customer of the day, Sammy Parkhurst, had just left. Bernwhaite, Pete, Archie, and a company technician were trying to fix a problem with the crusher. It would be a late night for them. Barker and Sleeper paced the ground around the truck, looking up at Teddy, eager for him to open the door and let them in. A light snow began to fall.

It was just about 5:30 and getting dark. Marcie was leaving. She waved at Teddy as she drove out. Teddy waved back.

"A-OK, Marcie," he called to her, smiling.

Now the store was closed and dark except for the dim night lights. Teddy could hear the crusher's angry growling and scraping as it fitfully started up and abruptly quit. Teddy was comfortable in the truck, cold but protected against the sharp wind. He sat back, settling in, pressing deeper into the seat, feeling that broken spring that he never could fix. *Like an ol' fren,* he thought. Teddy slid his hands around the steering wheel, feeling its cool smoothness, tapped his fingers on the dashboard and, as usual, the glove box door popped open. He smiled. He'd need to fix that, along with the broken seat spring.

Snowflakes blossomed on the windshield, turned into little water drops and ran down the glass like skiers on a slope. *Havin' a race,* Teddy smiled. The world dimmed, grew quiet. He relaxed, felt sleepy, softly surrounded by pleasant *picherbook* images of himself with Debbie, Sleeper, and Barker leisurely riding in his beautiful truck. His breathing slowed, his eyes closed. *Real nice,* he thought. *Real, real nice ...*

Then, it was time. Teddy sat up, making sure no one was watching, not wanting anyone to see what he was about to do, and maybe try to stop him. Carefully, he stepped on the clutch pedal, pushed it down, shifted into neutral like Archie had taught him, and felt the side-to-side slack in the long handle, just as it was supposed to feel. He pumped the accelerator pedal once, twice, and then, holding his breath, turned the ignition key and, with his left foot, stepped hard on the starter button on the floor.

A few growls from under the hood, then the old engine coughed, sputtered and roared like a lion, black smoke exploding from the exhaust pipe, to be snatched away by the eager wind. He thought that Mr. Beewite and Archie must have heard the noise and would come running to investigate. But the crusher's clanging and banging had covered the engine's roar. Another few moments and the engine settled down to a steady purr, and Teddy felt the reassuring vibrations as the old truck came back to life.

Slowly depressing the clutch and shifting from neutral to first, Teddy eased down on the accelerator and carefully maneuvered the truck away from his office, through the tall weeds to the driveway and out through the gates that Marcie had moments before left open. *Marcie not s'pose to leave gates open,* he thought. It was not until he reached the corner that Teddy realized that he, too, had left the gates open and he should go back and close them. But, with a guilty smile, he kept on going.

The snow was light, the road still dry and safe. The old truck rolled along smoothly, gaining speed: 20, 25, 30. *Nice,* Teddy thought, *real nice.* It was easy steering gently around the curves, up and down the little hills and over to the 9-W intersection. Yes, this was *really nice* he smiled. Just ahead, the traffic light turned red. Recalling a favorite game he and the twins had often played, Teddy knew, that "red light" meant "stop!" and he did, stepping on the brake and shifting into neutral.

When the light turned green, Teddy carefully depressed the clutch, shifted into first gear, accelerated, then shifted into second, then third. *Not so hard to do,* he thought. At the next corner he turned left, heading north on the narrow 9-W highway, not sure where he was going but, no matter, anywhere was wonderful when you're driving your shiny new truck. The streets were deserted. But now, safely out of Mr. Beewite's lot, he wished there were lots of people walking around to see him and admire his new truck.

Teddy had never driven before and was not familiar with the streets at this northern edge of town. He headed this way and that, not concerned where he was going, just enjoying his freedom of driving and discovering new places. After a while he found himself down in Nyack, on Main Street, near Franklin. He wasn't sure how he had arrived there, but he knew where he was, having walked these streets many times. A dark image popped up—*the Bad Thing* that had lurked here so many years ago—but that was long gone from his world, Pa had seen to that. He smiled, feeling sad but pleased, remembering Pa.

That made him think of Gar, *the Bad Thing* of so long ago. "Do you remember Gary?" Pa had asked him one day, looking up from the Journal News. "Well, you know, Gary joined the army, got sent over to Vietnam, to fight in the war. It says here that Gary is a hero, saved his platoon in a battle. Got medals for bravery. But he never came back from Vietnam, poor guy. Who would have thought that Gary would end up one of our town's heroes? Makes me think differently about Gary. You never know, I guess. The Legion's going to honor him in a ceremony at the park. I think we ought to go, pay our respects. It's sad that he didn't make it back."

Now, still thinking of Gary and Pa, Teddy drove slowly along Franklin Street. The sidewalks were empty, most stores closed and dark, but there were lights ahead. *Bob's Chicken Nuggets* was still open! *Nice* he thought, pulling over and parking at the curb, all thoughts of Gary evaporated. There were few cars at that hour, and he had plenty of room to park. Teddy climbed down from the truck, went into the store, and bought four take-out dinners, *Bob's Chicken Nuggets* being his favorite food. Well, maybe his second favorite, after Mr. Spone's *chawclit* ice cream sodas. When he climbed back into the truck the dogs, excited by the smell of deep-fried chicken, jumped all over him, poking their noses into the big paper bag.

Teddy gently pushed them away, laughing, "No, guys, not now. Later. After we go get Debbie!" But they persisted, Bob's Chicken Nuggets being their favorite food, too, and he finally had to lock the bags in the toolbox in the back of the truck. Teddy felt bad about disappointing his two little friends.

Teddy knew exactly where he was going. He made a U-turn on Franklin and drove back to Main Street, turned left and up the hill past Midland Avenue to Highland Avenue and left again to the group home where Debbie was waiting. The house was dark; everyone had gone to sleep. Debbie was hiding nervously in the shadow of the porch, waiting for him. When he pulled up she ran to the truck, opened the door, climbed in, and was jumped on by the wriggling dogs happily welcoming their friend. Finally peeling them off, she gently pushed them to the end of the seat and slid over to Teddy, pressing firmly against him, happy to see him, excited and scared, too, having broken the house rules by coming out at night without permission. *They might catch me,* she worried, *might even send a p'liceman to get me.*

Debbie pulled off her winter cap, causing her hair to fluff out and fill the truck with delightful perfume that surrounded Teddy and left him more than a little befuddled, but it was a nice kind of confusion. He loved it. Debbie leaned her head on his shoulder and looked up at him.

"Hi," she smiled.

Teddy, still befuddled, finally came up with, "A-OK, Debbie!"

The truck, so cold a moment ago, had filled with Debbie's warmth. *Nice,* Teddy sighed. *Real nice.* He wanted to stay there forever, like this, breathing the perfume of her hair, but he knew they must leave before someone caught them and made Debbie go back inside.

They drove with no destination, not saying much, having little need for talking, just enjoying this chance to be alone, warmly pressed against each other. Teddy put his arm around Debbie and, pulling her closer, nuzzled her hair. It had been nice before, but this was even nicer! Driving was difficult with one arm around Debbie, trying to shift gears. But that was *A-OK.*

The dogs, disappointed at not getting their Bob's Chicken Nuggets, which they knew were cruelly locked away in the toolbox, curled up on the end of the seat and went to sleep, small enough that they took up little space.

They drove slowly through Nyack's darkened neighborhoods, the streets empty, most people settled in watching after-supper television. The truck glided along. The streets, the town, the world, belonged to Teddy, Debbie, and the dogs, invisible in the darkness. They owned the night.

But their nighttime rambling through Nyack's quiet neighborhoods must have attracted attention because a flashing red light appeared in the rear-view mirror, far back but coming fast. Debbie, easily alarmed, raised her head, and looked back through the window.

"Oh no! It's a p'lece car, Teddy! Comin' to 'rest me 'cuz I broke the house rule! Teddy, I'm scared. Let's go home!"

Teddy felt a burst of protective anger. *Not nice!* he thought. *Makin Debbie scared,* and he knew he had to get Debbie away from that police car. Here was a new, exciting experience, a chest-expanding, manly determination to protect Debbie and an electric charge of danger and adventure.

Pulling his arm from around Debbie he grasped the steering wheel with both hands, stepped hard on the accelerator, and the old truck leaped forward: 40, 45, 50 miles an hour, a dizzying rush, the truck shaking with strain, causing the glovebox door to pop open again, startling Debbie and making Teddy laugh.

"Hang on, Debbie!" he shouted as she clung to him, her fright magnified to terror by their headlong speed. They blew across 9W, ignoring the red light, onto Route 59, heading west, toward Central Nyack. He knew that just ahead was Central Avenue, a dark street with no lights, where Aunt Macrie lived. If he could make a sharp turn there and race up to where the road ended in a dark wall of trees and shrubs at the edge of the woods, he might fool the policeman into thinking he had gone straight ahead on route 59.

"Hang on Debbie!" he shouted again. "Here we go!"

Teddy hauled on the steering wheel, making a sharp right onto Central Avenue. The careening truck leaned far over; its tires squealing, two wheels lifting off the road leaving them dangerously hanging in air. Debbie shrieked and Teddy clung desperately to the steering wheel, feeling the truck tipping over as the world tilted away from them.

"Nooooo!" he wailed.

The truck hung forever on two wheels, then fell heavily back down to all four and, under its own direction, swerved wildly through the next block, straightened out and roared up the hill to the dead-end where Teddy pushed on the brake pedal with all his might, stopping the truck just before it would have crashed into the woods. With no houses or streetlights, the truck became another shadow in the night.

The police car, siren shrieking, red lights flashing, raced past Central Avenue, the policeman having no clue where the truck had disappeared.

With engine and lights off, Teddy and Debbie clung to each other in the darkness, shaken and still trembling. The overheated engine ticked as it cooled. The dogs complained at having been thrown off the seat, grumbling but unharmed.

Debbie was sobbing in terror and laughing with relief. Teddy, adrenaline still surging, heart wildly beating, gulped for air. He struggled to steady his breathing, felt those *real bad* pains in his chest again and then, like the truck, began his own cool-down, relaxing, slowing. Encircling Debbie in his arms, he pulled her close, the warm embrace calming both of them.

Teddy gently stroked Debbie's hair, shoulders, arms. "A-OK, Debbie. A-OK," he said softly. Debbie's sobs slowed. She sighed, pressed against Teddy, tighter, wanting no space between them, feeling his warmth from every part of his body. They clutched each other, caressed, explored, kissed, discovering the delights of sharing themselves.

Teddy had no idea how long they had been in their embrace. Slowly returning to this world, they peeled themselves apart. A hint of dawn reached up from the east across the Hudson River. Debbie leaned her head on Teddy's shoulder, feeling deliciously tired and floating in a new contentment

Teddy wanted to stay there, together, forever, but he reluctantly started up the engine, shifted carefully into reverse, backed around, straightened out and headed down Central Avenue to the highway. He turned left and drove Debbie home. No one was awake yet and Debbie could slip inside undetected. As she was leaving the truck, Debbie stopped, slid back across the seat to Teddy, hugged him again and, in a whisper floating in wonderment, asked softly, "Are we married now?"

"I think so," Teddy said, still dazed in his own fog of delight.

Debbie smiled, kissed him lightly on the cheek, and disappeared into the house. It was a sweet kiss, light and soft. Teddy touched the spot, felt the glow of love that lingered there.

He was not aware of driving back to Bernwhaite's and was surprised to find himself going through the gates which were still open just as he had left them. He followed the driveway to his office, hoping to avoid attention although Mr. Beewite and the others must have gone home hours ago.

Teddy carefully parked the truck precisely as it had been before his nighttime ride, turned off the engine, pulled up the brake handle, and leaned back in the seat, again feeling that old broken spring in the cushion. *Gotta' fix it,* he thought. Teddy closed his eyes, smiled, sighed deeply and surrounded by sweet whispers of Debbie, floated off, enjoying the most glorious happiness he had ever known.

Chapter Twenty-Seven:

1976—Boxes

Three weeks later, on a Sunday morning early in December, Emily drove into Bernwhaite's lot to meet him as they had arranged by telephone. Bernwhaite greeted her solemnly with a gentle handshake and sad eyes. Barker and Sleeper wagged their tails in greeting, but without their usual exuberant welcome. "I packed up everything for you, Emily," Bernwhaite said. "Everything Teddy had. I put it all in his truck. Over there. Seven boxes. We can move them to your car."

"Thank you, Mr. Bernwhaite…"

"Karl, please."

"Karl, yes. Or as Teddy would say, "A-OK, Mr. Beewite."

They chuckled at that.

"You know, Karl, we owe you so much. I want to thank you for being so good to Teddy all these years, giving him his job, watching out for him. I know Teddy can be—could be—difficult…"

"No, no," Bernwhaite protested. "Teddy was never difficult, Emily, never a problem. Needed guidance now and then. But don't we all?"

"Yes, I guess we do," Emily said, smiling. "And I'm glad Teddy was no problem for you. He talked about you all the time, you know. About your breakfasts together, your trips to New York City, how nice you were to Barker and Sleeper, and everything. I know you didn't need to do all that for him, to treat him so nicely, but you did and, well, we can't thank you enough. He truly loved you, Karl, I want you to know that."

Bernwhaite turned away from Emily and wiped his eyes. "Speck o' dust must a' blown in," he explained in a muffled voice, still facing away.

After a while he turned back to Emily and smiled. "You know, Emily, whatever I might have done for Teddy, truth is, Teddy gave me far more in return. I'm the one who got the lion's share in that deal."

A deeply bittersweet expression come over him, shifting shadows of sadness and happiness. Emily saw it, recognized her own emotions in Karl's expression. "I know," she said. "Teddy gave us all so much. You know, Dr. Wharton, he's retired now, and his daughter, Dokkerdee as Teddy called her, agree; they admired Mom and Dad for how they enriched Teddy' life. But like you said, Karl, there's another side—how much Teddy enriched their lives, our lives. And I don't think Teddy ever realized how much he did."

"You know, Emily," Bernwhaite said. "Archie and Pete wondered why I hired Teddy and why I seemed to give him special treatment." Bernwhaite was remembering, with soft images from 74 years ago, when he was five years old in 1902: images, light and sweet and flowing gently like a movie that's been slowed just a bit. Little Karl and his big brother Davey, running through the pasture, Davey, laughing, twisting, turning, keeping just out of reach as Karl tried to catch him.

"Can't catch!" Davey sang.

"Yes, I can," Karl shouted, running after his big brother, triumphant when Davey paused just enough to let Karl to tag him. "Gotcha! Now, you're *It*, Davey!"

Then Karl, giggling, ran for his life across the green meadow as Davey, now the chaser, easily caught him with a happy shout, "Now Karl *it*!"

In those images Karl and Davey play forever in a green, sun-dazzled meadow of wildflowers and a sweet summer breeze.

But there are other images, dark and frightening; black smoke and writhing flames, shimmering waves of heat, shouting strangers struggling with water buckets, terrified animals running from the barn, whispered words, "just a matter o' time," "bound to happen," "kid like that," "kept at home an' all."

Five-year-old Karl, frightened, confused, clinging to his mother; Pa running from the collapsing barn, shouting in relief, "We got 'em all out!"

Davey, crying, cringing, surrounded by agitated people.

Then, Davey was gone. Their meadow fell silent and empty.

"I was just five years old when Davey went away," Karl said to Emily. "And he was just ten. Never had a chance to say goodbye, just a week later, one night while I was asleep. The next morning, he was gone. I didn't understand, kept asking, where's Davey? My ma said he went to live in a 'nice place where they can take good care of him.' I cried a lot after that, for my big brother, Davey. Everybody was sad for a long time.

"When Mrs. Jackson, the social worker, asked if I'd be interested in sponsoring Teddy, give him a chance to work, she showed me his picture. You know, Emily, they could've been twins, Teddy and Davey. Same round face, almond eyes, same big smile, same sweet disposition shining through. Of course, I agreed. Maybe I hoped Teddy might fill in some of the emptiness after Davey, even after all those years. And, you know, Teddy did. Teddy gave me so much, Emily. By rights, I should be thanking you."

They were silent for a while, sharing something deep and undefined, something *nice*. Emily gently touched Bernwhaite's arm. He put his hand on hers, smiled. They understood each other.

"Well now," Bernwhaite said, rousing himself. "Let's go on over to Teddy's truck. I'll show you what he left."

Bernwhaite pulled a box to the tailgate. "Here's what I found when I emptied Teddy's office. You know, Teddy had that big packing crate over by the fence, called it his 'office.' Painted the outside white like my double-wide. Spent a couple hours most afternoons in there when he wasn't working on his truck, waiting for me to finish up and drive him home. We all wondered what kept Teddy so busy in there. Archie asked him, but Teddy would just smile and say, "A-OK, Archie." He never did tell us, like he wanted to keep it a secret. Now that I know, I wish he had told us. I wish I had known. Anyway, Emily, here's what I found. Take a look."

Emily was puzzled. She opened the box and looked inside. It was filled with scrap material, various sizes and shapes of plywood, pine boards, a flat plastic tray with a broken end, pieces of dry-wall, and a smooth section of metal roofing. It seemed a random collection of construction waste. Bernwhaite had put everything neatly in the boxes, not thrown in or piled on top of each other but carefully placed, each on edge, like folders in a file drawer. They were different shapes, sizes, and material, but each had a flat, mostly smooth surface. And that's what Teddy had wanted; they were his blank canvasses.

Emily carefully pulled out a square of plywood. A beautiful pattern of color flowed across it. She pulled out another, then another. Each was gloriously painted: house paint, metal paint, exterior and interior, flat and glossy, oil and latex, liquid and spray paint, whatever partially-full paint cans and still-pressurized canisters Teddy could find in Bernwhaite's warehouse. The paint was brushed on, rolled on, sprayed, worked with fingers and palms, even just dripped on. But there was nothing random about the creations. Colors flowed like melodies, some soaring, others combining softly, showing a hint of familiar shapes. They were beautiful creations, colors and shadings, some melting smoothly together, others colliding, releasing rays of energy, gorgeous arrangements carefully worked onto each surface.

"Explosively colorful," some would say, "primitive," "formless," "naïve." And Emily's artist eyes saw beauty created by an unschooled talent that no one had ever suspected. *Teddy painted these?* she thought. *They're wonderful! And no one ever knew, never realized his talent!*

Eyes misty, hands trembling, Emily lifted out one painting after another, examining each, gently setting them face-up on the grass, careful not to damage them. After emptying the seven boxes and setting out the paintings, Emily and Bernwhaite were surrounded by 83 brilliant paintings, some small, some large, each unique, each on its own distinctively shaped "canvas." Teddy had worked the shape into each creation—the accidental shapes had become one with the painted art.

"Beautiful," Bernwhaite said, "like standing in a rainbow. They're not pictures of anything. I don't know what they're supposed to be. I almost know, just a hint. But the colors and all, how he put them together. Everything fits. And they're all different, see? Each one is something, but I don't know what. Beautiful, just beautiful."

Emily, too, was awe-struck. She knew that Teddy had no intellectual understanding of what "abstract" meant, had no words for it; but he had something that enabled him to pull bright, colorful and complicated images from somewhere, transfer them to his "canvasses," and create this beautiful art. But what was being abstracted? What were the images, ideas, memories from which Teddy had drawn his art? *What is he telling us?* Emily wondered. *And where had it all come from?* She was bewildered and then, walking among the paintings, catching a hint of meaning here, another, there, the answer took shape, and Emily began to see what Teddy was showing them.

Then, it all came together. Emily understood, and she abruptly sat on the ground and cried. Reaching out, as if to embrace all the paintings, Emily cried for her little brother who was no longer with them; she cried for his talent no one had suspected; and she cried for Teddy, alone, creating his beautiful paintings, never hearing a word of praise, support, or appreciation.

Bernwhaite, distressed by Emily's reaction put his hand on her shoulder. "Emily?" he gently asked. "Are you alright?"

"I should have seen it, Karl," she sobbed. "It was right in front of me, and I was too busy with my own life, my own career, to take the time to see it. I let him down."

In that moment of understanding and remorse, Emily resolved that Teddy would receive his long-delayed recognition. His had been a lonely art but, she knew, a fulfilling one. With that thought, Emily felt comforted, picturing Teddy during all those hours, finding pleasure and fulfillment in his creations. The artist in her understood that is what had kept him at it: the lonely but intense pleasure known by only a small minority of people, the rewards of creating beauty. Teddy never had the words to describe his creations, but he had the talent to create them.

"Karl," she said pointing at the paintings all around them "I know what this is! I know what Teddy is telling us! Karl, these are pages from Teddy's *picherbook!* Teddy tried but could never tell us in words what was in there. But now he's showing us. See? With his paintings. He's sharing his private *picherbook*, sharing Teddy's world with us!"

She lifted a painting in soft shades of white, like shifting clouds, with lightly brushed-in highlights of peach and yellow, glossy brown hints in the background and soft red brush strokes angled across the center.

"It's my wedding, Karl. My wedding colors, and the lovely mahogany of the church woodwork in the background. See? And the red carpet down the aisle. Teddy was so proud to be Best Man. This is his image of my wedding! To him, just like it was for our dad, it was the colors, always the colors; the colors that made Teddy's world, and it's all so beautiful!"

"And this one, see? It's a study in blue and silver, with this soft background of white clouds in the sunshine. This must be his portrait of Miss Ulie, our dear old friend. She had beautiful silver hair, like that, see? She was so elegant. And she liked to dress in these lovely blue shades.

"And here, Karl, look at this one. This is different from all the rest, see? Disturbing, dark, deep black, almost blue-black. And here, look here, these little soft touches, little feather touches of yellow and white and gray, like something small and vulnerable against this whole angry dark background. And here's this bright crimson pearl among the feathers. Gives me the willies. I wonder what the dark story is behind this painting."

They walked slowly among the paintings, a journey through time and Teddy's world, turning the pages of Teddy's *picherbook*. Barker and Sleeper followed them, careful not to step on the paintings.

Later, they packed up the boxes and put them into Emily's car, three in the trunk, four on the back seat. She lifted the largest painting, a two-foot by three-foot plywood rectangle. It was a striking black-and-white creation with a prominent and somehow foreboding dark metallic form just off center, blurred but dominating, and suggestions of rust-streaked boxy shapes in the background. Propping it against her car she asked, "Karl, what do you think Teddy's telling us here?"

He studied the painting, stumped for a few seconds, then his eyes widened in pleasure and recognition. "It's my car crusher! Teddy's *big cheese toaster*. He's turned that ugly machine into a beautiful painting."

Emily handed him the painting. "Take it, Karl. You should have this one."

He thanked her, immensely pleased. "I'll hang it in the store, in the middle of the big wall right across from the front door, and when customers come in, the first thing they'll see will be Teddy's painting!"

Emily smiled at that, liking the idea of each customer being greeted by Teddy's art. "Well, I guess that's it," Emily said. She leaned down to pet the dogs who had settled at her feet. Their tails thumped once or twice but not with their old, vigorous enthusiasm.

"Karl, what about Barker and Sleeper? What will happen to them, now? Without Teddy to take care of them?"

Bernwhaite sighed. "Poor little guys. They're grieving, sure do miss Teddy, keep looking for him every day, coming over to me like I can go get Teddy for them. It's sad. I can't keep them here, on the lot; trucks goin' in and out. I'm afraid they'll get hurt, roaming around here without Teddy to watch them. Or maybe run out in the street. They're getting' older, too, like the rest of us. Must be near ten years old by now." He paused, thinking. "For all those years, Teddy took good care of these little guys. I'd like to take them home, but Sarah, she can't have animals in the house, with her bad breathing problems." He looked away from Emily. "I hate to do it, but I guess I'll have to get rid of them."

Emily continued petting the dogs. "I'll be glad to take them home with me, Karl. We like these little fellas. They know us and our home, they been there enough weekends with Teddy over the years. And we have that big, fenced yard the kids used to play in. Be perfect for them. And you could come visit them whenever you want. Visit us, too. We'd like that, me and Ed. Anytime, Karl. You're invited, you know. Any time."

Bernwhaite cheered up and smiled at that, relieved about the dogs and pleased that even at his age he could find new friends like Emily and Edward. "Love to," he said. "I'll come and visit, Emily. I sure will."

Barker and Sleeper, as if knowing something important had just happened, eagerly jumped into Emily's car when she opened the door and motioned them in. They hopped into the back seat but, finding it crowded with boxes, scrambled up front, explored, sniffed around, and satisfied, poked their heads out the window, looking at Emily, wagging their tails and barking. And, with that, everything seemed to be settled.

Ready to leave, Emily looked back at Teddy's truck one last time. She paused and quietly asked, "Karl, that's where you found Teddy? In his truck?"

"Yeah. Saddest day of my life, Emily. So unexpected. It was around 5:30. I was working out back, on the crusher, with Pete and Archie and a company technician. Marcie had just left and waved to Teddy. He was sitting in his truck, waiting for me like he did every afternoon for me to drive him home after work. Everything seemed fine. Marcie says he waved back at her, smiled, like he always did. Marcie cried like a baby when I telephoned her about Teddy.

"Couldn't have been more than a few minutes after Marcie left when I heard the dogs. It was strange. They were whining, howling. It was eerie, gave me the willies. Something was wrong, so me and Archie, we ran up to see what was going on. The dogs were agitated, jumping at the truck like they were trying to get in, scratching at the door. Teddy was sitting there in the driver's seat like, you know, just sleeping peacefully. Doc even said it had been peaceful."

"I'm glad it was peaceful," Emily said. "And only a few minutes, you say, after he waved at Marcie? That's when you found Teddy? I wonder what was going through his mind in those last few minutes."

Bernwhaite smiled, remembering. "You know, Teddy liked sitting in his truck, especially when it was stormy, snowing like it was that day. I think he felt safe in there. And he liked to pretend he was driving someplace, maybe having an adventure, you know, in his imagination."

Emily thought of Teddy and his wonderful *mashinashin* that was fueled, not by words, but by his *picherbook* images.

"Yes," she said. "That's Teddy, probably imagining he was driving around somewhere. He loved that old truck. Told us a hundred times how he was fixin' it up, getting it running again and going to drive all around Nyack. Karl, I know this is a silly question, but could it be possible he might have really fixed it, got it working, maybe even driven it without you knowing about it?"

Karl smiled at that idea. "No way, Emily. Teddy didn't know how to drive. And anyway, that old Ford hasn't moved from that spot since Archie set it down there three years ago. True, Teddy pumped up the tires, cleaned the whole truck, washed it, made it look real good, even tried to polish it up. The old truck looks pretty good now, sittin' there, like it's ready to go. But under the hood, Emily, there's no battery, no fuel pump, no carburetor, no spark plugs; the engine block is all seized up solid; it's got no brakes, no transmission, no drive shaft. The Good Lord himself couldn't get that old truck running!"

There was not much more to say. Barker and Sleeper were restless, eager for Emily to get going. She stepped to her car, started to climb in.

"Oh, Emily, wait," Bernwhaite said, hurrying back to Teddy's truck. "There's one more thing." He opened the door and in the driver's seat, small and lonely, dwarfed by the big steering wheel looming over his head, sat an elderly Mr. Binky.

Emily was delighted. "It's Mr. Binky! Our Mr. Binky! Oh! I haven't seen him in years!"

"Yeah," Bernwhaite smiled. "Teddy brought him here, must a' been ten years ago, right around the time he rescued the two pups. And I think after the truck came into the lot the four of them liked to take their imaginary rides together."

"Four of them?" Emily asked.

"Yeah, you know, Teddy, Barker, Sleeper, and that little stuffed bear."

Emily smiled at the image of the four friends in the truck, pretending to drive around town. She picked up the old bear and hugged him, giving flight to a million sweet memories and a few more tears. "I guess you'll just have to come home with me, Mr. Binky," she told the little bear. He did not object to that.

Bernwhaite and Emily said goodbye, their lives seeming to separate at that moment but, in fact, coming together in a new friendship. They shook hands, smiled, not knowing what more to say. Bernwhaite felt that 'speck o' dust' in his eye again. Emily hugged him. "Thank you, Karl," she whispered. "Thank you for everything."

Emily climbed into her car and set Mr. Binky on the seat next to her. Barker and Sleeper sniffed and nuzzled the little bear, wagging their tails, greeting an old friend. Emily waved to Bernwhaite, and drove slowly out through the open gates, not knowing that her tires were erasing the remaining faint lines of perfect arcs in the dust that Teddy had made not very long ago. *"Wings,"* Bernwhaite thought, remembering. *"Big wings."*

He watched Emily go down the street and when she turned the corner, he saw Barker and Sleeper poking their noses out the window sniffing the air, enjoying the breeze and the new scents they were discovering on their way to their new home.

"So long, little guys," he whispered. "I'll come see you."

He stared at the empty corner for a moment, watching a little whirlwind of dust fade away. Then he turned, walked slowly back toward his office. He stopped to look at Teddy's truck, at Teddy's "office" in the big packing case, and at the doghouse that Teddy had painted like a circus tent. He stood there for a long time, remembering.

Finally, he sighed, feeling his sadness, his fatigue, an old man confronting his 79 years. Taking another look around, he carefully picked up Teddy's painting of the car crusher, stepped into his now silent and lonely office, and said, "Damn, Teddy. We're sure gonna' miss you around here."

Epilogue

On Tuesday, November 16, 1976, Teddy's funeral was to be a small family gathering. But Bernwhaite, Marcie, Archie, Pete, Doc Wharton and *Dokkerdee*, Mr. Streppone, Debbie, Miss Jane, and Teddy's house mates came. So many of Bernwhaite's customers came to pay their respects that the motorcade to the cemetery numbered thirty vehicles, and anyone seeing that long, slow procession led by Nyack's police cruiser with its red and blue lights flashing must have thought, "There goes somebody important, somebody *really, really* important."

Early the next year, true to her promise to bring recognition to Teddy's art, Emily arranged several exhibitions in Rockland County. The paintings generated excitement over this new-found local artist, especially after the Nyack *Journal News* ran a special edition featuring Teddy and his art.

In her studio Emily made color folios of Teddy's 83 paintings, with notes about each, and framed several large prints of Teddy's most interesting paintings.

Connie and Emily kept four paintings, gave the car-crusher to Bernwhaite, another to the Whartons, and two to the Nyack Library for permanent exhibit. That summer Emily organized a committee of local artists and business owners to arrange a charity auction at the Country Club. Several hundred items were donated by the public for auction. The featured items were Teddy's 75 remaining paintings, twenty framed prints, and a dozen of Emily's folios. The auction was a great success, generating $25,000 (about $135,000 in 2025) to support programs for special-needs children. Teddy's art alone brought in $19,000 ($90,000 in 2025).

A Final Note—January 2025

A supremacist world view, its cruelty ranged throughout history, remains embedded in our world indelibly and powerfully, even in our own nation.

I am superior to you: therefore, I have rightful dominion over you!

Supremacist attacks can be large-scale: an ethnic group, one religious sect against another, half of a country oppressed by Jim Crow laws, or a virulent political party warring against darker-skinned immigrants and asylum-seekers.[1]

Genocides are large-scale supremacist attacks: our 19th-century campaign to exterminate Native Americans, Germany's 20th-century Holocaust, and Russia's 21st-century invasion of Ukraine. History is filled with supremacist-driven genocides.

Supremacism also drives attacks on individual targets: each police killing of an unarmed Black man, each violent attack on an LGBT person, each derisive word hurled at "foreigners" and those with disabilities, each bully proclaiming superiority over his victim.[2] Whatever the scale, large or small, they all claim *I am superior to you!*

And they continue; every-day incidents, powered by fear, hate and cruelty.

About The Author

ANTHONY M. GRAZIANO, Ph.D., is Professor Emeritus, State University of New York at Buffalo. He holds degrees from Columbia, Michigan State, and Purdue Universities, a Clinical Psychology internship, and a post-doctoral fellowship in Child Clinical Psychology.

His academic and clinical career includes university teaching, psychological research, and clinical treatment of children with psychological and/or developmental disorders. From 1960 to 1969, critical of the psychiatric theories and treatments for children with autism—a condition then little understood—he developed a radically new treatment approach that contrasted sharply with standard psychiatric practice. It was, arguably, the first multi-dimensional behavior modification program of treatment and education for children with autism and other developmental disabilities. The program included his "programmed relaxation" procedures to teach emotional self-control to children with autism.[1] Over the years he refined and extended those procedures to other groups of children.

Graziano was one of many young psychologists in the 1960s and later who explored the clinical application of behavioral theory as an alternative to traditional psychiatric treatment. His challenge to psychiatric orthodoxy created a decade of local professional controversy. That program and the controversy it stirred is detailed in *Child Without Tomorrow* (1974) and in several articles.[2]

Among many clinical research projects, he created and tested methods of at-home training of parents and children in psychological self-control procedures to eliminate severe childhood phobias and disruptive family problems.[3]

In 1993 he received a Guggenheim award for his research on the prevalence of parents' use of physical punishment in childrearing.[4] (He is opposed to any physical punishment of children.)

Graziano's writing includes 24 books, numerous laboratory manuals and instructional CDs, a hundred conference presentations and professional journal articles, and dozens of newspaper and magazine articles. *Research Methods*, a textbook of scientific research[5] co-authored with his long-time colleague and friend, Michael Raulin,[6] has been adopted in college courses for over 30 years.

Three of his recent books are for general readership. *La Bell' America* (2009) is a family retrospective and discussion of Italian immigration in the early 20th century.[7] *McKinley's Ghost and the Little Tin Truck* (2016) is a novel about a farm family in the 1920s, a decade that foreshadowed the ethical, political and social corruption that consumes the United States today. *Teddy's World* continues his interest in family and cultural issues. The three books are set in the Hudson River town of Nyack, New York, and he thinks of them as his "Nyack Trilogy."

Graziano enjoys painting, operas, history books, science-fiction, and detective novels, roaming the Chautauqua woodlands, and preparing elaborate Italian meals for family and friends. He plays chess, tennis, and poker—"none of them too well," he admits. At 93, he continues writing and adding to a list of books and articles to be written.

"Over many decades," he says, "I have happily lost myself in construction projects, like renovating two old country homes and their surrounding acres. Digging in the ground, planting trees, clearing fields, working cement, laying up bricks and concrete blocks, hammering, sawing, building up or knocking down walls and building things like patios, porches, kitchens, bathrooms, fireplaces, and chimneys, keeps one young or, perhaps, just too busy to notice the years creeping up."

In 1957 he and Sheila Ginsberg, a fellow graduate student, married. Sheila became an attorney representing clients in sex discrimination cases. They have three children and three grandchildren whom they brag about at every opportunity.

"And" he adds, "over the years, numerous homeless dogs, lost cats, a little snake named Elmer, several orphaned gerbils and one forlorn little hamster also joined our family."

Endnotes

Chapter One

1. In the early 1950s television was new, screens were small, and the black and white images flickered, wavered, faded in and out, as if in a snowstorm.

2. "A-OK" was a popular expression in the 1950s, perhaps because of its use in the space program.

Chapter Two

1. The song "A Tisket, a Tasket," composed in 1938 by jazz singer Ella Fitzgerald and songwriter Al Feldman, was based on a nursery rhyme and children's game from the 18$^{th.}$ century or earlier. Fitzgerald and Feldman composed the music and altered the lyrics but stayed faithful to the original storyline. Fitzgerald's 1938 recording is an American jazz standard.

2. In the 1930s the Chrysler Corporation developed the first streamlined automobile, the Chrysler *Airflow*. Inspired by new aircraft designs, Chrysler employed Orville Wright to evaluate wind-tunnel testing of the design. Superior to other cars, it was a commercial failure and was discontinued in 1938, a radical concept far ahead of its time. A few remained on the road in the 1950s.

Chapter Three

1. In Greek mythology when Pegasus, the gods' flying horse, first struck a hoof on earth, a fountain of water gushed from the ground. The symbolism for striking oil was too much to resist and Pegasus,

painted bright red, has been the advertising image for the Mobil Oil company since 1911.

Chapter Four

1. A cigarette burns at 900 degrees C (1800 degrees F). Each cigarette is a tiny factory producing a thousand chemical compounds, many of which are carcinogenic, including formaldehyde (embalming fluid), arsenic, and lead.

2. In the 1950s radio, television, movies, newspapers, and magazines celebrated smoking. Tobacco companies advertised furiously to addict ever-younger children, gatherings were clouded with enough cigarette smoke to make eyes weep and lungs spasm. Waiting rooms and church steps were littered with smoking's detritus. Careless smokers were burned to crispy lumps in their beds; homes and forests were destroyed.

Over 40% of U.S. adults were regular smokers. Americans lived in an insane culture of tobacco addiction. In 1900 women did not smoke, and per capita annual consumption by U.S. males was 54 cigarettes, about one cigarette a week. By 1960 annual consumption by men and women peaked at 4,171 cigarettes per capita, about 80 a week, decreasing to 1,078 in 2015, about 40 a week, where it had been in the mid-1930s. In 2015, 265 billion cigarettes were consumed in the United States. In 2022 there remained 49 million adult U.S. smokers. The highest consumption states were West Virginia, Kentucky, Louisiana, and Tennessee.

The growing scientific evidence of tobacco's dangers was neutralized by the tobacco industry's decades of lying, suppressing, and distorting scientific information. In the 1950s we loved our cigarettes and embraced the industry's lies. Televised anti-smoking segments began in 1967, required by the Federal Communications Commission.

Chapter Five

1. The Second World War opened on September 1, 1939, with the invasion of Poland by Germany and Russia. The United States

was neutral until the December 7, 1941, Japanese attack on the U.S. naval station at Pearl Harbor. Germany surrendered on May 7,1945; Japan on September 2, 1945, after Hiroshima and Nagasaki were destroyed by a single atom bomb on each city, killing more than 200,000 people. Emperor Hirohito announced Japan's surrender in the face of the unimagined devastation by "a new and most cruel bomb." Tens of thousands more died from radiation poisoning. The "Nuclear Age" had opened. WW II caused an estimated 20 million military and 40 million civilian deaths. The Allies' suffered 85% of the deaths, the Axis, 15%. The difference is due to the large scale killing of civilians by Germany and Japan.

Chapter Seven

1. "Idiot" and "Imbecile" were not pejorative in the early 20th century (Jirik, 2019; Trent, 1994). In the 19th century, *feebleminded* meant persons of low intelligence. By the late 20th century, it was replaced by *mental deficiency*, *mental retardation*, and *intellectual disability*. The common terms M*ongolism*, *Mongoloid* and *Mongolian Idiot* were replaced by *Down Syndrome.*

2. Francis Galton (1822-1911) coined the term "eugenics"—meaning "well-born"—for his proposed new science aimed at elevating humanity by controlling and accelerating evolution. This would be done by encouraging propagation of the "most fit" and discouraging it in the "least fit." (See Galton, 1904.)

3. In the early 20th century, the eugenics movement swept through the country. The Eugenics Records Office (ERO) opened 1910 in Cold Springs Harbor, N.Y., funded by the Carnegie Foundation to conduct research in eugenics. In 1939, the Carnegie Foundation, after reviewing ERO's three decades of genetic research and public campaigns, concluded that eugenics was "without scientific merit," withdrew its support, and ERO closed. See: Stern (2005). *Eugenic Nation: Faults and Frontiers of Better Breeding in Modern America;* D'Antonio: (1957). *The State Boys Rebellion*; Lombardo (2011). *A*

Century of Eugenics in America: From the Indiana Experiment to the Genome Project.

4. *The Black Stork* is a 1917 silent film promoting eugenics in the U.S., authored by Hearst journalist Jack Lait, produced by The Wharton Studios in Ithaca, N. Y. Dr. Harry Haiselden—the country's foremost proponent of euthanasia for severely disabled babies—was co-author and leading actor. It was re-released in 1927 with the new title *Are You Fit to Marry?* and continued showing until 1945. In 1941 Joseph Goebbels' Nazi Propaganda Ministry produced a film with the same message of eliminating "defectives" in order to preserve the integrity of the Aryan blood, entitled *Ich klage an (I Accuse).* See: Taylor (2016). *The Black Stork: Eugenics Goes to the Movies;* Archibald (2022). *The curious and tragic case of Dr. Haiselden and the Baby Bollinger;* Pernick (1996). *The Black Stork: Eugenics and the Death of "Defective Babies" in American Medicine and Motion Pictures Since1915.* Note: *The Black Stork* can be viewed on YouTube.

5. The *sanctity of life,* the proposition that human life is sacred is an ancient Christian and Hebrew idea. *Euthanasia* is another ancient idea that under some conditions human life may morally be deliberately ended.

6. See Orr, et al. (1997). "Use of the Hippocratic oath: A review of twentieth century practice."

7. See Dowbiggin (2005). *A Concise History of Euthanasia;* Dowbiggin (2003). *A Merciful End: The Euthanasia Movement in Modern America.*

8. Anencephaly (*without a brain*) is an extreme developmental defect in about 1/10,000 births (compared with 1/700 births for Down Syndrome). In most cases both cerebral hemispheres, top of the skull and skin have failed to develop. Most do not survive beyond a few hours. (Graziano, 2002. *Developmental Disabilities: Introduction to a Diverse Field.)*

9. Clarence Darrow commented on Dr. Harry Haiselden's role in the 1915 "Baby Bollinger" case, as reported in the *Washington Post*, November 18, 1915: "Chloroform unfit children. Show them the same mercy that is shown beasts that are no longer fit to live."

The baby, John Bollinger, was born with multiple severe deformities. Haiselden, the hospital's chief surgeon, determined the baby was too deformed for a meaningful life and should be left to die. Five days later Baby Bollinger, without treatment or nutrition, died of starvation. Haiselden became a major proponent of eugenics and for euthanizing deformed children.

Chapter Eight

1. *There but for the grace of God go I.* This phrase expresses compassion and relief in view of another's misfortune. It is attributed to various people, mainly to John Bradford (1510-1555) who, observing a group of condemned prisoners being led to their execution, supposedly said, "There but for the grace of God goes John Bradford." Perhaps he was paraphrasing Corinthians 15:10 (KJV, "But by the grace of God I am what I am …") Bradford was burned at the stake in 1555 for heresy during the four-year reign of Mary Tudor—called "Bloody Mary" for the 400 people she ordered burned alive for heresy.

Chapter Nine

1. At Teddy's birth in 1938, physicians and society in general believed that "feebleminded" children should be given up for lifetime institutionalization. The most influential child-care book of all time, Benjamin Spock's *The Common-Sense Book of Baby and Child Care*, first published in 1946 when Teddy was 8 years old, helped spread that message: "If (the baby) merely exists at a level that is hardly human, it is much better for the other children and the parents to have him cared for elsewhere." That advice was still given to parents by physicians as late as the 1980s (see Stumbo, 2019).

Chapter Ten

1. The 2023 rate of Down Syndrome births was 1/700 births (See CDC, *Data and Statistics;* de Graaf, Buckley, Skotko, 2017.) In the 1920s and 1930s, life expectancy of a Mongoloid child was about 9 years, with intellectual deficiency and severe physical problems including congenital heart defects, respiratory disorders, and childhood leukemia. By 2023, with improved infant care and medical treatment, enlightened expectations, better social support, education, and guidance, life quality for Down Syndrome has improved and life expectancy increased to nearly 60 years (National Association for Down syndrome).

Chapter Eleven

1. In 1972, a half century after Alice Paul and Crystal Eastman's proposal, the Equal Rights Amendment (ERA) passed both houses of Congress and was sent to the states for ratification. Opposition by Republicans and labor unions slowed its progress. By January 2023, more than a century since its introduction, the ERA had been ratified by the required 38 states. But opposition to the final step—Congressional certification—continues. As of 2025, 105 years after it was introduced in Congress, it remains to be seen if Paul and Eastman's 1920 proposal will ever become the 28th amendment to the Constitution, despite President Biden's declaration at the end of his term that the ERA is now "the law of the land."

2. Since 1872 many women have sought nomination for U.S. president and vice president, and many have been successfully nominated by political parties. It was not until the 20th century that women were nominated by a major political party. In 1984 Geraldine Ferraro (Democrat) ran for the vice presidency but lost. Sarah Palin (Republican) ran for the vice presidency in 2008 but lost. Kamala Harris (Democrat) ran successfully for the vice presidency in 2020, becoming the first female U.S. vice president. Only two women have run for the presidency on a major party ticket,

both Democrats, and both lost to Donald Trump: Hillary Clinton in 2016 and Kamala Harris in 2024

Chapter Twelve

1. The Second World War began on September 1, 1939, with the German invasion of Poland, followed on September 17 by the Russian invasion of Poland, based on the Nazi-Soviet non-aggression pact of August 1939. The lead-up to World War II had been seething for twenty years in Germany's humiliation over their defeat in WWI and the German people's drive for revenge. The rise of Italian and German fascism, the Spanish civil war, Russia's communism, Japan's aggression in the Pacific, and growing worldwide tensions all led to the war.

2. Germany and Russia used modified buses and trucks to pump engine exhaust into hermetically sealed passenger compartments, efficiently killing people in about ten minutes as the engine idled. At first used in the late-1930s German eugenics program to kill feebleminded children and adults, the mobile gas chambers later were used to kill Jews, Romas, Poles, and others. It is estimated that more than 100,000 people were killed in the *Gaswagens.* See Naimark (2010). *Stalin's Genocides;* Friedlander, H. *The Origins of Nazi Genocide: From Euthanasia to the Final Solution*; Bartlet K. (2018). *Architects of death; the family who engineered the death camps*; Browning, C. (2003) Initiating the final solution.

3. The goals and methods of eugenics were supported by many Americans, including: Luther Burbank, Alexander Graham Bell, Henry Ford, Helen Keller, Margaret Sanger, Theodore Roosevelt, Woodrow Wilson, Warren Harding. See: Lombardo (2011). *A Century of Eugenics in America: From the Indiana Experiment to the Genome Project;* Stern (2005). *Eugenic Nation: Faults and Frontiers of Better Breeding.*

The American eugenics movement influenced German leaders, helping to fuel the Nazis' eugenics-based "racial cleansing" program. German death camps were discovered and liberated in 1944 and

1945. At Bergen-Belsen 60,000 emaciated, barely living prisoners were found; 13,000 were so ill they died even as they were being liberated; another 13,000 decaying corpses littered the area. See: United States Holocaust Memorial Museum (2019). *Liberation of Bergin-Belsen*; Bartlett (2018). *Architects of Death.*

4. Early on Sunday morning December 7, 1941, the Japanese repeated a tactic they had used successfully against Russia 36 years earlier. Without warning, while in peace negotiations with the U.S., Japan launched a massive naval and air attack on Pearl Harbor, destroying the U.S. base, sinking much of the U.S. navy, and killing more than 2,300 civilians and military personnel. President Roosevelt called on Congress to declare war on Japan. The attack on Pearl Harbor was also modeled after the successful British raid a year earlier (November 11, 1940) on the Italian navy moored in the port of Taranto—21 torpedo bombers were launched from an aircraft carrier in the Mediterranean, causing severe losses to the Italian navy. That highly successful surprise attack by the English navy was the world's first aircraft-carrier-based air attack, combining naval and air force units. The Japanese studied the British tactic, saw the parallels with Pearl Harbor—while the U. S. military and Intelligence services did not—and based their Pearl Harbor raid on it. That novel tactic changed forever the nature of warfare.

5. In the United States the consensual age for marriage and sex is set by states. Prior to 1900 it ranged by state from age 7 to 12; by 1920, 14 to 18; today it is 16 to 18 years. Exceptions make younger ages possible. See La Barge (2013).

6. By 1900 20% of children, many under the age of 10, worked in factories, mines, mills, farms, home workshops, in domestic service, in street trades and other occupations. See Schuman (2017).

7. Cat O' Nine Tails is a leather whip with a single handle from which extend several leather straps with a hard leather knob on each tip. As a youngster in the 1930s the author had a friend who was whipped by his grandmother with a Cat O' Nine Tails.

8. For discussions of the Better Babies movement see: Gerais (2017); Oveyssi (2015); Pernick (2002); Seldon (2005); Stern (2002); Uenuma (2019).

Chapter Thirteen

1. Just before and after World War I, U.S. immigration and internal migration caused a surplus of labor in northern states creating severe employment and housing competition. More than a million Black Americans, including former slaves and their descendants, fled north and west, escaping the South's Jim Crow segregation and seeking jobs in the North. (See Lemann, 1991. *The Promised Land: The Great Black Migration and How It Changed America.*)

2. By the mid-1920s millions of European and Asian immigrants had "invaded" the country. Americans saw them as having crude and unclean habits, shocking lifestyles, a propensity for drunkenness, violent crime, and "reproducing like rabbits." Bolstered by the eugenics wave, anti-immigrant sentiment soared in the 1920s, resulting in the 1924 Johnson-Reed Act that sharply limited immigration from some European countries (Italians and Poles were particularly targeted) and ended all immigration from Asia.

3. In the First World War 380,000 Black Americans served in the military, all in racially segregated units. Most were assigned to support duties (e.g. chauffeuring, kitchen duties, officer valets, janitorial and burial details) and saw no combat because the high command had no confidence in the discipline or bravery of Black men. One all-Black unit, however, the *Harlem Hell Fighters,* (369th Infantry Regiment) was assigned to combat and fought with outstanding bravery and success equal to that of the best all-White units.

4. "I'm free, White, and twenty-one!" was a common boast of young men and women for over a hundred years, into the 1970s, in everyday conversations and motion pictures. It was the ultimate statement of White privilege, superiority, and White entitlement. "Free" may be a reference to slavery or to being unencumbered by relationships

like marriage. "White," suggested a privileged social position. (The author recalls, when growing up in the 1930s and 1940s, hearing the comment frequently in daily conversations and even trying it out a few times himself.) It was so offensive that it was eventually banned from motion pictures and died out in general use, its demise spurred by the civil rights movement of the 1960s.

The boast may have originated as a statement of White voting privileges. In 1828, when there were four million enslaved people in the country, the phrase gained legal meaning when the voting requirement of property ownership was dropped, leaving the right to vote to free, White males of at least twenty-one years of age.

(There is a fascinating montage of motion picture clips on YouTube. See Jezebel, Free White and 21, YouTube.) Also see: Heisel, Andrew (2015). The Rise and Fall of an All-American Catch Phrase: "Free, White, and twenty-one."

5. From 1900 into the 1920s many erroneously-named "Black riots" erupted. Nearly all were White rioters murdering Black citizens. Massacres occurred in: Atlanta; Chicago; East St. Louis; Ocoee, Florida; Rosewood, Florida; Springfield, Illinois; Tulsa, Oklahoma. Igniting the White riots were rumors of Black men raping White women, conflicts over jobs and, in Ocoee, Florida, the rumor that a Black man had tried to register to vote. More than 500 Black men, women and children were murdered as well as about 50 White rioters. (See Black, 2003; Dray, 2002; Ellsworth, 1992; Hirsch, 2002; Madigan, 2001; McWhirter, 2012.)

Black persons and others were lynched by White mobs singly or in small numbers. A total of 4,743 men women and children (3,446 Black) were lynched in the U.S. from 1882 to 1968 (See Tuskegee University, 2016), an average of more than one a week for 80 years. (See, DeLucia, 2003; Dray, 2002; Tuskegee University, 2003.)

Blacks were not the only victims of massacres; other ethnic groups (e.g., Chinese, Mexican, Italian, Native Americans) were also killed by White gangs and, in some cases, by police units.

6. On May 31,1921, in Tulsa, Oklahoma a rumor spread that a Black man raped a White girl in an elevator. It was false, even the supposed victim denied it. A young Black man was arrested but released when the police found it had not happened. But the rumor was enough; gangs of enraged White men, many deputized, armed and encouraged by Oklahoma officials swarmed into the prosperous Black district of Greenwood, known as "Black Wall Street." For two days they chased, dragged, clubbed, slashed, and shot Black residents, looted, and burned their homes, stores, banks, schools, and workplaces. In war surplus airplanes they bombed neighborhoods and shot fleeing people. Some Black war veterans fought back and were arrested for rioting. Police rounded up more than 6,000 Black residents. Thirty-two deaths were officially acknowledged but more than 300 were suspected. More than 800 people were admitted to hospitals, ten thousand Black men, women, and children were driven out of Greenwood, losing everything but the clothes they wore. The White mobs destroyed over 30 million dollars of property (in 2024 dollars) leaving a smoldering wasteland of 40 square blocks of once peaceful and prosperous Black neighborhoods. Only the Black "rioters" had been arrested. Officials and journalists reported that the Black residents had rioted and destroyed their own neighborhoods.

For 75 years, Oklahoma officials blocked investigations. But in 1996 the state legislature began investigating, concluding in 2001 that Tulsa officials and White mobs had conspired in the massacre.

On the 100th anniversary of the massacre, June 1, 2021, President Joe Biden was the first and only sitting president to visit the site. He said, "For much too long, the history of what took place here was told in silence, cloaked in darkness…while darkness can hide much, it erases nothing … Some injustices are so heinous, so horrific, so grievous, they can't be buried, no matter how hard people try." (See Rascoe & Wise, 2021.)

Chapter Fifteen

1. The 1928 U.S. population was 120,000,000.

2. Herbert Hoover. Acceptance speech for the Republican presidential nomination. August 11, 1928, Palo Alto, California.

3. See Alston (1983). The post-war U.S. farm depression began in the early 1920s, long before the rest of the nation realized what was happening to the working classes. Farm income plunged, farmers defaulted on loans and lost their farms. Many small banks failed and the economic situations for farms and banks worsened. Farmers who had owned their land became tenants or unemployed and fell into poverty. Before1920 annual farm foreclosure was about 3.2%; in 1933 it reached 39%. From 1929 to 1932 farm income dropped by 60%. In 1933 alone, nearly a quarter million U.S. farms were foreclosed. President Hoover created the Farm Bureau to deal with the problem but allocated insufficient money and his program failed. It was left to President Roosevelt to create effective farm programs. Farmers had felt the deep sting of economic depression nearly a decade before anyone else. In those ten years, three successive Republican administrations (Harding, Coolidge, Hoover) did little to help the farmers.

4. Hoover, H. (1929). Message Regarding Black Thursday. Transcript: UVA Miller Center; Presidential Speeches. https://millercenter.org/the-presidency/presidential-speeches/october-25-1929-message-regarding-black-thursday.

5. See McElvaine (1993). *The Great Depression: America, 1929-1941;* Wilson (1975). *Herbert Hoover: Forgotten Progressive;* Smith (1970). *The Shattered Dream: Herbert Hoover and the Great Depression.*

6. Comments by Hoover and other Republicans infuriated people. Hoover said: "Nobody is actually starving. The hoboes are better fed than they ever were." (See Smith & Wallach 2004, *The ordeal of Herbert Hoover.*) Hoover's Secretary of the Interior, Ray Wilbur, was booed for saying the depression might be "good" for adolescents,

teaching them to stay at home, get closer to their families and rely on themselves.

Chapter Sixteen

1. A century of labor struggles around the world preceded the first U.S. minimum wage law, enacted by Massachusetts in 1912. Several states followed. But in 1923 the Supreme Court ruled the Massachusetts' minimum wage law violated the Constitution's Fifth Amendment, thus invalidating all the state minimum wage laws in the country. Over the next 10 years workers had no guarantee of a stable minimum wage. In 1933 FDR and the Democrats provided that wage guarantee passing the National Recovery Act which included labor reforms and encouraged industries to set wage standards. Many states then re-instituted minimum wage laws.

In 1935, the Supreme Court again struck down minimum wage laws setting off a political conflict over labor rights and welfare, pitting Republicans against Democrats. Two years later, in 1937, the Supreme Court, then with a Democratic majority, reversed itself with a narrow 5-4 decision upholding federal minimum wage laws.

Then, in 1938, Congress proposed 40 cents an hour minimum industrial wage. But, facing opposition from southern states and Republicans, Congress scaled it back in order to get *any* minimum wage legislation passed, and in 1938 set the minimum wage at twenty-five cents an hour.

2. Following Germany's defeat in World War I, Kaiser Wilhelm II ran off to Holland. A constitutional federal republic (Weimar Republic, 1918-1932) was formed. Relentlessly attacked by Nazis and other anti-democracy groups, the German experiment in democracy died in 1933 when Hitler took power.

3. Austria-Hungary declared war against Serbia on July 28, 1914. On August 1 and 3, Austria's ally, Germany, declared war on Russia and France. The next day, Britain declared war on Germany, and the First World War was on.

4. In Munich in February 1920, Hitler and the new Nazi party announced their 25-point platform specifying their goals for Germany, including:

"Only a member of the race can be a citizen. A member of the race can only be one who is of German blood ... Consequently, no Jew can be a member of the race."

"If it is impossible to sustain the total population of the State, then the members of foreign nations (non-citizens) are to be expelled from the Reich."

"Any further immigration of non-citizens is to be prevented. We demand that all non-Germans, who have immigrated to Germany since August 1914, be forced immediately to leave the Reich. (See: United States Holocaust Memorial Museum, 2022.)

5. As Sophie Krivitz had hoped in 1935, Hitler did fail, committing suicide on April 30, 1945. But while in power (1932-1945) Hitler led the Germans to world-wide destruction and murder of four-to-six million people in one of history's greatest waves of destruction, atrocities and mass murder. (See, Evans, R. (2009). *The Third Reich at War;* Goldhagen, D. (1996). *Hitler's Willing Executioners: Ordinary Germans and the Holocaust*; Kershaw, I. (2000). Hitler: 1889-1936. Vol. I Hubris I; Kershaw, I. (2000). Hitler:1936-1945. Vol. II Nemesis II; Koenigsberg, R. (1975). *Hitler's ideology: A study* in *Psychoanalytic Sociology*; Koenigsberg, R. (2000). Review essay of the Nazi doctors; Kuhl, S. (2001). The Nazi connection: Eugenics, racism and German National Socialism; Lifton, R. J. (1986). *German doctors and the final solution*; Lifton, R. J. (2000). *The Nazi Doctors: Medical killing and the Psychology of Genocide;* Ross, A. (2018). *How American Racism influenced Hitler;* Shirer, W. (1960). *The Rise and Fall of the Third Reich.*

6. In the 1920s there were thousands of Nazi supporters in the United States and several large Nazi groups and business collaborators. For example, Ford and GM subsidiaries are alleged to have produced military vehicles for the Nazi regime in WW II. See:

Dobbs (1998). *Ford and GM scrutinized for Alleged Nazi collaboration.* Diamond, S. (1974). *The Nazi Movement in the United States;* Hart, B. W. (2018). *Hitler's American Friends: The Third Reich's Supporters in the United States;* Hull, K. (2021). *The Machine has a Soul: Sympathy with Italian Fascism*; Lee, A. (1980). *Henry Ford and the Jews*; Rudin, A. J. (2014). *The Dark Legacy of Henry Ford's Anti-Semitism;* Silverstein, K. (2000). Ford and the Fuhrer; Whitman, J. O. (2017). *Hitler's American Model: The United States and the Making of the Nazi Race Law.*

7. The phrase, "make (our country) great again," is a common slogan used by political campaigners. Hitler and other authoritarian leaders have used the phrase, but it is not exclusive to them, and has been used by Barry Goldwater, Ronald Reagan, Bill Clinton, and Donald Trump. Trump was so enamored of the phrase *Make America Great Again* that in 2015 he had it registered by the U.S. Patent and Trademark office for his exclusive use. The slogan is imprecise and virtually meaningless, but Trump's "MAGA" is one of the most successful campaign slogans in U.S. history.

8. Are some social trends in the United States converging toward a "superior" class of people to control the country? See: Black, E. (2003) *War against the Weak: Eugenics and America's campaign to Create a Master Race.*

9. In the 1920s and 1930s many Americans supported euthanizing children with disabilities. (See: Archbald, 2022; Black, 2003; Dowbiggin, 2003, 2005; Lombardo, 2011, 2022; Pennick,1996; Taylor, 2016.) Some children were euthanized but it was the Germans who developed the largest and most efficient child-killing program, *Aktion T-4* disposing of 150,000 "defective" children from 1939 to the war's end in 1945. The aim was to cleanse Germany of people who were of no value, who did not deserve to live. Atkion T-4 began by killing defective newborns, then older children in institutions and to adults. Some 300,000 children and adults were killed. Aktion T-4 was a "testing ground," for technical developments such

as efficient gas chambers later used in Germany's holocaust, killing over 4 million Jews and others.

The Weimar Republic (1919 to 1933, Germany's brief postwar democracy) had initiated sterilizing and institutionalizing of 'defective' children. But later, under Hitler's direction, it was more cost effective to kill the children. Psychiatrists selected children to be killed by marking a box on a standard form. Transported by bus from hospital wards and homes to the "special clinics," the unsuspecting children were welcomed by nurses who then killed them by physical abuse, starvation, gassing in special "showers," or injecting them with lethal chemicals. The children's brains were removed and preserved for later study (Weindling, et al, 2021; Weindling, 2006; Blakemore, 2017.) Parents received a small urn of ashes from a common ash pit and were told their child had died of "natural causes" (U.S. Holocaust Museum, 2021).

There is a heart-wrenching photograph of a crying 4-year-old Richard Jenne—the last child killed in the program—being restrained by Head Nurse Sister Worle, possibly as she was killing him by lethal injection on May 29, 1945, at the Kaufbeuren-Irsee child-killing facility in Bavaria. Sister Worle admitted to having personally killed "at least" 211 children. An estimated 150,000 children were killed in the euthanasia centers. See: Nichols (2005). *Cruel World: The Children of Europe in the Nazi Web*; U.S. Holocaust Memorial Museum (2021); Perry, (accessed 2024) The Nazi euthanasia program that killed 300,000.

Aktion T-4 was driven by Hitler's obsession with Jews and "defectives" being "disease within the body of the people," "poisoning our blood," like viruses or bacteria which must be removed for the health of the "national body." See Koenigsberg (2000). Review essay of the Nazi doctors; Kuhl (2001). *The Nazi Connection: Eugenics, Racism, and German National Socialism*.

There is a large literature on Aktion T-4, e.g., AHRP (2024). Medicalized mass murder; Kaelber, L. (2012). *Child Murder in Nazi Germany: The memory of Nazi medical crimes and commemoration of children's euthanasia victims at two facilities*; Nichols, N. H. (2005).

Cruel World: The Children of Europe in the Nazi Web; Ost, S. (2006). *Doctors and Nurses of Death: A case study of Eugenically motivated killing under the Nazi euthanasia programme;* Rotzoll, M., et. al. (2006). *The first National Socialist extermination crime: The T-4 program and its victims.* Sereny (1983). *An Examination of Conscience*; U.S. Holocaust Memorial Museum (2021). Euthanasia Program and Aktion T-4.

10. Europeans "discovered" the American Continent and waged a 400-year war on Native Americans that has been called "the worst human holocaust the world has ever witnessed," "the greatest sustained loss of human life in history, a genocidal slaughter, a war of extermination. (See: Stannard, 1992; Alvarez, 2015; Woolford et al, 2014; Hine, et al, 2017; Ostler, 2015.) Some estimate that one hundred million Native Americans were killed throughout the continent including thirteen million in what is now the United States (Smith, 2017). Smallpox, measles, and typhus devastated the natives who had no natural immunity to the European pestilence. (See: Anderson, 2005; Lindsay, 2012; Madley, 2016; Norton, 1979; Thornton, 1990; Saurman, 2012).

The U.S. Cavalry and gangs of ranchers, farmers, and hunters massacred entire native villages down to the last child. Forced relocation of tribes brought starvation, sickness, and death (Flavelle, 2021). They were wars of extermination: "… a war of extinction will continue to be waged between the races, until the Indian race is extinct (California Governor Peter Burnett, 1851).

Killing Native Americans, seizing their land, destroying their governments and religion, forcing them into isolated, barely habitable reservations, was not enough, and the Canadian and U.S. governments partnered with Catholic and Protestant churches in more than a century-long campaign to destroy what remained of Native American culture. They forced an estimated 150,000 indigenous children from their families to distant government-church Indian schools. Their goal: to civilize and 'Christianize' the savages; to "kill the Indian in the child" to destroy their cultural futures and to train the children to become docile laundresses, maids, and manual laborers (Pratt, 1892.)

An early morning knock on the door.
The police, a social worker, or a priest.
Sometimes, all three.
"It is time!" they say. "Come!"
And they take away your children.
There is nothing you can do about it.
It is the law!
The government bus drives off.
And takes away your children.

The schools had complete control; children had no contact with parents, no champions to monitor their welfare. Parents had neither rights nor power. Many children were never again seen by their families. "They ran away," the parents were told. "We don't know where they are."

Parents asked about their missing children, doctors urged reforms, but the schools were shielded by government power and religious deceit. Most people remained ignorant of those events until the 1980s when distressing reports of the schools began leaking out.

By 2007 some reforms were enacted. But, even as reforms brought some relief, people were not prepared for what exploded in the summer of 2021 when a thousand missing children were found in mass graves. Then the sordid story of virtual kidnapping, abuse and death became known. A 2022 U.S. Government report suggests that child deaths in the U.S. schools might be in the thousands or tens of thousands (Newland 2022; Austen, 2023). As of this writing (2025) some 2,000 child bodies have been unearthed, some have been returned to their families, but most remain unnamed. Even as I write this, a *Washington Post* article has been published (Hedgepeth, et al, 2024) on their year-long investigation. They report many more children died in the Indian schools than have been admitted by the two governments: 4100 children in Canada, and 3100 in the U.S.

The reports of abuse and death continue, and the search for children's graves goes on. (See: Newland, 2022; Austen, 2023; Hedgepeth, et al, 2024).

There is a growing literature on the history, the harm and the attempts to understand what the two governments in partnership with religions did to our Native Americans. (See: Canadian Truth and Reconciliation Commission, 2012, 2015; Bush, 2015; Deer, 2019; Pember, 2021; Horowitz & Austen, 2022.) In 2019 the Anglican Church apologized (Hiltz, 2019).

How can we ever understand the actions of government and religious officials who carried out their intentional destruction of a culture and did so by attacking and abusing the children?

Chapter Seventeen

1. Composed in 1929 by Milton Ager and Jack Yellen, the song "Happy Days are Here Again" was used in several motion pictures, became FDR's theme song in 1932, and a Democratic campaign standard.

2. Indoor bathrooms were rare when the house was built, but "water closets" were appearing, a flush toilet, its copper-lined oak tank high up on the wall at the ceiling, and a long pull-chain for flushing. It was enclosed in a bedroom corner, just large enough for the toilet and a small sink.

Chapter Eighteen

1. In the 1930s and 1940s there were no parenting books about children like Teddy; no support groups and no internet with information, advice, and parent networking. There were few—if any—pediatricians, psychologists, or other professionals ready to help the parents at home. The first comprehensive parenting book for "normal" child rearing was Benjamin Spock's *Baby and Child Care*, 1946, with 50 million copies in ten editions over more than 75 years.

2. In much of the twentieth century the industrial work week was 60-80 hours. Change came after FDR's 1932 election. In 1940 Congress amended the Fair Labor Standards Act, limiting the industrial work week to 40 hours. It took time for some industries to adjust to the mandated limits.

3. In 1944 Frank's annual salary was $3,100.00. The hospital bill, $3,200.00, was staggering, equivalent to $57,000.00 in 2024. There was little health insurance in 1944, no Obama Care, Medicare, employer-based insurance, or assistance for children with disabilities. Families were on their own.

4. The Millers' story is told in Graziano, (2016). *McKinley's Ghost and the Little Tin Truck.*

Chapter Nineteen

1. The title of this chapter is borrowed from the book, *The Spaces Between Us* by Michael Graziano.

2. A popular song, "Doing what comes naturally" by Irving Berlin, sung by Ethel Merman in the 1946 Broadway show, *Annie Get Your Gun*. (Deborah refers to the song two years before it became popular—anything can happen for the sake of the story.)

3. The amount left for the Gardners to pay in 1944 ($320.00) is equivalent to about $6,000.00 in 2025.

4. "Mongolism" acquired a negative, destructive meaning - a "useless sub-human." When applied to a newborn with developmental disabilities it further burdened the child who had an already burdened life. In 1965 the World Health Organization advised replacing the terms Mongoloid, Mongolism and Mongolian Idiot, with *Down Syndrome* in honor of Langdon Down. The old terms dwindled slowly, lingering into the 21st century.

5. To the best of our knowledge, these lines are original in this work. We searched diligently to make a proper citation if it had been published earlier, but could find nothing like it.

Chapter Twenty

1. In the mid-1860s Down discovered and described two conditions, *Mongolism* (now Down Syndrome) and *Polysarcia,* a genetic disorder known since 1956 as Prader-Willi Syndrome. Characteristics of Polysarcia noted by Down: extreme obesity by age 7, insatiable appetite, aggressive food seeking, and marked cognitive impairment. Down's clinical descriptions 150 years ago are accurate today. (See: Black, 1999; Down, 1865.)

2. The treatment of mental patients has a sordid history interrupted at times by brief reform movements. One movement—about 1775-1825–was part of the humanitarian revolution of the late 18th century. Named "moral treatment," it emphasized the dignity and humanity of patients, respectful and kindly treatment in small living units. (See Bockoven, 1963. *Moral treatment in American psychiatry.*) In the 1860s Down, in essence, revived moral treatment. See: Van Robays (2016). *John Langdon Down (1828-1896).* This is an excellent article about Langdon Down and Mary Crellin.

3. The hospital closed in 1997. Today its famous theater is the site of England's Down Syndrome Society.

4. The 1950 UNESCO statement on science, concluded that "race" is a *social construct* with no scientific support. Early 20th century racial science held that the "Caucasian race" is biologically superior to all others, an idea which justified colonialism, wars, slavery, economic and social inequities, even genocide. Modern science holds that humans are biologically a single group. However, belief in "race" remains in the general public and is a major rationale of our supremacist world views.

The "racial science" of the 19th and early 20th centuries developed largely from Christian thought. See Keel (2018) *Divine Variations: How Christian Thought Became Race Science.*

5. World War II did not end Racism and xenophobia; they continue globally and in our own country are growing to an alarming

level of attacks on women, ethnic minorities, LGBT, the disabled, immigrants, and other vulnerable targets.

Chapter Twenty-One

1. See Tjio & Levan (1956). For a history of research, see Gartler (2006).

2. This account of Marthe Gautier's work has been drawn from two publications: Gautier & Harper (2009). *Fiftieth anniversary of trisomy 21: Returning to a discovery*; Engel (2013). *Meet Dr. Marthe Gautier: The scientist who discovered trisomy 21*. Also see Benderly (2015). *A Scientist Saint?*

3. The Lejeune foundation has acknowledged that Gautier "contributed to" the discovery but denies Gautier's account. The Foundation has presented its evidence of Lejeune's claim of the discovery—handwritten laboratory notes and personal letters between Gautier and Lejeune.

Given current ethical standards for acknowledgement of scientific work, the views of the scientific community on the trisomy 21 discovery have shifted to recognition of Gautier's primary role. Our reading of the historical record leads us to accept Marthe Gautier, and not Jerome Lejeune, as the discoverer of trisomy 21.

4. Engel (2013). *Meet Dr. Marthe Gautier*; Benderly (2015). *A Scientist Saint?*; Seidel (2022). *Jerome Lejeune, the Saint who Stole the Scientific Spotlight*.

5. Engel (2013). Recognition came late but Marthe Gautier was honored with The French Legion of Honor, 2014, Grand Prize of the French Federation of Human Genetics, 2014, The National Order of Merit, 2018. Dr. Gautier died in Paris on April 30, 2022, at the age of 96 knowing that she had, finally, been recognized for her discovery.

6. Life expectancy in Down syndrome has increased from nine years when Teddy was born in 1938 to nearly 60 years today. With

longevity, aging problems have accelerated particularly in cognitive loss. Alzheimer's disease is earlier and more prevalent in Down syndrome as are other aging issues such as cataracts and cardiac disorders.

Chapter Twenty-Four

1. The Nyack ice pond at 9-W and Route 59 survived into the 1940s. It had been created in 1869 by impounding natural underground springs. Over the next half-century it produced ice, 350 tons a year at its peak. In the winter months the pond was taken over by enthusiastic young ice-skaters but in 1925 a refrigerated ice-producing plant was established in South Nyack, ending the ice-pond's commercial value. The town maintained the pond for ice-skating for the next twenty years, promising never to sell it to commercial interests.

But in the mid-1940s as World War II was ending, the town sold the acreage to developers who filled in the pond. The old ice pond is now a motel and car wash lying in the shadow of a towering New York Throughway, surrounded by traffic on route 59, 9-W, Highland Avenue and Main Street. In our story, however, those acres hold our fictional Bernwhaite's Salvage Company where Teddy worked for twelve years. (For a true history of the ice pond, see Hayes, 2020).

2. Motion-detection security technology was not well-developed then. Equipment was expensive, unreliable, and the tapes difficult to work with. It was a great challenge to Teddy and probably of doubtful value for Bernwhaite.

3. DeSoto automobiles were manufactured by the Chrysler Corporation from 1928 to 1961. Over 2 million were manufactured.

Chapter Twenty-Five

1. The 1953-1956 Ford F-100 pick-up trucks are now collector's dreams, possibly the most sought-after of all pick-up trucks.

A Final Note

1. See: Buchanan, Wolgin & Flores et al (2020). *The Trump Administration's Family Separation Policy is Over;* Vinson (2020). *Family Separation Policy Continues.;* Southern Policy Law Center (2021). *Family separation under the Trump Administration.*

2. Millward (2023). *Fury as Donald Trump Says Immigrants 'Poison Blood of US'*; McAfee, T. (2017). Trump's Mockery of a Disabled Journalist. People.com/politics/trump-denies-mocking-journalist-disabled-watch-video//

About The Author

1. Graziano, Anthony M. & Kean, Jeffrey E. (1968).

2. Graziano, Anthony M. (1972). *Child Without Tomorrow.*

3. Graziano, A.M., De Giovanni, I.S., & Garcia, K. (1979). Behavioral treatment of children's fear: A review.

Graziano, A.M., Mooney, K.C., Huber, C., & Ignasiak, D. (1979). Self-control instructions for children's fear reduction: A multiple case study; Graziano, A.M. & Mooney, K. C. (1980). Family self-control instructions for children's nighttime fear reduction.

4. Graziano, Anthony M. (1993). Guggenheim Foundation research award: *Understanding Family Sub-Abusive Violence Against Children.* Jan—Dec. 1993.

5. Graziano, Anthony M. & Raulin, Michael L. (2021). *Research Methods: A Process of Inquiry. 9th. ed.*

6. Michael L. Raulin, Ph.D., Associate Professor of Psychology, Youngstown State University.

7. Graziano, Anthony M. *La Bell' America.* (2009). Teaticket, MA.: Leapfrog Press; Graziano, Anthony M. (2016). *McKinley's Ghost and the Little Tin Truck.* (2016). Ontario, CA: Guernica Editions.

References

AHRP (2024). 1939-1945 Medicalized mass murder, children first. *Alliance for Human Research Protection*. AHRP.org/1939-1945-medicalized-murder/

Alston, Lee J., (1983) Farm Foreclosures in the United States during the interwar period. *The Journal of Economic History,* Cambridge University Press, vol. 43(4), pages 885-903, December.

Alvarez, Alex (2015). *Native America and the question of genocide.* N.Y.: Roman and Littlefield. ISBN-13: 978-1-442-25646-0

Anderson, Gary C. (2005). *The Conquest of Texas: Ethnic Cleansing in the Promised Land, 1820-1875.* Norman, OK: University of Oklahoma Press. ISBN- 13: 978-0-890-96867-3

Archibald, Matthew (Retrieved 2022). The curious and tragic case of Dr. Haiselden and the Baby Bollinger. *National Catholic. Register.* https://www.ncregister.com/blog/the-curious-and-tragic-case-of-dr-haiselden-and-the-baby-bollinger Retrieved 01/23/2022.

Austen, I. (2023). More evidence of children's graves is found in former Indian school. *N.Y. Times,* Jan. 19, 2023.

Barry, J. M. (2004). *The Great Influenza: The Epic Story of the Greatest Plague in History.* N. Y.: Viking Penguin. ISBN-13: 978-0-670-89473-4

Bartlett, Karen (2018). *Architects of Death: The Family Who Engineered the Death Camps.* N.Y.: St. Martin's Press. ISBN-13: 978-1-250-11770-0

Benderly, Beryl Lieff (2015). Updated: A scientist saint? *Science.* American Academy for the Advancement of Science. 24 Feb., 2015. Doi 10.1126/science.credit.a1500051.science.org/content/article/updated-scientist-s aint

Black, Edwin (2003). *War Against the Weak: Eugenics and America's Campaign to Create a Master Race.* N. Y.: Four Walls, Eight Windows. ISBN 978-0-914-15329-0

Black, J. (1999). "John Langdon Down 1828-1896: A Caring Pioneer". Journal of the Royal Society of Medicine. 92 (6): 322–323. doi:10.1177/014107689909200621. PMC 1297222.

Blakemore, E. (2017). German scientists will study brain samples of Nazi victims. *Smithsonian Magazine* May 5, 2017. Accessed 12/29/2024.

Bockoven, J. S. (1963). *Moral treatment in American psychiatry.* N. Y.: Springer. ASIN: B0007DTPQA

Browning, Christopher (2003). *Initiating the final solution: The Fateful Message of September-October 1941.* Ina Levine Annual Lecture. March13, 2003. US Holocaust Memorial Museum Studies. Center for Advanced Studies. HTTPS://ashmm.org/m/pdfs/20050728-browning.pdf

Buchanan, Maggie B., Wolgin, Philip E., Flores, Claudia (2021). *The Trump Administration's family separation policy is over.* Center For American Progress. Americanprogress.org/article/trump-administration-family-separation-polcy/

Burnett, Peter (1851). State of the State Address. Jan. 06, 1851. Presented to the California Senate and Assembly.

Bush, Peter G. (2015). The Canadian churches' apologies for colonialization and Indian schools. 1986–1998. *The Canadian Journal of Peace and Conflict Studies.* Vol. 47, No. ½, 2015, 47-70.

Canadian Truth and Reconciliation Commission. (2012). *They Came for the Children: Canada, Aboriginal Peoples, and Residential*

Schools. Truth and Reconciliation Commission of Canada. ISBN: 978-1-100-19994-8

Canadian Truth and Reconciliation Commission. (2015). *Honoring the Truth, Reconciling for the Future. Summary of the Final Report of the Truth and Reconciliation Commission of Canada.* Executive_Summary_English_Web.pdf

D'Antonio, Michael (1957). *The State Boys Rebellion.* N.Y.: Simon and Shuster. ISBN 13: 978-0-743-24512-8

Deer, K. (2019). Anglican church of Canada apologizes for spiritual harm to indigenous peoples. CBC/ca/news/Indigenous/anglican—church—apology—spiritual—harm

de Graaf G., Buckley F., Skotko B. G. (2017). Estimation of the number of people with Down syndrome in the United States. *Genetics in Medicine*, 19, 439-447. doi:10.1038/gim.2016.127

Delucia, Catherine (2003). Getting the story strait: Press coverage of Italian American lynchings from 1856 to1910. *Italian Americana.* 21(2): 212-221.

Diamond, Sander (1974). *The Nazi Movement in the United States: 1924-1941.* Ithaca, N.Y.: Cornell University Press. ISBN 13: 978-0-801-40788-8

Dobbs, Michael (1998). Ford and GM scrutinized for alleged Nazi collaboration. *The Washington Post,* Nov. 30, 1998

Dowbiggen, Ian (2003). *A Merciful End: The Euthanasia Movement in Modern America.* N. Y.: Oxford University Press. ISBN 13: 978-0-19515-443-6

Dowbiggen, Ian (2005). *A Concise History of Life, Death, God and Medicine.* N.Y.: Rowman and Littlefield. ISBN 13: 978-0-19515-443-6

Down, John Langdon (1866). Observations on an ethnic classification of idiots. *London Hospital Reports*, 3, 1866, 259-262.

Dray, Philip (2002). *At the Hands of Persons Unknown: The Lynching of Black Americans.* N.Y.: Random House. ISBN 978-0-37550-324-5

Ellsworth, Scott (1992). *Death in a Promised Land: The Tulsa Race Riot of 1921.* Baton Rouge, LA: Louisiana State University Press. ISBN 978-0-80711- 767-5

Engel, R. (2013). Meet Dr. Marthe Gautier: The scientist who discovered Trisomy 21. *PCUC (People Concerned with the Unborn Child).* https://www.pcuc.org/trisomy-21 Accessed August 18, 2021.

Evans, Richard J. (2009). *The Third Reich at War.* N.Y.: Penguin. ISBN 978-0-71399-649-4

Flavelle, Christopher (2021). Forced Relocation Left Native Americans More Exposed to Climate Threats Data Show. *New York Times,* Oct. 28, 2021.

Friedlander, Henry. *The Origins of Nazi Genocide: From Euthanasia to the Final Solution.* Chapel Hill: University of North Carolina Press, 1995, ISBN 978-0-8078-2208-1.

Galton, Francis (1904). *Eugenics: Its Definition, Scope and Aims.* Paper presented at the Sociological Society, London University, May 16, 1904. Printed in *The American Journal of Sociology,* 10 July 1904, No. 1.

Gartler, S. M. (2006). The chromosome number in humans: A brief history. *Nature Reviews/Genetics.* Aug. 2006, Vol. 17, 657-659.

Gautier, Marthe & Harper, P. S. (2009). Fiftieth anniversary of trisomy 21: Returning to a discovery. *Human Genetics.* 126 (2) 317-324. doi: 10: 1007/00439-009-0690-1.

Gerais, Reem (2017). Better Babies Contests in the United States (1908-1916). *Embryo Project Encyclopedia.* (2017-07-19). ISSN:190-5030 http//embryo.asu.edu/handle/10776/12566.

Goldhagen, Daniel J. (1996). *Hitler's Willing Executioners: Ordinary Germans and the Holocaust.* N.Y.: Knopf. ISBN 0-679-44695-8

Graziano, Anthony M. (1974). *Child Without Tomorrow.* Elmsford, N.Y.: Pergamon. ISBN 0-08-017722-0.

Graziano, Anthony M. (1993). Guggenheim Foundation research award: *Understanding Family Sub-Abusive Violence Against Children.* Jan—Dec. 1993. N.Y.: Guggenheim Foundation.

Graziano, Anthony M. (2002). *Developmental Disabilities: Introduction to a Diverse Field.* Boston; Allyn & Bacon.

Graziano, Anthony M. *La Bell' America.* (2009). Teaticket, MA.: Leapfrog Press. ISBN 0–205–32206–9

Graziano, Anthony M. (2016). *McKinley's Ghost and the Little Tin Truck.* Ontario: Guernica Editions. ISBN 978-1-77183-138-3

Graziano, Anthony M., DeGiovanni, I. Susan, & Garcia, Katherine. (1979). Behavioral treatment of children's fear: a review. *Psychological Bulletin,* 86, 4, 804–830.

Graziano, Anthony M. & Kean, J. E. (1968). Programmed relaxation and reciprocal inhibition with psychotic children. *Behaviour Research and Therapy,* Volume 6, Issue 4, November 1968, Pages 433-437.

Graziano, Anthony M. & Mooney, Kevin C. (1980). Family self-control instructions for children's nighttime fear reduction. *Journal of Consulting and Clinical Psychology.* 48, 206-213.

Graziano, A.M., Mooney, K.C., Huber, C., & Ignasiak, D. (1979). Self-control instructions for children's fear reduction: A multiple case study: *Behavior Therapy & Experimental Psychiatry*, 10, 221-227;

Graziano, Anthony M. and Raulin, Michael L. (2021). *Research Methods: A Process of Inquiry.* 9th ed. New York: Pearson. ISBN 13-978-0-13-570505-6

Graziano, Michael S. A. (2018). *The Spaces Between Us: A Story of Neuroscience, Evolution and Human Nature. N. Y.: Oxford University Press.* ISBN 978–0-19-046101–0

Hart, Bradley W. (2018). *Hitler's American Friends. The Third Reich's Supporters in the United States.* N. Y.: Saint Martins/Thomas Dunne books. ISBN 10: 125-0-14895-2

Hayes, Mike (2020). Nyack People and Places: Nyack Skating Pond. https://nyacknewsandviews.com/blog/2020/01/nyack-people-places-nyack-skating-pond

Hedgepeth, D., Horwitz,S., Sohyun Lee, J., BaTran, A., Tabrizy, N., Chikwendiu, J. (2004). More than 3100 students died at schools built to crush Native American cultures. The Washington Post, December 22, 2024. https://www.washingtonpost.com/investigations/interactive/2024/native-american-deaths-burial-sites-boarding-schools/

Heisel, Andrew (2015). The rise and fall of an all-American catch phrase: free white and 21. *Jezebel.* Jezebel.com

Hiltz, Fred (2019). *An apology for spiritual harm.* The Anglican Church of Canada. Vancouver, British Columbia, July 12, 2019.

Hine, Robert V., Farragher, John M., & Coleman, Jon T. (2017). *The American West: A New Interpretive History.* 2nd. ed. New Haven: Yale University Press. ISBN 13-978-0300-1851-70

Hirsch, James S. (2002). *Riot and Remembrance: The Tulsa Race War and its Legacy.* Boston, MA: Houghton Mifflin. ISBN 978-0-618-10813-0

Hodal, Kate (2016). One in 200 people is a slave. Why? *The Guardian.* May 31, 2018.

Hoover, H. (1929). Message Regarding Black Thursday. Transcript: UVA Miller Center; Presidential Speeches. https://millercenter.org/the-presidency/presidential-speeches/october-25-1929-message-regarding-black-thursday

Horowitz, Jason & Austen, Ian (2022). Pope Apologizes in Canada for Schools that Abused Indigenous Children. *The New York Times,* July 25, 2022.

Hull, Katy (2021). *The Machine Has a Soul: Sympathy with Italian Fascism.* Princeton: Princeton University Press. ISBN 978-0-691208-12-1

Jezebel (2015). Free White and 21. YouTube, September 10, 2015.

Jirik, Katrina N. (2019). *American Institutions for the Feeble-minded, 1876-1916.* Doctoral Dissertation, University of Minnesota.

Kaelber, Lutz (2012). Child murder in Nazi Germany: The memory of Nazi medical crimes and commemoration of children's euthanasia victims at two facilities (Eichberg, Kalmenhof). *Societies*, 2012, 2(3), 15-194. Https://doiorg./10.3390/soc2030157

Keel, Terrance (2018). *Divine Variations: How Christian Thought Became Racial Science.* Stanford, CA: Stanford University Press. ISBN 978-0-80479-540-1

Kershaw, Ian (2000). *Hitler: 1889-1936. Vol. I Hubris I.* N.Y.: W. W. Norton. ISBN 978-0-1402-72390

Kershaw, Ian (2000). *Hitler: 1936-1945. Vol. II Nemesis II.* N.Y.: W. W. Norton. ISBN 978–0–393–32252–1

Koenigsberg, Richard A. (1975). Hitler's Ideology: *A Study in Psychoanalytic Sociology.* N. Y.: *Library of Social Science.* ISBN 10: 091-5-04201-0

Koenigsberg, Richard A. (2000). Review essay of the Nazi doctors. *Library of Social Science.* (libraryofsocialscience.com/reviews/published/lifton.html

Kuhl, Stephan (2001). *The Nazi Connection: Eugenics, Racism and German National Socialism.* N. Y.: Oxford University Press. ISBN 978-0-19514-978–4

La Barge, Margaret W. (2013). Age of Consent in European and American History. *Discover the Truth. Discover-the-truth.com/2013/09/09*

Lee, Albert (1980). *Henry Ford and the Jews.* N.Y.: Stein and Day. ISBN 978-1-89162-052-2

Lemann, Nicholas (1991). *The Promised Land: The Great Black Migration and How it Changed America.* N.Y.: Knopf. ISBN 978-0-33356-584-1

Lifton, Robert J. (1986). German doctors and the final solution. *N.Y. Times,* Sept. 21, 1986, Section 6, page 64.

Lifton, Robert J. (2000). *The Nazi Doctors: Medical Killing and the Psychology of Genocide.* N.Y.: Perseus Book Group. (Basic Books). ISBN 078-04650-490-5-9

Lindsay, Brendon (2012). *California's Native American Genocide, 1846-1873.* Lincoln, NEB: University of Nebraska Press. ISBN 978-08032-402-1-6

Link, Stefan (2011). Rethinking the Ford-Nazi connection. *Bulletin of the GHI.* (German Historical Institute) (49) Fall 2011.

Lombardo, Paul A. (Ed.) (2011). *A Century of Eugenics in America: From the Indiana Experiment to the Human Genome Era.* Indianapolis: Indiana University *Press.* ISBN 978-0-25335-574-4

Lombardo, Paul A. (2022). *Three Generations - No Imbeciles: Eugenics, the Supreme Court, and Buck v Bell.* Baltimore: Johns Hopkins University Press. ISBN 13: 978-1-42144-318-8

Madigan, Tim (2001). *The Burning: Massacre, Destruction and the Tulsa Race Riot of 1921.* N.Y.: St. Martin's Press. ISBN 978-0-31227-283-8

Madley, Benjamin (2016). *An American Genocide, the United States and the California Catastrophe, 1846-1873.* New Haven: Yale University Press. ISBN 13: 978-0-300-18136-4

McAfee, T. (2017). Trump's Mockery of a Disabled Journalist. People.com/politics/trump-denies-mocking-journalist-disabled-watch-video//

McElvaine, Robert S. (1993). *The Great Depression: America 1929-1941.* N.Y.: Times Books. ISBN 10-081-29232-7-8

Mc Whirter, Cameron (2012). *Red Summer: The Summer of 1919 and the Awakening of Black America.* N. Y.: St. Martin/Griffin. ISBN 979-82003-673-2-0

Medosch, Emily (2021). Not just ICE: Forced sterilization in the United States. *Immigration and Human Rights Law Review.* May 28, 2021.

Millward, David (2023). Fury as Donald Trump Says Immigrants 'Poison Blood of U.S.' The Telegraph. Oct 06, 2023. https://www.telegraph.co.uk/world-news/2023/10/06/donald-trump-far-right-immigrants-poison-blood-us/

MMWR (1999). Achievements in Public Health 1900-1999: Healthier Mothers and Babies. *MMWR Weekly.* October 01, 1999/48(38); 849-855. *Morbidity and Mortality Weekly Report-*Centers for Disease Control and Prevention.

Naimark, Norman M. (2010). *Stalin's Genocides.* Princeton, N.J.: Princeton University Press. ISBN 978-0-691-14784-0

National Association for Down syndrome. *Facts About Down Syndrome.* nads.org/resources/facts/ Accessed 12/10/2021.

Newland, B. (2022). *Federal Indian Boarding School Initiative Investigative Report.* U.S. Department of the Interior, May 2022. P. 93.

Nichols, Lynn H. (2005). *Cruel World: The Children of Europe in the Nazi Web.* N. Y.: Knopf. ISBN 978-06797-766-3-5

Norton, Jack (1979). *Genocide in Northwestern California: When our Worlds Cried.* San Francisco: Indian Historian Press. ISBN 0-913436-26-2

OECD (2022). Infant Mortality Rates (indicator). Doi:10.17871/83dea506.en (Accessed on 12 February 2022). (Organization for Economic Cooperation and Development).

Orr, R. D., Pang, N., Pellegrino, E. and Siegler M. (1997). Use of the Hippocratic oath: A review of twentieth century practice and a content analysis of oaths administered in medical schools in the U. S. and Canada in 1993. *The Journal of Clinical Ethics*, 8, (Winter): 377-388.

Ost, Suzanne (2006). Doctors and Nurses of Death: A case study of eugenically motivated killing under the Nazi euthanasia programme. *Liverpool Law Review* (2006) 27:5-30.

Ostler, Jeffrey (2015). Genocide and American Indian History. *Oxford Research Encyclope*dia. (https://doi.org/10.1093/acrefore/9780199329175.0133. Published online March 02, 2015.

Oveyssi, Natalie (2015). Forgotten stories of the Eugenic Age #1: How Better Babies became Fitter Familes. *Biopolitical Times*, July 07, 2015.

Pember, Mary Annette (2021). A history not yet laid to rest. *The Atlantic.* November 24, 2021. https://www.theatlantic.com/ideas/archive/2021/11/native-american-boarding-schools/620760/

Pernick, Martin S. (1996). *The Black Stork: Eugenics and the Death of "Defective Babies" in American Medicine and Motion Pictures Since 1915.* Oxford: Oxford University Press. ISBN 978-01950-773-1-5

Pernick, Martin S. (2002). Taking better baby contests seriously. *American Journal of Public Health*, 92 (2002): 707—708.

Perry, B. P. (accessed 2024). The Nazi euthanasia program that killed 300,000. https://www.history.co.uk/article/aktion-t4-the-nazi-euthanasia-programme-that-killed-300000

Pratt, R. H. (1892). The advantage of mingling Indians with Whites. *Proceedings of the national conference of charities and corrections.* Denver Colorado June 23,1892. https//hdl.hndle.net/2027/wu.89030648919hathitrust.org. Accessed 01/29/2023

Rascoe, A. & Wise, A. (2021). Biden says the Tulsa Race Massacre can't be buried no matter how people try. NPR: Biden Visits Tulsa on anniversary of race massacre. June1, 2021. www.npr.org › 2021/06/01 › 1001380354.

Ross, Alex (2018). How American Racism Influenced Hitler. *The New Yorker.* April 30, 2018.

Rotzoll, Maike; Richter, Paul; Fuchs, Petra; Hinz-Wessels, Annette; Topp, Sascha; & Hohendorf, Gerrit (2006). The first National Socialist extermination crime: The T-4 Program and its victims. *International Journal of Mental Health.* Vol. 35, No. 3, The Holocaust and the Mentally Ill: Part I: Extermination (Fall 2006), pp. 17-29

Rudin, A. James (2014). The Dark Legacy of Henry Ford's Anti-Semitism. *The Washington Post*, October 10, 2014.

Saurman, George (2012). *We've Done Them Wrong! A History of the Native American Indians and How the United States Treated Them.* Bloomington, Indiana: iUniverse. ISBN 978-14759-448-9-1

Schuman, Michael (2017). History of child labor in the United States—part 1: little children working," *Monthly Labor Review*, U.S. Bureau of Labor Statistics, January, https://doi.org/10.21916/mlr.2017.1

Seidel, Carol A. (2022). Jerome Lejeune: The Saint Who Stole the Scientific Spotlight.Casdinteret.com/2022/10/Jerome-lejeune-the-saint-who-stole-the-scentific-spotlight/#:

Selden, Steven. (2005). Transforming Better Babies into Fitter Families: Archival Resources and the History of the American Eugenics Movement, 1908–1930. *Proceedings of the American Philosophical Society* 149, no. 2, 199-225 (June 2005).

Sereny, Gitta (1983). *Into That Darkness: An Examination of Conscience.* N. Y.: Vintage Books. ISBN 978-0-394-71035-8

Silverstein, Ken (2000.) Ford and the Fuhrer. *The Nation.* January 24, 2000. (thenation.com/artcle/archive/ford/-and-fuhrer)

Smith, David, M. (2017). Counting the Dead: Estimating the loss of life in the indigenous holocaust, 1492-present. University of Houston *(A-NAS-2017.Proceedings-Smith.pdf)*

Smith, Gene (1970) *The Shattered Dream: Herbert Hoover and the GreatDepression.* N.Y.: William Morrow.ISBN 978-00705-847-4-7

Smith, Richard N. & Wallach, Timothy (2004). The Ordeal of Herbert Hoover, Part II. *Prologue Magazine.* Summer 2004, Vol. 36, No. 2, archives.gov/publications/2004/summer/hoover-2.html

Southern Poverty Law Center. (2021). *Family Separation Under the Trump Administration.* Southern Poverty Law Center. https://www.splcenter.org/our-issues/immigrant-justice/family-separation

Spock, Benjamin. (1946). *The Common-Sense Book of Baby and Child Care.* N.Y.: Duell, Sloan and Pearce. ISBN 0671770012

Stannard, David E. (1992). *American Holocaust: The Conquest of the New World.* N.Y.: Oxford University Press.

Stern, Alexandra M. (2005). *Eugenic Nation: Faults and Frontiers of Better Breeding in Modern America.* Berkeley: University of California Press.

Stern, Alexandra M. (2002). Making Better Babies: Public Health and Race Betterment in Indiana, 1920–1935. *Am J Public Health.* 2002 May; 92(5): 742–72. doi:10.2105/ajph.92.5.742

Stumbo, Ellen (2019). The mothers of kids with Down syndrome who went before us and fought for our kids. https://themighty.com/topic/down-syndrome-institution-history-parent-advocacy/

Taylor, Stephen J. (2016). The Black Stork: Eugenics goes to the Movies. *The Hoosier State Chronicles.* Feb. 04, 2016.

Thornton, Russell (1990). *American Indian Holocaust and Survival: A Population History Since 1492.* Norman, Oklahoma: University of Oklahoma Press. ISBN 978-0-80612-220-5

Tjio, J. H. & Levan, A. (1956). The chromosome number of man. *Hereditas,* Vol. 42, 1-2, Pp 1-6. May 1956.

Trent, James W. (1994). *Inventing the Feeble Mind: A history of Mental Retardation in the United States.* N. Y.: Oxford University Press. ISBN 9780199396184

Tuskegee University. (2016). *Lynching Whites and Negroes, 1882-1968.* (PDF) Tuskegee University. Archived from the original (PDF) on March 13, 2016.

Uenuma, Francine. (2019). Better babies contests pushed for much needed infant health but also played into the eugenics movement. *Smithsonian Magazine,* Jan. 17, 2019.

United States Holocaust Memorial Museum. (2019). *Holocaust Encyclopedia: Documenting the Number of Victims of the Holocaust.* Feb. 4, 2019. U.S. Holocaust Memorial Museum, Washington, D.C. (encyclopedia.ushmm.org.)

United States Holocaust Memorial Museum. (2021). Euthanasia Program and Aktion T-4. encyclopedia.ushmm.org/content/en/article/euthanasia-program.

United States Holocaust Memorial Museum. (2022). The Nazi Party Platform. encyclopedia.ushmm.org/content/en/article/nazi-party-platform

Van Robays, J. (2016). John Langdon Down (1828-1896). *Facts, Views, and Vision in ObGyn.* 2016, June 27; 8(2):131-136. PMC5130304. Published online 2016 June 30.ncbi.nim.nih.gov/PMC5130304.

Vinson, L. (2020). Family Separation policy continues two years after Trump Administration said it ended. Southern Policy Law Center, June 18, 2020. *Splcenter.org/news/2020/06/18/family-separation-policycontinues-two-years-after-trump-administration-claims-it-ended.*

Weindling, Paul Julian (2006). *Nazi Medicine and the Nuremberg Trials: From Medical War Crimes to Informed Consent.* Basingstoke: Palgrave Macmillan. ISBN 978-0-23050-700-5.

Weindling, P., Hohendorf, G., Huntelmann, A. C., Kindel, J., Kinzelbach, A., Loewenau, A., Neuner, S., Palacz, M. A., Zingler, M., Czech, H. (2021). The problematic legacy of victim specimens from the Nazi Era: Identifying the persons behind the specimens at the Max Planck Institutes for Brain Research and Psychiatry. *Journal of the history of the Nuro sciences,* 32 (2), 218-239. https://doi.org/10.1080/0964704X.2021.1959185

Whitman, James Q. (2017). *Hitler's American Model: The United States and the Making of the Nazi Race Law.* Princeton: Princeton University Press.

Wikipedia. Ages of Consent in the United States. https://en.wikipedia.org/wk/ages-of-consent-in-the-united-states. Accessed July 7, 2023.

Wilson, Joan Hoff (1975). *Herbert Hoover: Forgotten Progressive.* Boston: Little, Brown. ISBN 978-0-3169-4416-8.

Woolford, Andrew; Benvenuto, Jeff; & Hinton, Alexander (2014). *Colonial Genocide in Indigenous North America.* Durham, N.C.: Duke University Press. ISBN 097-8082-2357-79-7

MIX
Paper
FSC® C100212

Printed by Imprimerie Gauvin
Gatineau, Québec